PRAISE FOR LAU

You Shouldn't Be Here

"A hip, fresh, mind-bending mystery with characters you'll love to pieces. Madelyn is incredibly real, and her clever sleuthing skills bring to mind a modern-day paranormal Nancy Drew—righting serious wrongs and bringing justice to the land. Not to mention she's the perfect foil to the jaw-droppingly yummy Alex. Loved it!"

—J. T. Ellison, *New York Times* bestselling author

"*You Shouldn't Be Here* is the best kind of dual timeline story—where everything is connected, nothing is as it seems, and I never saw the final twist coming. Lauren Thoman's latest is the perfect blend of authentic characters and page-turning mystery: unsettling, surprising, and deliciously satisfying."

—Jessica Strawser, *USA Today* bestselling author of *The Last Caretaker*

"*You Shouldn't Be Here* will touch your heart in ways you could never expect. Thoman has created a charming but tense story that drew me in and wouldn't let go. I was riveted from the first page."

—R. J. Jacobs, author of *This Is How We End Things*

I'll Stop the World

"Lauren Thoman's *I'll Stop the World* is a whip-smart mystery with a vibrant cast of characters that gives off great eighties vibes. I was absolutely dazzled by this unputdownable genre-bending novel that's equal parts coming-of-age suspense and an emotional tale of forgiveness and second chances."

—Mindy Kaling

"Thoman's ambitious timeline of events is both expansive and compressed, with the storyline unfolding over the course of both one week and thirty-eight years, and her portrayal of teenagers in varying degrees of crisis is sympathetic. A novel look at strange (and stranger) things."

—*Kirkus Reviews*

"Thoman's sweeping debut defies categorization. A multigenerational mystery, a compulsively readable love story, an intricately woven sci-fi—whatever it is, *I'll Stop the World* is the mind-bendy time-travel eighties romp we all need right now. I'm obsessed with this book."

—David Arnold, *New York Times* bestselling author

"*I'll Stop the World* layers mystery upon mystery, from the everyday secrets in the lives of teens coming of age in a small town now to the dark shock waves still radiating out from deaths that took place decades before. Lauren Thoman's debut novel is a time-bending page-turner packed with twists no one will see coming. This is a story that continues to resonate long after you finish."

—Gwenda Bond, *New York Times* bestselling author of *Stranger Things: Suspicious Minds*

"In this standout debut, Lauren Thoman takes the reader on a wild ride, deftly wrapping a coming-of-age story with a clever mystery, sprinkled with eighties nostalgia that'll have you reaching for your Bubble Yum. As I tore through the pages, I fell in love with the cast of flawed and funny characters, who felt as real as the friends I grew up with. Best of all, Thoman delivers an impossibly satisfying ending in a way only the very best time-travel storytellers can. This one should go at the top of everyone's must-read list!"

—Brianna Labuskes, *Wall Street Journal* bestselling author

"A brilliant, thought-provoking page-turner that so deeply sucked me into a world of richly drawn characters and fast-paced action that I never wanted to leave."

—Sonali Dev, *USA Today* bestselling author of *The Vibrant Years*

"A page-turning, time-bending mystery full of heart. *I'll Stop the World* gave me a chance to solve a cold crime from a refreshing new perspective. Lauren Thoman is an exciting new talent not to be missed!"

—Kara Thomas, bestselling author of *That Weekend* and *Out of the Ashes*

YOU SHOULDN'T BE HERE

OTHER TITLES BY LAUREN THOMAN

I'll Stop the World

YOU SHOULDN'T BE HERE

A NOVEL

LAUREN THOMAN

This is a work of fiction. Names, characters, organizations, places, events, and incidents are either products of the author's imagination or are used fictitiously. Otherwise, any resemblance to actual persons, living or dead, is purely coincidental.

Published by Thomas & Mercer, Seattle

www.apub.com

ISBN-13: 9781662517686 (hardcover)
ISBN-13: 9781662517693 (paperback)
ISBN-13: 9781662517709 (digital)

Cover design by Caroline Teagle Johnson
Cover image: © Ingrid Michel / Plainpicture

Printed in the United States of America
First edition

To Greg, who has always believed in me enough for the both of us. I promise to never stop sneaking dinosaurs into my books for you.

That didn't happen.
And if it did, it wasn't that bad.
And if it was, that's not a big deal.
And if it is, that's not my fault.
And if it was, I didn't mean it.
And if I did, you deserved it.

—*"The Narcissist's Prayer" by Dayna Craig*

"Be curious, and try to make sense of what you see. We live in a universe governed by rational laws that we can discover and understand. Despite recent triumphs, there are many new and deep mysteries that remain for you to solve."

—*Stephen Hawking in an interview with Radio Times, 2016*

"For those of us who believe in physics, the distinction between past, present and future is only a stubbornly persistent illusion."

—*Albert Einstein in a letter to the family of Michele Besso, 1955*

"One need not be a Chamber—to be Haunted,
One need not be a House—
The Brain has Corridors
surpassing
Material place."

—*Excerpt from "One need not be a Chamber—to be Haunted" by Emily Dickinson, 1862*

PROLOGUE

It was probably nothing.

Piper swiped her key card through the reader and heard a soft beep as the lock released. Her pulse roared in her ears as she pulled open the gate, the metal of the chain-link fence rattling like firecrackers as it scraped the packed earth.

What are you doing, you shouldn't be here, no one is supposed to be here, it's probably nothing anyway, you're going to get into so much trouble, you're going to get fired, you should go home, it's not like you're going to find anything, go home, go home, go home.

The constant stream of mental objections continued as she stepped past the AUTHORIZED PERSONNEL ONLY sign, into the site.

She'd swapped out her work heels for rubber-soled running shoes in her car. Now she moved quietly, aiming for the green office trailer by the lot for C Building.

One day, North Ridge would be a sleek office park of mirrored glass and glistening metal, with C Building towering over the others like a chrome crown. Now, though, the structure was just a tall grid of metal beams that sliced the setting sunlight into lines, casting long shadows across the ground like prison bars.

The portable metal steps clanged in protest as she ascended to the door, but no one was around to hear. Another swipe of her card, and she was in.

The office wasn't much to look at. A desk, a couch, two upholstered armchairs with negligible padding, all in varying shades of discount brown. Her employer was never one to spend money in places where no one important would notice. A small metal cart sat against a wall, holding a Keurig and a sleeve of Styrofoam cups. Her own from earlier that day was still in the plastic trash can beside it.

She slid open the bottom desk drawer, holding her breath. Multicolored file folders lined up neatly in front of her, separated by handwritten tabs. She pointed the flashlight on her phone into the drawer as her fingers walked through the labels, searching for the one the site manager had open on his desk earlier today when she'd forgotten to knock. The one he'd slipped into a drawer before she'd gotten a good look at it.

For months, the numbers on this project hadn't made sense. Her boss kept telling her not to worry about it. But it was her job to make them make sense. She didn't know *how* to not worry about it. She'd been quietly keeping a record of all the documents that didn't add up, just in case, but there were some things she didn't have access to from her work computer. Some things she could only find here.

There it was, a plain manila folder tucked inside one of the bright hanging sleeves. She pulled it out, thumbing through the contents.

She wedged her phone under her chin, aiming the light at the papers in her hands. She flipped back and forth through the folder's contents, confused at first as her fingers skimmed the pages. She'd never seen these invoices before. She hadn't heard of these vendors. She recognized the amounts, but—

The truth clicked into place. Her eyes widened. The blood drained from her face.

Now she understood why the numbers weren't adding up.

She shouldn't be here.

She was not supposed to see this.

The door creaked. Someone else was here.

Piper jumped, sending her phone clattering to the floor, the flashlight shining up at the ceiling. A figure stood in the doorway, barely visible in the darkness. He stepped into the trailer, one hand in his pocket. With the other, he shut the door behind him.

"Well," he said, almost conversationally. "What are we going to do with you?"

She recognized that voice. *Get out,* her brain screamed. Trembling, she bent to pick up her phone. She needed to see. Needed to get to the door.

"Leave it," he said, his voice turning harsh. He stepped closer to her as she froze, midcrouch, hand extended toward the floor. As he got closer to the light, she realized that his hand wasn't in his pocket after all.

"I didn't see anything," she said, her voice trembling.

A soft click came from inside his jacket.

"I think we both know that's not true," he said.

Run.

She threw the folder at his face and bolted for the door, her heart racing. Her fingers groped for the handle, invisible in the darkness. *Please please please.*

The shot exploded with a crack that split the darkness. She screamed, but couldn't hear her voice over the ringing in her ears.

Was she hit? She didn't think she was hit.

There. Her hands found the door handle and wrenched it open. She stumbled out into the night, her teeth chattering. She couldn't feel her limbs. Her foot slipped, and she tumbled down the metal stairs. Her head hit the railing, and bright light burst through her vision.

Get up! Move!

She got her arms under her, pushed herself up. Nothing hurt, but her legs weren't working right. She crawled forward, dragging herself across the ground as her feet scrabbled clumsily behind her.

She was okay, though. She was pretty sure she was okay.

She didn't hear him behind her. Maybe he wasn't following.

Her car wasn't far. She could make it.
The ground was wet. Her face was wet.
When did it get so cold? She didn't remember it being cold.
She was okay, though.
She was pretty sure she was okay.

PART ONE

That didn't happen

CHAPTER ONE

Among the projects that have ground to a halt due to the pandemic is the much-anticipated North Ridge Business Park in East Henderson, which was set to open sometime in 2022. The Raymond Realty Group's 100-acre park, which was in the early stages of construction, has been in development since 2018 and was projected to create nearly 2,000 jobs. "It's a real shame," Doug Raymond, CEO of Raymond Realty Group, told us on a Zoom call. "North Ridge would've been a beautiful addition to East Henderson, and we're so sad to let it go. But in the current economic and cultural climate, we just didn't see a viable way to proceed." Raymond clarified later on that he was indeed referring to the number of businesses who pulled out of the project due to financial hardship, and not to the state of his company, which he assured us is "chugging along just fine."

—Excerpt from the *Philadelphia Inquirer* story "Coronavirus Takes a Wrecking Ball to Construction Plans," September 2020

—

"I'm telling you, it's a ghost."

Angie twirled around her bedroom, arms splayed wide as if to scoop up the paranormal energy like a sail, brown hair swishing around her face. "Can't you *feel* it?"

Her best friend dropped into the deflated black beanbag in the corner, a tangle of dark hair falling across his forehead. "I feel like you have reached an impressive new level of boredom."

"Bas," Angie groaned, placing her hands on her hips and glaring down at him. "I'm serious."

"So am I. I think you've finally let East Henderson get to you. In like, a clinical way."

"I'm not imagining it. My house is actually haunted."

She hadn't been sure at first, but now she was. It started with small sounds while she was alone in the house: a book dropping or a door closing, little things that could be blamed on neighbors or wind or her own brain playing tricks on her. But over the past couple of days, it had grown into more than that. Food smells when no one was cooking. Snippets of muffled conversation, like she was listening through a door.

And then last night, singing. Only a few notes, and too faint to make out the lyrics, but this time, she was sure it hadn't been a figment of her imagination. The voice was female, bright and beautiful, and completely unfamiliar. It came from right outside her bedroom door, drifting down the hall, like it was walking to her father's room. But when Angie checked, there was no one there.

She'd heard it a couple of times since, never lasting for more than a few seconds, always just barely out of reach. No other explanation made sense. It had to be a ghost.

Bas—short for Sebastián, but his parents were the only ones who called him that—leaned forward, bracing his long arms on his knees. The cuffs of his jeans leaped higher, exposing several inches of his bony brown legs. He'd gone through a growth spurt that summer, shooting up to tower nearly six inches over Angie. She was still getting used to it. In elementary school, *she'd* been the taller one, and for most of middle and high school, they'd been eye to eye. When she looked at him now, his chin was where his eyes should be. It was weird, and she didn't think she liked it.

His clothes were having a similar problem adjusting; everything was too tight, too short. He tried to disguise it with hoodies and long socks, but he wasn't fooling anyone except himself.

She wished he could give some of that unwanted lankiness to her. Now, next to him, she felt like a toadstool. Her legs were too short, her face too round, making her look younger than she was. A few times that summer, people had actually assumed she was his little sister, which had felt both mortifying and vaguely racist. Bas was Mexican and deeply tanned, while Angie was a quarter Chinese and held a rather vampiric attitude toward sunlight. But apparently some people just saw two non-white teens with dark hair and assumed they were part of a matched set.

"Have you considered the more obvious explanation?" Bas asked, tugging his socks up again.

"Which is?"

He raised a thick eyebrow. "The voice you've been hearing . . . it's a woman, right?"

Angie narrowed her eyes. She had a feeling she knew where he was going, and willed him to make a U-turn. "Yeah . . ."

Bas shrugged. "Maybe your dad is dating."

"He is *not*."

"Angie, I know you don't want to hear this, but your dad having a girlfriend is actually preferable to your house being haunted."

"That's debatable," Angie grumbled.

"Plus," Bas went on, "it's been, what, two years since your mom left? How long do you expect him to go without . . . you know, companionship?"

"First of all, gross," Angie said, wrinkling her nose. "And second of all, my dad is not the type to bring some random woman home without telling me. And third of all, *gross*." She sat down on her bed, the cheap spring mattress creaking under her weight, and covered her eyes with her hands. "Why would you put that image in my head?"

"Come on, it's never occurred to you that he might not want to be alone forever?"

"He's not alone. He's got me. As he likes to remind me every freaking day."

"You know that's not the same thing."

"Where would he even *meet* anyone?"

"Apps?"

Angie snorted. "I shudder to imagine the type of woman who would go for my dad's dating profile. 'Favorite food: frozen egg rolls. Favorite book: *Star Trek* novelizations.' His photo is probably a bathroom selfie of him giving the Vulcan salute in a short-sleeved button-down."

"Your mom went for him."

"My mom *left*." The words came out sharper than she'd intended, their edges filed to points. But even though she hadn't meant to, she kind of hoped they'd drawn a little blood.

Maybe if they had, he'd let it go. And she wouldn't have to admit that before her mom left for good, she'd been gone all the time. And now her dad was gone all the time. And the one thing they had in common was Angie.

Maybe she drove them away.

Bas opened and closed his mouth wordlessly, deciding against whatever he had planned to say. He dipped his head to scratch the back of his neck.

Angie gazed out the window over her bed, through the lacy cream curtains her mom had hung just two months before she'd left. *They'll brighten up the place,* she'd said. *See? Aren't they pretty?*

Angie should probably take them down. They didn't go with anything else in her room. Not the CHVRCHES and Lorde and MCR posters on her walls. Not the piles of ripped jeans, graphic tees, and chunky sweaters that littered her floor. Not the haphazard rows of horror and sci-fi novels erupting from her floor-to-ceiling bookshelf, their spines spiderwebbed and pages soft from countless rereads.

Not Angie herself.

Maybe the curtains had been the last straw. Beautiful, delicate, and completely out of place, just like her mom. Maybe her mother had looked at them in Angie's messy cave of a room and seen how much they didn't belong there.

How much *she* didn't belong there, with Angie.

The irony was that Angie looked like her. But in all the wrong ways. She had her curves, but not her height. Her bold features, but not the sophistication to pull them off. Her wavy hair, but not the skill to tame it.

Her daughter. But not the one she wanted.

Angie reached out, bunching the gauzy fabric in her fist. They looked stupid anyway. She'd never liked them, even before her mom left. They just weren't her. Not that her mom had ever really seen *her*. She'd only ever seen the daughter she wished she'd had. The daughter whose room looked nice with lace curtains.

Rip them down.

Angie's fingers fell away from the curtains. Before she'd even processed that she hadn't done it, the fabric had settled back into place as if she'd never touched it at all.

She closed her eyes. Maybe Bas was right. Maybe the voice she'd been hearing was just a real-life woman her dad had been hiding from her. Maybe he didn't want her to know he'd moved on, when she still hadn't.

Except . . . it didn't feel right. Even though she hadn't been able to make out anything the voice had said yet, she couldn't shake the sense that it was talking *to* her. It wasn't something she'd overheard. It was something she was *meant* to hear.

She wished it would say something now. If Bas could hear it, he'd understand.

And then she realized, he *could.*

She whirled around. “Bas, I’m brilliant.”

He raised an eyebrow. “Congratulations?”

“We’re going to prove it’s a ghost.”

“We?”

“We just need to get a few things first.” Angie’s brown eyes glimmered. How had she not thought of this before? It was so obvious. She pretended she didn’t notice Bas’s frown, and stepped back into her combat boots, discarded earlier at the foot of her bed. “How much money do you have?”

CHAPTER TWO

Coming Soon! Darley Estates: Luxury living in the heart of scenic East Henderson. Floor plans starting at $1.4M. Invest in your family's future, today!

—billboard for Raymond Realty Group, near exit 320 on the Pennsylvania Turnpike

—

The graveyard of Wawa coffee cups on the floor of Madelyn's rented U-Haul bordered on obscene. The drive from State College to East Henderson wasn't that far—a little under three hours, if you obeyed speed limits—yet she'd burned through enough salted caramel lattes to fill one of those champagne tubs in the Poconos.

One of those tubs that Ralph—the world's biggest phlegmwad—had always insisted would be *so* romantic, despite her fear of heights and bewilderment at the very concept of a seven-foot-tall tub.

"How many fluids do we think are floating around in that pool?" she'd asked, wrinkling her nose the last time he'd pulled up the "Champagne Tower Suite," with its private heart-shaped pool, on his phone.

He'd shrugged. "It's chlorinated, babe." As if that had anything to do with it.

At least she'd figured out who he really was before she'd handed over six hundred bucks for him to book a weekend getaway she didn't want. Let him go marinate in his cloudy pool with someone else.

For probably the hundredth time since she'd gingerly pulled out of the parking lot of her former apartment complex, she glanced in her rearview mirror to make sure her car was still back there. She'd never towed anything before—never driven a truck before—and kept having nightmares of her little Honda Fit slipping off the trailer hitch and getting smashed to pieces without her noticing. She managed to catch a glimpse of metallic yellow bouncing along behind the bulky box truck and felt a temporary wash of relief.

Her audiobook paused and her earbud beeped, alerting her to an incoming call. She glanced at her phone, rattling around in the gray plastic cup holder, then tapped her ear to accept. "Hello! I'm almost to the exit." She had to shout to be heard over the truck's windy growl.

"Wonderful! I'll be heading over in a few minutes." Her landlord, Doug Raymond, sounded different than she'd expected. Based on the photos on his website, he could've moonlit as a Santa Claus, with his round wire-rimmed glasses and neatly trimmed snow-white beard. But his voice was nasal and thin, almost whiny, with a hint of a southern accent. "How's the drive been?"

"Great," she said. "I mean, you know. Uneventful." She did wish the turnpike exits were closer together—she had to pee *so bad*—but she wasn't about to tell her landlord that. She did not need this man to think she was weird when he was the only reason she would have a place to live when school started on Tuesday.

She'd submitted an application to Raymond Realty Group a few weeks ago for one of the very few houses listed in her price range. A quick internet search had made it clear that if she wanted a place in East Henderson, they were the ones to talk to. And not just to rent—they seemed to own the vast majority of the property in town, from rentals and residential properties to commercial complexes.

Her search also informed her that their CEO, Doug Raymond, was a "proud supporter of the second amendment"—one of the photos on his Instagram was of him and his family all grinning and holding assault rifles—was heavily involved in local politics, and was rich enough to buy his own small country if he wanted. Not the type of person she'd typically choose to rent from, but her options were limited.

A couple of days after she'd submitted her application, Doug Raymond had called her personally to tell her that the house she'd applied for was unfortunately already leased, but he might have a different property for her. He said it was a house that he owned personally, not through Raymond Realty. He'd been using it as a short-term vacation rental for the past couple of years, but was thinking of switching it over to a regular rental property, since he'd decided the home-share industry was "more trouble than it's worth," and liked the idea of renting it to "a sweet little lady such as yourself." The only downside was that it wouldn't be available until Labor Day weekend.

While she didn't love being referred to as "a sweet little lady," or the idea of moving three days before her first day of work, she told herself it would all be worth it once she was there. She agreed on the spot.

"Thank you again so much for this," Madelyn said. "I don't know what I would've done without your help."

"That's no trouble, sweetheart," Raymond said.

Madelyn made a face, but didn't say anything. She hated when men talked to her like she was a piece of candy. However, she needed Doug to like her, so she'd force herself to smile through his sugary epithets. Or at least make him *think* she was smiling.

They ended the call, promising to meet up in a few minutes in front of Madelyn's new home. Madelyn wriggled forward in her seat, willing the last few miles to pass more quickly. Those Wawa lattes were pounding down the walls of her bladder like a Trojan army.

Eight minutes later, she turned into the driveway of 906 Gazelle Lane, an adorable two-bedroom cottage in one of the older neighborhoods in East Henderson, which had recently exploded with new construction. The house was one story, with white siding and bright-blue trim, and a wide front porch that would be perfect for a rocking chair.

Doug Raymond's car—a sleek black BMW—was already parked on the street, blocking her mailbox. He waited for her by the front door.

Sweating, Madelyn inched the truck into the short driveway, terrified she might ding his expensive car. She parked with the nose of the truck nearly touching the garage door, her Fit sticking into the cul-de-sac like a thorn.

"I'll move it!" she promised as she slid out of the truck. "Just need to use the bathroom first."

"That's fine," Raymond said, shielding his eyes from the early-September sun with a manila folder. "It can wait until after I show you around and we go over this paperwork."

"But the neighbors," Madelyn said, gesturing at the houses on either side of them. Her car wasn't blocking their driveways, but it would still make driving through the cul-de-sac awkward. She didn't want to give them a reason to be annoyed with her on her very first day as an East Henderson resident.

"They'll be fine," he insisted, unlocking the front door and holding it open. "They can wait a few minutes. I've got somewhere to be after this."

"Oh, okay. Sorry." He took up half the doorframe, forcing Madelyn to turn sideways in order to get inside.

"This is the living room, obviously," Raymond said, gesturing around them. The front door opened to a square, sunny room with white walls and beige carpet, crisp lines on the floor indicating that it had been vacuumed recently. Sunlight streamed in through a large picture window beside the door, facing the street. Beyond the living room was a small dining area with a black metal chandelier, with the door to the garage on its left and the galley kitchen to the right, just beyond the hallway that Madelyn assumed led to the two bedrooms. A glass-paned door at the back of the dining room led to the fenced-in backyard.

Raymond started narrating the interior of the house. "It's been given a fresh coat of paint, new carpet, and—"

"I'm so sorry," Madelyn interrupted, shifting from one foot to the other, "but I've had a lot of coffee and I was wondering if I could, uh . . ."

Raymond frowned, but nodded, gesturing toward the hallway to their right, off the back of the living room.

The one and only bathroom was located on her left, across the hall and a few feet past the second bedroom, which Madelyn planned to use as her office.

Like everything else in the house, the bathroom was small, decorated simply with white tile and a two-door vanity painted hunter green. No shower curtain or rings, which Madelyn didn't yet own; she opened her phone and started a THINGS TO BUY list in her Notes app as she emptied her bladder. Thankfully, there was toilet paper on the holder, although no soap by the sink. She added it to her list, since she had no idea which box her bathroom stuff was in.

She should have time to run to the store after Raymond left, assuming she could figure out how to get her Fit off the tow dolly. Her best friend and former roommate, Syzygy, would be arriving soon to help her unload, but judging by their last few texts, they were at least an hour away still.

"So what brings you to East Henderson?" Doug called through the closed bathroom door.

Madelyn bit her lip. Was he really talking to her while she was on the toilet? "Work," she called, keeping her voice bright.

"Yes, I remember you mentioned a teaching job in your application," he said. "Is that it? No family in town, friends, anything like that?"

She was not doing this. She was not having a conversation with this man through a bathroom door while urinating. She simply was not.

He rapped on the door. "Maddie? Hello? You okay in there?"

Dear lord. Now she was "Maddie"? She abhorred that name, along with people who just assigned other people nicknames without asking first. "I'm fine!"

"Okay, I was just wondering since you didn't answer."

"Just work," she said, hoping that would placate him. "Nothing else."

She finished up as quickly as she could, scrubbing her hands under hot water and drying them on the sides of her jeans. When she opened the door, Doug Raymond stood directly in front of her, close enough that he could've heard every drop of pee hitting the porcelain sides of the toilet.

Gross.

"You look different than I expected," Raymond said as she squeezed around him, pressing her back to the wall to avoid her chest brushing against his arm. That was code, she knew, for *I thought you'd look more Asian*.

It was her surname: Zhao. People never cxpected someone with a Chinese last name to be biracial. But while it was hard to miss the suggestion of her Asian heritage in her face, especially in her eyes, which looked like they had been copied and pasted directly from her Chinese father's face onto her own, plenty of her mother's features had worked their way into her appearance. She was there in her sharp nose, her full lips, her thick chestnut hair.

"Yeah, it's my voice. It's too low for my face," she said with a smile. She knew the road he wanted to go down, but refused to set a single toe on it.

Raymond frowned. "No, I wasn't talking about your voice. It's—"

"The place looks great," she said, moving into the living room like she hadn't heard him. "I can't wait to start decorating. I've never had a place of my own before."

Raymond cleared his throat, rocking back on his heels. "Well, about that, I did want to call your attention to a couple of the terms in your lease before making things official."

Madelyn kept her smile in place as her heart kicked into double time. She'd expected to simply hand over a check, sign her name, and be handed the keys.

Was there more to it than that? Could Raymond really decide not to rent to her *now*?

Raymond turned around the end of the hallway into the small kitchen, recently renovated with blue-flowered tiles and stainless steel appliances. He slid the contents of the manila folder out onto the white granite counters. "As we discussed, this is a one-year lease, with your last month and first month payable up front, along with your security deposit of three thousand dollars."

Madelyn nodded. So far, he hadn't said anything she didn't already know, although her stomach tightened at the mention of the money. Her parents had helped her out with the deposit, but this was still the most money she'd ever paid to live somewhere. She knew she could cover the rent on her salary—she'd start on Tuesday as the new chorus director for East Henderson Middle School—but calculating her budget on her laptop felt very different from actually handing over the giant check in her purse.

"You're the only tenant, of course, and it needs to stay that way. No roommates, boyfriends, or—oh, I'm sorry, am I supposed to say *partners* or some other PC nonsense now?" He said that last part with a chuckle, but something in his tone sounded like a threat.

Madelyn gave him a tense smile. "No problem."

Something in his eyes darkened, like she'd just failed some sort of test, but it lasted only a second before his expression cleared. "And of course, no pets," he went on.

She nodded again. "Yup." That was the one clause she intended to break, but he'd never notice. She and Syzygy hadn't had any trouble keeping Potato a secret in their previous apartment, and she didn't see why that would be any different now. That was, assuming that she managed to get Raymond to leave before Syzygy and Potato showed up.

Raymond went through the terms of the lease one by one, with Madelyn nodding along. It seemed a bit harsher than he had implied it would be—an interest rate that went up half a percent every *hour* the rent was past due seemed ridiculously steep—but she didn't think it would be a problem. She was a pretty neat and organized person, lived alone, and didn't know anyone in town. And Potato was tiny, house trained, and didn't shed—a key factor in keeping her existence hidden from nosy landlords. Between the two of them, they'd barely even compress the carpet fibers.

"And the last thing," Raymond said, leaning so close she could see the slight yellowing of his teeth from what she assumed was the tobacco on his breath. "You do understand that you are not to make *any* alterations to the physical structure of the home whatsoever, yes?"

She nodded.

"No paint, wallpaper, screws, nails, et cetera. If you want to hang things up, get those double-sided whosiwhatsits, you know, those strips with the tabs."

"Sure thing," she said, suppressing the urge to roll her eyes. She understood him not wanting her to wallpaper the whole place, but how hard was it to patch a couple of nail holes? Still, if the barrier to entry here was Command Strips, she'd use Command Strips. "I'll be so unobtrusive, the walls won't even know I live here."

Raymond chuckled. "Well, they may not, but I will. I've got your address, after all. And your signature, if you'll put it right here."

Madelyn took the pen he offered, gripping it awkwardly by the nib to avoid touching his fingers. His nails were neatly manicured, the cuticles expertly trimmed and moisturized. She signed the lease, hand wobbling slightly under the pressure of his eyes boring into her.

She'd barely finished filling in the final *4* of the date when he snatched the paper out from under her fingertips, leaving a faint inky streak across the bottom of the sheet where she hadn't finished lifting the pen.

"We're all set," he exclaimed jovially, sliding the lease back into the manila folder, followed by her check. He reached into his pocket and held out a royal-blue Raymond Realty Group key ring with two brass keys dangling from it. "Welcome home."

She held out her hand to accept the keys. They were still warm from his pocket; she quickly deposited them on the counter. She glanced at the folder holding her lease. "Don't I get a copy?"

He shook his head, pressing his lips together. "We've got a great system for handling things at the office. Very organized. The very best one on the market, actually. All you need to do is call, and Barbara will get you the information you need in a jiffy."

That wouldn't work for Madelyn—she'd spent far too long letting Ralph "handle things" and had sworn she'd never give a man that sort of control again—but she decided she'd rather take it up with Barbara than argue with Raymond.

"I'm sure I'll be great," she said, walking to the front door and opening it for him. She stuck out her hand, offering a handshake. "Thank you *so* much for coming by and going over the lease with me, Mr. Raymond. And for renting this place to me. It's lovely. I know I'll love living here." Her cheeks hurt from how widely she was smiling.

A shadow flickered across Raymond's face, but then he took her proffered hand, shaking vigorously and squeezing a tad harder than was necessary. Madelyn matched his grip, waiting for him to let go first, all the while smiling sweetly.

After holding on several seconds too long, Raymond pulled his hand away, sticking it in his pocket. "You're welcome, sweetheart. Pleasure to meet you. And remember, if you need anything, you've got my number."

She nodded, closing the door behind him as hurriedly as she could without slamming it. Once she heard the latch click, she breathed a sigh of relief, then pulled out her phone to send a text to Syzygy. Survived my first Doug Raymond meeting.

And?

About what I expected. I can handle him. How's the spud?

Full of french fries and farting up a storm. Neither one of us can wait to get her out of this car.

That's what you get for feeding her french fries.

I was desperate. This dog could shatter glass with her whining.

Well, soon you won't have to deal with her anymore. Her new home is all ready for her.

For the record, I still think this is a really, really bad idea.

What, hiding Potato? We've never had a problem before.

You know what I mean. Just please promise me you'll be careful.

She was typing her response when a loud knock sounded at the front door, startling her. Good grief. Raymond hadn't even been gone for three full minutes yet.

She was still standing in the entryway, so she didn't even have to move to let him in. She pasted a smile on her face as she opened the door. "Did you forget—"

But there was no one there. She leaned out, peering around both sides of the house, but the only movement was the azaleas in the flower bed, swaying gently in the late-summer breeze.

She closed the door again, turning the dead bolt this time. "That was weird," Madelyn said out loud. A shiver traced down her spine, but she shook it off. She was anxious, that was all. Probably just imagining things.

She looked at her phone to see Syzygy had sent one more text while she was answering the door.

Remember, you can't help anyone if you become a target too.

CHAPTER THREE

I don't believe in so-called "affordable housing." You want to afford housing, you get a job and work for it. Our clients have earned the right to live in beautiful homes, and we help them find exactly what they're looking for. I'd rather reward winners than give handouts to losers.

—Doug Raymond on the *Luxury Living* podcast, September 14, 2012

Angie sat in chemistry with Bas, their lab table covered in the soft pretzels that they were somehow supposed to be melting over the Bunsen burner that sat between them. However, Bas wouldn't stop eating them. Angie—dressed, inexplicably, in a marching band uniform—kept swatting them out of his hand, reminding him that these were for *school*, not for snacks, but he didn't seem to care and only continued tearing off giant bites with his teeth.

Irritation built to a boil inside her, and she was getting ready to climb on top of the table and start screaming—what that would accomplish, she wasn't sure, but it felt like the right thing to do—when a girl at the table behind her began to sing.

Angie recognized the tune, although the lyrics remained fuzzy. It was from an animated movie she'd watched with her parents when she was little, back before she'd developed her own taste and they'd subsequently given up on family movie nights. This movie was one of the few she'd liked: *Anastasia*, about a lost Russian princess with amnesia.

She turned around in her chair, searching for the singer, but her face remained stubbornly out of focus, caught in Angie's peripheral vision. Her voice was pretty, though, and oddly familiar, although Angie couldn't remember where she'd heard it before. Angie strained to make out the words, leaning toward the girl until she was crawling over the table to get to her, coarse salt digging into her palms. Desperate, she called out to the singer. *Who are—*

"—you?"

Her own sleepy murmur met her ears as darkness settled in to wipe away the classroom, the pretzels, Bas. A dream, she realized. Just a dream, shattered by the sound of her own voice.

Her room was still dark, and the clock on her nightstand read 1:43 in glowing green. Plenty of time until morning. She rubbed her eyes and flopped over in her bed, re-fluffing her pillow and burrowing deeper into her blankets.

It wasn't until she stilled, waiting to sink back into sleep, that she realized the singing hadn't stopped.

Angie sat up straight in her bed, heart pounding. It was the same voice from her dream, singing the same song, "Once Upon a December." The lyrics were still a little muddled, dulled by multiple doors and the spray of the shower.

"No way," she muttered, swinging her feet onto the floor. Bas was right. Her dad had a woman over, and she was *singing* in the freaking *shower* at 1:43 in the morning.

She could not believe this. How dare he invite some stranger to spend the night without even *mentioning* it to Angie? This was her house too. And they both used that bathroom. If her dad's gross sleepover friend was using Angie's Aveda Smooth Infusion shampoo and conditioner that cost her nearly fifty bucks, she may actually have to perform a citizen's arrest.

But almost as soon as the anger flared up, it was gone, replaced by a cold, twisting sensation that coiled through Angie's insides like a snake. For a few long seconds, she sat motionless, listening, her toes feeling glued to the worn beige carpet. There was a woman in the bathroom. Presumably naked. There was only one person who could have invited her into this house.

Her mom had been gone for nearly two years. She was never coming back. Angie knew that.

So why did this hurt so much?

As Angie sat there on the edge of her bed, the woman finished "Once Upon a December" and shifted to a different song, something pleading and mournful that she didn't recognize. It was all Angie needed to remember how to move. She stood, feeling her way through the dark room to the door.

She wasn't sure what she intended to do. March down to her dad's room—the room he once shared with her mom—and confront him? And say what? *How dare you move on when I haven't yet?*

But as soon as she stepped into the hall, she froze.

The bathroom door was open.

The light was off.

The room was silent.

Angie tiptoed to the bathroom doorway, gooseflesh rising on the back of her neck. *What the hell?* With a trembling hand, she reached around the doorframe and fumbled for the light switch.

In the split second between flicking the switch and waiting for her eyes to adjust, all sorts of awful images flashed across her imagination. A pale figure with stringy black hair standing in her path. A blood-smeared body in the bathtub. A bony hand draped in tatters of hanging flesh, fingers inches from her face.

But there was nothing. The bathroom was empty. Everything was exactly as she'd left it when she got ready for bed, down to the empty

Dixie cups on the counter and her maroon towel flung carelessly over the shower curtain bar. Angie shuffled far enough into the room to peer into the tub. Still a few lingering droplets from her shower a few hours ago, but mostly dry.

She'd heard the shower. She could've *sworn* she heard the shower. A high-pitched hum underscoring the woman's voice.

And where was the woman? Angie's heart pounded against the walls of her chest like a fist on a door, insistent and relentless, as she flipped off the bathroom light, then forced her feet down the hall to her father's room.

He always slept with the door cracked, despite her repeated requests that he close it. *I want to be able to hear if something happens,* he always said. He never said what that something might be.

Holding her breath, she pushed his door open, giving her eyes a second to adjust from the light of the bathroom. Her dad was face down on the left side of his bed, one leg hooked around the outside of the comforter. Deep, steady snores rumbled out from where his face was buried in his pillow. The right side of the bed, as it had been for the past two years, remained smooth and untouched.

Angie's mind spun as she hurried back to her room, her breath coming in shallow gasps. Locking her door, she pulled the nanny camera down from where she'd stuck it on top of her bookshelf earlier that day. Bas had thought she was insane when she dragged him into Best Buy for surveillance equipment that afternoon, but this was *exactly* why she'd done it. Something was living in her house. It was the only possible explanation. And now she'd have proof.

It took four attempts to eject the SD card from the camera and three more to insert it into her laptop. Her hands were shaking so badly that it was a wonder she didn't drop it. Paging through the tiny manual that had come with the camera, she found the section on *Reviewing Your Footage* and followed the instructions, which annoyingly involved downloading the camera company's proprietary video software first.

"Come on, come *on*," she muttered, her knee bobbing up and down as she waited for it to install. The progress bar crept forward at a glacial pace thanks to their bargain bin internet connection. Watching paint dry would be exciting compared to this.

Once it finally completed, she opened up the footage from that evening, listening intently . . . but there was nothing there. On the screen was her room, illuminated in shades of green thanks to the camera's night vision setting. She saw herself sit up in bed, pause for a minute, then walk to the door.

But there was no sound. She double-checked her computer speakers to make sure they weren't muted, then searched for a volume button on the video software but couldn't find one. She opened the manual again, flipped to the table of contents, then paged forward to the section on *Sound*.

She blinked a few times, disbelieving.

Note: Only the KidSafe Camera Pro records sound. All other KidSafe Camera models record video only. Before purchasing a camera that records sound, please check with your state to ensure compliance with local wiretapping laws.

"God*dammit*," she yelled, throwing the manual across the room. She'd asked for the best nanny camera they had—and then quickly revised it to the best nanny camera they had under a hundred bucks—and the stupid Best Buy employee had sold her one that didn't even record sound? What the actual hell?

"Angie?" Her father's groggy voice drifted down the hall. "Everything okay?"

"I'm fine," she called back. "Sorry. Bad dream."

"Okay. 'Night. Loveyouuuu." His words were already slurring together as he sank back into sleep.

She didn't answer, dragging the slider on the video uselessly back and forth as if she could pull "Once Upon a December" out of her computer speakers through sheer force of will. She watched herself pop silently in and out of bed like a jack-in-the-box. Nothing else in the room so much as stirred. Nothing to indicate that her house was haunted by an actual singing ghost.

Closing her laptop, she flipped her bedroom light back off and flopped onto her bed. The only sound in her room now was the loud thumping of her heart, fueled more by frustration than fear. Tomorrow, she'd exchange her stupid video-only nanny cam for one that also recorded sound, but that didn't help her at all tonight.

She reached for her nightstand and grabbed her phone, unplugging it from its charger and opening the Voice Memo app. Her finger hovered over the Record button as she strained to hear the ghost's voice. Seconds turned into minutes, yet the night remained stubbornly silent.

"Who *are* you?" she asked again. This time, the only voice she heard was her own.

CHAPTER FOUR

It's official—starting next month, I'll be working as an Accounting Specialist at Raymond Realty Group! I am SO excited to begin this next chapter in my career at one of the fastest-growing businesses in my community. Thanks so much for everyone who was rooting for me in my job search. Can't wait to crunch some numbers!

—Facebook post from Piper Carden, July 2018

Once Syzygy arrived with Potato, it didn't take long to unload. Madelyn didn't have that much large furniture that required two people to move; the biggest thing she owned was her upright piano, which her parents had paid to have professionally moved from their house in Tennessee. It was scheduled to arrive later that week. Aside from that, she just had her bed and mattress, one of the couches and a coffee table from their apartment, and a round white dining table.

Everything else was small enough to move on her own, so whatever wasn't clearly labeled with a destination—which was most of it, since Madelyn had gotten overwhelmed with packing pretty early in the process and started dumping things in random boxes in an effort to be done as quickly as possible—she and Syzygy piled in the living and dining rooms, which then overflowed into the garage for her to deal with later.

As they worked, Potato bounced from room to room, gleefully sniffing every inch of her new home that she could reach on her short little legs and, as promised, making the whole house smell like flatulent dog. Since Madelyn had no idea where any of her scented candles were, she opened all the windows instead, grateful for the mild late-summer breeze.

Syzygy decided to stay over that night, since they were too tired to attempt the three-hour drive back to State College. They were working on their graduate degree in psychology at Penn State, so they'd renewed the lease on their apartment for the next year. After they'd returned the rental truck, the two of them drank boxed wine out of paper cups and watched episodes of *The Great* that Madelyn had saved on her laptop until they both passed out on her bare mattress on the floor, Potato curled up happily between them.

In the morning, Syzygy stuck around long enough to run to Wawa for coffee and breakfast sandwiches, but then had to make the trek back home. They wanted to squeeze in a nap before their marathon bartending shift that night. "Nothing says 'let's celebrate the working class' like working until five a.m., eh?" they said wryly around a bite of pancake sausage Sizzli.

"Do you at least get Monday off?"

"And miss out on the opportunity to let a bunch of drunk businessmen educate the poor ignorant Brit on the superiority of American capitalism? Not on your life." Syzygy winked. "I may even femme it up a bit. Break out the glitter." They waggled their eyebrows, giving their shoulders a little shimmy.

Typically, Syzygy's style was probably best described as chaotic gender neutral; they gravitated toward bold prints, bright colors, and piles of eclectic accessories, which they would mix and match into surprising ensembles that seemed equal parts clothing and performance art. Today, they wore a flowing patchwork linen skirt over black cargo pants, a loose purple tank top, a jungle-print necktie, and a brown knit beanie with a multicolored pom-pom on top. Madelyn wasn't sure if they'd packed this outfit intentionally, or just scavenged it together using whatever they could find in the trunk of their car. Either seemed equally likely.

But occasionally, Syzygy would decide to don more traditionally feminine attire: sundresses, jumpsuits, corsets, rompers. Once, a full ballgown, which they had worn to all their classes that day. Not for any real reason, they'd told Madelyn when she'd asked. Just because that's what they felt like wearing.

Madelyn laughed. "Does glitter equal better tips?"

"It doesn't hurt," Syzygy said. They gestured to the sea of boxes scattered around the house. "Well, good luck with this. I don't envy the unboxing of whatever is in all of these. You are positively rubbish at packing, you know that?"

"Yes, but I have many other fine qualities."

"Do you?" Syzygy furrowed their brow, tapping their chin with a finger. "May have to think on that."

Madelyn rolled her eyes as she pulled Syzygy in for a hug. "Be safe, okay?"

"I will if you will." They took her by the shoulders, holding her at arm's length. "I meant what I said before. *Promise* me you'll be careful."

"I promise."

"Do you want me to leave Jubilee with you?" Jubilee was Syzygy's Taser, named for the X-Men character who shot sparkles out of her hands. She lived in Syzygy's glove compartment.

"I wouldn't know the first thing to do with her."

"That's always her problem, poor girl."

"I'm going to be fine," Madelyn assured them. Even her parents were not as protective as Syzygy.

They frowned, clearly displeased with Madelyn's lack of doomsdaying. "He has a lot of money."

"I know."

"And a lot of guns."

"I know."

"And as a general rule, it is not a good idea to piss off people with a lot of money and guns."

"Syz, I *know*. I swear, I too want me to stay out of trouble."

"You just have a funny way of showing it sometimes," they said with a sigh. "Just be smart, okay?"

"I'm glad you reminded me, because until now I was planning to be *very* stupid."

"You know what I mean."

"I do. Thanks, Syz. Text me when you get home, okay?"

"Okay, but you know we're still sharing our locations. So you can literally just watch me drive the whole way home."

"Sure, if I wanted to be super weird about it." She should probably turn that off. It had made sense when they were sharing an apartment and Syzygy was working overnight shifts, but less now that Madelyn had moved nearly two hundred miles away.

"Whatever, stalker."

They hugged again, and Madelyn swallowed tears as she watched them drive away. It hadn't felt real until she'd said goodbye to Syzygy. But now it washed over her like a bucket of ice water. For the first time in her life, she was truly on her own.

She looked down at Potato, who was staring at the spot where Syzygy's car had been and wagging her tail hopefully. "Nope, they're not coming back," Madelyn said. "It's just you and me now, spud."

Potato kept wagging. She didn't understand, of course. It was one of the things Madelyn loved about her. There was no need to ever justify her actions or save face with her dog. No need to explain or defend or impress.

Dogs weren't complicated. Not like people. It was safe to love a dog. Dogs would always love you back.

She scooped up Potato and snuggled her face into her soft fluff, admitting in a whisper what she couldn't tell anyone else. "I really hope this wasn't a mistake."

CHAPTER FIVE

> Look for the RR Platinum seal, our patented ninety-nine-step guarantee. Remember, if it's not platinum, it's not anything.
>
> —Raymond Realty Group radio spot, 2023

If not for a coupon code, Madelyn may not have ever applied for a job in East Henderson.

It was New Year's Eve, the final day of 2020, and Madelyn had gone over to Ralph's house to watch the ball drop on TV. They were halfway through their freshman year of college at Penn State, where Ralph had already declared his intention to major in business management, while Madelyn was still undecided. She was leaning toward teaching, but hadn't told Ralph, since she knew he wouldn't approve.

She'd spent most of the break with him, getting in as much "quality time" as possible, or at least Ralph's definition of quality time. She would've liked to spend time with some of her friends from high school—most had gone to school in Tennessee or the surrounding states, and it would've been nice to see them again, especially since their senior year got cut short due to COVID—but Ralph pointed out that the two of them rarely ever got any time alone at school, between classes and roommates and homework.

He was right, of course. She felt kind of guilty when he had to point it out to her. She needed to do a better job of prioritizing their relationship.

So she didn't object when he suggested spending New Year's Eve at his house, even though they'd be driving back to school in two days, and Madelyn had turned down invitations to two other parties in order to say yes to Ralph. His parents weren't home, so they'd have the house all to themselves. And at least with each other, they wouldn't have to wear masks. He was right; it was too good an opportunity to pass up.

Madelyn noticed the brochure on the kitchen table early in the evening, but didn't work up the courage to ask about it until Ralph had already had a few glasses of champagne, which he claimed he'd gotten as a gift from work. Madelyn had her doubts about whether the Olive Garden would give their nineteen-year-old servers bottles of alcohol, but knew better than to challenge him.

"What's this?" she'd asked when Ralph seemed pleasantly inebriated.

He'd glanced at the brochure. "Oh, nothing. My dad got my mom this stupid genetic testing thing for Christmas." He scoffed. "Parent gifts are so boring."

Madelyn neglected to point out that his Christmas gift to her had been a gold locket with a picture of his face inside. Hardly the pinnacle of creativity. Which had not been improved when he'd leaned into her ear and whispered, "Of course, we can totally swap that out with a more *intimate* photo if you want," then glanced pointedly at his crotch.

She wondered if any girl in the entire world would be tempted by that offer. It was possible, she supposed. But unlikely.

"I've always kind of wanted to do one of those tests," Madelyn said carefully. "They're just really expensive."

Ralph rolled his eyes. "Seriously, babe? Why? Spoiler alert, you're Chinese."

Madelyn bit her tongue as he laughed at his own joke. "True," she agreed, "but my mom isn't. And since she's adopted, it might be nice to learn a little bit about that side of the family."

"Oh yeah," Ralph said. "I'd forgotten about that."

Of course he had.

"So," Madelyn ventured, "it looks like there's a referral code here. Do you think your parents would mind if I used it?"

Ralph shrugged. "If that's how you want to spend your money, knock yourself out." He'd sat up then, wagging a suspicious finger at her. "But remember, I already *gave* you your Christmas present. So I'm not paying for this too."

"Of course," she'd readily agreed. "I wasn't going to ask you."

"I mean, I *would*, you know, if you'd told me that was what you wanted," he said, relaxing back into the couch. "But you didn't. And that necklace wasn't cheap."

"It's really nice," Madelyn said, brushing her fingers against the locket at her neck.

Ralph had given her a lazy grin, beckoning her back to the couch. "Nothing but the best for my girl."

The next morning, she'd filled out the order form online as Ralph snored through his hangover, using the Metsons' referral code for 50 percent off. And a few weeks later, she'd received her results, which told her she was half Chinese, a quarter German, 15 percent Welsh, 5 percent Czech, and 5 percent all sorts of other things—and that she had a cousin she'd never met.

She'd messaged her right away, and heard back later the same day. Before long, the two of them were corresponding regularly, and even exchanging occasional texts. Her cousin's name was Piper Carden, she was about six years older than Madelyn, and she worked in the accounting department of a company in East Henderson, Pennsylvania. Piper had been excited when she'd heard Madelyn was attending Penn State, and told her that if she ever wanted to travel to the eastern side of the state, she was welcome to stay with her.

Soon, that invitation morphed into solid plans, and Madelyn was set to visit East Henderson over spring break, while Ralph went to Europe with his parents. She hadn't told Ralph about Piper. He wasn't close with any of his extended family, and wouldn't see the appeal of Madelyn trying to forge a relationship with hers. So his vacation felt like the perfect time for them to finally meet.

Except one week before Madelyn was set to visit, Piper stopped responding to texts and emails. Her phone went straight to voicemail. Madelyn considered going anyway, but she didn't have Piper's address, and besides, she didn't want to just show up if Piper had changed her mind. Spring break came and went, and without anywhere else to go, Madelyn spent the week crashing on the couch of a friend who lived off-campus.

For a long time, she assumed that Piper had chosen to cut her off. Maybe she had come on too strong. Maybe she was too young, too immature. Maybe Piper had simply gotten sick of her.

She tried not to let it bother her. After all, she barely knew Piper. They'd talked for only a couple of months. It wasn't a big deal. Or at least, it shouldn't be.

Then, during her junior year, she got an email from a lawyer in East Henderson.

I'm representing Kelsey O'Donnell in a lawsuit against Raymond Realty Group, the email said. At first, Madelyn had been confused. She didn't know anyone named Kelsey O'Donnell.

> I was given your name as a possible contact of Piper Carden. As you may already be aware, Piper went missing in the spring of 2021, and the circumstances surrounding her disappearance may be material to my client's case. I was wondering if you would be open to a conversation regarding your interactions with Piper, either on or off the record.

Madelyn felt like she'd been punched in the stomach. By then, Piper had been missing for two years. Madelyn should've known something was wrong instead of making it about herself. She emailed the lawyer back right away, agreeing to help in any way she could.

Kelsey O'Donnell turned out to be a former administrative assistant at Raymond Realty Group who was fired shortly after Piper disappeared. Not long after that, the company sued her for divulging trade secrets. In response, O'Donnell had countersued for wrongful termination, claiming that her firing and the subsequent lawsuit had been manufactured for spurious reasons, and that she was actually fired in retaliation for asking too many questions about the sudden departure of another employee—Piper Carden.

Piper had been the one to help Kelsey get the job at Raymond Realty. She'd come aboard during the pandemic, after being furloughed by her previous company, and although she wasn't thrilled about having to come into the office while most other companies went remote, she enjoyed seeing Piper every day. For the ten months they worked together, they met for lunch daily and texted regularly.

Until one day, Piper didn't show up. She'd missed work before, of course, but had always texted Kelsey to let her know why. This time, there was no text. No email. No response when Kelsey called. Piper was simply . . . gone.

A coworker said they'd heard she quit. And it wasn't unusual for employees to leave without a word—turnover was pretty high—but Kelsey wasn't just a coworker. She and Piper were friends. And for her to suddenly go dark felt very, very wrong.

Kelsey went to Piper's house, but it seemed abandoned. She checked with mutual friends, but no one had heard anything. So she started asking questions around work, until, as her attorney put it, "she was instructed to let it go."

It wasn't long after that when Kelsey found herself pulled into a meeting with her boss, where she was unceremoniously fired for poor job performance, which Kelsey found shocking since her performance reviews up to that point had been "glowing." Two days later, she was served with a lawsuit for "the solicitation of proprietary information" and "the knowing and willful dispersal of trade secrets."

Confused, Kelsey contacted an employment attorney—T. J. Melitz, who had emailed Madelyn—and explained her situation. "Off the record," Melitz told Madelyn during a Zoom call, "it's unsurprising to me that Raymond Realty would resort to such tactics. It's consistent with their reputation for being extremely litigious."

However, he thought Kelsey had a case if they could make a solid connection between Piper's disappearance and Kelsey's firing. "Which is where you come in," he said. "Any insight you can give us into the weeks leading up to her disappearance would be helpful. Especially if she mentioned anything about work."

But Madelyn hadn't been able to help much. Going back over her messages with Piper, she realized that most of it had been about her. Her family, her life, her school. *Maybe* Piper seemed a little more reserved than usual in the weeks leading up to her disappearance? But Madelyn could also chalk that up to her forgetting to ask any meaningful questions.

Since her information was mostly useless, Melitz agreed to keep it off the record. A few months later, the entire lawsuit was placed under seal. Madelyn never heard anything else about it, and her internet searches revealed nothing.

She felt awful for Kelsey and sick over Piper. She wished she'd been able to help.

But at least keeping her talk with Melitz off the record meant that her name was never submitted as a possible witness. Which meant that Doug Raymond had no idea who she was.

Which was why, when she'd been offered the job in East Henderson, her first call was to Raymond Realty. Having her application kicked straight up to Doug Raymond himself was just an unexpected bonus.

She had told Syzygy the truth. She was here for a job. And that *was* her top priority.

But she now had a direct line to Doug Raymond. And if he had answers about Piper . . .

Well. It couldn't hurt to at least poke around a little. Right?

CHAPTER SIX

Mayor Whitburn and Doug Raymond cutting the ribbon at the new Raymond Realty Group headquarters in East Henderson, Pennsylvania. The company's new campus boasts a food court, a fitness center, and a select number of "focus rooms" for employees wishing to minimize distractions. In 2020, Raymond also suggested these rooms might double as solutions for employees with mild or asymptomatic cases of COVID-19 who wish to return to work. Raymond Realty Group began the $200 million renovation of the facility, previously the East Henderson Municipal Business Center, in mid-2019.

—Photo caption in the *East Henderson Herald*, March 19, 2021

By Tuesday morning, Madelyn was ready to relinquish custody of the dog back to Syzygy.

"Potato, *no*."

Bouncing on one foot, Madelyn scooped up the little dog with one hand while attempting to zip her ankle boot with the other. For the past two and a half days, while Madelyn attempted to unpack as much as possible before school started, Potato had been obsessed with the wall outside the bathroom. For reasons understandable only to dogs, her new favorite activity was digging at the smooth ecru paint with her tiny claws.

Maybe she didn't like the new house. Not that Madelyn could blame her at the moment. It looked like it had been picked up and shaken like a snow globe. Whatever good intentions she'd had about unpacking in an organized and orderly fashion had been abandoned about an hour after Syzygy drove away. As overwhelming as packing had been, it was nothing compared to unpacking.

Somewhere along the way, Madelyn had gotten it into her head that she couldn't figure out where things went unless she could see all of it at once. So she'd opened up every box within arm's reach, dumped their contents out on the floor . . . and then realized she'd made a horrible mistake.

Maybe she just needed to embrace living in squalor.

Fortunately, Potato was about as vicious as her namesake, and she hadn't managed to leave a mark on the wall yet. A mess, she could clean up, but paint and drywall were another story. The last thing Madelyn needed was for Doug Raymond to kick her out for letting her contraband dog scratch up his precious walls.

Potato had been an impulse buy the week after she'd broken up with Ralph. The apartment that she'd shared with Syzygy didn't allow pets either, but they'd had only a few months left on their lease, Potato didn't shed, and neither one of them had much willpower when it came to small, fluffy dogs. One look at Potato's big round eyes and stubby wagging tail, and they'd both been goners.

Plus, Ralph hated dogs. Which should have been her first clue that he was a mistake.

"Alexa, add dog spray to my shopping list," she called, dodging a minefield of half-unpacked boxes as she deposited Potato in her bedroom and shut the door. She'd get some of that stuff that was supposed to make dogs stop licking themselves and spray it on the wall. Hopefully it would smell worse than whatever Potato was so fixated on. Probably soup spilled by the previous tenant or something equally gross.

"Okay," Alexa chirped, *"I've added doll trays to your shopping list."*

Madelyn rolled her eyes as she swiped on lipstick in the bathroom mirror. Given all the concern over the past few years around AI technology, she would've expected it to be a little more intelligent by now.

High-pitched barking pierced her heart as she turned the dead bolt to unlock the front door. She checked her watch, then walked back to the bedroom. Potato bounced frantically around her legs when she opened the door, begging to be picked up. "Okay, just *one* more cuddle," Madelyn said, picking her up. Immediately, Potato calmed, snuggling into her chest.

"I promise I'll come back," Madelyn said into her soft brown fur. "It'll be okay. But now I've got to go."

Potato let out a mournful yip as Madelyn set her back on the floor. Madelyn's heart gave a flutter of regret as she closed the door again. "I wish you could come with me too."

Sighing, she returned to the front door, then paused, confused. It stood wide open, letting in a bright beam of morning sunlight. Had she opened it before walking to the bedroom? She thought she'd just unlocked it.

Madelyn shook her head, reminding herself never to move three days before starting a new job ever again. It was clearly breaking her brain. She desperately hoped there was more coffee at school. Preferably in the form of an intravenous drip.

She kneaded her hands on the steering wheel as she navigated toward the school, remembering too late that she'd forgotten to take her prescription Effexor that morning. Her stomach felt tight, her heart tapping a swift beat against the walls of her chest.

Perfect. Just what she needed on her first day of her first real job: constant, simmering anxiety.

She missed the turn-in for the school on her first pass, forcing her to drive around the block before pulling into the teachers' lot, which was already full of cars. No one else was in sight, meaning they must all be inside already. She hadn't even made it through the doors yet, and she was already underperforming.

Madelyn pulled out her phone as she hurried inside, triple-checking the email from the principal.

> Welcome back, teachers! We'll kick off our in-service day in the library with a welcome breakfast, meet-and-greet, and a short address from yours truly at 8:00!

She swiped down from the top of her screen to check the time. 8:04.

Crap crap crap.

She'd been inside the school only once before, during her interview two months earlier, but thought she remembered where the library was from her brief tour with Principal Hayes. Moving as quickly as she could without breaking into a run, she walked through the lobby, turning right once she reached the hall.

At least she would have missed only the first few minutes of the breakfast and meet-and-greet. She'd slip in, grab a plate, and strike up a conversation with whoever was nearest. Maybe no one would even notice she was late.

"Oh thank God," she said as she recognized the bright mural on the wall leading to the library. Eventually, she'd love to spend more time taking it all in, identifying every single literary character and book reference that decorated the hall, but for today, she rushed past Narnia and Wonderland and Camp Half-Blood without a second glance. She didn't even bother to look in through the half-light double doors before throwing them open and stepping into the library.

Which, she quickly realized, was a mistake.

Madelyn stumbled to a mortified halt as every head in the library swiveled to face her. All the teachers were seated at the various tables, with the principal standing up in the center of the room. A table off to the side held three open boxes of Dunkin' donuts, a couple of cardboard catering jugs of Wawa coffee, and a mostly empty tray of breakfast sandwiches.

"I-I'm sorry," Madelyn stammered. "I thought it started at eight?"

"We go by the school schedule for in-service days," Principal Hayes said, her voice cool. "First bell is at 7:34."

Of course. So everyone had gotten there half an hour ago, eaten breakfast, and then settled in for the principal's remarks.

Everyone except her.

"Everyone, this is Miss Zhao," Principal Hayes said, addressing the room. She pronounced it *zay-ho*, which was possibly the most egregious mispronunciation of her last name that Madelyn had ever heard. "She's going to be our new choir director."

Madelyn forced a smile, unable to work up the courage to correct Principal Hayes in front of everyone. "Hello," she said, giving a small wave. A few teachers responded with lukewarm greetings; most just smiled or nodded.

Great. Now she was going to be Miss Zay-ho to the rest of the school. That's what she got, she supposed, for showing up half an hour late to in-service.

"So sorry," Madelyn said again, desperately scanning the room for an empty seat and coming up short. *Oh no oh no oh NO,* a voice in her head repeated, growing more and more frantic as she realized she'd have to remain standing for the duration of the meeting. Like an awkward Venus de Milo, standing there metaphorically naked and armless in front of everyone.

In the back of the room, one of the teachers rose from his chair and gestured to it. "Here, you can take my seat," he said with a small smile.

Madelyn shook her head. "Oh no, it's fine, I'm fine here." She shifted from one foot to the other, hugging her stupid messenger bag to her chest like a life vest as she waved him off. *What are you doing, you idiot,* the voice in her head screamed.

The other teacher—young, tall, and *painfully* cute, she realized with a mortified little flutter in her stomach—placed both hands on the chair and pulled it out a little farther. "Please, I needed to stand up anyway. Leg cramp." He shook out his right leg with a grimace, as evidence of his absolutely-not-real cramp, and raised his eyebrows at her expectantly.

Everyone was staring at her, waiting for her to stop disrupting their morning, and she had the feeling that this chivalrous guy with the annoyingly handsome face would not be the first one to flinch. "Okay," she said with a nervous smile, weaving around the room to the proffered chair.

The closer she got, the more the flutters in her stomach turned into bona fide flapping. Of *course* it would be her luck that the very first thing she did in her brand-new job was make an absolute fool of herself in front of the most beautiful man she'd met in months. He wore dark jeans and a green button-down shirt the color of wet grass. His sleeves were rolled halfway up his forearms, baring rich brown skin, and he had a pair of bright-blue sunglasses perched on top of his head, nestled in waves of thick, dark hair.

"Thank you," she whispered, sinking into the chair as gracefully as she could as Principal Hayes began speaking again.

"No problem," he whispered back. "How do you take your coffee?"

"One cream, two sugars," she answered automatically, before realizing what he was really asking. "But you don't have to—"

It was too late; he was already halfway to the food table, where he poured coffee and creamer into a paper cup and grabbed a couple of sugar packets, along with a napkin and a donut, before making his way back to her. "Hope you like jimmies," he said, handing over the coffee and the donut: chocolate with rainbow sprinkles, or "jimmies" as she'd learned Pennsylvanians liked to call them.

She nodded gratefully. "Thank you. Again."

"Anytime," he said with a slightly crooked grin that revealed a dimple in his left cheek. "And you really didn't miss much. She'd only been talking for a minute when you came in."

She let out a relieved breath. "Thank goodness. I was afraid that—"

Beside her, a square-jawed woman with thinning brown hair pulled into a low ponytail cleared her throat, shooting Madelyn an irritated look.

"Sorry," Madelyn whispered. Biting her lip, she turned her full attention to Principal Hayes, tearing her eyes away from her rescuer. Once she felt certain that the woman beside her was placated, she risked a glance behind her, searching for him, but he'd moved away to lean against a low bookshelf, and was watching Principal Hayes intently. She was surprised to find that she was disappointed; she'd hoped he'd stay near her.

But that was silly. He'd been polite, that was all.

Still, throughout the rest of the principal's remarks, she caught herself repeatedly glancing in his direction. Once or twice, she thought she felt his eyes on her, but when she checked, he was still staring straight ahead. Did he know she was looking? Did he *like* that she was looking?

Get it together, Madelyn.

It was only once Principal Hayes had finished speaking and people started to rise from their chairs that Madelyn realized she'd missed absolutely everything the principal had said. Her heart began to race as she stood, sliding the strap of her bag onto her shoulder and trying her best to mirror what everyone else was doing, which she assumed was heading to their classrooms. She followed the ponytailed woman out of the library and into the hall, but wasn't sure which way to go beyond that. She couldn't remember where the choir room was in relation to the library and didn't want to ask after the horrible first impression she'd already made.

Arbitrarily, she picked a direction and started walking, pulling out her phone as she pretended she knew the way. Maybe there was a map of the school on the website.

"Um, hi, do you know where you're going?"

She knew that voice. Madelyn scrunched her eyes shut for a long second, then turned around. Sure enough, there he was again, her knight in shining skinny jeans, giving her a somewhat bemused smile.

She tried for a smile and completely overshot her attempt at "sunny," landing on something that felt more akin to "caught in a bear trap." *Too many teeth. Abort, abort!*

"Sure!" she chirped, a little too brightly. "I was just headed to the, uh . . ." She pointed down the hallway in the direction she'd been going. "Oh, wow, what's it called? I *always* forget what it's called," she said, stalling in the absurd hope that maybe there actually *was* a logical destination with a weirdly complicated name somewhere in this general direction.

"Gym?" he said. His mouth twitched, like he was fighting a smile.

She blinked at him. "Is that really all that's down there?"

"Yup."

"Oh God." She buried her face in her hands, hoping that maybe when she looked back up, the day would have reset from the beginning. "I swear I am not normally like this."

"Like what?"

"A wreck." Madelyn dropped her hands and sighed. "I was going to be so professional today," she said wistfully.

"The day is still young," he said, grinning adorably at her. It was truly not fair that he could be so chill and lovely while she was . . . whatever she was.

He pointed over his shoulder with his thumb. "Well, if you change your mind and wanted to head down to the arts wing, I'm going that way."

She nodded gratefully, following as he began walking in the opposite direction. "So you teach an arts class too?"

"Language arts, yes," he said. His stride was long, and she hurried to keep up. Now that she was able to study him more closely, she realized that what she had thought was generic texturing on his shirt was actually a subtle dragon print, twining through the fabric like vines. "I teach Spanish."

"Oh. I took Spanish in high school, but I don't remember much," she said, searching her memory. "Um, me llamo Madelyn." Wow, her accent was *terrible*. This was definitely not the way to impress him.

But he smiled, touching his own chest. "Mucho gusto, Madelyn. Me llamo Alejandro. Or as the kids call me, Señor García."

"Mucho gusto, Alejandro," she said, hoping he wasn't going to want to keep conversing in Spanish. The rest of her vocabulary consisted mostly of menu items from Taco Bell.

"You can call me Alex, though," he said, much to her relief. "Some of the teachers like to call me Alejandro because they think it sounds more ethnic."

She looked at him, wondering if he was joking or annoyed, and he winked at her. Joking, then.

"So how *do* you pronounce your name?" Alex asked. "Because I doubt it's *zay-ho*."

Madelyn groaned, burying her face in her hands. "I should've said something," she said. "Now it's too late."

"Nah," Alex said, waving away her concern. "I'll just make a point to call you by name every time I see you. Couple weeks, people will get it right. Although Hayes may be a lost cause. So is it . . . *zow*?" He pronounced it to rhyme with *cow*.

A grateful laugh escaped through Madelyn's fingers. "You're close. It's Zhao," she said, dropping her hands from her face. "The *zh* in Chinese is pronounced like a *j* in English."

That was actually an oversimplification too, but it was as close as most Americans could get. The actual *zh* sound in Mandarin was more of a mix between a *j* and a *ch*, but farther back in the mouth. And the Mandarin pronunciation didn't really rhyme with *cow* either, but Madelyn had learned the hard way not to try to teach people to say it with the longer Chinese *o*, since that always ended in them calling her Madelyn Joe. Which was almost as bad as Madelyn Zay-ho.

Madelyn didn't mind the common pronunciation of her last name, though, as long as people were trying. The truth was, she had a little trouble saying it correctly herself. She'd never had any interest in learning Mandarin as a kid, and once she got a little older, it felt too daunting to try. Her mouth had never quite learned to make the sounds that should have been natural for her. She could get pretty close, but she knew she still had a heavy American accent.

Which made it easier most of the time to simply embrace the American pronunciation. Even though Americans looked at her and saw a Chinese person, she knew Chinese people listened to her and heard an American. That would always be the case. No point in fighting it.

"This is you, Miss Zhao," Alex said, stopping by the choral room that Madelyn remembered from her tour. She felt a little thrill to hear her name on his lips—pronounced correctly, or at least as correctly as she'd explained it.

"Thank you very much, Señor García." She opened the door, pleased to see MISS ZHAO—CHOIR printed on a nameplate on the wall.

"I'm right down that hall, room 117," he said, pointing past her. "And then back the way we came, if you turn left and then take your second right, you'll find the teachers' lounge."

"Right," she said, nodding. "Got it."

She didn't, of course. She was certain she'd find buried treasure before she'd successfully navigate her way to the teachers' lounge. But she'd already been enough of a disaster that morning, and wanted him to think she was at least somewhat competent.

He nodded, adjusting his bag on his shoulder as he stepped away from her, walking backward. "Room 117," he said again. "Let me know if you need anything."

She nodded again. "Gracias, señor." Dear lord, she *had* to stop with the terrible Spanish.

But his smile widened. "I told you, call me Alex."

"Right. Alex," she confirmed, pointing at him like a dork.

"Madelyn," he said, pointing back before spinning on his toe and continuing toward his classroom.

Tearing her eyes from him, she walked into the choir room, dropping her bag by her desk and sinking into the ancient swivel chair that still held the imprint of her predecessor in its cracked faux leather. Her heart pounded. She pulled out her phone and opened the Messages app. Help, she typed. I met a guy.

The response from Syzygy came immediately: 😲.

He works down the hall from me.

🍿

I made a total ass of myself in front of everyone and he rescued me. And brought me coffee. And a donut.

What kind of donut?

Chocolate. With sprinkles. I'm sorry. "Jimmies."

Solid. Go on.

Cute. Tall. Dark hair. Latino, I think. Teaches Spanish.

Oh and he was wearing a shirt with the sleeves rolled up. You know. In the good way. And his shirt had dragons on it. Not like, weirdo dragons. Hot dragons.

Marry him.

Madelyn laughed out loud, shaking her head. We WORK together. I am not allowed to have a thing for him.

Fine. But I'm gonna at least need pics. To confirm the hotness.

I cannot stalk my coworker.

You dweeb, get his IG.

Oh. Right.

She pulled up Instagram and started to type his name into the search bar, but before she finished, a notification popped up.

@salexgarcia has requested to follow you.

OMG HE FOLLOWED ME ALREADY.

ARE YOU SERIOUS?

I AM FREAKING OUT.

Dibs on Human of Honor at your wedding.

Shut up.

YOU texted ME.

I have to go work now.

Oh right. Me too. Go be a grown-up.

Right. Um. How does one do that?

Hell if I know.

Madelyn put her phone face down on her desk, then thought better of it and tucked it into her bag instead. As she busied herself getting her classroom ready, she kept catching herself glancing toward the door, hoping Alex might stop by, but of course he didn't. He was working. Just like she was supposed to be.

She sighed as she opened her laptop and connected to the school Wi-Fi, forcing herself to keep her eyes on the task at hand. She did *not* have a crush, she told herself. She didn't even know this guy. He was probably a serial killer. Or a narcissist. Or a gun enthusiast. Or one of those people who cut their toenails in the living room.

She was better off on her own.

It didn't take long to decorate the room. She'd thought she had brought too many posters and pictures and knickknacks, but it turned out that what seemed like a lot in her boxed-up apartment in State College looked like barely anything in her empty classroom. Still, she did what she could, making a mental note to check out the local thrift stores soon to try to find a few more items to liven up the space.

Once the room was as ready as she could get it, she busied herself composing a welcome email to her students and another for their parents, uploading her syllabus, and adding concert and audition dates to the school calendar. She snapped a photo of the most decorated corner of the room for her newsletter—ideally she'd love to send one out every week, but maybe she should aim for every other week to start—

An email notification popped up on her screen.

FROM: Kelsey O'Donnell
SUBJECT: Are you here?
Want to meet up?

CHAPTER SEVEN

Dear Piper,

This feels like such a strange thing to be typing, but I guess we both signed up hoping for this, so here goes: I think I'm your cousin. Or I guess, I KNOW I'm your cousin. DNA doesn't lie, right? It just sounds weird to say it like that, like I'm sure, when this all is so new and unfamiliar. But science is science, right? So here goes. According to our results, your mom was my mom's sister. I don't know what your experience was, but here's mine.

My mom was adopted. She made a decision not to find her birth family, which I respect. But I have always been curious, obviously. My mom is amazing. She majored in art history, but works as a paralegal. She loves to crochet. Her favorite movie is Point Break, which is just too ridiculous for words. The first time I ever got my period, she let me skip school and took me to Sonic, where we ordered milkshakes and she told me about a time she snuck out of a friend's house during a sleepover and wound up spending the night in a cemetery. There's more to that story, but it's better in person.

I am currently a freshman at Penn State. I haven't declared a major yet, but I'm leaning toward music ed. I have one younger sister, although I think she'd prefer we weren't related. I've been dating my boyfriend Ralph since our junior year of high school, and we are planning on getting married after we graduate college. My dad is Chinese, which makes me half-Chinese, but I don't speak the language, although I wish I did. My favorite things are sci-fi novels, string cheese, and the smell of fresh cut grass. I would love to get to know you better. I have so many questions.

Sincerely,
Madelyn Zhao

Not long after the lawsuit fizzled out, Kelsey O'Donnell moved to Lancaster, nearly an hour west of East Henderson. Madelyn considered doing a Zoom call or waiting until the weekend to meet, but eagerness got the better of her. She and Kelsey had spoken a couple times on the phone during the lawsuit, but this was their first opportunity to meet in person, and Madelyn was dying to talk to her without the court case looming over them.

Half an hour after finishing up at the school, Madelyn buckled Potato into her harness in the front seat of the Fit and pulled up directions to Lancaster.

The drive out to Kelsey's was peaceful, the scenery shifting from highways to town roads to long stretches of farmland with houses and barns dotted in between the farther west she traveled. With a few miles to go, traffic slowed to a crawl, and Madelyn wondered if there had been an accident. But when the cars in front of her finally managed to work their way around the obstruction, she was treated to the sight of a black buggy pulled by a brown horse.

Potato yipped excitedly at the horse—who she probably assumed was a very large dog—through the cracked passenger-side window as Madelyn wove the car around them.

She couldn't help but look over at the driver as she passed, and was surprised to see a young boy, probably no older than sixteen and wearing suspenders and a wide-brimmed hat, perched on the driver's seat with the reins in his hands. He touched a hand to his hat when he noticed her looking, and Madelyn smiled back, unsure of the etiquette.

By the time she arrived at the coffee shop Kelsey had picked, Kelsey was already there. Madelyn found her sipping tea at a black metal table in a small seating area bordered by an iron gate lined with flowers.

Madelyn hurried to her table, hugging Potato to her chest, her leash wrapped around her hand.

Kelsey sprang up from her seat, wrapping Madelyn in a tight hug. "I'm sorry, I don't know if you're a hugger," Kelsey said, her chin still on Madelyn's shoulder. "I just feel like I know you."

"I do too," Madelyn said, squeezing her back.

They separated, and Kelsey looked down at Potato, wriggling eagerly in Madelyn's arms, desperate to meet this new human with her new smells. "And you must be Potato," she said, scratching her behind the ears.

Potato increased her squirming, attempting to climb out of Madelyn's arms and into Kelsey's.

"I think you're her new best friend," Madelyn said, placing the little dog down on the cobblestone patio, where she immediately began pawing at Kelsey's ankles. A small dish of clean water was already set out under the table. Kelsey must have told the staff that she was meeting someone with a dog. "Thank you so much for picking a place where I could bring her."

"No trouble. Lots of pet lovers in this area."

"I actually passed a horse and buggy on my way here."

Kelsey chuckled. "Even in Amish country, you'd be hard pressed to find a coffee shop that will let you bring in a horse. But dogs are easy peasy."

Madelyn sat in the chair across from her and pulled a couple of toys out of her bag for Potato, who had lost interest in Kelsey and was now busy sniffing the ground. Madelyn knew from experience that she'd take a few trips around the table, tangling the leash into a complete mess, before settling down by her feet.

In person, Kelsey looked different from what Madelyn had expected from her social media. In those photos, she favored dark lip colors and smoky eyes, dangly earrings and loose hair. But that was clearly an image she had curated for internet. Today, Kelsey didn't seem to be wearing any makeup, and although she was only in her early thirties, she already had the beginnings of shadows under her eyes. Her dark curls, pulled into a messy ponytail at the nape of her neck, had slivers of gray weaving through them, and she wore a faded blue hoodie and purple leggings with black sneakers, like she was planning on taking a walk or heading to the gym.

"I'm so glad we finally are getting a chance to meet in person," Madelyn said after running inside to place her order, assured by Kelsey that she was fine with Potato on the patio.

"Me too," Kelsey said. She sighed, pulling one foot up on the seat in front of her and using her bent knee to prop up the arm holding her tea. She stared at her cardboard to-go cup, rotating her wrist to send the contents swirling lazily inside. "I think you might be the only other person in the world who cares that she's gone."

Madelyn wanted to protest. Piper was young, pretty, smart, funny. Her emails had talked about going out for drinks with coworkers, attending birthday parties and baby showers, going on first dates.

But there was a difference between being liked and being cared for. Piper was single, lived alone, and didn't have any family. Her mother—the sister Madelyn's mother had never known she had—had died while

Piper was in college, and she'd never known her father. Neither of them knew their grandparents.

Kelsey had been the only person who was in her life enough to truly feel her absence when she was gone. To everyone else, she was just a friend they lost touch with, a coworker who moved on, a woman they dated briefly.

The cousin they'd emailed for a couple of months.

"I wish I'd gotten a chance to know her better," Madelyn said.

"I do too," Kelsey said. She smiled sadly. "She was so excited to find you. She always wanted a sister. I think she hoped that you might one day have that sort of relationship."

"She had you," Madelyn said.

"There's a difference between loving someone like family and *being* family," Kelsey said. "Especially for someone like her, who never really knew her birth family. All she had was her mom, and they weren't close."

"What was her mom like?" Madelyn hadn't told her own mother about Piper. Maybe she would someday. But her mom had made a choice not to search for her birth family, and Madelyn didn't know if she'd want to learn about a sister and a niece that she'd never meet.

Still, Madelyn wished she'd gotten a chance to meet her aunt. Piper had shown her a picture once. The sisters looked so similar. Madelyn wondered if their voices sounded alike, if they moved the same way, if they laughed at the same jokes.

Kelsey shrugged. "She didn't really talk about her much. I'm sorry. I wish I could tell you more."

"That's okay," Madelyn said, her heart sinking. She'd known it was a long shot, but it was still disappointing that she'd never know more about that part of her family.

But that wasn't why she was here, she reminded herself. "Listen," Madelyn said, leaning forward and folding her hands on the table between them. "I understand if you don't want to talk about what happened. But—"

"It was never that I didn't want to talk about it," Kelsey said, her forehead creasing. "It's that they made me sign an NDA as part of my settlement. I can't so much as *think* the name Doug Raymond without them coming after me."

"I was wondering about that," Madelyn said. "So you can't tell me anything?"

"Oh, I'm not worried about talking to *you*," Kelsey said. "At least not out here. That was one of the reasons I had to move. Too many people in East Henderson who work for Doug Raymond, or have a friend who works for him, or whose kids go to school with his grandkids. He's got that whole town wrapped around his finger. Couldn't even go to the grocery store without worrying I was going to run into one of his flying monkeys."

"That sounds terrible."

"It was for a while. Did I tell you I lost thirty pounds between when Piper went missing in 2021 and when we settled the lawsuit in 2023? I was afraid all the time. I wasn't sleeping, I wasn't eating. My lawyers took my case on contingency, but I still blew through every penny of my savings going to therapy three times a week." Kelsey rolled her eyes. "People kept telling me I looked great. As if the worst grief and trauma of my life was some great new diet."

She took a long sip of her tea. "When I moved out here, I was just trying to get away from all of that. My therapist thought a change would be good for me, and she was right. But I realized something after I'd been here for a while." She leaned forward across the table, as if she were sharing a secret. "Outside of East Henderson, nobody cares about Doug Raymond."

She leaned back, shaking her head incredulously. "I know that's probably obvious to you already, since you're not from around here. But it blew my freaking mind. Living in that town, I felt like he was the most powerful man in the world. It felt like he could do anything to anyone and get away with it."

"But he does, doesn't he?" He was still doing whatever he wanted, while Piper was gone. It sure felt like he had gotten away with it to Madelyn.

"That's the thing," Kelsey said. "He does, but only because he's convinced everyone he's too big to knock down. But I feel like if the right people looked at the right time, they'd see straight through him. And then his whole house of mirrors would shatter."

"Except like you said, no one in East Henderson is going to be the one to do it, and no one outside East Henderson cares," Madelyn said.

"Which is where you come in," Kelsey said. "I'm under an NDA, but you're not. No one even knows you have any sort of connection to me or Piper. You can ask questions, poke around. Maybe you'll find something I missed."

"If you couldn't find anything with a whole legal team helping you out, I don't know what I'm going to do," Madelyn said hopelessly. The more she thought about it, the sillier she felt thinking that she could just rent a house from Doug Raymond and somehow use that connection to find her missing cousin. This wasn't a Nancy Drew book. He wasn't just going to leave clues lying around her house for her to find, or casually incriminate himself while she eavesdropped around the corner.

In the real world, everything had a price. And Doug Raymond was rich enough to buy whatever reality he wanted. Including one in which he was invincible, and anyone who questioned him simply ceased to exist.

"Hey," Kelsey said, "don't count yourself out before you've even started. I know their playbook now. You can be more prepared than I was, make better choices."

"I doubt they'd do the same thing twice in a row."

Kelsey let out a bitter laugh. "Madelyn, they have been pulling the same crap for *years*. It never changes. They've just convinced everyone not to compare notes. Or made them sign away their right to talk about it at all." She knocked back the rest of her tea in a long gulp, then tossed the cup overhand into a trash can by the coffee shop door. "But screw them. I'll say what I want to say."

"I don't want to get you in trouble," Madelyn said.

"I was in trouble the second I applied for that job," Kelsey said with a shrug. "Maybe if you can figure out what they did to Piper, we can keep someone else from getting into trouble with them in the first place."

The first step in the playbook, Kelsey said, was gaslighting. When she first started asking questions about Piper, she was made to feel like she was crazy. *People quit their jobs all the time,* her managers told her. *She probably wants to move on. Stop taking it so personally.*

But after a while, it was obvious to everyone that she hadn't just quit. Kelsey sighed, fixing Madelyn with a fierce look. "You know it took *weeks* for them to even look for her? Weeks. I started asking questions on day one, but by the time anyone took me seriously, the trail had gone cold." She shook her head, lip curling in disgust. "What kind of people would *do* that?"

That was the question Madelyn was trying to answer.

Looking back, Kelsey thought they'd been doing it to Piper too. A couple of months before she disappeared, Kelsey noticed she was acting strange. "Not the type of strange anyone else would notice," Kelsey said. "But strange for her."

Piper stopped talking about work. Maybe that was normal for other people, but she and Kelsey always used to discuss their respective projects at lunch. They liked their jobs, and found their work interesting. But over time, Kelsey realized she was the only one who ever brought up work. And when she asked Piper about what she was working on, she'd change the subject.

"It wasn't like her," Kelsey said. "She *loved* what she did. I didn't get it, but numbers were like chips and queso for her. She couldn't get enough of them. So for her to suddenly not want to talk about budgeting forecasts and data analysis was like . . . if The Rock one day just stopped talking about his workouts. Like, it may not be everyone's thing, but if *he's* not talking about it, you know something weird is going on."

Kelsey had tried to ask her what was wrong, but Piper brushed her concerns aside. "She told me it was nothing, that she was being ridiculous, that she was probably just confused by stuff that was above her pay grade." Kelsey shook her head, pressing her lips together. "She was so smart. And they made her feel stupid."

After Piper disappeared, Kelsey demanded answers. She wasn't looking to her employer at first. But after being stonewalled by the police, she started digging at work. "It was so bizarre," Kelsey said. "People *liked* Piper. You'd think they'd want to know what happened to her. But every time I asked a question, people would just shut down. It was like I'd announced I had leprosy or something."

It didn't take long for Kelsey to become a pariah at work. Conversations ended when she entered a room. Meetings disappeared from her calendar. Several times, she saw people she didn't recognize coming and going from the senior leadership offices, but when she'd ask who they were, no one would tell her.

Eventually, after a few weeks, her supervisor called her into a meeting and told her in no uncertain terms to let it go. "He said that I needed to accept that Piper had moved on, and that I was making myself look bad and making people uncomfortable with all my questions," Kelsey said bitterly. "That's step two in the playbook. If they can't convince you you're crazy, then they'll just straight-up lie and dare you to not believe them."

But Kelsey didn't believe them. She kept pushing for answers, refusing to buy the company narrative that Piper had quit, until she eventually got called into her final meeting, where she was told she was being let go. "We all knew it was bullshit," Kelsey said. "They just wanted an excuse to get rid of me. And get me under an NDA. They offered me six months of severance if I signed."

"Can they even do that?" Madelyn asked. "Isn't that coercion? Or duress, or something?"

Kelsey shrugged. "Probably. But that's a legal issue, which I'd have needed a lawyer to argue, if I was even thinking straight enough to realize what was happening at the time. And lawyers cost money. Which I didn't have, because I was being fired."

"But you didn't sign," Madelyn said. "So you were thinking straight enough to tell them no."

"For a while, anyway," Kelsey said, her words tinged with regret. "But they wore me down eventually."

By that point, Kelsey had been certain Raymond Realty Group had something to do with Piper's disappearance. "They were like little kids yelling not to look in their room," she said. "Maybe you weren't going to before, but you sure as hell will *now*."

But before she had a chance to figure out her next move, they came at her with the next phase in the playbook: intimidation.

One day, as Kelsey was looking at job postings online, a letter was hand-delivered to her at home, telling her to cease and desist from discussing the company's proprietary information. "Credit where credit is due," she said. "Calling getting rid of an employee and covering it up 'proprietary information' is an impressive display of creativity."

After speaking to an attorney—"apparently every lawyer within a hundred miles of East Henderson already knows that Raymond is the freaking Antichrist, except for the people working for him," Kelsey said—she decided to countersue. But even with her lawyers working on contingency, the lawsuit was costly.

"No one would hire me," she said. "I don't know if they called places telling them not to hire me, or if everyone just knew I was the bitch who dared to question Doug Raymond, but either way, I was blacklisted. Couldn't even get an interview anywhere."

Meanwhile, Raymond's legal team threw up every barrier in the book, stalling and obfuscating until she'd burned through every last penny of her savings. "That's when they went for the kill shot," she said dryly.

Once Kelsey had exhausted her willpower and her resources, Raymond Realty Group offered to settle, paying her attorney fees and even offering her a modest severance, on one condition: that she would sign a nondisclosure agreement prohibiting her from ever discussing the case again, under any circumstances. Feeling as though she had no other choice, Kelsey signed.

"I've regretted it every day since," she told Madelyn. "Nothing is worth your voice. Nothing. Should've known that from the freaking *Little Mermaid*, but you do all sorts of stupid shit when you're broke and terrified."

"I'm so sorry," Madelyn said again. She'd lost track of how many times she'd said that. Her insides were coiled into knots. All Kelsey had done was ask questions, and they had tried to destroy her life.

Did Madelyn stand a chance against these people? Did she even want to try?

"So after all that," Madelyn said, "did you at least get *some* information that could be helpful? Do you have any theories?"

Kelsey shrugged, blowing out a long breath. "I have theories, yeah. But nothing concrete. I'm convinced it had something to do with money. She worked with a lot of major accounts, managing millions of dollars. Something must have grabbed her attention. I told you she loved numbers; she needed things to add up. It's why she was so good at her job. Nothing got past her." Kelsey frowned at her hands, picking at her cuticles. "'I'm guessing she went to her manager, and was fed some bullshit story, same as I was. But like I said, Piper was smart. She would've kept digging. Eventually, they must have realized there was only one way to keep her quiet."

"I wonder what she found," Madelyn said.

"I have no idea," Kelsey said. "I should've pushed more, convinced her to tell me what was wrong. I knew it was about work. I knew it was tearing her up. Maybe if I'd said something, I could have helped her. But I didn't. And now she's gone."

"It wasn't your fault," Madelyn said softly. She couldn't bear the thought of Kelsey taking responsibility for what had happened to Piper, especially when she'd tried so hard to save her.

But Kelsey gave her a wry smile. "Wasn't it?" she asked. "I was her best friend. I saw her every day. And I knew something was wrong, but I convinced myself it was none of my business. Maybe part of me thought I was giving her space, but if I'm honest, I also didn't want to know something that might threaten my crappy paycheck and shitty health insurance." She gave a bitter laugh. "Ironic, huh?"

"That's on *them*. Not you," Madelyn argued. She hated that Kelsey had been torturing herself over this, when the leadership at Raymond Realty probably hadn't ever given her or Piper a second thought.

Kelsey fixed her in a thoughtful gaze. "I wish it was that simple," she said. "But it's not. I would never have hurt Piper. But maybe that doesn't matter. I had the opportunity to protect her, and I didn't. I didn't ask questions until it was too late. And I have to live with that."

Madelyn shook her head, but couldn't find any more words to argue. Was she any better, living in one of Raymond's houses, giving him money and trying not to think about what he did with it? She was afraid she knew the answer, even if she didn't want to face it.

Kelsey leaned forward in her seat, holding Madelyn's gaze. "They beat me," she said, "but they haven't beaten you yet. Keep looking. And whenever you find what you're looking for, don't let them silence you the way they silenced me." Her lips twitched into a semblance of a smile. "Do it for Piper."

"I will," Madelyn promised, even though she had absolutely no idea how she was going to keep it.

PART TWO

And if it did, it wasn't that bad

CHAPTER EIGHT

I believe in three fundamental rights. The right to free speech. The right to bear arms. And the right to spend my own money any way I damn well please.

—Tweet from @DougRaymondOfficial, March 2, 2021

"Well, you're all dead now. I hope you're happy."

Angie and Bas exchanged a disbelieving look as they crawled out from under their desks, along with the rest of their Personal Finance class. Across the room, their substitute teacher flipped on the classroom lights, looking annoyed.

In the row in front of Angie, Bethany Matthews glared at the sub as she got to her feet and dusted off her black jeans, running a hand through her bright-pink hair. "You can't just *say* stuff like that," she muttered under her breath. "It's traumatizing."

The sub frowned, her eyes narrowing. She was probably in her forties and built like a public mailbox, with square shoulders and a wide mouth like a carp. She'd written her name on the whiteboard at the beginning of the period: Mrs. Madison. "You know what's traumatizing?" she said, pitching her voice to project over the low din of the shuffling students. "Getting shot because you couldn't keep your mouths shut."

Bethany's mouth dropped open while a few other students exclaimed in protest, including Bas. "Mrs. Madison, come on. Don't you think you're being a little harsh?" he said, holding out his hands plaintively. "We all know what these drills are for. There's no need to make them worse."

"That's right, dude," Wyatt Schaeffer said, brushing his stringy blond hair out of his face and clapping Bas on the shoulder. "You tell her."

Angie wrinkled her nose, wondering whether Wyatt had left a grease print on his shirt.

Mrs. Madison glared at them, her face rapidly turning the color of a bruised tomato. Instead of responding, she picked up the phone receiver at the front of the classroom. "Hi, yes, this is Mrs. Madison subbing for Mr. Lange today. I'm sending some students to the principal's office, uh . . ." She picked up the clipboard of the seating chart and scanned it with one finger, the phone wedged between the side of her head and her shoulder. "Um, yes, Sebastián García, Wyatt Schaeffer, and Bethany Matthews. Yes, thank you." She hung up and crossed to Mr. Lange's desk, picking up a notepad. "You give this to the principal," she said, scribbling furiously. "Take your things."

"Yo, you guys, this is messed up," Wyatt protested loudly—mostly, Angie suspected, to score points with Bas, who was one of the only kids in their class who didn't make a point of avoiding him.

"Cut it out," Bas hissed under his breath as he shrugged on his backpack. In front of Angie, Bethany did the same, looking like she was about to shoot lasers out of her eyes.

Mrs. Madison held out the note, pinching the paper at the very edges. Her mouth twitched like it was filled with live beetles as she handed it to Bethany, who read it and then let out a disgusted snort, rolling her eyes. Angie wondered what it said.

As the three of them shuffled out of the classroom, Angie wished she'd been brave enough to say something too. Sure, the class hadn't exactly been *silent* during the intruder drill, but that was no excuse for what Mrs. Madison said. As a sub, she probably had no idea how draining it was to have to do this over and over again every year. None of them needed to be reminded that if the stakes were real, they could die. If anything, they could use some more help forgetting that grim reality.

Even though they'd been doing these drills since kindergarten, they always left a sour lump in Angie's stomach. If there was a real shooter, of course, she knew she and her classmates would be silent. Or at least, as silent as they could be while crying and panicking and texting their families goodbye. No one was under any sort of illusion that hiding under their desks or turning out the lights would do much to stop a hail of bullets shot from a weapon made for war zones.

But the drills were their own thing, and everyone got through them as best they could. Some huddled up silently, exactly as they were supposed to. Some played games on their phones or watched YouTube videos. A few kids in the back of the room played a hushed game of Mafia.

Today, Angie and Bas had texted one another from underneath their desks, their notifications set to silent. She told him about the singing in the middle of the night, and her realization that the nanny cam they'd bought didn't record audio. He reiterated his theory that her dad had a girlfriend, which made her want to pluck his phone from his hand and hurl it across the room.

She'd wanted to talk with him more after class, but their mini-revolution against Mrs. Madison had shot that plan to hell. When the bell rang, Angie was out the door before it finished sounding, hoping to catch Bas before his next class. He should be done in the principal's office by now; it had been nearly twenty minutes.

Sure enough, she spotted him in the hallway outside the band room and hurried to intercept him. "What happened?" She was already breathing heavily; that was probably the most cardio she'd voluntarily participated in since they'd gone to see Paramore and Fall Out Boy that summer in Camden.

Bas shrugged. "Not much. We told them what Mrs. Madison said, and they agreed that it was inappropriate and said they'd talk to her. I kind of get the impression they don't really like her either."

"So no detention or anything?"

"Nope."

Angie sighed, half in relief, half because she was still a little winded. Bas *never* got in trouble at school. His parents would flip if he got detention for talking back to a teacher, even if talking back was completely warranted. "In that case, do you think your parents will let you borrow their car to drive me to Best Buy after school? I need to get an audio recorder. Then maybe we can do a movie night?" After researching it, she'd learned that getting a separate recorder for audio was a much cheaper option than buying a decent security camera that also recorded sound.

Bas's mouth twitched as if he were fighting the urge to say something snarky, but he nodded. "Sure, but maybe we can do dinner at my house in between? No disrespect to your dad's frozen egg rolls, but my mom is making pollo entomatado."

Angie's mouth watered. It wasn't even that her dad didn't know how to cook; he'd kind of given up after her mom left. Bas's mom was her only source of food nowadays that wasn't previously frozen, freeze-dried, or canned. Plus she always sent her home with a Costco-size sour cream or margarine tub full of leftovers for her and her dad to share. "Deal, but then back to my house for movie night. We still have so many more *Paranormal Activity* movies to watch. Plus, I feel like the ghost might do something tonight."

Bas laughed. "You really don't see the irony in that, do you?"

Angie wrinkled her nose. "It's totally different."

"You're setting up surveillance equipment to capture paranormal activity in your house. It's literally the exact plot of the movies."

"Well, yeah, when you put it like *that*, but you're forgetting one important thing," Angie said, wagging her finger at him as they parted ways at the arts wing. "I know better than to stick around once things go sideways."

CHAPTER NINE

Dear Madelyn,

Congratulations on getting a role in your friend's production! I'm not familiar with Songs for a New World (not much of a musicals person, alas!) but I will be sure to listen to the soundtrack right away. I'm so excited for you. Maybe I can even drive out to Penn State to see you in it? When are your performance dates again? We are in the middle of a big project at work, so I'm not sure how much time I will have, but I will take a look at my calendar and try to make it work. In the meantime, I'm cheering you on from afar!

Love,
Piper

—

"Pay attention," Madelyn reminded her sixth period music appreciation class over the soaring soprano of Mozart's "Queen of the Night" aria coming from the classroom speakers. The talking ebbed for a few seconds before the volume began to creep back up. It was probably a lost cause trying to get seventh graders to listen to Mozart during the first month of school, but she had intentionally planned a light class period, knowing she wouldn't be able to focus.

She was already on edge from that morning. She'd finally remembered to email Barbara at Raymond Realty a couple of days ago, asking for a copy of her lease, and the response had arrived while she was getting ready for work.

> If you would like to stop by the office, I can print you a copy. But if you just have a question, most of our tenants prefer to ask those over email, where we can respond specifically and promptly.

Madelyn had replied that she'd stop by one day after school. Barbara had written back that she should let her know if she changed her mind. It was all very polite, but Madelyn could sense an implied *you asshole* at the end of each of Barbara's sentences.

Not a great way to start a day that was already bound to be stressful, thanks to the drill scheduled for sixth period.

She wiped her sweaty palms on her skirt, glancing at the clock above the door again. 1:22. Three more minutes.

She didn't know why she was so nervous about the intruder drill. She'd participated in dozens of these as a student, flipping off the lights and hiding under desks or pressed into corners, passing the time whispering and texting and doing whatever else they could think of to take their minds off the horrific scenario they were practicing. It was never her favorite thing, but it also wasn't *that* big a deal. Just another unpleasant part of school, like dress codes and bad Wi-Fi.

But something was different about having to lead one as a teacher. For the first time, the full weight of the drill pressed down on her. Should the worst happen, she was responsible for the lives of these children. Not in the metaphorical sense, like some of her education teachers had liked to opine in college, telling their classes things like,

You will be molding young lives. If a person with a gun walked into their school, it was literally her job to keep her students alive.

She was a chorus teacher. Armed with a conducting baton and a tuning fork. It was absurd.

And yet, it was how it was.

The email had come in the day before. Teachers, be prepared for an intruder drill during sixth period tomorrow, beginning at 1:25 p.m. Please follow the safety protocols outlined in the handbook. If you need any reminders about what to do, please email me or stop by my office. The drill will last for approximately ten minutes. Following the drill, students will proceed to their seventh-period class.

The intercom beeped, signaling an impending announcement. Her students exchanged uneasy looks as Principal Hayes's voice came over the loudspeaker. *"This is an intruder drill. Students, please follow your teachers' instructions. I repeat, this is only a drill."*

"Okay," Madelyn said, raising her voice to be heard over the sudden chatter as she moved toward the classroom door. Her hands were shaking as she pushed it closed; she curled them into fists. "I'm going to turn off the light. I need everyone to get down on the floor and out of sight. Move against the walls here and here." She gestured to the sides of the room as students began to drop to the floor and crawl into place.

The classroom door was already locked, but that didn't feel like enough, so Madelyn pulled a chair over and wedged it under the handle before flipping off the light. The room still wasn't very dark; light streamed in the windows that faced the front lawn and parking lot. Sinking down onto her hands and knees, she crawled to huddle underneath her desk.

Once she was curled into place, she remembered that she hadn't told the kids to be quiet, but they didn't seem to need the reminder. The class was mostly silent, although some of the students still spoke in hushed whispers.

"We are *way* too close to the door," said a tall seventh grade girl off to Madelyn's right. She thought her name was . . . Ashleigh? Ainsley?

She'd been working on memorizing the names of her students for the past few weeks, but there were so many of them. It was taking longer than she'd anticipated.

"I *told* you we should go over by the window," another girl with spiky brown hair said. Jenna, Madelyn thought.

"I was just trying to do what Miss Zhao said," a third girl said, thankfully pronouncing her name correctly. It was still a coin toss whether people would get close or butcher it beyond recognition. This girl, Madelyn knew, was named Candice. She'd introduced herself after the very first day of class, and sat in the center of the front row, giving off the vibes of a puppy hoping for treats. "Next time, we can go by the window."

"I'm going *out* the window," Ashleigh-or-Ainsley said.

"Are you nuts?" Candice hissed. "What if he comes in here while you're climbing out the window? You'll be stuck."

"I'd rather take my chances than squat in here like a sitting duck."

"If he comes in here, I think we should attack," Jenna said. "Just like . . . swarm him. He can't take us all."

"That is the stupidest thing I have ever heard," Ashleigh-or-Ainsley said. "There is no way you would swarm a shooter. And if you did, you'd get shot."

Jenna shrugged. "If he comes in here, I'm getting shot anyway. May as well go down fighting."

Candice looked from one to the other, shaking her head. "You are both insane."

"Think on the bright side. If one of us dies, you will be free to use our body as a shield."

Madelyn curled into herself, biting her lip. These students were twelve years old. They shouldn't have to think like this. No one should *ever* have to think like this.

The ten minutes of the drill grated past like nails on a chalkboard. Madelyn focused on 4-7-8 breathing exercises—four seconds in, hold for seven, exhale for eight—to help calm her anxiety, although she could do them for only a few minutes before she started feeling lightheaded. After that, she moved on to a sensory grounding technique she'd learned from Syzygy, counting down things she could see, touch, hear, smell, and taste. She was trying to come up with a second thing she could smell—the spotty deodorant habits of her preteen students unfortunately crowded out most other scents—when Principal Hayes's voice boomed over the loudspeaker.

"*Thank you to everyone who participated in today's successful drill. We appreciate your cooperation. Students should now proceed to their seventh period class.*"

And just like that, it was over.

Moving stiffly, Madelyn unfolded herself from under her desk. Her whole body ached. She must have been tensing her muscles without realizing.

She turned on the lights, her hands numb. Unlike her, Jenna, Candice, and Ashleigh-or-Ainsley sprang to their feet with ease, their minds already on other things. They scooped up their backpacks and flowed out the door with their classmates, chattering about their next class as though nothing had happened.

And nothing *had* happened, Madelyn reminded herself. She had participated in these drills plenty of times as a student. So why was she so anxious?

Two periods later, once her classroom finally emptied for the day, she wandered over to the ancient upright piano and sank onto the bench. A stack of sheet music sat on top of the piano: the various pieces Madelyn was considering for the semester. She picked up the piece on top and opened it on the music rack, staring at it blankly, her fingers resting lightly on the keys.

"You all right?"

Madelyn jumped, pulling her hand into her lap like the piano had tried to bite her. Alex stood beside the bench, canvas bag slung over his shoulder. She blinked up at him, confused. "Heading out already?" He normally waited for the buses to pull out before heading to his car at the end of the day.

Not that she'd been paying attention, of course. It wasn't her fault that his classroom *happened* to be right down the hall from hers, or that she noticed when he walked by. The motion caught her eye, that was all. No other reason.

"Already?" He raised a thick eyebrow. "Last bell rang fifteen minutes ago."

"What?" Madelyn looked uncomprehendingly from him to the clock on the wall, to the music on the piano. Had she really been sitting there staring into space for fifteen minutes?

"Let me guess. The drill got to you?"

Everything was getting to her. The drill, starting a new job, moving into a new place, the knowledge that her landlord may have somehow been involved in her cousin's disappearance. Although of course, she couldn't tell him about that last part. "I've just got a lot on my mind," she said.

"It's okay," he said, his eyes gentle. "The first one tends to get to people. After my first drill as a teacher, I couldn't stop shaking. I went to my car during my free period and screamed as loud as I could into my jacket. Spent the rest of the day hoarse."

She bit her lip and nodded, her stomach in knots. "Yeah," was all she could find to say. He wasn't wrong; she hated everything about the drill, from the way her students casually talked about dying to the sinking helplessness that enveloped her as she huddled under her desk. She just wished that were the *only* thing wrong right now.

"Listen," he said, tilting his head toward the open door of her classroom. "You want to go grab a cup of coffee and talk?"

"Oh." Madelyn looked at her hands, clenched on her lap. She'd been casually fantasizing since the first day of school about Alex asking her out, but taking pity on her following an active shooter drill was not really the romantic outing she'd had in mind. "You don't have to—"

"There's this place I really like that's not too far away. I was going to stop in there on my way home anyway. And I could use the company." He gave her a small smile, dark hair falling across his eyes, and she almost believed that he was inviting her to coffee for his sake, and not hers.

Plus, even if it was only because he felt sorry for her, coffee with Alex seemed much more likely to cheer her up than the alternative: live-texting Syzygy all her complaints about the latest *Grey's Anatomy* while sipping a glass of cheap boxed wine.

"Sure," she finally agreed, smiling for what felt like the first time that day. "Coffee sounds great."

CHAPTER TEN

> Not everyone is going to like the way I run my business. And those people can go back to selling shacks and being poor.
>
> —Doug Raymond on the *Straight Shooter* podcast, November 8, 2018

"This doesn't freak you out?"

"What do you mean?" Angie asked, blinking herself back to consciousness. She hadn't realized she was drifting off until Bas spoke. She scrubbed a hand across her face, hoping she hadn't drooled.

"I mean . . ." He gestured at the screen, where a teenage girl was levitating out of her bed while unconscious. "This isn't hitting a little too close to home for you? You've already passed the 'things go bump in the night' and 'planting cameras' phases of these movies. All that's left is for your ghost to start killing people. Only question is who's going to get possessed in order to set up the sequel."

"Technically the second and third movies are prequels."

Bas frowned. "I'm serious. If you really do have a ghost—and I'm not saying you do—aren't you worried at all that it might be dangerous?"

"No."

"Why not?"

Angie picked the remote up off the coffee table, pausing the movie, even though she'd probably missed the last half hour already. "It just . . . doesn't feel that way to me. I know you don't get it, but my ghost feels a little more Casper than Tobi. You've got to trust me."

Bas dropped his head back against the couch cushions and yawned, but his expression still seemed irritated. "I just feel like you're playing with fire."

"Look, if I'm wrong and she does start messing with us in creepy ways, then that's it," Angie promised. "I'll show my dad the footage and convince him to leave, and we'll be fine."

Bas rolled his eyes. "Yeah, I'm sure it'll be that easy."

Angie bit her lip, wishing she could explain in a way he could understand. "Besides," she said, unable to keep a tinge of sadness from her voice, "you don't believe in any of this anyway."

"I do sometimes. I'm just . . . not sure this is how it works." He turned to give her an apologetic smile, his brown eyes half-shut. "But maybe I'm wrong. Pretend I didn't say anything. Let's turn the movie back on."

"No, it's fine," she said reluctantly. She didn't feel like watching anymore. Between Bas's concern and his doubt, she'd lost her enthusiasm for the movie. "We're both falling asleep anyway. We can turn it off." She leaned forward, aiming the remote.

Before she pressed a button, the TV switched off.

Angie pulled her hand back like she'd touched an open flame.

Bas stretched obliviously, reaching up over his head and arching his back. "In that case, I'm gonna go," he said, yawning again.

"No, Bas, did you not see that?"

He blinked sleepily at her. "What?"

"The TV turned off."

"Well, yeah. We'd agreed to turn it off." His brow crinkled, confused. "Right? I didn't fall asleep, did I?"

Angie shook her head, feeling like she was losing her mind. "It turned off by itself. I didn't do it."

"Didn't you use the remote?"

"No. I mean, I touched the remote, but I didn't press anything."

"Are you sure? Those buttons can be sensitive sometimes."

"Bas, I would know if I pressed a button." She narrowed her eyes at him. Skepticism she could handle, but she wasn't an idiot.

He shrugged, spreading his hands. "I'm trying to think of a logical explanation."

She tilted her head and gave him a pointed look. "I knew you didn't believe me."

"It's just . . . I told you, I don't think this is how it works. It's a TV. There are a million reasons why it could have turned off. Maybe there was a power glitch, or the remote malfunctioned, or maybe your dad has an app on his phone—"

"Shhh!" Angie held up a hand, her eyes going wide. "Do you hear that?"

Bas looked around the room, hands out by his sides like he was off-balance. "What?"

"Singing."

It was her again, Angie was sure of it. The ghost. Once again, she didn't recognize the song and couldn't make out the lyrics, but the melody was clear. She edged toward the hall, listening intently. "The shower's on again too," she whispered.

Bas shook his head, his expression bewildered. "I don't hear anything."

Angie stared at him, uncomprehending. "Really?"

Bas took a couple of steps toward her, looking concerned. "Angie, I'm getting worried about you."

She stepped away from him, her heart pounding and mind racing. The closer she got to the hall, the clearer the sounds of the shower and the singing were. It was impossible not to hear them. "No, I'm okay, just listen." She listened for a few seconds, then hummed a few bars, echoing the melody as best she could. "How can you not hear that?" She had to raise her voice to even be heard over the singing.

"There's nothing to hear," Bas said quietly.

Angie shook her head, then dashed to the bathroom, jumping into the open doorway. "Aha!" she called, flipping the light on.

But the shower was dry. The singing stopped. The room was empty.

Again.

Bas came to stand beside her, his phone in his hand. "I think we need to—"

"Wait!" The phone reminded her. She actually had proof this time. Exchanging the nanny cam for one that also recorded sound turned out to be *way* too expensive, so instead she'd kept it and purchased a cheap audio recorder. It was in her bedroom. "Just . . . just hold on a sec."

She retrieved the recorder and rewound a few minutes, then played it back.

". . . knew you didn't believe me." Her tinny voice came through the miniature speaker.

"It's just . . . I told you, I don't think this is how it works," Bas's answer came, small and quiet, but clear. Angie clutched the recorder with white knuckles, ears straining. Any second now, it would start.

"Do you hear that?" she heard herself say.

"What?"

"Singing."

There were a few seconds of staticky silence. *"The shower's on again too."* Her recorded voice was quiet, barely more than a breath, but she could still hear it.

Where was the singing? It had been so loud, so clear.

How could she possibly be the only one who could hear it?

"How can you not hear that?" Her voice echoed on the recording, raised to practically a yell.

Angie switched off the recorder, her fingers numb. Tears filled her eyes as she looked at Bas. "I'm not crazy," she whispered. "She's *here*. I can hear her. I don't know why you can't."

He shook his head. "I don't think you're crazy," he said softly.

She wished she weren't so good at knowing when he was lying.

CHAPTER ELEVEN

It was love at first sight. Just took a little while to convince her of that. [laughs] She worked in the pro shop at my daddy's club, and I was smitten with her from the moment I saw her. But she was very professional, wouldn't give me her number. So I just started coming back. Every weekend, Saturday mornings, I was there. Always asked for her number. She'd always say no. I'd buy something every time, you know, to be polite, toss her some commission. Think I probably wound up with enough shoelaces to lasso the moon by the time she finally said yes. But I think now, she'll finally admit she was just playing hard to get. Played that game for a lot longer than I would've liked, to be honest, but I'd say we both won in the end, wouldn't you, sweetheart?

—Interview with Doug and Stacey Raymond on the *First Kisses* podcast, February 2013

"It just all seems so *pointless*," Madelyn groaned, scrubbing at her fingers with her napkin to erase the last remnants of her chocolate croissant. "We are traumatizing these kids, and for what? Does anyone really think that turning off the lights and pressing a pathetic doorknob lock is going to make a difference to someone with a weapon that can blast its way through any door he wants?"

If she hadn't been sitting across from a guy with eyes like polished topaz and hair that looked soft enough to curl up and nap in, she would've licked her fingers clean. But although part of her felt like she'd known Alex for months already rather than just a few weeks, she wasn't ready to be quite *that* casual yet.

Alex nodded, taking a slow sip of his chai latte. They were both on their second drinks; the first round had been on Alex, but when their mugs were empty twenty minutes later, Madelyn had insisted on picking up the second. These beverages, she noticed, were taking them both a lot longer to work through. Was Alex also trying to draw out their time together? Or was he just a slow drinker?

Also, should she be thinking about any of this, given their topic of conversation?

Almost definitely not. But she couldn't help it. Every time she looked at him, her insides turned to warm jelly while her brain disappeared entirely, replaced by something most closely resembling a drooling emoji.

Earlier, when Alex had gone to the bathroom, she'd texted Syzygy to get their opinion.

Ask him out, came their response.

We are out.

Not like, OUT out.

I'm not going to ask him out at all. Especially not right after a SCHOOL SHOOTING drill.

Fair. Hardly the type of story you want to tell the grandkids as you tuck them into their radiation suits at night.

Alex had returned before Madelyn had been able to reply to Syzygy's pithy doomsdaying, and Madelyn had hurriedly dropped her phone back into her bag so that he wouldn't think she was getting bored. It was honestly a testament to the type of friend that Syzygy was that they went along with Madelyn's romantic fancies at all, considering that their personal compass had its needle stuck on nihilism. A tattoo that wound around their forearm like a snake read COMEDAMUS ET BIBAMUS, CRAS ENIM MORIEMUR: *let us eat and drink, for tomorrow we die.*

Madelyn had asked once why they'd left out the "be merry" part of the saying when they'd translated it into Latin. Syzygy had deadpanned, *Remind me which part of our own imminent and entirely avoidable demise we're supposed to be merry about.*

"I know," Alex said with a sigh, tipping his chair back slightly on two legs and folding his arms across his chest. "I tried to tell Principal Hayes when I started that these drills hurt more than help. She's old enough that she never had to do these as a student, but I've been doing them my whole life. And I think that the biggest effect they have is increasing anxiety in students. But she said we didn't have a choice. That decision is made at the school board level."

"Then we should petition the school board," Madelyn said, knowing she sounded naive but unable to rein herself in. Also, she realized as she clocked her racing heartbeat, she probably should have reconsidered that second caramel macchiato.

"The school board won't care," Alex said, frowning. "They're all bought and paid for."

"By who?" School board positions were supposed to be voluntary.

He shrugged. "Rich parents and local business owners looking out for their own interests, would be my guess. Board members don't draw a salary, but let's just say that some of them have a lot of 'friends' with deep pockets." He drew air quotes around the word *friends*.

Madelyn sighed. "Sounds like Tennessee." She'd always heard growing up that she attended school in the top county in the state, but that school board now seemed to be populated largely by individuals who, by all indications, loathed children, parents, schools, and the very concept of education. It was hard to fathom why they even *wanted* their positions, but they seemed determined to keep them.

It was one of the reasons she hadn't wanted to stay there to teach. She'd hoped Pennsylvania would be better, but she should've known that it wouldn't be that easy. Of course people like that existed in every state.

She sipped her drink, then stared into her mug hopelessly. When she'd declared her music education major during her sophomore year of college, practically everyone she'd known had tried to talk her out of it. The pay was too low, the workload too high, the red tape too thick, the public resentment too strong. Even her parents, while not explicitly asking her to change her major, had reminded her numerous times throughout college that *it's never too late to change your mind* and that *it can't hurt to leave your options open.*

But she loved teaching. Or at least, she loved the idea of it, loved her semester student teaching, loved her dreams of what her program would be like once she'd had more than a few weeks to build it.

She just didn't love all the other stuff that came with it.

"It's not that bad," Alex said, even though he couldn't possibly know all the thoughts swirling around in her mind. "We always do the first intruder drill close to the beginning of the year, but we'll probably only do a couple more between now and the end of school. And the first one is the worst. It'll get easier after this, I promise."

"It's so messed up, though, isn't it?" Madelyn asked. "That we have to do this at all?"

Alex gave her a wry smile. "People love their constitutional freedoms."

"Interesting definition of *freedom*."

"According to some people, it's the *only* definition of *freedom*," Alex said, rolling his eyes. "I'm sure you've seen the billboards. They're . . . special."

"Oh yeah?"

"There's one up toward the Poconos that has a picture of Jesus geared up like Rambo, fighting zombies."

Madelyn snorted, fully able to picture it in her mind, then slapped a hand over her mouth, mortified. Could she not just laugh like a normal person? Did it have to come out like she was part warthog?

Over Alex's shoulder, a curvy red-haired woman in purple cat-eye glasses glanced up and gave her a tiny smirk, before returning her gaze to the book on her lap.

"My landlord probably paid for some of them," Madelyn said, remembering the pictures on his social media. "I tried not to think about that too much when I handed over my gigantic rent check."

"Who's your landlord?"

"Doug Raymond. He owns this company called—"

"Raymond Realty Group. Yeah, I know who he is, although I've never met the guy," Alex said, his mouth twisting like he'd eaten something bitter. "What's he like in person?"

"He's, um," Madelyn said, trying to think of what she could say without sounding paranoid or insane.

Possibly a murderer? No.

Potentially a crime lord? Definitely not.

A lot like my ex-boyfriend? Not in a million years.

"A little intimidating," she finally said. "Self-involved. Kinda sexist. Dead behind the eyes."

Alex let out a puff of air that halfway resembled a laugh. "That tracks."

"How do you know him?"

"Oh, he's everywhere around here. Commercials, radio, park benches, Little League jerseys. He's even got this ad that plays at the movie theater before the trailers where he pretends to interview people who bought houses from him, and they all look like they're being held hostage. I always want to tell them to blink twice if they need help."

Madelyn thought of Piper, and her smile faded. The more she learned about Doug Raymond, the bigger the knot in her stomach grew. What had he done to her? And would Madelyn ever be able to find out the truth? She felt like a mouse up against a lion. Or something scarier than a lion. One of those bizarre engineered dinosaurs from *Jurassic World*, maybe. The ones that were inexplicably bred to be as deadly as possible.

She had a lot of side-eye for the *Jurassic World* scientists. So, she imagined, would their literary counterparts.

Alex leaned forward, looking at her with concern. "Is everything okay? Your face just fell hard enough to split concrete."

Madelyn scrambled for an explanation that didn't have anything to do with Piper. "I hate that I have to give this guy half my paycheck every month," she said. It was the truth; she didn't even want to think about what her money was being used for.

"Just try to stay on his good side," Alex said. "He's ruthless. You ever been over to his offices?"

Madelyn shook her head. She still needed to go there to get a copy of her lease, but had been putting it off until she had her feet under her at school a little more.

"It's *intense*. He's got armed security at the doors and a bodyguard stationed outside his office. And someone told me once that he makes all his employees sign super-broad NDAs before he'll hire them."

"What the hell? Is he operating a secret branch of the CIA over there or something?"

He laughed. "Pretty sure he's just a megalomaniac."

Madelyn shook her head. "Well, I guess that explains the lease."

"Yeah, what *is* the lease like?" Alex asked, leaning forward across the table.

Madelyn tried her best to summarize Doug Raymond's despotic rental agreement, from its moratorium on nail holes to the four paragraphs devoted to paint colors. "Like, it's *beige*," she finished up. "How precise does it need to—oh *shit*."

Somehow, in her exuberant gesticulating, she'd managed to hit the bottom of her coffee cup with her free hand, sending the entire cup and its contents spiraling through the air—and across her shirt. Her cream-colored cardigan now carried a bold splatter of dark Colombian roast. For a second, she froze, her eyes fixed straight ahead, her brain racing to find a way to salvage the coffee dripping from the table onto her lap, the mug shattering across the floor, the dark spray of liquid on her face.

"I am *so* sorry," Madelyn said, aghast. She slid out of her chair, crouching on the floor as she tried to gather the broken pieces of her mug into her hand.

"Let me take care of that," Alex said, pulling napkins from the dispenser at the center of the table. "You go get cleaned up."

"Are you sure?" Madelyn stared at the porcelain shards on the floor, willing them to fuse back together.

"Absolutely," he said, gently tipping her hand to deposit the pieces into his, sending a little sizzle of electricity through her. "I've got this."

Mustering as much dignity as she could, Madelyn hurried to the restroom, hoping, against all odds, that the damage wasn't that noticeable. But the second she caught the gaze of her reflection, her heart sank. If possible, it was worse than she had feared.

Dark-brown coffee stained her blouse and cardigan, and also dripped from her chin and coated the bottom few inches of her hair, turning it stringy and limp. But by far the worst thing was where the stain had landed: in a bold splotch right smack over her left boob, rendering her white shirt transparent and putting her utilitarian tan bra on full display to the entire coffee shop. To Alex.

"Noooooo," Madelyn groaned, leaning forward over the sink until her forehead rested against the mirror. The first time he had asked her to do something outside of work, and she had to spill coffee all over herself and show off the world's most boring underwear.

She deeply wanted to start this day over. Only this time, she would simply not get out of bed.

The bathroom door swung open, and Madelyn straightened, grabbing a handful of paper towels and dabbing ineffectually at her shirt. It was no use. There was no paper towel in existence that was absorbent enough to make her shirt less see-through.

Instead of going into a stall, the woman who had entered the bathroom—the woman with the purple glasses, the one who had caught her eye earlier—walked straight up to Madelyn, rummaging through her purse. "I always carry a change of clothes with me," she said by way of introduction, "in case I decide to go to the gym, which I never do." She pulled out a clean black T-shirt, folded and rolled into a neat bundle, and thrust it toward Madelyn. "Here."

Madelyn stared at her for a second, uncomprehending. "Excuse me?"

"I saw your, er," the woman said, flailing her arms to imitate Madelyn's erratic movements. Bright-red hair bounced around her face, cut off bluntly at her jawline. She wore an off-the-shoulder black shirt and cutoff denim shorts with cowboy boots, and would've looked right at home singing in a rooftop bar in Nashville.

The woman leaned closer, lowering her voice, even though Madelyn was certain they were the only two in the restroom. "Are you on a date?"

Madelyn shook her head, probably a little too emphatically. "He's a coworker," she said, hating how formal that sounded.

The woman raised her eyebrows. "If you say so."

"He *is*," Madelyn insisted, wondering why she was fighting so hard against what she wanted to be true. "It's not like that. I just started a few weeks ago. He's just helping me get my bearings."

"Gotcha," the woman said, pulling more paper towels from the dispenser. She ran them quickly under water and then held them out toward Madelyn. "For your hair," she said.

"Thank you." Madelyn squeezed her coffee-soaked hair between the wet paper towels, attempting to wipe out as much of the stickiness as possible.

Deciding it was as good as it was going to get, Madelyn tossed the wad of paper towels into the trash. The woman offered the shirt again, and Madelyn accepted it gratefully. Once she'd pulled it on, she realized that it had a graphic of a flower-covered skull on it, which was not something she would typically pick. But at least it was comfortable, and although it was a few sizes larger than Madelyn typically wore, it still looked pretty good. Flattering, even. And definitely better than the alternative.

She wadded up her blouse and cardigan to stuff into her purse. "Thank you again so much," she said.

"Happy to help. Looks good on you," the woman said, giving her a small smile. "You'd better get back to your . . . coworker." She hesitated a second, then said, "Hey, can I make a totally unsolicited, probably too personal observation?"

"Um, okay?"

"That guy you're with. The coworker."

Madelyn felt heat rush to her cheeks, and trickle down her stomach. "Yeah?"

"I'm not sure *he* thinks you're just coworkers."

Madelyn shook her head, her heart giving a nervous little flutter. "What?"

The woman shrugged. "I just got a vibe. Maybe I'm wrong. But just . . . if you're really not into him, you should let him know. Before things get awkward."

Madelyn swallowed, unsure how to respond to that. She *was* into him. She just . . . shouldn't be. And despite whatever vibe this woman thought she'd picked up on, she was almost positive he wasn't into her.

He was being helpful. That was all. And that's the way it should be.

"Okay," she muttered, eager to change the subject. "Can I get your number?" Madelyn pulled her phone out of her back pocket. "So I can return your shirt."

After a brief hesitation, the woman nodded. "Sure," she said, procuring her own phone from her purse. "My name's Nat."

"Madelyn," Madelyn introduced herself automatically, navigating to the contacts screen. She held her phone out to Nat. A few seconds later, Nat's phone buzzed.

Nat handed the phone back to Madelyn with a smile. "I texted myself. And created a contact."

Madelyn glanced down at what she'd entered. Nat—fashion police. "I'll give the shirt back to you tomorrow," she promised.

Nat shrugged. "No rush."

"Seriously," Madelyn insisted. "I promise."

Nat smiled. "I believe you."

As abruptly as she'd entered, she pushed open the bathroom door and hurried out.

Madelyn stood there, slightly stunned, staring at her reflection in the mirror and her flowery skull T-shirt, wondering what Alex would make of her midcoffee wardrobe change.

Taking a deep, fortifying breath, she exited the bathroom and made her way back to Alex.

All traces of the coffeetastrophe had been wiped clean, and a fresh, frothy beverage sat steaming at Madelyn's place. Alex also seemed to have a fresh drink; he smiled at her over the rim of his nearly full mug as she dropped into her seat. "Welcome back," he said.

"I'm so sorry about that. Thank you for cleaning it up."

He waved a hand. "Barely did a thing. Staff jumped in to help right after you left." His eyes fell to her top, and he grinned. "I like the shirt."

"It's not mine," she said automatically, before mentally berating herself. Why on earth did she feel the need to share that she was wearing a stranger's clothes? But now she was already in too deep; she had to keep going. "A woman in the bathroom gave it to me."

"Really? Who?"

Madelyn looked around the coffee shop, but there was no trace of Nat. "I think she left."

"A regular superhero, then," Alex observed. "She swoops in to save the day and then disappears without a trace. Wonder if she's single." He winked, making it clear he was joking.

Madelyn forced a tight laugh. "I'll be sure to ask her next time I see her."

She shoved aside the pang of unexpected jealousy that arose in her gut. She was being ridiculous. He was just being silly. And besides, Alex wasn't *hers*. She needed to get a hold on herself. Alex was being nice to her, a good friend, nothing more.

She remembered what Nat had said. *I'm not sure he thinks you're just coworkers.*

But whatever vibe she'd picked up on was obviously wrong. If he was into her, would he have made a joke about being interested in someone else? Definitely not.

They were coworkers. Maybe even on their way to becoming friends. Unless she screwed it all up with her stupid crush.

She cleared her throat and straightened her shoulders, determined to keep things between them professional. "So," she said, folding her hands in her lap. "What were we talking about?"

CHAPTER TWELVE

Not everyone deserves to be a homeowner. If you can't save up a down payment, if you think it's the government's job to take care of you, you don't deserve to own a house. You don't deserve anything. Stop whining, get up off your ass, and go earn a living like the rest of us.

—Tweet from @DougRaymondOfficial, February 2019

Angie stopped at the door to her room, blocking it with her body as she turned to face Bas. "I need you to promise to not freak out."

He widened his eyes, looking alarmed. "Why would I freak out?"

"Just . . . I don't know. Be cool, okay?"

"Angie . . ."

She sighed, wishing she hadn't warned him. "Come on," she said, grabbing his sleeve and dragging him into her room.

"Okay," he said once the door was shut. "What's the big deal?"

Taking a deep breath, Angie picked up her green canvas shoulder bag from her desk chair, and dumped the contents out on the floor.

He was already shaking his head before the bag was empty. "You have got to be kidding me."

"What?" She shrugged innocently. "It's just a few things."

"Did you rob an occult store?" He waved an arm at the floor, on which was now displayed an impressive assortment of herbs, crystals, talismans, incense, candles, and a Ouija board. Everything her online searches had suggested might help her communicate with her ghost, or at least, everything she could afford within her rapidly dwindling budget.

"Come on, it's not that much." And it really wasn't, considering the vast panoply of options out there.

"Angie, I really don't like this." Bas crossed his arms across his chest, stepping back toward the door. "And my abuela would *kill* me if she knew you were doing this, or that I was helping you."

"It's not like we're summoning a demon, Bas."

"You don't know *what* it is," he said. His head wagged back and forth, steady as a metronome.

"I honestly don't think it's anything bad," Angie insisted. "I mean, it sings show tunes! How scary can it be?"

"That's my whole point," Bas said through clenched teeth. "You're so sure that you know what you're dealing with, but you don't. You're messing with things here you don't understand. You're not being respectful."

"I didn't think you believed in any of that stuff."

"It's not that I don't believe in it at all. I just think there might be another explanation here. But that doesn't mean I want to do . . . whatever this is."

Angie sighed, grabbing his arm. His skin was warm through the thin cotton fabric of his sleeve. She searched his dark eyes, hoping that whatever he saw in hers would reassure him. "Look, I know you think I'm losing it."

"I don't think that," he said.

"But I promise you, there's something here," she pressed on. "I don't know why I'm the only one who can hear it. But it's real. It's not in my head. And if I can't prove it by recording it, maybe there's another way."

"Or maybe you should leave it alone."

Angie took a breath, letting it out slowly. "If nothing happens today, I'll let it go. Okay? Will you help me if I promise that this will be the end of it?"

He studied her face, a crease forming between his eyes. "You absolutely *promise*? No more ghost stuff at all?"

"If nothing happens, yes. No more ghost stuff at all." Her stomach clenched as she desperately hoped he wouldn't have to call her bluff. "But something is going to happen," she said, more a wish than a promise.

"If it doesn't," he said, "I want you to come talk to Aunt Liliana with me."

Now it was Angie's turn to shake her head. "I thought you said you didn't think I was crazy." Bas's aunt was a psychologist with a small practice in Malvern, about twenty minutes away.

"I *don't* think you're crazy. But I am worried. Just talk to her. Maybe it's, I don't know, stress or something."

"You think stress is making me hear a woman sing songs from *Anastasia* in my shower?"

He spread his arms in a show of helplessness. "I don't know! I have no idea what any of this means. But that's my condition. I will help you do this if, when nothing happens, you talk to Liliana."

Angie's face scrunched as she considered Bas's proposal. "Fine," she said finally. "But when something *does* happen, you have to believe me, and help me figure out what's going on. Deal?"

Bas briefly cast his eyes to the ceiling, as if looking for wisdom from above. "Deal," he agreed.

They settled on the Ouija board first, placing it between them on the floor and both placing fingers on the planchette.

"What will we do if your dad comes home?" Bas asked.

Angie rolled her eyes. "That would be a first." Her dad was gone so much lately that she was beginning to wonder if he technically still lived there anymore. How many hours constituted a legal residence? Or was it more accurate now to say that he lived at work?

She rolled her shoulders, anxious to get started. "What should we ask?"

"Maybe how Hasbro has a direct line to the spirit realm?"

"Hey. You said you'd help."

"Sorry." He cleared his throat. "It's your ghost. You should come up with the question."

Angie nodded nervously. Her fingers tingled with anticipation. She adjusted her position, keeping her back straight and her arms as loose as she could. "Hello? Ghost? Are you here?" she asked in a loud, clear voice.

For a moment, nothing happened. Then the planchette started to move, edging toward one of the few complete words on the board.

No.

"Bas," Angie groaned.

"I didn't do it!"

"Well, *I* didn't do it."

"Try asking another question."

"Fine. But don't mess it up this time."

"I didn't mess it up the first time."

Angie growled under her breath, shifting on the floor again. She wiped her sweaty palms on her jeans, then placed her fingers back on the planchette, willing the ghost to reveal itself. She swallowed. "Who are you?"

A

N

G

Angie yanked her fingers off the planchette and jumped to her feet. "If you're not going to take this seriously, then you should leave. I'm sorry I asked." Her face was hot. She'd really thought he would help her, even if he didn't believe her. She hadn't prepared herself for how much it would hurt to be wrong.

"Angie, I swear I wasn't doing it."

"Then who was? And *don't* say it was me."

Bas shrugged. "You know this is all based on subconscious movement, right? Maybe your subconscious is trying to tell you something."

"Or maybe you're just an asshole." She stomped to her bedroom door and flung it open. "Get out."

Bas's jaw dropped open. "*What* did you call me?"

"You're. An. Ass. Hole," Angie repeated, enunciating every syllable. "You're supposed to be my best friend, and instead you're making fun of me."

"*Supposed* to be your best friend?" His hands were fisted at his sides, his jaw twitching. "Are you kidding me?"

"No, Bas. Unlike *some* people here, I've been totally serious this whole time. Now get. Out." Angie's teeth were clenched so hard she was giving herself a headache.

Bas gaped at her for a second, then walked quickly out of her room and down the hall, his arms and legs held stiff, like his joints were rusted. He paused at the front door, looking back at her, but she remained in the hall, arms crossed, jaw set. She could feel cracks spiderwebbing through her insides, but she refused to give him the satisfaction of seeing her shatter.

He shook his head again, his eyes falling from her face, then walked out the door.

Angie stood where she was, unmoving, counting the seconds silently in her head until she could be sure he wasn't coming back.

Slowly, she walked to her room and closed the door, staring at the discarded Ouija board on the floor, the planchette still circling the letter *G*. She picked it up and turned it over in her hands. Just a piece of cheap plastic. Bas was right. It was never going to help her talk to her ghost. Maybe nothing would.

It wasn't until the tears started to drip onto the clear plastic circle at the center of the planchette that she realized she was crying.

CHAPTER THIRTEEN

Dear Madelyn,

No I have not read Dune! But I agree that the trailer looks very good (and I do love Jason Momoa), so I will definitely do my best to get to it before the movie comes out. Although I just looked up how many pages it is, and let's just say, that's going to be an ambitious goal for me. But I feel up to the task!

I actually haven't been to the movies since before the pandemic, if you can believe that! I do try to squeeze in an episode of TV here and there, but work just has me so busy all the time that it's hard to make time for it. I did really enjoy The Great. It takes some fairly broad historical liberties, but I think it is very well done, and it makes me laugh a lot. If you haven't watched it, I think you'd like it.

Love,
Piper

The dryer buzzed, and Madelyn reached for the remote, pausing her episode of *Derry Girls* right as Nicola Coughlan scrunched up her nose like she was about to sneeze. She grabbed the laundry basket off the floor and padded in her slippers to the garage.

She had pulled half the dryer contents into the basket before she registered that it wasn't dry. Not even close. She looked at the dial and immediately realized why. It still had half a cycle left. That must not have been the dryer buzzer she'd heard after all.

Sighing, she restarted the dryer and returned to the living room, which was gradually beginning to resemble an actual room more than a natural disaster site. The first couple of weeks of unpacking had felt like living in a cardboard war zone, but now her house appeared at least marginally inhabitable. "I think I'm losing my mind, spud," she told Potato, unpausing the episode. She listened more than watched as she folded towels and T-shirts and yoga pants into stacks.

When the pile had diminished to nearly a third of its original size, the dryer buzzer went off again—or maybe for the first time—and this time, the clothes inside were actually dry. She retrieved them and returned to the couch, adding them to the laundry heap. She reached for the nearest item, a black T-shirt, and turned it right-side out. A skull grinned at her.

She blinked at it, confused. This wasn't hers.

At once, she remembered: the coffee shop, the spill, the red-haired woman in the bathroom. Madelyn had promised to return her shirt. The woman had put her number into her phone as something silly, what was it?

Pulling up her contacts, Madelyn scrolled until she found Nat—fashion police.

> Hey, this is Madelyn from the coffee shop. I've got your shirt! Thanks again so much for letting me borrow it. Where can I meet you to return it?

Only a few seconds passed before the response came in.

Of course! Can you meet me back at Bean Juice at 11?

Madelyn glanced at the clock. It was only a little past nine a.m., giving her a couple of hours until then. Perfect. She could finish up the laundry and still have plenty of time to get dressed and make it across town to Bean Juice. She texted Nat confirming the plan, then returned her attention to Netflix.

Once the episode concluded, she gathered a stack of towels and headed to the bathroom, where her towels lived in a shallow basket under the sink, wedged in beside two rolls of toilet paper and the pipes. Overall she liked her house, but storage was a serious problem. She wished it had a linen closet, but even a bigger vanity would be helpful.

She froze at the doorway to the bathroom. There was water all over the floor. Quickly, her eyes scanned the room, but the sink and tub were off and the toilet wasn't running. Something must be leaking.

Bracing herself for what she might find, she opened the vanity doors and groaned. It was definitely the sink. Her spare toilet paper was soaked. Where there used to be two neat rolls now sat a swollen, white mess.

As if summoned by the prospect of new mischief, Potato rushed into the bathroom, tail wagging. Without hesitation, she dived straight into the cabinet, scooping up a mouthful of soggy toilet paper and smacking her jaws happily.

Madelyn considered fishing it out of her mouth, then decided to leave her alone. Wouldn't be the first time her dog had eaten toilet paper. And at least it was meant to break down. Could be worse.

Dropping her clean towels to soak up the water, she pulled out the mushy white lumps of former toilet paper and dumped them into the trash with a wet plop. Next she pulled out the rest of the towels—also sopping; apparently she wasn't done with laundry after all—and piled them on top of the others on the floor.

As Potato feasted on wet white blobs, Madelyn stuck her head under the sink to see what was leaking. It didn't take long to find a persistent drip originating from the bottom of the U-shaped pipe, although she had no idea how to fix it.

Once she had mopped up as best she could, positioned a pot under the leak, and deposited the wet towels back into the washing machine, Madelyn returned to the bathroom, frowning at her phone.

It was Saturday, which meant the Raymond Realty Group offices were closed. So much for calling Barbara. Plus, this was technically Doug Raymond's house, not his company's. He was the one responsible for dealing with this. She kicked herself for not having a copy of her lease yet. It would have been nice to have the exact wording available when she called him, since she suspected it was not written in her favor.

Of course, she'd have to make sure all traces of Potato were out of here whenever he sent a plumber over, but that was still a better option than hiring one herself with money she didn't have.

Wrinkling her nose, she dialed his number. He answered after three rings. "Doug Raymond here."

"Hi, Mr. Raymond, this is Madelyn Zhao—"

"Ah, Maddie, yes! How's the house treating you? Settling in all right?"

"Actually, sir, that's why I'm calling. The house is great, but I think there might be a problem with—"

"I'm going to stop you right there, sweetheart. I had my people go over that place with a fine-tooth comb before you arrived. You noticed the RR Platinum decal in the front window, I assume?"

"Um—"

"That means that the property held up under the highest level of scrutiny. We inspect everything. Leave no stone unturned. And my people are the best in the business. If there were any issues, we would've found them."

"I appreciate that, sir, but—"

"Now in my experience, honey, when something goes wrong after we've signed off on it, it's almost always user error. You know what that means?"

"Yes, but—"

"That said, I don't mind sending one of my guys out to take a look at whatever isn't working right for you. Absolutely happy to do that if need be. But my guys aren't cheap, and I don't pay to fix user error. That's one of the terms of your lease, if you'll recall. Still, just say the word, and I'll have someone out there lickety-split."

Madelyn gritted her teeth, glad that Raymond couldn't see her face right now. "Actually, you're right," she said, keeping her voice bright. "I think I was just being silly. Sorry to bother you."

"No trouble at all, sweetheart. Call anytime."

Madelyn hung up the phone, wishing she owned a punching bag. RR Platinum. Right. She looked down at Potato, who lay belly-up on the floor, paws poking at the air as she attempted to scratch her back on the carpet. "If he actually had someone inspect this place before I moved in," Madelyn said, "*I* will eat a roll of toilet paper."

Potato paused in her rolling, peering up at Madelyn. Probably wondering if she was going to get another soggy white snack.

Madelyn sat on her bathroom floor for the next twenty minutes, watching home repair videos on YouTube. If Raymond wasn't going to take care of his own property, she'd have to fix the leak herself. Fortunately, it didn't seem *that* hard. As best she could tell, she needed a couple of new parts and cheap tools from the hardware store, and she should be able to patch things up decently. It may not look professional, but as long as it wasn't soaking her toilet paper, she didn't care.

She decided against makeup, since she'd be gone for only a few minutes. Swapping out her pajama pants for jeans and a *Stranger Things* hoodie, Madelyn swept her dark hair up into a messy ponytail and declared herself ready to go.

It wasn't until she was standing in the store, staring down what felt like endless aisles of tiny metal and plastic parts that all looked varying degrees of the same, that she worried she might be in over her head.

She considered calling her dad, but he probably wouldn't be much help. He was notorious for tackling repair projects himself only to later hire a professional, claiming he "just didn't have the time to spend on it anymore." Madelyn and her sister had both long suspected that this was code for him not having any idea what he was doing in the first place.

Biting her lip, Madelyn pushed herself down the aisle labeled PLUMBING and attempted to make sense of the dozens of tiny labels for more joints and fittings than she could ever hope to comprehend.

She was standing in front of a row of bins of PVC fittings, staring at her phone as she rewatched one of the videos in the hopes that it might magically tell her which one she was supposed to buy, when someone touched her shoulder. "Hey."

She jumped, dropping her phone with a clatter. "Oops."

"Let me get that for you." The voice sounded familiar.

Madelyn turned to see Alex standing behind her, smiling sheepishly. He also wore jeans and a sweatshirt—his was unzipped, revealing a blue-and-white Sixers jersey for player 21, whoever that was—but somehow looked a thousand percent more put together than she did. As he bent to pick up her phone, she yanked the elastic out of her hair, finger-combing it over her shoulders. She tugged on the bottom of her hoodie, trying to make it look less bulky. *Why* exactly had she decided to leave the house looking like she was allergic to personal hygiene?

"Sorry about that," he said, returning her phone to her. "I didn't expect to see you here."

"I didn't expect to be here," she said, "but my sink decided today was a good day to just . . . give up."

He gave her a commiserating smile. "And you don't want to call your landlord?" He asked the question like he already knew the answer.

"Oh, I did. He made it very clear that there was nothing wrong, but if there was, it was my fault and he wasn't paying for it."

"Sounds like Doug Raymond," Alex said. "Nothing is ever his fault."

For some reason, Madelyn felt like that was an opening. "Do you know anything about *Raymond Realty Group v. O'Donnell*?"

Alex narrowed his eyes thoughtfully. "Which one was that?"

"It was a lawsuit from two years ago. Doug Raymond's company sued—"

"Oh right." Realization dawned in his eyes. "The woman who was trying to find her friend."

Madelyn raised her eyebrows. "Technically it was about proprietary information, but yeah, that was the real issue. How did you know that?"

He smiled sheepishly. "I may occasionally fall down the rabbit hole of the Rotten Raymond subreddit."

Madelyn studied his face, but he didn't look like he was kidding. "There's a subreddit devoted to Doug Raymond?" She'd been looking into Doug Raymond for a year and even she hadn't stumbled across the Rotten Raymond subreddit.

"There's a subreddit devoted to everything. There's one that's just people rating their own poops."

"Ew." Madelyn wrinkled her nose, but couldn't help laughing. "I don't think I wanted to know that."

"Sorry. Now that's a piece of unwanted knowledge that *you* get to randomly share with people against their will," Alex said, grinning.

"So what kind of people post on the Rotten Raymond subreddit?"

"Some claim to be former employees, or people that know him or his family personally. Others . . ." He sighed, running a hand through his gorgeous hair. "I think that sometimes, there can be a lot of appeal to anonymity," he said carefully. "Some people need a place to talk where no one will know it's them."

"Why *are* people so afraid of him around here?" She knew what Kelsey thought, but she was curious to find out what someone who hadn't had any personal interaction with Raymond's company would say.

"Let's see." Alex started ticking off items on his fingers one by one. "He's friends with the mayor. He desperately *wanted* to be friends with the governor, but his guy didn't win. He'll try again next time, though. He plays golf with half the judges in the county. He hosts barbecues at his house for the entire police department. He practically self-funded the sheriff's last campaign. Plus he's got an arsenal in his basement and is richer than God."

"You make him sound invincible."

"Around here? He kind of is. Plus, he's mean. By the time he was done with the poor woman in that lawsuit, she was lucky they left her with the clothes on her back."

Interesting. That wasn't what had happened with Kelsey—Raymond had paid *her*—but of course, Madelyn wasn't supposed to know that. Yet somehow, Alex, or maybe the Rotten Raymond people, were under the impression that it was the other way around. She wondered if the company intentionally spread that rumor or if it took shape on its own.

But of course, she couldn't tell Alex any of that. She sighed, returning her attention to the endless bins of fittings. "Which brings us back to me having to learn plumbing through YouTube."

"Actually," Alex said, his cheeks reddening slightly, "if you wanted, I could come take a look at the sink."

She raised an eyebrow, enjoying watching the heat flushing his skin. Did she make him nervous too? "Do you moonlight as a plumber?"

"Not exactly. But I did work construction in college, so I'm handy enough," he said with a shrug, shoving his hands in his pockets as his blush reached his ears. "But only if you want help. I don't want to overstep."

Madelyn swallowed her instinct to say that no, she was fine, she'd do it herself. Why did she think that would impress him? And more importantly, why did she care about that more than getting her sink fixed? Because let's be real, she was not going to fix that sink herself. She couldn't even figure out what parts to buy. Even after half a dozen

YouTube videos, the people on her phone screen may as well have been waving magic wands.

Alex seemed to take her hesitation for offense, because he stepped back, holding up his hands. "Never mind. Obviously you're here because you wanted to do it yourself. I'm so sorry. I shouldn't have said anything." He was speaking fast, his words tumbling over one another in their haste.

"No!" she exclaimed, so loud that a woman at the end of the aisle jumped, then tossed her a dirty look. Madelyn cringed. *Sorry,* she mouthed as the woman pointedly turned away.

Alex was staring at her through round eyes, his hands still hovering halfway up between them. A smile tugged at the corner of his mouth, teasing out his dimple.

"No," Madelyn said again, intentionally measuring her tone this time, "I meant I'm *glad* you said something, because I would very much appreciate your help. Thank you."

"Oh, well, great," Alex said, his shoulders relaxing. The dimple was now on full display. "I've actually got some time now, if you wanted to show me the problem."

"Weren't you here for something?"

"Yeah, just grabbing some stuff for my parents. But they don't need it until this afternoon."

"In that case, sure," Madelyn said, maybe too eagerly. "Let me send you my address—*shoot.*" When she'd swiped to her messages, she saw she'd missed two from Nat.

5 minutes away!

And then seven minutes later: Got a table in the back, let me know when you're here.

The shirt. Bean Juice. She had completely forgotten.

"Everything okay?" Alex asked as Madelyn typed furiously, telling Nat she was almost there. The coffee shop was ten minutes away. Less if she didn't hit any lights.

"Yeah," Madelyn said, moving out of the aisle, toward the door. "I forgot I have somewhere to be. Can you come by in a couple hours? Wait, no, you said you're going to your parents' house."

Alex matched her pace. "I could tell them that something came up—"

"No, don't do that," Madelyn said hurriedly. "The leak's not that bad. It can wait until you're free." She pulled up directions to Bean Juice in her Maps app. East Henderson was still mostly a maze to her.

"How about tonight?" Alex suggested. "My parents' thing won't take that long."

"Yeah, that works." Nine minutes with traffic. Not too bad.

"Would you like to go to dinner first? If the sink isn't too urgent? I know this great cheesesteak place."

"Yeah, sure, whatever," she said, staring at her phone. She tapped out a message to Nat. Sorry, traffic, be there soon! They'd reached the front of the store, and she looked up from her phone, giving Alex a grateful smile. "Thanks again so much."

"Happy to help," he said. "I'll see you tonight?"

"Yup, text me the name of the place and I'll meet you there. Bye!" Madelyn gave him a parting wave before rushing out the doors. Jumping into her car, she plugged in her phone and threw the car into reverse.

It wasn't until she was on the road and replaying her conversation with Alex in her head that her eyes widened. Oh God. Had he asked her out on a date? For *tonight*? And had she really responded with *whatever*?

She knew she was supposed to be keeping it professional. But if she was honest, that was only because she'd been sure *he* wanted to keep it professional. If he was interested, she absolutely wanted him to know that she was too.

And instead she'd said . . . *whatever*.

At the first red light, after slowing to a stop, she lowered her head onto her steering wheel and groaned.

CHAPTER FOURTEEN

> Other folks can run their companies however they like, but if you're working for me then you'd better understand that it's my way or the highway. And I have absolutely no problem running you over.
>
> —internal company email from Doug Raymond, April 2020

Angie walked in the door, dropping her backpack and jacket in a heap on the floor.

Bas had been pissy in school. Which she guessed made sense, since she'd been kind of bitchy the night before, but come *on*. Obviously she was under a lot of stress. He needed to cut her some slack.

Except apparently not—he was too high on his principles or whatever.

And then, if that wasn't enough, driver's ed had *sucked*. Whose bright idea was it to invent parallel parking anyway? If cars were meant to park that way, the wheels would turn sideways. It wasn't *her* fault that she kept hitting the curb. It was simple physics. People who could do it *without* hitting the curb were witches or warlocks or maybe leprechauns or something.

She'd planned to do the dishes after school, but now she didn't feel like it. She also didn't feel like doing homework. She didn't feel like doing anything. Everything was horrible and she wanted to be far, far away from here.

Stepping over her pile of school stuff, she collapsed onto the couch, kicking her sneakers off before putting her feet up on the coffee table and turning on the TV. She was navigating the menu to Netflix, planning to drown her sorrows in anime, when her dad stomped into the living room from the hall. She hadn't even realized he was home.

"What the hell is this?" he said, his voice sharp. His hand jutted toward her, clenched around a piece of black plastic about the size of a baseball.

Crap. The nanny cam.

Angie's mind whirred for an explanation and came up blank. "Um, I don't know," she said. Playing dumb wasn't a great option, but it was the only one she had. "What is it?"

Her dad's eyes narrowed as he held the camera closer to her face. "It's a surveillance camera. It was in your room."

"Oh wow," she said, blinking in what she hoped was a convincingly innocent fashion. "That's weird." Belatedly, she realized that she should probably sound more upset about a camera in her room if she truly didn't know about it, but it was too late to pick that route now.

He shook his head, staring at her like she'd asked him to remind her what color grass was. "Yeah. It *is* weird. Why do you have this?"

"It's not mine!"

"Angelina Mei Stewart, do *not* lie to me. I know it's yours."

"Dad, I swear—"

"Bas already told me."

Angie's jaw dropped open. Bas *told* him? She knew things were off between them, but she never dreamed he would tell her dad. She would *never* betray him like that, no matter how mad she was.

Did she even know him at all?

"Well?" Her dad shook the camera at her like answers might fall out of it.

Angie swallowed. "What did Bas tell you?"

"Nope." Her dad shook his head, crossing his arms. "We're not going to play that game. You tell me exactly what you were doing with this, and you tell me *right now*."

Angie picked at her cuticles, dropping her eyes to the coffee table. She couldn't bear to see her dad's face when she told him. "I think our house is haunted," she mumbled, her lips barely parting enough to let the words squeeze through.

Silence stretched between them for excruciatingly long seconds. "Excuse me?" Her dad's voice was strained.

Angie cleared her throat. "I, um, think our house is haunted?" She risked a glance at him and wished she hadn't. He was staring at her like she'd sprouted antlers. "I hear things sometimes . . . at first it was just random sounds, but lately it's been, uh, singing?" She wished her explanations would stop coming out of her mouth like questions.

"You hear . . . voices," her dad said slowly, and she absolutely hated the way his own voice sounded. All the anger had drained out of it. Replaced by something much worse. Concern? No, even worse than that.

Fear.

"Not *voices*," she said. "One. A woman. And it's not just her voice. Sometimes she makes things happen. Like the other night Bas and I were watching a movie, and she turned off the TV." She shook her head, knowing how absurd she sounded, but once she started telling the truth, it was like a dam burst inside her.

Suddenly she wanted to tell him everything. Maybe then, he'd understand. Maybe he'd even experienced it too.

"I know it sounds crazy. Bas thinks I'm crazy. That's why I got the camera. To prove it to him. And, well, I guess to you too. But it turns out this camera only records video, not audio, so—"

She paused. She had been about to tell him about the audio recorder, but what if he didn't know about it yet? If he'd found it, wouldn't he have brought it in here too, along with the camera, when he confronted her? And if he didn't believe her now, it might be the only thing she had left that could help prove that she was telling the truth. It hadn't worked yet, but that didn't mean it never would.

If he already knew about the recorder, she'd admit it and hand it over, she decided. But that didn't mean she had to *volunteer* that information.

"—so it didn't help Bas believe me after all," she finished. "And I guess that's why he told you."

Her dad shook his head, looking stunned. "Angie, I . . . I don't know what to say."

"Do you believe me?" She knew the answer before the question finished leaving her mouth.

Instead of answering, her dad came around the coffee table to sit beside her on the couch. He placed the camera on the table in front of them, then turned to take her hands in his. "Honey, I know you've been really . . . stressed since your mom left. And I know that you wish your life was more exciting, but—"

She yanked her hands away. "Oh my God, Dad, I'm not doing this because I'm bored. Or stressed. It's not a mental illness, and I'm not making this up. There is something *here*."

"Come on, sweetheart, listen to yourself." He waved his arms, gesturing to the room around them. "We both know there's no one else here."

"How would you know?" She stood up, hands fisted at her sides. Hot tears pricked at the back of her eyes. "You're never here either."

His eyes narrowed. "That's not fair."

"So? Sometimes life isn't fair. Isn't that what you said to me when Mom left?"

"That was different. I'm trying my best. Being a single parent isn't easy, and—"

"You have *got* to be kidding me. How are you parenting? Name *one* way that you parent me." She was playing with fire and she knew it, but she couldn't stop now. Her mom had left; Bas betrayed her; even her freaking *ghost* seemed to be ignoring her. And now her dad was going to patronize her with a talk about how hard it was to be a single parent?

Nope.

She held up a hand, ticking items off on her fingers. "I grocery shop. I do the laundry. I do dishes. I clean. I get myself to and from school. I go to drivers ed. I do my homework." She shrugged, spreading her arms wide and letting out a dark laugh. "Seems like I've been parenting myself pretty well, Dad."

"Young lady, you do *not* speak to me that way." His face was turning red, a vein popping out of his temple like an angry purple worm. "Have you ever even *thought* about whose job it is to make sure you have money to buy groceries, or clothes to wash, or a house to clean? Have you considered *why* I'm not able to be home as much as I'd like to be?"

"Because you don't *want* to be here!" Angie yelled at him. The tears were falling freely down her cheeks now, and she swiped them away angrily with the heels of her hands. She didn't want him to see her cry. She didn't want to see him at all. "Ever since Mom left, you can't even stand to *look* at me."

"That's what you think?" Her father scrubbed a hand down his face, then slid it around the back of his neck and up into his hair, like he was brushing off invisible ants.

"It's the truth," she said, fighting to keep her lip from trembling. "I can't help that I look like her, you know. It's not like I enjoy the reminder any more than you do."

He shook his head, his jaw twitching. "You've got it all wrong," he said, his voice low.

"Of course." Angie threw up her hands in exasperation. "Like I'm all wrong about the ghost. Stupid Angie, wrong about everything."

"That's not—"

"Never mind," she said, snatching up her book bag from where she'd dropped it by the front door and slinging it over her shoulder. "Keep the dumb camera. I won't use it anymore. And I won't talk about the ghost either. Happy?"

"Angie." Her dad took a step toward her, his hand half outstretched, as if he weren't really sure he wanted to reach for her. After a second, he seemed to decide against it, putting his hand in his pocket. "Let's talk about this."

She shook her head, chewing the inside of her cheek and staring at the stained carpet. "I have homework," she muttered, turning away and walking to her room.

Once she was inside, she locked the door and pulled on her headphones, picking her loudest playlist and turning it up until it felt like the drums were trying to batter their way inside her skull. Setting her phone on silent, she pulled out her math homework and emptied her head of everything that wasn't polynomials, letting the music wash over her like a cleansing wave.

For a little while, she didn't want to know if her dad was still trying to talk to her, or if her ghost was singing to her, or if Bas was texting her to apologize. She told herself it was because she was mad at all of them. But no matter how loud she cranked her music, she couldn't drown out the fear that if she took the headphones off, she would be greeted only by silence. And that's what scared her most of all.

PART THREE

And if it was, that's not a big deal

CHAPTER FIFTEEN

I heard Doug Raymond makes all his employees sign a blood oath of loyalty. True?

—post by karvin4501 on r/RottenRaymond

"I am *so* sorry I'm late." By the time Madelyn flung herself breathlessly into the seat across from Nat at Bean Juice, she was nearly half an hour late. At first, she'd hoped that traffic would be enough of an excuse, but that was before she'd realized that Nat's shirt was still on her couch at home.

"Not a big deal. I've just been catching up on email," Nat said, snapping her laptop shut. The outside was covered in stickers: coffee cups, cartoon characters, pithy quotes, cat memes, and dozens of other brightly colored images and designs gave the impression of a graffiti wall. Overwhelming, but also artistic in its chaos.

Kind of like Nat. Today she wore a black motorcycle jacket over a crop top with a fluorescent unicorn on it, yellow plaid trousers, and orange Converse sneakers. A dark-gray pageboy cap hid most of her red hair, and she'd swapped out her purple glasses for round tortoiseshell frames. Madelyn felt like she and Syzygy might get along.

"So," Nat said, "what was the mysterious detour about?"

Madelyn sighed. All she'd texted was, Something just came up, be there as soon as I can. But after keeping Nat waiting for so long, she supposed she owed her an explanation.

"Well, the truth is, I kind of ran into that guy you saw me with the other day."

Nat leaned forward across the table, resting her chin on her hands in a show of exaggerated interest. "Oh *really*?"

"My sink broke, and I had to go get this part to fix it, and he happened to be at the store and—"

"Oh my gosh. Let me guess. He offered to fix it. You took him home with you. One thing led to another. 'Something just came up' indeed." She waggled her eyebrows.

"I was only half an hour late!" Madelyn protested, heat rising to her cheeks. "And for the record, that was just because I had to go home to grab your shirt, since I didn't think to bring it with me to the store. Oh, here you go, by the way. Thanks so much for letting me borrow it."

She pulled the freshly laundered shirt from her purse and handed it across the table to Nat, who dropped it in her bag without taking her eyes off Madelyn. "You can accomplish a lot in half an hour," she said, undeterred. "I mean, *something* definitely distracted you enough to lose track of time."

Madelyn sighed. "Honestly, the truth is way less fun than whatever you're picturing."

"Oh, so you *admit* it would be fun."

If Madelyn's face were any hotter, it would burst into flame. "We were actually talking about my landlord." A thought occurred to her. "Actually, if you've lived here awhile, maybe you know who he is too. Doug Raymond?"

"Womp womp," Nat sad-tromboned, flopping back in her chair. "You really could not have said two more buzz-killier words just now."

"So you do know him."

"Everyone does. He's the one dragging this town to gentrified hell in a bespoke handbasket."

"How so?"

Nat looked around with a sigh. "You're new, so you wouldn't know, but this place is practically unrecognizable from what it used to be. I mean, East Henderson was never cool, but at least it had character. Now it's like a Stepfordized version of itself, all polished and pristine with no personality whatsoever."

She pointed through the front window to the new commercial complex going up across the street, all crisp brick-and-stucco exteriors with giant industrial windows. "There used to be this comics store over there that I went to all the time. Owner was this awesome Nigerian dude who would set aside some of the new releases every Wednesday for kids who couldn't get there until after school. Then a couple doors down was Lotus House, the best Chinese restaurant in town. Amazing dim sum on the weekends." She shrugged, giving Madelyn a wry look. "Something tells me they won't be able to afford the rent in Silver Spoon Commons or whatever the hell that place is going to be called."

Madelyn squinted at the sign across the street. "I think it says Silver Spring Commons."

"Same difference."

"So I take it you're not a fan," Madelyn said.

Nat snorted. "That's an understatement. You say Raymond's your landlord?"

Madelyn nodded.

Nat frowned, leaning forward in her chair. Behind her thick glasses, her dark eyes were serious. "Then if you don't mind just a little more advice from a relative stranger, watch your back."

A chill rippled under Madelyn's skin. She tried to laugh it off, letting out a nervous titter. "You make him sound like a hit man or something."

Nat gave her a grim smile. "All I'm saying is that when it comes to Doug Raymond, I wouldn't rule anything out."

"Ohmigod, Potato, *stop*," Madelyn groaned, maneuvering the little dog away from the wall with her foot as she fastened her earrings into place. Tonight she was wearing her long, dangly gold stars, which Syzygy called her "stripper earrings," for reasons only they fully understood. Still, the moniker made them feel a little bit much for school, but perfectly fine for a date.

Which this was, right? An actual, bona fide date, not just a friendly, pre-plumbing dinner?

Dear God, *please* let this be a real date. She'd have a hard time justifying earrings that brushed her shoulders and a neckline that plunged halfway to her belly button if this was supposed to be a platonic dinner. Not to mention the half pound of makeup she'd caked on using a TikTok filter that, ironically, promised to give her a "natural glow."

Potato was already back at the wall, and Madelyn's stomach sank when she saw that her tiny claws had finally managed to work their way into the drywall, creating a rough indentation half an inch deep that may as well have been half a mile. Madelyn groaned, picking Potato up again and shutting her in the bedroom. She hadn't put her in her crate in a couple of months, but she may need to set it up again if Potato was going to keep doing this. In the meantime, the bedroom would have to do.

"Sorry, love you!" Madelyn yelled as she hurried out the door, shoving her hands down the front of her V-neck jumpsuit to adjust her boobs, which never seemed as perky in a strapless bra as she felt like they should. She was only twenty-three, for God's sake. Things were *not* supposed to be drooping yet.

She paused when she got to her car, glancing over her shoulder before sliding into the driver's seat. For a second, she'd felt like someone was watching her, but there was no one there. She must still be a little thrown by her conversation with Nat that morning. Even though she'd signed her lease knowing that Raymond may have had something to do with Piper's disappearance, Nat's warning had freaked her out more than she wanted to admit.

But that was silly. Even if he *was* involved in whatever had happened to Piper, that hardly made him a boogeyman lurking in her bushes. She just needed to chill out and focus on something else until she knew more.

Like her date with Alex.

Hunching over her steering wheel, she drove to the restaurant Alex had texted her, afraid to smush her hair, which she had spent forty-five minutes curling and which would probably go flat the second she walked into the restaurant. The joy of Asian genes.

If she ever got the opportunity to make whatever Faustian bargain Sandra Oh must have struck in exchange for her voluminous curls, she'd take it in a heartbeat. She'd commented on it so many times before moving to East Henderson that Syzygy had taken to calling *Killing Eve* "the hair show."

The Salt Shaker was an unassuming brown building with a pothole-marked parking lot that looked like it hadn't been repaved in decades. A metal pole at the front of the lot propped up a dingy white sign that proclaimed the restaurant's name in red block letters, next to a cartoon image of a dancing salt shaker.

After parking in what she *thought* was a real space—it was hard to tell, since all that was left of the painted lines were a few faded white flecks here and there—Madelyn checked her makeup in the rearview mirror, feeling significantly overdressed in her emerald-green jumpsuit and four-inch heels.

Her phone buzzed with a text. Here! Got a table toward the back. Turn right when you come in and keep walking until you hit a wall.

Ugh. *Keep walking until you hit a wall* was hardly a flirty text.

Her phone buzzed again. This time, there was a photo of a glass of red wine. They have some great local wines here, and I remembered you said you liked reds.

Madelyn blinked at the photo. Red wine was definitely a date drink. And she didn't even remember telling him she liked reds.

She closed her eyes for a moment, steadying her nerves. Casting one final glance in the mirror, she picked her way across the parking lot and entered the restaurant.

To her relief, the inside of The Salt Shaker wasn't quite as sketchy as the exterior, decorated with wide-plank natural wood floors, black-topped tables, and framed vintage artwork covering every spare inch of wall space. It was far from fancy, but it wasn't the dive she'd been fearing either.

True to his instructions, after turning right at the entrance, she found Alex in the back of the restaurant, tucked into a booth upholstered in dark-gray fabric, looking at his phone and chugging a tall glass of water. While he wasn't as dressed up as she was, he looked nice, dressed in dark jeans, a button-down lavender shirt, and a lightweight brown leather jacket. Two glasses of red wine sat on the table, along with a second water glass, all seemingly untouched.

She had nearly reached the table by the time he noticed her, dropping his phone face down on the table and practically leaping to his feet. "You're here!" he exclaimed with a grin that instantly warmed her to her toes. His eyes scanned over her, taking her in without lingering for too long, and his eyebrows raised approvingly as he returned his gaze to her face. "You look *amazing*."

"I may have gotten a little excited at the idea of a night of actual in-person human conversation, even if it does involve fixing my sink," she said, certain her cheeks must be glowing like live coals by now. "My most exciting social interaction of the past couple weeks was a Zoom game night with my college roommate."

Alex laughed, gesturing for her to sit first. "What games?"

She shrugged as she slid into her side of the booth, grateful to at least be able to tuck away her absurd heels. "Mostly Jackbox Games. They're good for long distance."

"Oh yeah." Alex nodded knowingly. "I played a bunch of those with my college roommates during the first year of the pandemic."

"Were you teaching then?"

He shook his head. "Nope. I was supposed to graduate that spring, but wound up having to redo my student teaching in the fall, since everything shut down before I could finish it up."

Madelyn shuddered. She'd been a senior in high school in the spring of 2020. Instead of a formal graduation, she'd had a Zoom ceremony in which she wore her cap and gown over pajama pants. Not exactly her fondest memory.

She did some quick math. "So you started teaching two years ago?"

He did a little shimmying shrug, wiggling his head indecisively. "More or less. Spring of 2021. Lots of openings back then. Easy to get a midyear job. Definitely a deep-end-of-the-pool situation, starting off with hybrid school and mask mandates, which made teaching a second language to eleven-year-olds *really* fun."

She cringed. "Wow. I'm sorry."

He shook his head, shooting her another radiant grin that set her insides boiling. "Nah, it's cool. Kept me from having to move back in with my parents after school, like a bunch of my friends had to do. And honestly, since I was brand new anyway, I didn't even have to pivot my teaching style. Hard mode for everyone else was my normal."

Madelyn felt the corners of her mouth tugging up. "Now I feel bad freaking out the other day. Didn't realize I was starting on easy mode."

"Oh no, those days are always hard mode," Alex said, his eyes losing a bit of their playfulness as he held her gaze. "No matter how long you've been doing this."

Madelyn swallowed, her throat suddenly thick. He was just so . . . *earnest.* Like he was somehow miraculously immune to bullshit. She didn't know how anyone managed that. In her experience, everyone had an agenda, everyone was working an angle. But Alex felt different. Not predictable, but . . . safe. Like a well-lit path in a crowded city.

Of course, after Ralph—the talking hemorrhoid—she knew better than to assume that red flags would always be visible right away. Some stayed tucked away until you were in too deep to find your way out. Others, you could look straight at them and see only a party.

So she'd keep looking. But she couldn't ignore the feeling in her gut that there weren't any to find.

She remembered her wine and took a long sip, unsure how to handle the strong and confusing emotions stirring inside her, with half of her wanting to get up and sprint away before he could rip off the mask and reveal the inevitable ugliness underneath, and the other half wanting to crawl across the table and lick his face.

The wine was good, fruity and deep with a touch of strawberry sweetness. She held up the glass and examined it. "You said this was a local wine?"

"From a vineyard in Avondale. You like it?"

She nodded, taking another sip. "I didn't know Pennsylvania wine was a thing."

"Almost as much of a thing as Pennsylvania mushrooms."

She raised an eyebrow. "Pennsylvania mushrooms?"

"Chester County is the mushroom capital of the world, you know."

"You're making that up."

He put a hand over his heart. "Madelyn, I am an *educator*."

The waitress came over then, holding a stainless steel pitcher and placing it on the table. Pulling an order pad and a pen from the black apron at her waist, she gave them both a wide smile. Her red nametag read SHERRY. "You guys ready to order?"

"Oh, whoops," Madelyn said, grabbing the plastic-covered menu in front of her and trying to inhale the whole thing in one visual gulp.

"We're going to need another minute, Sherry," Alex said.

"Sorry," Madelyn said, her face buried in the menu.

"Take your time," Sherry said.

Once Sherry was gone, leaving two freshly refilled glasses of water in her wake, Madelyn lowered the menu to find Alex staring at her. "Yes?" She glanced down, hoping she hadn't spilled wine down her cleavage.

"Tell me something about you," he said, folding his hands on the table. His position, combined with the deeply sincere way he spoke, made her feel like she was in a job interview. An interview with an incredibly cute interviewer whose jawline she wanted to nibble.

"Um," she said, every detail about her own life tumbling out of her head like water through a colander. She looked at the menu again, which may as well have been written in hieroglyphics. "I am very bad at deciding what to order at new restaurants."

He laughed, as if she'd said something genuinely delightful. "Are you a Whiz or provolone person?"

"I . . . don't know. I've never actually had a cheesesteak."

The expression on his face was like he'd been stabbed. "You went to *Penn State*." His eyes filled with horror. "Oh no. Are you a vegetarian?"

"No. I'm just from Tennessee. Cheesesteak wasn't much of a priority for me."

His features relaxed. "Oh good. I was extremely concerned that I had picked the absolute worst restaurant for our first date. I'm pretty sure the only vegetarian thing on this menu is the house salad, and even that is not a guarantee."

First date. Suddenly she felt a thousand pounds lighter.

"Yeah, about that," she said, leaning forward and lowering her voice. "Why *did* you pick this place?"

He wrinkled his nose conspiratorially. "Because they have the best cheesesteaks outside of Philly."

Madelyn spread her hands, at a loss. "Okay, seriously, what's the deal with you people and cheesesteaks? It's meat and bread and cheese."

Alex went extremely still, then reached across the table and took her hand. Electricity shot up her arm. His touch was soft and warm, and she fought the urge to cling to him like a baby koala. "Madelyn, I am about to change your life."

She should say something witty. He was being hyperbolic; that was the scripted response.

But the only word she could find was, "Okay."

After ensuring he had her permission, Alex ordered them both cheesesteaks with provolone, peppers, and onions, along with a basket of fries to split.

The fries came first, crinkle cut and perfectly crisp. Alex nestled them to the side of the parchment-lined basket so he could squirt in a blob of ketchup from one of the bright-red squeeze bottles that decorated every table.

"So Tennessee, huh?" he asked, dragging a fry through ketchup and popping it into his mouth. "What brought you to Pennsylvania?"

She could hear the crunch as he bit into his fry across the table, and snagged her own from the basket. Her eyes closed blissfully as it hit her tongue, her tastebuds singing a tune of salty, starchy goodness. "Wow," she said, her eyes fluttering open. "Those are *really* good."

"I told you," he said, looking pleased with himself.

"I think I was just tired of living in the South," Madelyn said in answer to his question, plucking another fry from the basket. "I always knew I wanted to be a teacher, but it's getting a lot harder to do that where I grew up." She watched him carefully, hoping that was enough; she didn't want to get into the book bans and funding problems and covert racism that had made her public school education a minefield. Nothing would kill the mood—assuming there *was* a mood—like that particular soapbox.

Alex nodded knowingly, and she breathed an inward sigh of relief. "My parents went to Penn State," she continued, "so it made sense to go there. And from there, it was easy to apply for Pennsylvania jobs."

"And you got a coveted East Henderson gig," Alex said with a grin. "Quite the achievement."

"Is it?" Madelyn asked. "I'm about ready to drop-kick some of my students straight into the sun."

Alex laughed. "Middle school is rough. They want to be treated like adults but have the maturity level of a whoopee cushion."

"They keep pranking me," she said. "Except the pranks are . . . so dumb."

"Like what?"

She sighed. "Once they stole all my staplers and put them in the cafeteria microwave."

"Oh dang, that was *you*? Wow, you have a lot of staplers."

"Yeah, I kept losing mine in college and so I'd buy another and then I'd find it, and that cycle repeated itself a few times." She shrugged. "This week they covered my whiteboard in Post-its, and underneath, it just said *SHIZZLE*. Like, what does that even *mean*, you little cockroaches?"

Alex grinned. "Sounds like they like you."

"They have a weird way of showing it."

"Nah," he said around a mouthful of french fry. "That's mild. They've got you on easy mode."

"What's hard mode?"

He shrugged. "Depends. When Mr. Sexton started, they covered his seat in superglue. And somehow changed his ringtone to a fart noise."

Madelyn laughed. "Wow, that's awful."

"Yeah, so is Mr. Sexton." Alex looked around. "Don't repeat that, please."

She ran her index finger and thumb across her mouth, miming pulling a zipper closed. "My lips are sealed."

"Anyway, middle schoolers are gonna middle school no matter where you are, but East Henderson is still a pretty solid place to land for your first job," he said. "Thanks in no small part to your esteemed landlord, real estate prices have nearly doubled in the past couple years."

"How much of this town does he own? I noticed the place going up across from the coffee shop."

"Yeah, he's got a few like that, along with most of the newer subdivisions," Alex said. "That brand-new neighborhood off the turnpike, with the model home that looks like a castle? That's his. But he also owns a bunch of strip malls, condos, that sort of thing on the outskirts of town. Lower-rent stuff that lets him get away with being a cheapskate while still making him money, because he knows his tenants can't afford to push back."

"So . . . everything."

"Pretty much. It's wild; ten years ago he was just a normal real estate agent and East Henderson was like any other town around here. Now we've got these giant houses and country clubs and high-end boutiques, and somehow he owns all of it."

"Business must be good."

"I guess. Although with the speed he built his business, you'd think he struck oil or something."

She was getting ready to ask another question when their cheesesteaks arrived in plastic baskets lined in checkered parchment, cheese oozing out between juicy slices of chopped steak. Her mouth immediately watered, and her eyes fluttered shut in delight as she sank her teeth into the chewy roll, flavor bursting across her tongue.

When she opened her eyes, Alex was grinning at her. "You get it now?"

Madelyn nodded, dabbing her lips with her napkin. She decided she could eat one of these every day and die happy. "I take back every skeptical thing I ever said about cheesesteaks."

Alex laughed, then dug in to his own. Juice dripped over their fingers and into the baskets, which were empty before Madelyn knew it. They polished off the last of the fries and ordered another round of wine. She'd originally intended to limit herself to a single glass, but she felt comfortable with Alex, and didn't want the night to end. But the second glass didn't last long, and it seemed that almost as soon as their glasses were refilled, they were empty again.

"Shall we go see about that sink?" Alex asked, and Madelyn reluctantly agreed. Originally, the idea of going to dinner before tackling her bathroom seemed great, since she wanted to look nice for their date and wouldn't have wanted Alex to see her putting the finishing touches on her hair and makeup while he crawled under her sink. Now, though, it felt like an incredibly unsexy way to end the evening.

Alex flagged down Sherry for the check. When it arrived, Madelyn pulled out her purse, but he waved her off. "My treat," he insisted.

"Are you sure?"

His dimple winked at her, turning her insides to jelly. "Of course." His tone was wine-warmed and flirty, and she couldn't help but feel that he was agreeing to more than just picking up the check.

As he walked up to the counter to pay, Madelyn checked her phone and was shocked to find that they'd been there for nearly two hours. It had felt like a quick bite, but apparently time moved twice as fast when she was with Alex.

He returned to the table rubbing his hands together. "Are you good to drive?"

She was—she was always careful to drink at least twice as much water as wine when she went out, and apparently they'd been here longer than she thought—but she found herself shaking her head. "Maybe we can walk around for a few minutes?" If she could make the date part of the evening stretch even a tiny bit longer, she would.

He suggested going across the street for dessert, which turned out to be water ice, another Pennsylvania staple Madelyn had never had.

"What were you *doing* in college?" Alex laughed as he handed over her small mango Gelati.

"Studying," she said, smiling playfully as she licked a tiny scoop of vanilla custard off her plastic spoon. Divine.

He raised his eyebrows. "Somehow I feel like that's not the extent of it."

She shrugged. She wasn't drunk, not even tipsy, but she almost felt like she was, loose and warm. She took a step closer to him and shrugged. "Maybe."

He held her gaze for a few agonizing seconds, causing her breath to catch in her throat. Was this it? Was he going to kiss her?

Instead, he took a comically big bite of his own blueberry lemonade water ice, then promptly winced. "Ow. *Ow.* Brain freeze."

Madelyn laughed, rubbing his shoulder as he pressed his palms to his head. A delicious shiver ran through her at the feel of his skin beneath the fabric of his shirt, making her want to get rid of the thin barrier entirely. *Slow. Down,* she reminded herself.

When his brain thawed, they walked back to the Salt Shaker parking lot, where they leaned side by side against the bumper of her car and talked until their cups of ice were empty. At some point that Madelyn couldn't quite recall, they'd drifted closer until her arm was pressed against Alex's from her shoulder to her elbow.

He grinned at her with blue-stained teeth. "What do you think, is it sink time?"

Madelyn took a deep breath, wanting nothing more than to say yes. But if they went back to her house now, the sink was the last thing on her mind, and she suspected the same was true for him. As much as she liked Alex, she couldn't forget that this was what had gone wrong with Ralph. She'd fallen for him too hard, too fast. The next time, she'd promised herself she'd take things slow.

This felt like the next time. And inviting him back now felt anything but slow. Even if it was ostensibly to fix her sink.

"Actually," she said slowly, "I think I need to call it a night. I'm sorry."

"No problem," he said quickly, although she thought she caught a flicker of disappointment in his eyes. "Some other time then."

"Are you free tomorrow? Maybe sometime after lunch?" Early afternoon felt like a much safer time to be alone in her house with him. Without the wine-and-dine flirty preamble. Maybe she wouldn't shave her legs tonight, as insurance.

"Perfect. Just text me your address and I'll be there." He reached for her empty water ice cup and his fingers brushed hers, lingering for a second as their eyes met again. She waited for him to turn away again, but instead, he leaned in, and her eyes fell shut.

The kiss was soft and sweet, his lips still cool from the water ice. She started to shift her body, wanting to melt into him, but then felt him pull away. As quickly as it had begun, it was over. The cup disappeared from her hands as Alex stacked it into his. "I'll see you tomorrow," he said softly, so close she could smell the blueberry sugar on his breath

"Mm-hmm," was all Madelyn could manage.

Somehow, she found her way into her car, and when she realized Alex was going to watch her until she drove away, she maneuvered her key into the ignition and located the gas with a wobbly foot.

When she got home, after letting Potato outside, she pulled out her phone to update Syzygy to find that she'd already missed two texts from Alex.

I had a great time with you tonight.

Can't wait to see you tomorrow.

Clutching the phone to her chest, she sank onto the couch with a groan. Potato jumped up to lick her chin, and Madelyn looked into her warm brown eyes. "Tomorrow would be taking it slow, right?"

Potato wagged her tail, and Madelyn took that as a yes.

CHAPTER SIXTEEN

> You know, we really don't lose that many people. I think it's because our hiring process is so effective. When you only hire the best, and you treat them well, that door just doesn't revolve very fast. I mean sure, sometimes we get some rats that manage to sneak their way in there, but we always manage to sniff them out. Rats don't last long in a lion's den.
>
> —Doug Raymond interview on *Business Talk* with Gabby Lee, October 3, 2017

"Hey. Jerkwad. I need to talk to you." Angie flung the words at the back of her former best friend like a knife. For the last few days, Bas had been avoiding her, but she wasn't going to let him get away with it anymore. Today, she'd sprinted out of Film Studies in order to catch him before he got to his bus.

Bas turned to face her, looking weary. "What is it now?"

Winded, Angie stumbled to a stop. She hadn't expected it to be so easy, but it was about time that *something* was easy. "What the hell did you say to my dad?"

He looked at the ground, a telltale sign that he felt guilty. "Did you get in trouble?"

"Do you *care*?"

"Of course I care. I'm worried about you."

"Really? Then why haven't you texted me in three days?"

His eyes narrowed. "You know why."

"Because you think I'm crazy."

"No! Because—" He glanced around, then took a step toward her, lowering his voice. "Because I didn't want to, I don't know . . . encourage you or something."

"Right. Because heaven forbid my best friend encourage me."

"You know what I mean. All that ghost-hunting stuff, it's not good for you. I think you may need some help."

"So you tattled to my dad."

"I didn't *tattle*."

"What would you call it?"

"I just told him that I had some concerns about you."

She laughed, high and shrill. "Concerns," she said, making air quotes with her fingers.

"Yes, *concerns*. It's not . . . not healthy, what you're doing."

Angie shook her head, glaring at him. "Great, so now I'm unhealthy *and* crazy."

"That's not what I said!"

"Well, you'll be pleased to know that he took my camera, and gave me a whole lecture about what a ridiculous, ungrateful child I am. So no more *unhealthy* ghost-hunting shit that you're so *concerned* about. Congratulations, you cured me. I hope you're proud of yourself."

"Oh, get over yourself, Angie," Bas said, his expression turning hard. "I'm not going to apologize, because I didn't do anything wrong. If you would take two seconds to consider this from my perspective—"

"That's rich, Bas," Angie said, crossing her arms. A crowd was beginning to gather around them, drawn by their raised voices, but she couldn't bring herself to care. "I could say the same to you."

"You don't think I've tried to see this from your perspective?" He was starting to talk with his hands, the way he did when he got upset, waving them about as his voice grew louder. "I spent *days* trying to help you out and giving you the benefit of the doubt. I even paid for half of your stupid nanny cam."

Angie rolled her eyes. "I'll pay you back."

"I don't care about the money!" Bas yelled, throwing his arms wide and nearly smacking a passing freshman in the face in the process. "I care about *you*! You're so bored that you've decided you're living in your own personal horror movie, and you don't even see how messed up that is! And you won't let anyone help you!"

"I asked *you* to help me."

"Not help you find *ghosts*, Angie, help *you*. Something is very wrong here, and you don't see it. You *won't* see it. So yeah, I talked to your dad, because I thought maybe he might get through to you since you won't listen to me."

"I would *never* betray you like that."

"I didn't betray you! I'm trying to *help* you."

"Well, I don't need your help!" Angie shrieked. "As a matter of fact, why don't you leave me alone forever?"

"Fine!" Bas yelled back without hesitation. "Have a nice life."

"Go to hell."

Angie turned away and stomped toward her bus, flopping into the first empty seat and slumping down until she couldn't see out the window. She didn't want to know if anyone was still staring, or if Bas was still standing there, or if he was looking for her, or if he wasn't looking for her.

That hadn't been what she'd planned at all. But she'd gotten so angry. And Bas . . . she'd never seen Bas that mad before. He was normally the calm one. He was the one who helped her cool down whenever she ran hot. She wasn't prepared for him to get as worked up as she was. And when he had . . . they'd both boiled over.

She sighed, pulling out her headphones and sliding them over her ears to block out the world. The bus pulled out of the school lot and wound toward her house. She wanted a do-over for this entire school year, and it was still only September.

When she got home, after dumping her school things by the door, the first thing she did was check the garage to make sure her dad's car wasn't there. She didn't want to be surprised by him again. But the garage was empty, as usual.

Good. She wasn't in the mood to talk to him, or anyone.

As quickly as she could, she unloaded and reloaded the dishwasher, then moved the laundry from the washer to the dryer. Once that was done, she shut herself in her room and pulled the audio recorder out of its hiding place, nestled between a tattered paperback copy of Shirley Jackson's *The Haunting of Hill House* and a Pennywise Funko Pop. She plugged it into the USB slot on her laptop. She'd been doing this every day after school, scanning through the hours of audio for any little blips. Fortunately, the playback software allowed her to view the audio waveform, so the process took only a few minutes rather than eight hours.

Unfortunately, those few minutes had been uniformly disappointing so far. Since her dad was at work, the only little sound wrinkles while she was in school each day were cars honking, a few snippets of conversation from people walking by outside, or neighborhood dogs barking. Once there had been a big spike, which had proved to be the doorbell chime.

The waveform bar finished loading, and Angie leaned back in her chair, lazily dragging her fingers across the trackpad as she watched the interminable flat line scroll by. Once again, absolutely nothing noteworthy to see here. She didn't understand. Why was the ghost only willing to interact with her? What did it want? And why couldn't anyone else hear it?

As much as she knew she'd never be able to convince Bas or her dad, she knew she wasn't crazy. This was real. It didn't make sense, but she knew it was true the way she knew she was awake after a vivid dream. There was never a question that maybe she was still asleep. She just knew.

She was nearly two-thirds of the way through the eight-hour waveform when she bolted upright in her chair, hurriedly pulling on her headphones from where they'd been draped around her neck. This was more than a blip; this was . . . *something.*

"—any choice," an unfamiliar male voice said. It was faint, like it was coming from another room.

The next voice was her father's. *"Please. I just need a little more time."*

Angie paused, heart pounding, and scrolled back to the beginning of the sound spikes. What was her father doing home in the middle of the day? Shouldn't he be at work? And who was he talking to? She turned the volume up as high as it would go and pressed Play.

The first few sound spikes were the doorbell, the high-pitched chimes piercing her ears, causing her to wince. She heard the door open, then her dad's voice, sounding tense. *"What are you doing here?"*

"Just passing by. Laird said he thought you might be home."

Laird was her dad's main foreman. He supervised the work on the jobsites while her dad handled his company's scheduling, materials, clients, and other more administrative tasks.

"Why were you talking to Laird?"

"Happy coincidence. Ran into him over at Mayday. Said he's got a lot of time on his hands lately."

"Couple jobs wrapped up early. Not a big deal."

"Laird seemed to think it was more than a couple jobs. He said you're behind on paying your crew, Cameron. Said he was worried he may need to look for another job."

Angie leaned in toward the screen, her hands pressed tight over her headphone speakers, as if that would help this conversation make sense. Who was this guy? What was he talking about? Her dad was never home. He was constantly working. His jobs weren't wrapping up early; if anything, they were always running late.

"I'm going to pay the crew." Her father's voice sounded strained. *"I was actually just getting ready to run by the bank."* There were a few seconds of silence. Angie tried to imagine what was happening. Then she heard her father's voice again, even quieter. *"I'll get you your money. I swear."*

"Glad to hear it. Because otherwise, well. You know what happens. I hate to do it, but you really haven't left me any choice."

"Please. I just need a little more time."

"How much more? I've been more than patient, Cameron. Too patient, some might say."

"A . . . a month? Or, no, no, wait." Her father was talking fast. Too fast. Arguing with an opponent only he could hear. *"Two weeks. Give me two weeks, Doug. Please, I'm begging you."*

"Two weeks," the man, Doug, said. *"But Cameron, this is the last time. I've tried my best to help you. I even tossed you some work. I don't do that for just anyone, you know. But you have got to do your part."*

"I will," her dad said, and her stomach dropped at the desperation in his voice. She'd heard him talk like this only one other time in her life: right before her mother left. *"Thank you. Thank you. I promise, Doug, you won't regret it."*

"I sure hope you're right," Doug said. *"You have a nice day, Cameron. I'll see you in a couple weeks."*

"Yes. A couple weeks. Thank you."

Angie heard the door close, and the waveform flattened for a few seconds. She could see one last spike coming up before the sound ended for good. She assumed it would be another door—maybe her dad went into his bedroom or the garage—and started to remove her headphones, but as she slipped them off her ears, she heard her dad yell *"Fuck!"* so loudly it made her jump and drop her headphones on the floor.

She couldn't remember that she'd ever heard her dad say that word before. She'd barely ever even heard him cuss.

For a while, after the audio finished playing, her mind felt blank, like it had forgotten how to form thoughts. She simply sat and stared at her screen, unable to comprehend what she had heard. Once her thoughts did begin to solidify again, they were a chaotic jumble, swirling around and crashing into each other like bumper cars, each impact spinning off a spray of new questions.

Who was Doug? Why did her father owe him money? What happened if he didn't pay? *Why* couldn't he pay? Where was he going all the time if it wasn't for work?

Angie picked her headphones back up off the floor and listened to the audio again. And again, and again, over and over as if maybe listening to the words enough times would make the meaning behind them finally become clear.

She didn't know how many times she'd listened when she finally heard the back door to the garage open and close. The clock on her nightstand read 6:23. Based on the time she'd started the audio recorder that morning, the conversation with Doug and her dad had occurred sometime around 1:00 p.m. If he wasn't working, where had he been for the past five and a half hours?

She walked out of her room to find her dad in the kitchen, ripping open the plastic packaging on a pack of frozen egg rolls. "Oh hey, honey," he said without looking up, shaking the egg rolls onto the toaster oven tray. "You want any of these?"

Angie shook her head wordlessly. Her tongue felt thick in her mouth, her throat dry. Taking a clean glass from the cabinet, she filled it from the water dispenser on the fridge and took a sip. It didn't help. "Dad?" The word came out soft and scratchy. She cleared her throat.

"Hmm?" He slid the tray into the toaster oven and twisted the dial to ten minutes. The temperature was already set; it was rare that their toaster oven was used for anything else.

"Why were you home this afternoon?"

He looked up from the mail, which he'd been shuffling through and tossing into the trash one piece at a time. "What?"

"You were home while I was in school. Why?"

"How did you know I was home?" he asked sharply. But before Angie could answer, he sighed, returning his attention to the mail. "I had a little break from work, that's all. So I came home for lunch. Why? Did one of the neighbors mention it?"

She swallowed again, willing him to volunteer the rest of what she wanted to know so she wouldn't have to ask. *Why do you owe someone money? Where do you go every day? What is happening to us?*

He finished with the mail, keeping one lone envelope, which he tucked into the back pocket of his khaki pants, then walked over to the fridge to pour his own glass of water. He glanced at her out of the corner of his eye. "Was there something else?"

"I . . ." Angie closed her eyes briefly, blowing out a long breath. "Who is Doug?"

Her dad froze, his glass of water halfway to his parted lips. Slowly, he lowered it to the counter, running his other hand through his hair. "Who?" His voice was quiet, and she thought she detected a slight tremor.

"I know a man came to see you today. His name was Doug. Who is he?"

Her dad looked around the kitchen, narrowing his eyes, then stepped out into the hall, looking toward the living room. "Do you have more of those cameras stashed around here? We talked about this." His tone was harsh, but he didn't sound angry, not exactly. He sounded . . .

Scared.

"No," she said, her skin growing hot as her pulse began to race. "Dad, what's going on? Who is Doug?"

He turned and looked at her, hands on his hips. His eyes were wide, and for the first time, she noticed the bags underneath. "No one you need to worry about," he said, speaking rapidly. "Just a business contact. That's all."

"He said you owe him money. He said—"

"How do you know that?" His eyes kept darting around the room, as if he expected a camera to jump out and attack him at any moment. "Tell me the truth."

Angie bit her lip, but knew there was no way to ask him about what she'd overheard without being honest about how she had heard it. "I have an audio recorder."

Her dad threw up his hands with a groan. "Angie, we *talked* about this."

"We talked about the *camera*," she retorted. She knew it was a flimsy excuse, but right now, she didn't care. "But also it's a good thing I was recording, because otherwise you'd keep lying to me, apparently. Who is Doug? Why do you owe him money? And what did he mean when he said you know what happens if you don't pay him? What happens, Dad?"

Her dad turned away from her, bracing his hands on the counter. His knuckles were white, his arms tense, like he was trying to push himself into another reality where he didn't have to have this conversation.

"Dad?"

"Just a minute," he said without turning to face her. "Just . . . give me a minute."

Angie swallowed the urge to ask him again, hugging her arms across her stomach as she shifted her weight from foot to foot. She didn't know what to do with her body. She didn't want to lean or sit; she had too much nervous energy for that. But their kitchen was too small to pace. All that was left was to stand awkwardly in place, and wait.

"Doug Raymond," her father said finally, his shoulders hunched away from her, "is our landlord."

"What?" Angie blinked. She'd figured he must have loaned her father money, or maybe paid him in advance for a job. Nothing like this. "But . . . we own this house."

"We *did* own this house," he said. His voice sounded small. "But when your mother left . . . you know she always made more money than me. I . . . I did my best, but I couldn't . . . it wasn't enough. I got behind and . . ." He turned around, eyes rimmed in red, hands clasped in front of him like a plea. He drew in a shaky breath. "Last year, Doug approached me. I'd done some work for him, and he got wind that I was having trouble making ends meet. He proposed that he buy the house and rent it back to me. The money from the sale would be enough to keep us afloat for a while, and we wouldn't have to move. I said yes. I didn't think you'd ever have to know."

"Dad," was all Angie could think to say. The blood had drained from her face. How had she not known? She'd thought they were fine. Everything was *fine.*

Her dad sniffed, rubbing a hand quickly across his eyes and clearing his throat. Angie had only ever seen her dad cry a couple of times. Seeing him fight tears now turned her stomach to ice. This must be really bad.

"I had a plan," her dad said, his voice thick. "I thought I could use a little of the house money to get us back on track and set the rest aside for your college. But . . . well, things with my business . . . materials prices keep going up and there are all these big companies that can buy in bulk and turn jobs around faster and cheaper and it's so hard to compete. I didn't want to lay anyone off and I figured that things would pick back up if I could hold on a little while longer—"

"You spent all of the money from our house," Angie said softly. It wasn't a question. She could clearly see where this story was headed. "And now we're broke, and you still don't have enough work."

He nodded miserably. "I got a job at McDonald's," he said, not meeting her eyes. "I pick up shifts whenever work is slow. And I started doing some jobs for Doug too. Errands, deliveries, that sort of thing."

Angie's eyes widened. "The McDonald's by my *school*?" All those afternoons and evenings when she had thought he was tied up on a jobsite, he was flipping burgers.

But he shook his head. "No, out near Conshohocken."

Twenty minutes away. He probably had to drive past three other McDonald's in order to get there. He must not have wanted anyone to recognize him. Probably not good for business to see that the contractor you hired to remodel your kitchen is so strapped for cash that he had to take a minimum-wage job.

"How are we still behind then?" Angie asked. Now that they were talking about this, she was determined to see it through, even if she hated what she found. "He said you hadn't paid your crew. Where is all that money going?"

"I've been doing my best," her dad said. "I pay them what I can. It's just . . . it's a lot of money, sweetheart. None of my jobs pay very much. But I swear, I'm working as hard as I can. And I'm almost caught up."

"But not on the house," she said. He was working three jobs, keeping him so busy that he was never home, but it wasn't enough. He was paying everyone's bills but his own. "Dad, how far behind are we on the house?"

It took him an eternity to answer. "Five months," he whispered.

"Five *months*? How on earth are you paying back five months' worth of rent in the next two weeks?"

"I have some things I can sell," he said. "Your mom left some jewelry, and we've got that old clock that belonged to my grandfather—"

"Dad, are you kidding? That stuff is worth like, a few hundred bucks, tops."

He shrugged helplessly. "I'm trying everything I know to do, sweetie. I'm so sorry. I never wanted you to have to find out about this."

"Dad," Angie whispered, her throat tight. She dreaded the answer to her next question. "What happens if you can't pay?"

He opened and closed his mouth a few times without any sound coming out, like the words were stuck in his throat. After a few false tries, all he managed was, "I'm so, so sorry, honey."

Angie took a step back, her legs banging against the kitchen table with a clatter. Her body had gone numb. She couldn't believe this was happening. Had been happening for months, while she'd been busy chasing ghosts.

And now it was too late.

They were going to lose their home. In two weeks, they'd have nowhere to live.

CHAPTER SEVENTEEN

Dear Madelyn,

I'm sorry about your fight with Ralph. That sounds awful. For what it's worth, I don't think you were being unreasonable to want to invite your friends to your birthday dinner. It's your birthday! You should get to spend it with whoever you want! But of course, I understand your point about all the planning he put into it, and that you didn't want to hurt his feelings. It sounds like you tried very hard to do the right thing for everyone involved, but I'm sorry it meant you didn't enjoy your birthday. I hope you get an opportunity to go out with your friends another time and celebrate!

(And please take all of my relationship advice with a grain of salt, since the last date I went on, the guy did not look up from his phone once the entire time we were at dinner, but then aggressively tried to make out with me outside the restaurant while I waited for my Lyft. So clearly I am not good at this!)

Love,
Piper

It took everything she had not to text Alex immediately when she woke up at 7:30.

Madelyn had promised herself last night that she'd wait to text him until the morning; well, it was morning. But 7:30 was a little *too* morning, and she didn't want to scare him off before they'd even gotten a chance to explore this thing between them. Instead, she forced herself to get out of bed and go through her morning routine first, taking her meds, making coffee, walking Potato, and showering before she even let herself consider sending a text.

At 9:47, she decided it was late enough to not be weird.

Good morning! Still on for this afternoon?

His answer came back right away: Of course! I was thinking around 2, if that works for you? My family likes to eat lunch together on Sundays.

2 is perfect. She'd prefer he come over in four minutes rather than four hours, but it wasn't like she could say that.

Awesome! Just need your address 🙂

906 Gazelle. It's the little white house with the blue trim.

Three dots appeared, indicating that he was typing his response, then disappeared.

That was weird. His answers had come through right away before. She waited, watching her phone screen, as the dots appeared, then disappeared, then appeared, then disappeared. It was like he was writing and deleting numerous responses without sending.

What was wrong? Had something come up? Was he going to cancel? Had he suddenly decided that actually, he should *not* have kissed her last night and that this was all a mistake?

Right as she was debating calling Syzygy to talk her down from the anxiety spiral, her phone buzzed with a new text.

Okay. See you at 2.

No emoji, no exclamation points. Tone was impossible to discern over text, that's what everyone always said, but this one felt strangely cooler than his previous communication. As if something had happened to extinguish his interest between her sending him her address and him confirming their plans.

She was probably reading too much into it. That's what Ralph always said she did. Syzygy insisted that he was full of shit—which he was—and that Madelyn should trust her gut when it told her something was wrong—of which Madelyn was less convinced.

The thing was, her gut lied to her all the time. If she always listened to her gut, she wouldn't have a degree or a job or a place to live, because she would have talked herself out of all of them. She wouldn't even have Syzygy, thanks to the voice in the back of her head that was constantly convinced that her friends secretly hated her.

It was precisely because she *didn't* trust her gut that she had any of the things she valued in her life. Her gut liked to remind her that any of those things could go away at any time. She'd spent the past year learning to rely on cues outside herself to keep her grounded, reminding her that just because she felt a thing didn't make it true.

So instead of allowing herself to spiral, she spent the next couple of hours cleaning and going over her lesson plans for the week. Alex didn't text again, but he *had* said that he spent Sundays with his family, so he probably wasn't on his phone. And, she reminded herself, *he* had kissed *her* last night. He wouldn't have done that if he wasn't interested, right?

Unless . . . she had made it *so* obvious that she wanted him to kiss her that he was just being polite? She ran back through the night in her head, looking for any indication that he was merely playing along with her clear desperation, but all signs pointed to the feeling being mutual, including his texts when she got home. Even this morning, he'd seemed eager to see her again.

Until suddenly, he wasn't.

But that was probably nothing. She was reading into it too much. All this thinking about Piper had her seeing conspiracies where there were none.

By 1:30, she'd finished cleaning up from lunch and had run out of things to do, so she stationed herself on her couch with the sci-fi book she'd been reading, determined not to spend the next half hour looking out the window and checking her phone. She refused to be *that* girl.

At 1:54, right in the middle of a particularly harrowing scene about potato farming—a subject she would never have considered even *could* be harrowing—she heard the sound of a car stopping in front of her house. Sliding in a bookmark to keep her place, she dropped the book on the coffee table. A glance out the window confirmed that it was Alex. Her stomach gave a nervous flutter.

But something was . . . off. He wasn't getting out of the car. She squinted around the edge of the curtain, hoping he couldn't tell she was watching him. He seemed to be talking to himself, and he looked agitated, kneading the steering wheel with his hands. Maybe he was finishing a phone call?

He shook his head, lips pressed together in a frown, then swung open the car door and got out. Instead of coming to the door, though, he stood in her driveway, staring at the house with a slightly nauseated expression. His shoulders and chest heaved like he was taking intentionally deep breaths.

What on earth was going on? Madelyn rushed to the front door and swung it open, stepping outside. "Alex? Are you okay?"

His eyes drifted from the house to her. "What is this?"

"What is what?"

"Is this some kind of sick joke? Are you messing with me?" His tone was getting darker. Angry.

Madelyn searched her memories for anything she might have done to upset him, but couldn't think of anything. "Is *what* a joke? I have no idea what you're talking about."

Alex glared at her, his face a thundercloud, nostrils flaring. "Who *are* you?"

CHAPTER EIGHTEEN

> We LOVE our new home. Doug Raymond was amazing to work with. He guided us through every step of the process, offering his expertise to make sure we got exactly what we needed. The neighborhood, the amenities, absolutely everything makes us feel right at home. Five stars!
>
> —five-star Yelp review of Raymond Realty Group

Angie perched at the edge of the driver's seat, too nervous to blink, her knuckles white on the steering wheel. She'd never driven at night before. And she'd driven into town only a couple of times, always from school with her driver's ed instructor in the seat beside her. This was totally different.

The sun hadn't finished setting yet, but it was dark enough that everyone had their headlights on. Their beams were an onslaught of blinding light, and she had to fight the urge to close her eyes to block them out or, worse, veer off the road to escape.

It didn't help that she was convinced that at any second, flashing lights were going to appear behind her. She had her permit in her wallet, but that wouldn't do her much good since there wasn't a licensed driver in the seat beside her. Would she be arrested for driving without a license? Her dad couldn't afford to bail her out of jail; he couldn't even afford to keep their house. And even if he could bail her out, he probably wouldn't, not after she grabbed the keys and ran out, ignoring his calls to come back.

What happened if no one came to bail you out? Did you just . . . *stay* there?

"Shit, shit, shit," she chanted under her breath, scanning the buildings around her for the blue awning of Raymond Realty. She knew it was around here somewhere. They drove by it all the time, so even though she'd never stopped there before, she had a solid idea of where it was. Her eyes darted to the speedometer every few seconds to ensure she was going the speed limit.

There. She spotted the awning with its white block lettering jutting out from a redbrick storefront. By the time she recognized it, though, there wasn't time to find a parking spot, and she didn't want to attempt to parallel park on the busy street anyway.

She continued down the street and pulled into the Wawa gas station on the corner, parking at the far end of the lot. The late-September air was crisp and cool, tinged with the smells of gasoline and freshly baked bread. Before she could lose her nerve, Angie locked the car and jogged down the sidewalk back to Raymond Realty.

She wasn't entirely sure what she planned to do. When she'd grabbed the car keys, she'd thought a plan would come to her in an adrenaline-fueled epiphany, but her mental tablet of ideas was still frustratingly blank. And realistically, the office probably wasn't even open right now. Most businesses in town closed around five, and it was nearly seven.

Still, she felt like she had to do *something*. And with only two weeks to come up with a solution, every second counted. She couldn't go to bed like everything was normal. If no one was in the office, well, she'd have to figure out what to do from there, but she needed to at least start by trying to reason with Doug Raymond, and this was the only place she knew to look for him. Her dad hadn't been able to buy them more time, but maybe she could. It was one thing to say no to a grown man; she hoped it was another to tell a teenage girl that she was about to be homeless.

The stenciled front window of Raymond Realty was dark as she approached, her steps slowing. Her stomach dropped. Of course no one was there. She had known that was probably going to be the case, but hadn't expected the cold wave of disappointment that washed over her.

So. That was that. She'd have to come back tomorrow.

There was no reason to stay, but she couldn't bring herself to leave yet. She raised her hands to the plate glass window, cupping them around her face to peer inside the darkened office. It was entirely ordinary: a few desks facing sets of upholstered armchairs, framed artwork of beautiful homes and sleek office buildings on the walls, geometrically patterned carpet, fake plants. A hall off the front office space led deeper into the building, but she couldn't see where it went. Probably just to more offices.

Sighing, she dropped her hands and took a step back, blinking back tears. It was silly to have thought she could do anything tonight, but she hated feeling powerless. She wanted to call Bas, tell him everything, have him tell her it was all going to be okay, but when she pulled out her phone, their argument after school came rushing back. It felt like so long ago.

Had she really said all those awful things to him? It all felt so stupid now. Who cared if her house was haunted; in two weeks, she wouldn't even live there anymore.

Where would they go? Would they have to leave town? Would she go live with her mom? Did her dad even know where her mom was? She'd granted him full custody in the divorce, and although her dad had said that it was because she was trying to keep things "consistent" for Angie, she knew he was covering for her. A mom who actually cared about consistency wouldn't disappear without a word. She would check in. She would stay involved. Text, call, FaceTime, something.

Last year, her mom had texted three times. Once on her birthday, once to send a photo of her pedicured toes on a lounge chair with an unspecified beach in the background with the words miss you and a kissy face emoji, and once to send her a photo of a museum display with the text not supposed to take photos in here but look! Your namesake!

The photo was of Chinese American actress Anna May Wong, a movie star from the 1930s her mom had always admired. Angie's full name, Angelina Mei, was her mom's tribute to Anna May but, as she explained it, "even more glamorous" and "truer to your roots." Angie had always thought there was something bizarrely performative about her half-Chinese mother changing the spelling of a famous Chinese woman's name as a way to "honor" her mixed-race heritage, but she never felt like she could bring it up without coming across as performative herself.

It didn't matter now, though. This year, there had been only the birthday text, and even that had come a week late. Her mom was basically a stranger. Angie couldn't imagine that she'd help them now.

As Angie tried to think through what might happen next, she remained on the sidewalk, staring blankly at the darkened window of Raymond Realty as people stepped around her. She wasn't really looking anymore; she just didn't have anywhere else to go.

It took her a few seconds to notice when a light in the back of the office turned on.

When the change finally registered, adrenaline surged through her body. She stepped forward, bringing her hands up to the window again and searching the office. Who was here? Was it Raymond? Could her haphazard plan actually have paid off?

She waited for someone to walk into the front of the office, hoping to catch their eye so they would let her in. Faint shadows moved in the hall, but no one came into view. Should she knock? Yell? She didn't want to make a bad impression. It was important he like her so that he would give them more time to pay off their debts. But if he left without ever knowing she was there, she would've missed her chance.

As she shifted from foot to foot, debating what to do, a yell came from the back of the office, accompanied by a dull thud, like something heavy had been knocked over. *What was that?* Angie squinted, shuffling to the side to try to get a better angle. Had he dropped something? Was he hurt? If Angie helped him, maybe he'd be grateful enough to give them an extension.

A woman stumbled into view from the back of the office, bracing a hand on the wall as she gingerly touched the side of her mouth. Dark-brown hair fell across her face, and her wraparound dress hung off one shoulder, but she appeared too dazed to notice. She wore tall, pointed heels, the kind Angie had never been able to walk more than three feet in without toppling over.

All thought of coming heroically to Doug Raymond's aid vanished from Angie's mind, replaced by horror. Who was this woman? What was happening? She didn't understand what she was seeing, but knew instinctively that something was very, very wrong.

The woman lifted her eyes, looking toward the window, and her eyes locked on Angie's. For a moment, they stared at each other, neither moving. The skin around one of the woman's eyes was beginning to darken. She opened her mouth, and Angie was certain she was about to say something to her, but before she could, she pitched forward, hit from behind by an unseen force, sprawling onto the floor behind the reception desk, out of sight.

A man emerged from the hall. He wasn't especially tall or broad; really, nothing about his appearance was particularly noteworthy. Short, lightly graying hair, neatly trimmed beard, generic business suit. In most ways, he was indistinguishable from any of the dozens of other middle-aged white men she passed in town every day who vanished immediately from her memory.

Except for the expression on his face, which turned Angie's blood to ice. It was pure, unfiltered rage. A dangerous, hungry look, one that didn't care about anything except its own satiation. In an instant, Angie knew that look would sear itself into her nightmares for the rest of her life.

She recognized him from the picture she'd found online before leaving her house. Doug Raymond.

His eyes remained locked on the woman on the floor of the darkened office like a bear stalking its prey. Picking up a round planter from the desk, he raised it up over his head, then brought it down and—

Oh God.

Angie's hand flew to her mouth, holding in a scream as she watched Raymond swing the planter down behind the desk again and again and again. Her whole body felt numb. She couldn't see the woman anymore, but her mind conjured horrible pictures of what she must look like now. She took a shaky step back, then another.

Her hand bumped into something—a parking meter. She looked down and saw she was still holding her phone. *911. I should call 911.*

Trembling, she punched in the passcode, but her fingers were shaking too hard and she kept entering it wrong. After three tries, her phone screen changed. *You have reached the maximum number of login attempts. Your device is now locked.*

"Crap," she said through clenched teeth, tears spilling down her cheeks. She glanced up at the window, but she had stepped too far away and it was too dark for her to see inside. All she could make out now was her own terrified reflection. She looked at the phone again, willing it to let her in.

Wait. A faint memory stirred in her brain. Wasn't there something about being able to call 911 on a locked phone? How did she do that?

Frantically, she swiped her fingers across the screen, poking at random in the hopes that she would magically touch the right thing. And to her amazement, it worked. She wasn't sure what she'd done, but suddenly the phone keypad appeared, glowing white like a beacon of hope.

Yes!

She glanced up at the window again as her thumb hit the 9—

And locked eyes with Doug Raymond, framed in the window, his face splattered with blood.

CHAPTER NINETEEN

Dear Madelyn,

I'm so sorry I couldn't make it out to Penn State for your show. I really wanted to go, but I just couldn't get the time away from work. I hope it went wonderfully well! If there are any recordings of your performance, please send them along. I would love to watch them.

But I'm so excited for your trip to East Henderson in a couple weeks! I can't wait to show you around town. I think my friend Kelsey may also join us on Saturday, if that's all right with you. You'll like her—she knows all the best places to eat! Of course I will have to work during the week, but I would love to show you around our new offices. If I can find my way around without getting lost, that is—they're so much bigger than our old ones!

Can't wait to see you soon!

Piper

—

Madelyn shook her head, baffled. What was Alex talking about? Why was he acting like he didn't know her—or worse, like he was mad at her? Did it have something to do with her relationship to Piper? But why would that matter?

Her heart hammered against her chest, and her feet felt glued in place. Most of the words she knew seemed to evaporate from her mind. "I . . . I'm Madelyn."

"But who *are* you?" Alex asked again. "What are you doing here? And don't lie. I *know* it's about her."

The questions flew at her like daggers, and she flinched with each one. Okay, so he *did* know about Piper. "I'm so sorry. I should have told you," she said. "I just didn't realize you knew her." She tried to think back to when they'd talked about Kelsey's court case. Had he mentioned anything about knowing Piper?

"*Knew* her? I was her best friend. And I don't believe you didn't know. *Everyone* knew. It's even in the freaking police report."

This wasn't adding up. Alex wasn't Piper's best friend. Kelsey was. She tried to recall whether Piper had ever mentioned having a close male friend in town.

And he definitely wasn't in the police report. Kelsey's lawyer had obtained a copy for her case, and she'd shown it to Madelyn. It was barely a page, and entirely useless.

"I swear, I didn't know," Madelyn insisted.

He narrowed his eyes, lip curling in disgust, then brushed past her into the house, not waiting for an invitation.

Madelyn stood frozen on the front step for a second before following him inside, hugging her arms around her middle to try to stop the violent churning in her stomach. She shouldn't be surprised that he'd turned on her. That was always the way it went.

But for some reason, stupidly, she'd thought he was different.

He stood in the middle of her living room with his back to her, slowly scanning the worn red sofa, the black-and-white flowered curtains she'd gotten from Target, the old upright Yamaha piano against the wall that she'd taken lessons on as a child. His fists clenched and unclenched at his sides, fingers flexing and twitching.

"Alex?" Madelyn said tentatively, still standing by the open door. She didn't want to close it yet. Just in case she needed to get away. "I really am telling the truth. If I'd known you were friends, I would have told you."

He turned to her, seething. "Stop. Just stop. You'd think after ten years, I'd be over this, but—"

"Ten years? What are you talking about?"

"Come on. You know how long it's been."

"I really don't." Piper had gone missing in 2021. Even by the laxest mathematical standards, that did not round to ten years.

He sighed, running a hand through his hair. Hair she had *really* wanted to run her own fingers through, before Alex had proved to be just as toxic and gross as every other guy she'd ever been attracted to. "I can't do this," he said, deflating. "Can you please just tell me what's going on? Why are you doing this?"

Madelyn sighed, mustering up her courage. "Piper was my cousin," she said slowly. "I only found her a couple years ago, right before she went missing. I came here because—"

"Wait," Alex said. "Who's Piper?"

Madelyn tilted her head. "My cousin?" It came out with a question mark, not because she wasn't sure of the answer, but because she was perplexed by the question.

"I know, you said that, but . . ." He scrubbed his hands over his face, through his hair. "This doesn't make any *sense*," he muttered into his hands.

"If you're not talking about Piper," Madelyn said, "who *are* you talking about?"

"You really don't know?"

"I have no idea." She folded her arms, bracing for the bullshit. Because that's what it always was after a guy blew up for no good reason, and realized he'd gone too far. Pure bullshit.

Slowly, Alex dropped his hands, and the look he gave her was distant, as if he were looking at her but seeing someone else. "Do you ever hear ghosts?"

He said it so softly, Madelyn wondered if she'd misheard. "Ghosts?"

He nodded, his Adam's apple bobbing as he swallowed. "In this house. I think . . . I think they might sing?" His tone was almost apologetic.

Madelyn wrinkled her forehead. Nothing about this conversation made sense.

He sighed, nodding to himself. "Okay. When I was in high school . . ." he said, then covered his face with his hands. "Oh God," he muttered, his voice muffled.

Madelyn waited, but he didn't say anything further, so she prompted him. "Yes?"

He cleared his throat, dropping his hands to his sides and looking at her clearly for the first time. "When I was in high school, my best friend went missing. One night, she and her dad disappeared without a trace. No one ever heard from them again. I was the last one to ever speak to her, so the police brought me in for questioning."

"Oh wow." So they'd both had someone they cared about go missing in this town. What were the odds?

"No charges were ever filed. They eventually ruled out foul play." Bitterness edged his voice.

"You don't agree?" She hadn't forgotten that he owed her an apology, but she was also intrigued. Just how often did people go missing in East Henderson?

Alex shook his head. "Something weird was going on with her. Before. She thought her house was haunted. I didn't believe her. But once she was gone . . ." He swallowed again, his face strained, like the words were thick and sharp, caught in his throat like a bone. "I never told the police this," he whispered. "But I went to her house late that night. She'd called me and I hadn't picked up, and then I called her and it went straight to voicemail. Then I tried texting her dad and it didn't go through. I got worried. So I came over to check on her. And . . . I heard it."

Madelyn was completely lost now. "Heard what?"

"The ghost." His eyes were distant, staring into the past. "She'd tried to get me to hear it so many times before, and I never had. But I did that night." He looked at the floor, shuffling his feet. "After that, I stuck around for a while, hoping I would hear it again, but that was the only time. I found their phones on the kitchen counter. I had a bad feeling, but I didn't tell anyone then. But when she didn't show up at school the next day, I told my parents that I was worried, and they called the police."

"Why are you telling me this?" Madelyn asked. She was having a hard time processing what he was saying. Obviously he wasn't talking about Piper. Whatever he'd experienced had happened long before her. But she also couldn't wrap her head around whatever he *was* saying.

"She lived here. This was her house." He looked around the room again. "I was standing right here when I heard it."

He looked at her, his expression haunted. "I'm sorry I yelled at you. I shouldn't have done that. I just couldn't believe that I was back here. Of all places."

A chill ran down Madelyn's spine. She'd assumed he was mad about Piper, but this . . .

This was worse.

The front door opening, the dryer buzzer, the knocking with no one there. She'd written it all off as the wind, the neighbors, sleep deprivation, anxiety over living alone. There were so many normal explanations for what she'd experienced.

Or just one paranormal one.

The hair on the back of her neck stood up. Her eyes darted around the room, half expecting to land on a translucent figure rising out of the floor.

She was so freaked out by the thought of living with a ghost that she almost missed the next thing Alex said.

"Her name was Angie," Alex said. "And as of last week, she's been missing for ten years."

PART FOUR

And if it is, that's not my fault

Ten Years Ago

Abigail Norris-Graham deserved a raise.

She hated these visits to small-town offices with their eight-bit players. It felt cheap, and she was not cheap. If her bosses wanted her to grease some tiny wheels, then grease she would. That grease should just cost extra.

But her bosses were not people that one could simply ask for more money. Not without giving something in return. And that something always came with a steep cost. One that Abigail was not in any hurry to pay.

So she greased them too. It wasn't the first time, and it wouldn't be the last. Abigail was used to quietly building her own corporate ladder, one carefully crafted rung at a time. She climbed it lithely, with none of their clumsy scrambling, so that they barely even noticed she was moving.

Soon enough, they'd think it was their idea to move her into a different role. One that didn't involve buttering up small men with big egos and outsize ambitions. One that didn't require her to smile at men like Doug Raymond.

She'd dealt with a lot of insufferable blowhards in her line of work, but Raymond was especially vile. She was tired of pretending she didn't notice. But her superiors seemed to think that this guy might be important, given the right opportunities. It was her job to make that a reality.

"That's right," she confirmed to her employer over the phone as Raymond unlocked the rear entrance to his office. "Twenty percent, he'll handle customs, we'll take care of PENNDOT."

"Can't believe you sold him on twenty. I swear, woman, you could negotiate the gills off a fish."

Abigail smiled to herself. She'd been authorized to go up to thirty, but she prided herself on never hitting her cap.

"Tell Raymond we'll send a courier over tomorrow to grab his signature on a few things so we can wrap this up, but no need for you to stick around for that. Excellent work, Abigail. As always."

"Thank you, sir." Abigail tucked her phone back in her purse. "We're all set," she said to Raymond. "Courier will be by in the morning with the paperwork."

"Wonderful," Raymond said, holding the door open for her.

She stepped into the office, looking around in mock admiration as he flipped on the lights. "Wow, this place is great."

It wasn't. Everything felt generic, from the bargain-bin carpet to the open-source artwork on the walls. But guys like this needed to feel like they had good taste. Like they stood out from the crowd.

Honestly, it was embarrassing. They didn't stand out from the crowd; they *were* the crowd.

Abigail hadn't wanted to return with him to his office. She would much rather be back at her five-star hotel, where she could ditch her Manolo Blahniks and shapewear and bloodred lipstick, and sink into a bubble bath in the giant Jacuzzi tub. But Raymond had a bottle of champagne he'd been saving for a special occasion, and insisted she come in for a toast.

One glass, she'd agreed. She'd toss it back, then get the hell out of there.

The champagne was in a minifridge behind Raymond's desk. He opened it with a flourish and filled two gold-rimmed flutes, handing one to her. "To our new partnership," he said, raising his glass to clink against hers.

She sipped as quickly as she could without being obvious, wishing she were alone so she could take time to savor. Dom Pérignon was not meant to be chugged.

"That artwork cost ten K," Raymond boasted, pointing to a forgettable painting of flowers in an ornate frame. "We believe that top-dollar work deserves top-dollar price tags."

"I can see that," Abigail said admiringly, pouring more champagne down her throat, and counting the seconds until she could excuse herself. Every minute with this idiot made her feel like she'd aged ten years.

"Actually," Raymond said, moving closer to her, "I've noticed that *you* are a top-dollar gal."

Abigail knew the sound of an exit cue. She finished her champagne as she sidled around him. "Congratulations again, Doug," she said, setting down her glass. "I need to get going, but we'll be seeing a lot more of each other, I'm sure. I look forward to working with you."

"We could see a lot more of each other right now," he said with a wink.

Gross. Did he really think that was a good line?

She gave him a noncommittal laugh and moved to the door, trying the knob. Locked.

She closed her eyes, clenching her teeth. This was the last thing she felt like dealing with tonight.

She turned to smile at him. "Doug," she said, keeping her tone playful, "did you lock the door?"

"Didn't want to be interrupted," he said, his thin lips curling into a hungry smile.

Abigail batted her lashes. He wasn't the first man to have interpreted a business deal as something more. She knew how to handle herself. "You know I'd *love* to stay," she said sweetly, "but I promised my husband I'd call in time to say good night to our daughter."

Of course she wasn't married and didn't have any children, but he had no way of knowing that.

"No wedding ring," Raymond observed, running a hand down her arm.

"I take it off to travel," she said without missing a beat. "Don't want to risk losing it."

She tried the door handle again, but it remained stubbornly locked. What sort of nightmare office locked the doors from the inside?

Raymond moved even closer, pinning her back against the door. Abigail's heart hammered in her chest. She clutched her purse in front of her, fumbling inside for her pepper spray. "Doug, I'm flattered," she said, keeping her smile glued on. "But I really do need to get going. Please unlock the door."

Where was her pepper spray? She never left for a business meeting without it. She knew too well the types of men she dealt with.

"You don't have a husband," Raymond said, his voice husky. "Come on. Stop playing games."

Abruptly, he leaned in, mashing his chapped lips against hers, his stubby hands grabbing at the front of her dress, yanking at the ties that held it shut.

Wedging her arms between them, she pushed him away. "Mr. Raymond, this is inappropriate. I'm here only to negotiate—"

"You and I both know what you're here to do. And you're not leaving until we've closed the deal."

Shit. Abigail dug in her purse, frantic. She *knew* she'd put the pepper spray in here tonight. She'd checked twice before leaving her hotel. How could it not be here?

But somehow, it was gone. She'd need to get out of this another way.

Abigail was taller than Doug. Probably in better shape. She doubted he got much exercise in; she went to the gym five days a week. She'd taken self-defense classes; he probably thought he was invincible.

Still, she knew better than to underestimate ruthless men. Fighting was always a last resort. Running was safer.

The back door was locked, but the front door probably had a standard dead bolt on it. If she could get to the front, she could get out. Call a car, return to her hotel, and graciously accept his inevitable excuse that this had all been a drunken mistake, even though one glass of champagne was hardly enough to cloud either of their minds. Everything would be fine.

As he leaned in for another sloppy kiss, she ducked under his arm, twisting out of his grip. But before she could take more than a couple of steps, her head snapped back, pain lancing through her scalp. She lost her balance, and cried out as he released his grip on her hair to slam her head against the wall.

The room tilted around her, a sour taste filling her mouth. Ringing filled her ears.

"Lying bitch," Raymond snarled, pressing himself against her. "You're not better than me."

Mustering her strength, she shoved him back and thrust out with the heel of her hand, aiming for the bridge of his nose. Even if she didn't break it, the blow should cause his eyes to tear, buying her a few seconds to get away.

Or at least, that should've been what happened. But she was sluggish and off-balance, and her hand glanced off his cheek instead. He took a step back, but she could tell that she hadn't done enough damage to truly slow him down.

She lurched away from him, head spinning, bracing one hand against the wall to keep from toppling over. She blinked as she stumbled into the dark reception area of the Raymond Realty offices, her vision swirling.

A fuzzy figure stood at the window. A girl. A woman. Herself? All of the above?

Help, she tried to call. Did she make a sound? She couldn't tell.

Light exploded through her vision as something hard collided with the back of her skull. Her head screamed in pain. She stumbled forward, hands fumbling for purchase, even as a part of her mind protested that this was *stupid*, Doug Raymond was *nothing*, he was the type of pathetic, self-important pustule that she popped every single day without batting an eye, he did *not* have the upper hand, she *always* had the upper hand, this was absolutely *not happening*.

Abigail's knees hit the cheap carpet, followed by her hands, scraping the skin off her palms. She'd probably torn her fifty-seven-dollar nylons, the ones that were guaranteed not to rip, the ones that made her legs look goddamn Amazonian.

He would pay for that.

She turned to tell him. "You stupid motherf—"

Fireworks burst behind her eyes. All at once, she couldn't feel her hands anymore. Or her face. Or her legs.

Oh God. Is this—

CHAPTER TWENTY

Appreciate what you have before it turns into what you had.

—Sebastián A. García, senior quote, East Henderson High School 2015–16 yearbook

---

"What did it say to you?" Madelyn whispered. "The ghost."

She ran her hands over her legs, pressing her palms to her thighs. She felt jittery, like she needed to run, hide, maybe scream. Anything but just stand there in her probably-haunted house.

Alex squinted slightly, like he was looking into his memories. "It said, *Angie needs your help.*"

"You're sure? It mentioned her by name?"

His eyes were glassy as he spread his hands. "Her name was clear, like someone spoke it right into my ear. The rest was sort of hazy, kind of fading in and out like a dying microphone. But yeah, I'm sure."

"What happened to her?"

"I'm not sure," Alex said. "We had a huge fight that afternoon. That's why I didn't pick up when she called. We said some pretty nasty things to each other, and I was still mad at her."

"What was your fight about?"

His mouth pressed into a grim smile. "The ghost. I told her it was all in her head, and that she needed professional help. And she told me to go to hell." He chuckled softly. "Ironic, huh? If I'd believed her, we never would've fought, and I would've picked up the phone. But the only reason I believe her now is because I went over that night, and the only reason I went over was because I didn't pick up."

"Do you think the ghost did something to her?" She couldn't bring herself to speak above a whisper.

He shook his head. "I know this is going to sound extremely woo-woo, but I just got this . . . this *feeling* that the ghost genuinely wanted to help. Angie always said she thought it was friendly, and I was always skeptical, but as soon as I heard it, I understood why she felt that way. I felt it too."

"Unless the ghost *wanted* you to feel that way so you'd let your guard down."

Alex looked at her, narrowing his eyes. "Wait. Who did you think I was talking about?"

Madelyn had gotten so wigged out by the ghost conversation that she'd almost forgotten. "I had a cousin who used to live in East Henderson. Piper. She disappeared a couple years ago. I thought you must have known her. That's one of the reasons I applied for a job here. I was hoping I might find some answers about what happened to her."

He shook his head slowly. "I don't think so. Wow. So we both know someone who went missing from this town."

"But years apart," Madelyn pointed out. "Probably not related." She felt distracted. Her mind was still stuck on the ghost. Alex's friend thought her house was *haunted*? That was not a thing she needed to hear if she ever wanted to sleep again.

As if he'd read her mind, Alex said, "I don't think Angie's disappearance had anything to do with the ghost."

"No?"

"No." Alex sighed, running a hand through his dark waves. "It turned out that her dad didn't actually own this house. Doug Raymond bought it shortly after Angie's mom left, when her dad was having trouble paying the bills, and they rented it back from him. I don't think Angie knew. I feel like she would've said something if she did."

"So he only owns this house because of them," Madelyn said, the pieces clicking into place.

"Yup. And they probably left because of him," Alex said. "Apparently her dad had fallen way behind on his payments, and they were getting ready to be evicted. The police figure he jumped the gun, skipped town before Raymond could kick them out."

"Do you think that's what happened?" Should she tell him that she also suspected Raymond of being involved with Piper's disappearance? Or would that only serve to open up old wounds?

He sighed, his shoulders slumping. "Maybe. I thought for a while that maybe something more was going on, but I think I just wanted to believe that she wouldn't have left like that on purpose. Not without saying goodbye. But looking back, that's probably what happened. The last thing we did was fight. I think she was just . . . done with me."

"Did you ever try to do what the . . . the voice said?" She had a hard time saying *ghost*.

He spread his hands. "I tried, but I didn't know what to do. I tried texting her, calling, emailing. Nothing ever went through. Her social media went quiet. I've googled her on and off over the years, but nothing ever comes up." He sighed. "Eventually I had to take the hint. She didn't want to be found."

"How old was she when she disappeared?"

"Sixteen. It was the beginning of our junior year. She'd finally gotten around to getting her driver's permit over the summer." He gave a tight smile. "She was always talking about how much she wanted to get out of this town. We'd talked about taking a road trip that next summer, where we'd drive across the country and see all the things. We were going to call it the Banjo Tour." He noticed her confused expression, and explained, "I went by my first name in high school. Sebastián. Angie called me Bas. Bas plus Angie became Bangie, which became

Banjo. But once she was gone, that name didn't feel right anymore. So I started going by my middle name. Alejandro."

Madelyn remembered his Instagram handle: *@salexgarcia*. Sebastián Alejandro. If she scrolled back far enough, would she find pictures of him and Angie?

"So . . . what do you think the voice meant?"

He gave her a rueful smile as he looked around the room, as if the answer might be written on the walls. "If I'm honest, I think it meant that I was a hormonal teenager who desperately wanted everything happening in other people's lives to have something to do with me."

"You think you imagined it?"

"I didn't at the time. I was positive I heard something. And enough weird stuff had happened with Angie that I'd half convinced myself that maybe she was right and there really *was* some sort of spirit or something here. But now . . . I don't know." He sighed. "I fight with my best friend, she goes missing, and then I immediately hear a voice telling me to find her?" He shrugged. "Sounds like chronic teenager main character syndrome to me."

"But what if you *didn't* imagine it?" Madelyn pressed. "What if it's real?"

Alex raised an eyebrow. "Have *you* heard any voices since you moved in?"

She hesitated, then shook her head. No, she hadn't heard any voices. But she couldn't deny that some of the things she'd experienced since moving in were . . . strange. Not that she wanted to tell him that now, if he needed to believe it was all in his head.

"Then there's nothing to worry about," Alex said, leaning back in his chair.

"And yet ten minutes ago you were screaming at me."

He hung his head. "I'm so sorry about that. It really threw me when you texted me her address. I felt like you were messing with me somehow, even though obviously you weren't. It took me a long time to be okay after Angie, and then all of a sudden I felt like I was being dragged back to that time. But that's not an excuse. I shouldn't have acted like that."

"It's okay," Madelyn said. "It was a lot to process."

"It's not okay. But thank you." He let out a long, shaky breath, then looked at her, his expression almost startled. "And I'm so sorry. I completely glossed over what *you* said. Your cousin went missing too? What happened? Are you okay?"

"I'm fine," she assured him. "I didn't really know her very well." She wouldn't tell him about Piper's connection to Doug Raymond, she decided. Not yet, anyway. Maybe if she found out something new, she might bring it up. But for now, it felt like telling him would just stir up a lot of old anxiety, and she didn't want to do that to him.

"Are you sure? We can talk about it, if you want," he said.

She shook her head, pressing her lips into a smile. "I'm sure. I'm good."

"In that case . . ." He shook out his limbs, like he was trying to reset his body. "Let me make it up to you. I was promised a leaky sink?"

It felt so strange switching back to the original plan for the day after talking about ghosts and missing people, but the sink *was* still broken, and she still couldn't afford to hire a plumber. After he retrieved his tools from his car, Madelyn showed Alex to the bathroom, scooping up Potato to keep her from attack-kissing his face as he crawled into the cabinet under the sink.

As he poked at the pipes, Madelyn realized with a jolt that she didn't need to show him around at all. Because he'd already been here countless times before, as a teenager.

Stepping into the hall, she pulled out her phone and opened Instagram, keeping one eye on the bathroom door to make sure he didn't see what she was doing. Navigating to Alex's profile, she scrolled back, back, back, watching him age backward through college and high school. She watched him grow and remove facial hair, morph through various fashion trends, and go through a handful of what she assumed were girlfriends, although none seemed to last for very long.

Finally, during a teenage phase with a lot of scarves and knit caps and open button-downs, the same girl's face started appearing in photo after photo. Dark hair and eyes—maybe part Asian? Did Alex have a type?—wry smile, round cheeks, black fingernail polish. There she was throwing a peace sign from the front seat of a car, grinning while holding two slices of watermelon on top of her head, lying on a floor with Alex, the tops of their heads touching and their bodies pointed in opposite directions.

Madelyn slowed to read the captions.

@no_angiel got her learner's permit, clear the roads

"I'm summer Mickey Mouse" @no_angiel

This is ART or whatever (@no_angiel)

She clicked on the handle, but nothing came up. Her profile must have been deleted at some point. Madelyn clicked back to Alex's profile and stared at the photos of Angie.

"What happened to you?" she whispered.

"What?" Alex called from the bathroom. "Did you say something?"

"Nothing, sorry," she said, hurriedly closing the app in case he came out.

Then she held her breath, listening for the ghost, just in case.

CHAPTER TWENTY-ONE

I mean, development felt like a natural space for us to step into. This area is getting ready to explode over the next few years. Lots of families and businesses looking for their next big step up. We can provide that. I think we're in a really good position to make that happen.

—Doug Raymond television interview, *East Henderson in the Morning*, May 12, 2015

Whatever Madelyn's hopes were for Alex's visit, they'd been sufficiently quashed by his dramatic arrival. After he fixed the sink—he'd just had to "clean the O-ring," whatever that meant—he didn't waste time sticking around, making up an excuse about grading tests that she was 100 percent sure would not have been a factor if the whole Angie thing hadn't come into play.

Once he was gone, Madelyn poured herself a glass of boxed wine and stood in the middle of her living room, working up her courage. Angie didn't think the ghost was dangerous. Alex didn't think the ghost was dangerous, if there was even a ghost at all.

So there was no need to be anxious. Regardless of what her brain thought.

"If you're out there," Madelyn said, trying to inject some authority into her voice, "I need you to behave. Okay?"

She listened, but heard only silence.

She looked at Potato. "This is ridiculous," she declared. Potato wagged her tail in agreement.

Madelyn got out her laptop, determined to get some answers. First up: Angie and her dad, whose name Alex hadn't provided, but which Madelyn's investigative skills quickly assured her was Cameron.

That route proved disappointing. Every relevant piece of information was from 2014 or earlier; everything since then was pure speculation or bot-driven drivel. Apparently a single dad and his daughter skipping town over credit problems wasn't much of a headline in 2014, or ever. Too common to waste the ink, Madelyn supposed.

She'd already read everything she could find on Raymond before moving to East Henderson—except, of course, the Rotten Raymond subreddit, which she'd thoroughly perused after learning about it from Alex—but searched for him again. This time, rather than wading through hundreds of articles with titles like OPINION: Is Doug Raymond actively TRYING to kill us all, or is that just a fun bonus and Raymond Realty Unveils Plans For Former Site of Beloved East Henderson Bookstore (Spoiler: It's More Luxury Condos), she limited her search to results published prior to 2015, since she doubted she'd find anything relevant to the Stewarts after that.

An hour later, Madelyn was no closer to answers than she had been when she started. She looked up from her computer to see Potato digging determinedly at the seam between the carpet and the wall outside the bathroom, tiny paws cycling furiously. "Tater!" Madelyn reprimanded her, pushing herself to her feet—*whoops*, she may have had a little more wine than she'd thought—and rushing over to where her dog was laser-focused on forfeiting Madelyn's security deposit.

"No," she said, scooping the pup up with one hand. After wandering through every room in her house searching for her leash—it was in a basket by the front door, same as it always was—Madelyn clipped it onto Potato's collar and looped the other end around her ankle, tethering them together.

She looked down at Potato, who wagged her stubby tail expectantly. "You're a menace," Madelyn said.

Potato licked her chops, certain she'd just been praised.

After weaving into the kitchen for a glass of water—damn, was she drunk? That would be fun to explain to seventh graders tomorrow—she returned to the couch and her laptop, dragging Potato behind her like an overeager anchor. Her fingers wriggled over the keyboard, searching for inspiration. What to google? She'd searched for Angie and her dad, for Doug Raymond . . . why not for Alex?

Gulping water, she typed in *Alex García*, then deleted *Alex* and typed in *Sebastián*, recalling that anything from around the time of Angie's disappearance would probably use his first name. Sure enough, the findings were older, but didn't seem to have anything to do with Angie. She added Angie's name, then *disappearance*, then the year, but nothing noteworthy turned up. She decided to toss Piper's name into the mix, but that just led to more dead ends. No matter what combination of search terms she entered, she couldn't find anything useful.

"There's nothing *here*," she groaned to Potato, flopping onto her back on the cushions. Her head swam in a wine-soaked haze. "This is all pointless," she said as Potato climbed onto her chest and licked her chin. "Tell me why I thought I could solve this by myself again?"

Potato turned in a circle, lost her balance, and tumbled into the thin space between Madelyn's body and the back of the couch. She let out a plaintive whine, followed by an exasperated snort.

"Well said," Madelyn mumbled, throwing an arm across her face. She needed to think. Which may have been easier if she hadn't downed half a box of Cabernet first, but she was where she was.

So. Google was useless. Not much of a shock, since if the answers were on Google, the Rotten Raymond people probably would have found them already.

She could try interrogating Doug Raymond. But she would probably have more luck getting straight answers from Potato.

She could go to the Raymond Realty Group offices. She needed to go there anyway to get her lease. Which should really have happened already, but oh well. She'd get to it soon. But it felt pretty far-fetched to think that she'd just waltz into Doug Raymond's office and stumble upon the clues that would make all this make sense. Looking at the Raymond Realty Group website, she saw their offices were enormous. She wouldn't even know where to begin.

What was left? The police station? She'd looked at the police report on Piper. Maybe the report on Angie would have more answers, but based on what Alex had said, she doubted it.

The county courthouse? Kelsey's case was sealed. There was never a case about Angie at all. So that was a dead end.

The library?

Madelyn pursed her lips, one hand buried in Potato's fluff. She'd given up trying to wiggle out of where she'd fallen, and was now snoring with her paws sticking up in the air, Madelyn's fingers scratching her belly. The library could be useful. They kept old newspapers, local documents, county archives. There might be something there that she couldn't find online.

It was worth a shot.

"Alexa," she said, her arm still draped over her eyes, "remind me to go to the library tomorrow for . . . investigative purposes." She was drunk enough to know she might not remember this tomorrow. And to know she should drink more water. But too drunk to want to go *get* that water.

"Okay. I'll remind you tomorrow to go to the library for a vest and a porpoise."

"Alexa, why do you suck so much?"

"Here's something I found on WebMD dot com—"

"Alexa, stop." She rolled over, burying her face in the couch cushions. Potato grumbled in protest at the sudden lack of belly scritches, flipping onto her tummy and squirming forward, coming to rest with her face in Madelyn's armpit.

Madelyn knew she should go to bed. She should wash her face and put on moisturizer and brush her teeth and make sure she had clean clothes for school tomorrow.

She should do all those things. Absolutely.

But she didn't want to. And there was no one around to make her.

"Alexa, wake me up at six a.m.," she mumbled into the couch.

"Alarm set for six a.m."

Huh. For once, it actually did something right.

Hugging the couch cushion to her chest, pretending she'd already turned off the lights, Madelyn went to sleep.

CHAPTER TWENTY-TWO

Kelsey O'Donnell 11:46 AM: Heading down to the cafe in 5.

Piper Carden 11:46 AM: Sorry, meant to text. Totally swamped. I'll grab something from the vending machine.

Kelsey O'Donnell 11:47 AM: Again??? You can't keep subsisting on granola bars and string cheese.

Piper Carden 11:49 AM: I just want to get this project finished up before my cousin comes so I can work normal hours that week.

Kelsey O'Donnell 11:50 AM: I'm looking forward to meeting her! And to seeing you for more than 30 seconds at a time.

Piper Carden 11:50 AM: ME TOO!

Kelsey O'Donnell 11:52 AM: In the meantime, eat a piece of fruit or something. You've been at your desk so long I'm afraid you'll get scurvy.

Piper Carden 11:53 AM: LOL. I promise.

—Slack exchange between Kelsey O'Donnell and Piper Carden, February 2021

Monday's hangover ached like regret and stupidity.

School was a slow drip of torture. Madelyn hadn't realized before how loud middle schoolers were. Or how high pitched their voices were. Or how often they dropped things, causing her teeth to rattle with every bang and thump and crash.

The smells were also an issue. Preteens did not smell good, which was an objective fact most days, but felt like a pointed taunt today. Like they all *knew* her stomach was a delicate lattice of fragility, and they had all decided not only to forgo deodorant but also to skip brushing their teeth, en masse, *on purpose*.

And why were the lights so *bright*? It was like the interrogation of Picard in this school. *There are four lights! And they are all! Too! Much!*

Madelyn wanted to give her previous night's self a swift punch in the nose. Except that thought made her current self's head hurt.

She would also like to travel back in time four years and tell herself not to major in music, so that she wouldn't have to endure eight periods in a row of prepubescent singing while hungover.

But since none of that was possible, she opted for the largest cold brew that Bean Juice had to offer and three tabs of ibuprofen, since two felt like a joke.

The day crawled by like a snail through wet cement, made even more insufferable by the fact that Alex didn't stop by her room. You'd think the least he could do after dropping an atomic bomb on her the day before would be to say hello, but on the other hand, she was not at her best today, and should probably be grateful that he didn't see her like this. When she was finally able to shut herself in her Fit at the end of the day, she breathed a sigh of relief at the blissful silence.

"Here's your reminder: go to the library for a vest and a porpoise!"

"Screw you," Madelyn mumbled, resisting the urge to hurl her phone into the parking lot.

But Alexa—jerk that she was—was right. She'd forgotten, as she knew she would, but now it all came rushing back. She did need to go to the library. Even though she deeply did not feel like it right now.

Seventeen minutes later—it would've been seven, but her hangover required that she detour through the McDonald's drive-thru for a basket of fries—she heaved herself up the stairs to the second floor of the East Henderson Public Library. The map by the front door showed that Local Archives was a small section in the very back of the building. Madelyn hoped it might contain a better record of the town scandals of 2014 than the internet did.

It took her a few minutes to find the small plaque identifying Local Archives, and a few minutes more to get her bearings once she was there. Metal shelves filled with newspapers and magazines lined the walls, and in the middle of the space was a table divided into four cubbies, each with its own computer station. Against a back wall stood a shelf holding hundreds of white boxes of microfilm.

Unsurprisingly, there didn't appear to be anyone assigned to the area, and Madelyn gulped at the white wall of microfilm, hoping she wouldn't have to scan dozens of old newspapers one by one to find what she was looking for.

"Need some help?"

Madelyn jumped at the voice, and spun to see Nat standing behind her. Today, she wore ripped jeans, combat boots, and a loose-fitting tank top. Around her waist, she'd tied a faded blue-and-black plaid flannel shirt.

Madelyn's jaw dropped. "What are you doing here?" she asked, her voice carrying a little too loudly.

Nat smiled with a corner of her mouth, holding a finger to her lips. "Ultimate Frisbee," she said dryly, with a pointed glance at the books surrounding them.

Madelyn laughed. "I just didn't expect to see you here."

"I don't live in the coffee shop, you know."

"So you work here, then?"

"I don't know that I'd call it *work*," Nat said with a wink, leaning a hip against the table and crossing her arms. "Mostly, I read."

Madelyn shook her head, reevaluating her mental image of Nat. She'd taken her for an artist of some sort, maybe a musician. *Librarian* probably wouldn't have been anywhere in her first hundred guesses, but right now, she was grateful to be wrong. "I'm actually really glad you're here," she said. "I could use some help." Along with a bottle of water and a couple more ibuprofen, but that was probably an overshare.

Nat stretched her arms out in front of her, cracking her knuckles. "Awesome. I love helping. What are we looking for today?"

Madelyn sighed, turning her attention to the rows of shelves. "I'm trying to find more information on a local family who went missing about ten years ago. Before they disappeared, they lived in the house I'm renting."

"The one you're renting from Doug Raymond?" Nat asked. "Is that why you were asking about him the other day? You think he may have had something to do with it?"

"I'm not sure," Madelyn admitted. "Right now I'm just trying to connect all the dots."

"That is the point of dots," Nat agreed with a somber nod. "Ten years ago, you said?" She was already sliding into a chair at one of the workstations, waking up the screen with a shimmy of the mouse. As she hunched over the keyboard, two tiny wing tattoos peeked out from the back of her tank top above her shoulder blades. "How big of a deal was this disappearance?"

"Not very," Madelyn admitted. "The police think they skipped town to sidestep creditors."

"Ah, yeah, the FICO mafia is definitely a thing," Nat said. "But I'm gathering that you don't buy it?"

"I think something happened to them," Madelyn said. "But I don't know what."

"Gotcha. What were their names?"

"The dad was Cameron Stewart. And then his daughter was Angelina, but she went by Angie."

"Ten years back is right on the line," Nat said, typing into the computer, "but most of the local newspapers had gone digital by then. Shouldn't have to break out the microfilm for this one."

"Oh good, because I have no idea how to use it," Madelyn admitted.

"Fortunately for you, I do," Nat said. "But even more fortunately, we won't have to. Take a look."

She pushed her chair away from the computer, gesturing at the screen, where half a dozen results had popped up. Madelyn pulled up a chair and clicked on the first, scanning it with eager eyes, then the second. As she worked her way down the list, though, her hope quickly dwindled. She'd assumed it would've been a fairly big deal in a small town for a family to disappear, but the articles Nat had found barely even mentioned the Stewarts. Four predated their disappearance; three of those were press releases about construction projects Cameron's company was working on, and one was a story about the 2012 East Henderson Film Festival, in which Angie appeared in a grainy photo selling refreshments alongside two other members of the high school film club.

Of the remaining two, only one had anything even remotely interesting. Both articles highlighted local development projects involving Stewart Construction, but one mentioned that after the owner, Cameron Stewart, disappeared, it was later acquired by Raymond Realty Group.

So not only did Doug Raymond own their house but he also bought Angie's dad's company. That didn't feel like a coincidence.

Madelyn pointed at the screen. "That's interesting, right?"

Nat squinted over her shoulder. "It's not *not* interesting," she agreed.

"I wonder what was in it for him," Madelyn mused. It felt suspicious to her, but she didn't want to jump to conclusions. Just because Kelsey suspected Raymond of having something to do with Piper's disappearance didn't mean that he had anything to do with Angie's. Maybe there was a perfectly normal explanation for him and his company quietly eradicating every trace of the Stewart family from East Henderson. "I guess it makes sense that a real estate company would branch out into development," she begrudgingly admitted. "And that he'd own investment property."

"You just gave Doug Raymond enough credit to buy a timeshare. Dude is fishier and dirtier than the Schuylkill."

Madelyn raised an eyebrow. "You think it could have something to do with what happened to them?"

Nat shrugged. "I'm just saying that this is a man who once threatened to sue trick-or-treaters for trespassing. He's not a reasonable guy, so I wouldn't assume reasonable explanations."

"Speaking of which, can we look up a lawsuit?"

"Sure. What's the case?"

"*Raymond Realty v. O'Donnell.*"

"Oh yeah, I remember that one. She made a lot of noise for a while there, before they got to her."

"Got to her?" It felt like everyone in this town had heard a different version of Kelsey's case.

Nat shrugged. "I mean, one day she was shouting from the rooftops that Raymond was shady as shit, and the next she's quieter than a funeral in a library. Gotta figure something happened."

Madelyn wished she could tell Nat how close she was to the truth. "I wondered if there may have been some local reporting on the case that wasn't available online." Maybe there was something Kelsey or her lawyer had missed, something that didn't feel relevant at the time but might now, in light of what she'd learned about Angie.

"Unfortunately, there really isn't much," Nat said, pursing her lips. "Most of her stuff was on social media, which then got deleted. And it never gained much traction with local journalists because no one from the company would talk about it. So pretty much all of the news coverage was just quotes from her lawyers. It fizzled out pretty fast."

"Ugh," Madelyn groaned. Another dead end. "Did you know her friend? The one who went missing."

Nat shook her head. "Never had the pleasure."

Me neither, Madelyn thought. She wished she'd gotten the chance.

"Must be nice, though," Nat said thoughtfully. "To have a friend willing to go to bat for you like that."

Madelyn looked at her curiously. "You think?"

"Well, yeah," Nat said. "In case you haven't noticed, Doug Raymond is kind of like the Godfather of East Henderson. People don't just cross him for no reason. But this girl's friend did. Even if he won, someone like that is worth their weight in gold."

Madelyn made a mental note to pass that along to Kelsey. She thought she'd appreciate it. "Do you think it's weird?" she asked. "He owned the house of this family who disappeared. And then a few years later, a woman from his company goes missing, and her friend insists he has something to do with it. You think they could be related?"

Nat laughed, then shrugged. "You ever meet a clinical asshole? Not garden variety, but the type who makes it their entire brand?"

Ralph's stupid face flashed across Madelyn's mind. "Yup."

"Then you know that with these guys, it's always a pattern. They love to screw people, and they never learn any new moves. So I don't know if it's *related* related, but in my experience, when you see someone standing in a ring of fire, chances are they set at least a few of them."

"I just wish I could find anything concrete on any of it."

"Maybe not in the newspapers, but you can't be as dirty as he is and not leave *some* sort of a trail," Nat said. "He may have all sorts of powerful friends, but no one actually *likes* him. If you keep digging, you're sure to hit something that will lead to some answers about your house ghosts."

"They're not ghosts," Madelyn clarified. "They just disappeared; they're not dead." *At least I hope not,* she added silently.

Nat gave her a tight smile. "They lived in your house, disappeared, and now you're in the cobweb section of the library sniffing for clues." She spread her hands as if indicating the obvious. "Sounds like a haunting to me."

CHAPTER TWENTY-THREE

That whole aw-shucks happy grandpa persona isn't real. I worked at that company for five years, and let me tell you, the second the cameras turn off, he goes dead behind the eyes. Absolutely dead.

—post by FinallyFree24 on r/RottenRaymond

"Hola, Señor García!"

"Hola, estudiantes!"

Madelyn looked up from her desk at the sounds of her exiting third period choir students greeting Alex outside her classroom. She had her planning period next, followed by lunch, which she typically ate at her desk to give her more time to work. But Alex's planning period wasn't until the afternoon, which made his presence in her doorway unusual.

"Don't you have a class?" she said as he stepped into the choir room, still waving to the students in the hall. High-pitched giggles floated in after him. Madelyn suspected that half of the kids in the school had a mild crush on Alex.

"I'm only stopping by for a second." His smile looked slightly strained. She wondered if Sunday had ruined the easy rapport between them, and if they'd be able to get it back. "I wanted to ask you . . ." He glanced over his shoulder, toward the hall, like he was checking to make sure no one was hovering behind him. "Are you free this afternoon?"

She nodded slowly. Last week, that question would've set her heart racing, but this didn't sound like he was asking her out on another date. His voice was low and almost . . . furtive.

"I was going to stop by my landlord's office for a copy of my lease, but that shouldn't take long," she said. She'd been procrastinating for ages, hoping that Barbara would just give in and email her a copy, but her latest emails had gone unanswered. *Hint taken, Barbara.* "After that, I just need to take Potato on a walk."

"That's perfect. You know Hillspring Park? It's not far from your place. There's a dog park in there."

"Yeah." She took Potato there sometimes, although she let her off her leash only when it wasn't crowded or when the other dogs were small. The big dogs made her nervous. She worried they'd think Potato was a squirrel or some other tiny animal that they should chase. Potato would think that was great fun, but Madelyn didn't want to see what would happen if they caught her.

"Would you meet me there once you've gotten back from Raymond's office? There's something I need to show you."

"What is it?"

He shook his head. "I'll explain later. It's complicated. Just text me when you're getting ready to head out."

"Okay."

As soon as Madelyn agreed, Alex bade her a hasty goodbye and was out the door. He was making her nervous. Like they were planning a bank robbery, not walking her dog in the park.

The rest of the day passed slowly, curiosity about what Alex wanted to show her gnawing at Madelyn. She didn't see him again before the final bell rang, and his car wasn't in the lot. Had he left school early? What on earth was going on?

She made her stop at the Raymond Realty Group offices as brief as possible, although it still took longer than she would have liked. The location was really more of a compound than an office, with multiple redbrick buildings arranged around a central courtyard. She hadn't expected it to be so large, since the company had relocated from its original spot in the town center only a few years ago. She knew they'd moved to accommodate their rapid expansion into the development market, but she hadn't realized it was a Big Bang situation.

Madelyn parked in what she assumed was the main lot, only to discover that she was actually in the visitor lot, and that if she wanted to interact with Doug Raymond's office directly, she needed to navigate to the other side of the complex and park in the employee lot. Alex was right; there were armed guards at the entrance, although they didn't appear to be doing much other than staring down the people entering the building.

Inside, she asked a blonde receptionist for directions to Doug Raymond's office, only to be informed that he wasn't in today. "Actually, I just need to see Barbara," Madelyn clarified, and the receptionist rattled off a list of directions.

Her instructions didn't seem too complicated, but Madelyn still managed to get turned around and wound up in the employee cafeteria, which reminded her a lot of the dining commons at college. Except at college, there were a lot more women; outside of the receptionist, judging by the employees she saw, Raymond Realty Group was overwhelmingly male.

Since Raymond was out of the office, Madelyn didn't get a chance to see if Alex was right about the bodyguard. Barbara turned out to be a silver-haired woman with maroon lipstick and a sizable chip on her shoulder, who printed off Madelyn's lease only after making it extremely clear that she was exponentially more irritating than all Raymond Realty's other tenants, who, to be clear, Barbara also did not like.

Madelyn's chest felt tight the whole way home, imagining Piper going to work there. It was easy to imagine how someone could go missing from that place and no one would care. It was so big, most people probably wouldn't even notice.

Potato was already running in excited circles when Madelyn arrived home, her little tail wagging furiously. Their routine was the same every day, with a short walk before school and a longer one in the afternoon, yet the way Potato acted, you'd think she was finally escaping prison after nineteen years.

After wrestling the fluffy dog into her purple plaid harness and shoving a handful of training treats into her jacket pocket, Madelyn swapped out her black school flats for worn gray running shoes and headed out the door.

The day was overcast, dark clouds piling up overhead as a cool breeze shook the treetops, already beginning to show signs of warming color in preparation for fall. The forecast didn't predict rain for another couple of hours, although the humidity hanging heavy in the air and the darkening sky seemed to be building a compelling argument to the contrary. Potato, blissfully oblivious to the imminent storm, led the way to the park, her claws tapping on the sidewalk like typewriter keys.

The dog park wasn't huge, maybe half an acre of green space surrounded by a chain-link fence. Only a couple of dogs were there today, probably because of the weather: a smiling golden retriever catching an orange Frisbee thrown by a middle-aged man in a Phillies jersey, and a squash-faced brick of a dog that was probably some sort of pug mix. He was determinedly sniffing his way around the entire perimeter of the fence as his pink-haired owner checked her phone on one of the green metal benches near the entrance.

Although both dogs were significantly larger than Potato, Madelyn decided there was enough open space to allow her to run for a little while. As soon as she unclipped the leash from her harness, Potato lost her tiny mind, bouncing gleefully in place a few times before tearing off to chase after the golden retriever, yapping joyously.

Madelyn winced, taking a few nervous steps after her, but the golden's owner caught her eye and smiled. "She's okay. Stella loves puppies."

"Thank you!" Madelyn called, her shoulders relaxing slightly. She was still fairly new to dog ownership, and although Syzygy kept assuring her that she wasn't screwing it up, Potato was just so *small*. Madelyn constantly found herself imagining all the terrible things that could happen to her. As soon as she brought her home from the rescue, suddenly the whole world looked like a death trap.

Syzygy—who'd majored in psychology, and was currently working on their master's—told her that she needed to push herself out of her comfort zone before she was ready, to prove to herself that it wouldn't be as bad as she thought. Which was why Madelyn took the ten-pound dog on two walks a day, even though she probably wasn't big enough to require that much exercise.

So far, it had been good. They both enjoyed the time outdoors, and although they'd both been frightened a few times by speeding cars or lunging dogs, Syzygy had been right. Nothing terrible had happened.

Yet, Madelyn's brain always added. But she tried her best to keep that voice from being too loud.

She settled in on an empty bench, keeping her eyes glued on Potato. She couldn't even begin to keep up with Stella, and had taken instead to running in circles in the middle of the larger dog's Frisbee path, jumping and nipping at Stella each time she ran past.

"Thanks for meeting me." Alex's voice came from beside her. Madelyn jumped at his sudden presence; she'd been so focused on Potato, she'd filtered out everything else.

He sat down on the bench beside her, hugging a worn green bag in his lap. She hadn't realized it in school, but up close, he looked terrible. His eyes were bloodshot, with slight shadows underneath, as though he hadn't slept well, and his wavy hair was a little flatter than usual. Had he forgotten to shower?

Madelyn breathed in through her nose as subtly as possible, and was relieved that she didn't detect any whiffs of day-old grossness.

He looked out at Potato bouncing exuberantly in the grass. "She good?"

"Yup. She would live here if I let her."

Alex nodded, then looked down at the bag. "So Sunday night, a little while after I left your house, my mom called. Just, you know, mom things." He waved his hand, indicating his own nebulous definition of *mom things*. "Anyway, I mentioned that you lived in Angie's old house, and she said that reminded her of something and that I should come over. So I went by yesterday after school, and my mom gave me *this*."

He patted the bag in his lap. It was a messenger bag with a frayed canvas strap and chunky brass buckles, covered in patches and pins, most of which Madelyn didn't recognize. She could identify the clown from *It*, Jack Skellington from *The Nightmare Before Christmas*, Harley Quinn, a T. rex, and a Pride pin, but the rest were a mystery to her. It looked like the type of thing a kid in high school might have. Thick Sharpie letters across the front read *BAS*.

"Was this yours?"

"It was hers. Angie's."

"Oh." That explained the way he was clutching the bag, like he was afraid it might disappear. "Why'd your mom have it?"

He shook his head, letting out a soft, humorless laugh. "You know how I was talking about the irony of Angie's disappearance? Well, apparently there's another layer I didn't even know about. It turns out that the night she went missing, she stopped by my house."

Madelyn's jaw dropped. "You're kidding."

"I wish. My parents were out to dinner that night, but when they came home, this was on our doorstep. I guess Angie had come by my house on her way out of town. And no one was home, because I was over at her house."

"That's . . . wow. Why didn't they give it to you back then?"

Alex rolled his eyes, frowning. "Have I mentioned how religious my parents are?"

"No?"

"Well, they're super religious. That's why we do the Sunday lunch thing, because my parents like to follow up church with a big family meal. Anyway, they looked inside and decided that Angie was into 'witch things,' and was trying to get me involved in the occult." He made finger quotes around *witch things*.

"Was she?"

"No. Angie wasn't really into much of anything supernatural, except for the ghost. Which I have a feeling is what's in here."

"The ghost?"

"No, her ghost-hunting supplies. She was obsessed with trying to get it to talk to her. I think she googled 'how to talk to ghosts' and ordered everything she could afford."

"Ah," Madelyn said, a clear mental picture coming into focus.

"Anyway, they didn't want me to be like, pulled over to the dark side. So they hid the bag up in the attic and never told me about it."

"Even when Angie went missing? They didn't think that maybe there'd be a clue in there?"

Alex shrugged, making a frustrated sound in his throat. "I asked. They said they didn't want to get me in trouble."

"How would *you* get in trouble?"

"They thought it was full of witchcraft supplies. To them, everything about it was trouble. They said that while they loved Angie, they loved me more and needed to protect me." He frowned, eyes narrowed. Clearly, he was not a fan of his parents' reasoning.

Madelyn could feel her face twist into a similar expression and worked to smooth it back out. This all sounded a little too close to the community where she'd grown up in Tennessee.

"Then I guess they forgot about it until I brought up Angie and it reminded my mom that she still had it," he continued. "Apparently now that I'm an adult, she's no longer afraid that I'll be corrupted by demonic forces." He said it flippantly, but there was a bitter edge to his words.

"Have you looked inside yet?"

He sighed, then shook his head almost guiltily. "No. I couldn't do it. We fought so much about the stuff in here, and what it meant. This is the reason I wasn't there for her on that day. I just . . . I don't think I can. It brings up too many hard memories."

"That makes sense." Madelyn stared at the bag, trying to picture the contents. Crystals and candles, she guessed, maybe some tarot cards or herbs. Clearance rack at Hot Topic–type stuff, the kind she and her friends might have grabbed on a whim during a trip to the mall in high school and then forgotten about in a week. Nothing that should carry this much weight a decade later. "So . . . that's why you wanted to meet me today? To tell me about this?"

"Actually, I wondered if . . . would it be okay if I gave it to you?" His eyes met hers briefly, then dropped to the ground. Embarrassed? Ashamed? She couldn't tell.

"You want me to take Angie's bag?" Madelyn didn't know how she felt about that. On one hand, it seemed almost like an honor to be entrusted with the last thing his best friend had given him. On the other, it also felt kind of like a curse. Something awful had happened that night, and she wasn't sure she wanted to be part of it, no matter how much she liked Alex.

"I know it's a weird thing to ask," he said, still not meeting her gaze. "But you're the only one I've ever told the full story of that day. And you live in her house. It feels right, giving it to you."

"Okay," she said, feeling like she didn't have any option but to agree. Not that she worried that he'd get mad if she didn't. He wasn't like Ralph—the sentient skin-flap—who would fly off the handle at the smallest perceived slight. It was more that he already looked so sad, she couldn't bear to make him sadder.

He started to hand her the bag, then hesitated. "One more thing. If it's not too much trouble."

"Sure." This was already so bizarre, she didn't feel like anything he could say would make much of a difference.

"Would you actually go through it? I think I already know what's in there, and it's been ten years, but in case Angie added something that might be a clue to what happened . . ."

Madelyn nodded. "Of course." She didn't ask how she was supposed to know whether something was a clue or out of place without knowing their history, or point out that the bag was meant for Alex and that he might find meaning in its contents that she could miss. It felt more important to just say yes than to get tangled up in logistics.

And as much as she hated to admit it, seeing how much anguish this was causing him . . . she was kind of dying to see what was inside.

CHAPTER TWENTY-FOUR

FROM: chelseawongacts@gmail.com
TO: sebastianag@gmail.com
SUBJECT: re: Question

Sebastian, hello! Of COURSE I remember you! So lovely to hear from you. In answer to your question, no, I don't have any other contact information for Angelina or her father besides what you mentioned, and I haven't spoken to either of them recently. If you do see my daughter soon, please tell her that her mother loves her very much! It's been a bit since we've chatted—life in LA keeps me very busy, as I'm sure you can imagine! Sorry I can't be more help! Please tell your parents I said hello!

Sparkles and sunshine,
Chelsea Wong
Actress, musician, model
IMDb
official website

—

Back at her house, Madelyn dumped the contents of Angie's bag out on her kitchen table. As she'd expected, it looked like the clearance bin at a strip mall witch shop. In addition to a full-size Ouija board, there were candles, incense, packets of herbs, a fabric satchel of crystals, and a couple of pocket guides to contacting spirits. No tarot cards, surprisingly. Maybe Angie's money had run out.

As Potato flopped down on her floor pillow and fell immediately asleep, tuckered out from her exploits at the park, Madelyn sifted gingerly through Angie's ghost-hunting supplies, looking for anything that could possibly be a clue. But half of it still seemed brand new, no dust or fingerprints or worn edges from frequent handling. It was like she'd bought all her supplies but never used them.

The Ouija board was open, but appeared similarly unhandled, as if Angie had simply taken it out of the plastic only to immediately put everything away. The pocket books didn't even look like they'd been thumbed through.

Madelyn sighed, her shoulders slumping. She hadn't realized how much she'd hoped that the bag might contain answers. And not just for Alex—for her. She couldn't shake the feeling that Angie's and Piper's disappearances were somehow related, and that if she could just catch a break on one of their cases, she would find answers to both.

But after going through everything in the bag twice and closely examining each item individually, she was no closer to understanding what had caused Angie and her dad to up and vanish overnight. So Madelyn turned her attention to the bag itself. It was clearly one Angie had owned long before she gathered her supplies, covered with tokens of her interests, its hems frayed and softened from use. She pictured Angie moving through the crowded halls of her school, bag slung over her shoulder and bulging with spiral-bound notebooks, mechanical pencils, chewing gum wrappers, tinted ChapStick.

As she expected, the bag had several smaller pockets sewn into its lining. In one, Madelyn found a stubby pink eraser and a wad of Starburst wrappers. In another, two plastic-wrapped Tampax tampons.

In a third, two Sharpie markers and a small silicone duck wearing sunglasses.

She was prepared to call it a wash when she unzipped the last pocket and found a cell phone–size audio recorder tucked inside.

She remembered Alex mentioning that Angie had been trying to capture proof of her ghost. This must be what she'd used. And for some reason, she'd wanted Alex to have it.

Heart racing, Madelyn reached for her phone, then hesitated. What if it contained something time-critical, something that could've helped Angie ten years ago but was useless now? Would it help him to know that, or hurt him more?

She should check it first. It was the kind thing to do.

Grabbing her laptop from her school bag, Madelyn plugged it in and ejected the memory card from the recorder, only to realize she didn't have an SD card reader on her computer. She had an external drive she could use, but all her dongles were still boxed up in her office, which she'd only half unpacked.

She groaned, resisting the urge to simply give up and call it a day. With every box she unpacked, the less desire she had to keep going. Cardboard boxes were a viable organizational system, right? People used decorative bins all the time. Hers would just all be corrugated and held together with packing tape. She could say it was warehouse chic.

But if she didn't find out what was on that recorder, she knew the curiosity would nag at her forever.

She spent the next twelve minutes digging through boxes unhelpfully labeled Office—Misc, which had felt like a time-saver when she was dumping stuff into repurposed liquor boxes a month ago, and completely dunderheaded now.

Finally, she found the dongle she needed in a box underneath a pile of old college textbooks that, for some reason, she'd decided to move across the state instead of selling back to the campus bookstore. Returning triumphantly to her computer, Madelyn plugged in the drive, inserted the memory card, and clicked open the contents.

The drive was full of audio files, identified only by strings of numbers with no discernible meaning, most likely assigned by the recording software. Madelyn checked the file sizes and groaned. There were dozens of hours of audio here and no way of knowing whether any of it was relevant other than listening to it.

She glanced at the clock. It was nearing six, and she still had to eat dinner and finish working on her lesson plans for the week, after being derailed by Alex's revelations over the weekend. Might as well multitask.

Hitting Play on the first recording, she put in an earbud and listened for a few minutes. It started with a female voice, she presumed Angie's, saying the date. *"September twelfth, twenty-fourteen."* But after that was mostly ambient noise, with some rustling and shuffling sounds, and occasional voices saying nothing much.

"Morning."

"You want one of these?"

"Have you seen my blue notebook?"

This was going to take a while.

Setting the player to 2x speed, Madelyn went to the kitchen to start scavenging dinner.

She kept the recordings going as she piled a plate with sliced cheese, a few chunks of the cold rotisserie chicken that had been two-for-one at Giant last week, and half a sleeve of Ritz crackers. As she ate, she pulled up her lesson plans and got to work.

When one recording ended, she'd start the next one, only half paying attention as she went about her evening. Each one began with Angie's voice stating the date, and Madelyn had to admire her commitment to her project, even as day after day passed with nothing to show for her efforts. The recordings didn't appear to be playing in order, with the dates jumping forward and backward in time, causing Madelyn to wonder disinterestedly how the software came up with the file names if they weren't sequential.

She finished her lesson plans and checked the clock. It may be hard to watch an episode of TV before bed while listening to the recordings, even if they were mostly white noise, so she opted for a video game instead, pulling out her Switch and resuming her exploration of the kingdom of Hyrule.

Midway through her third shrine of the night—one of the ones where they took all her armor and weapons and food away, her least favorite kind—Madelyn froze at a familiar voice.

"Test test test. I think it's on."

Alex. His voice was a little shallower, a little higher, but it was unmistakably him. She slowed down the playback speed and listened closer. On the Switch screen, her unmoving avatar was summarily executed.

"This is Angie Stewart, recording on September fifth, twenty-fourteen."

"You probably don't need to say your name every time."

"Well, yeah, but this is the first one."

"Right, I meant for the next ones."

"Yeah, probably."

"So . . . now what?"

"We let it run, I think. And then I'll listen later to see if it picked up anything."

"Should we check to make sure it sounds okay?"

"Oh yeah, that's a good idea. One sec."

After some rustling, the recording stopped, by far the shortest one she'd listened to yet. She clicked on the next recording on the list, holding her breath.

"Okay, take two. Angie Stewart, September fifth, twenty-fourteen."

"Man, I ate too much chicken. And too many beans. This may be a very stinky movie night."

"That'll be a great opening to the documentary."

"This part won't be in the documentary."

"How do you know?"

"They always cut out the boring shit."

"Not all of it. They have to keep some in for human interest."

"My bean farts are human interest?"

"I don't know, Bas. Humans are gross."

Right. Angie had called him Bas. It was so strange to hear him like this. Like he used to be a whole different person.

"Did you want to watch the movie?"

"Yeah. I want to make popcorn first, though."

"I thought you just said you were too full from dinner."

"Not my popcorn stomach."

"Fair."

Their voices faded in and out as they moved around the house, and Madelyn pictured teenage Alex and Angie in the kitchen by the microwave, then moving to the couch, the bowl of popcorn between them. Earlier, when Alex had told her about Angie, she'd wondered whether there was more to their relationship than strictly friendship, but based on the recording, she doubted it. Their interaction was easy and light, but not flirty. Just comfortable. Almost more like siblings than friends.

They reminded her of her and Syzygy. She felt a pang of intense sympathy for Alex, and also for Kelsey, knowing how much it would hurt if her best friend suddenly disappeared without a trace.

From their intermittent comments, Madelyn gathered that they were watching a *Paranormal Activity* installment, that they'd been working their way through the franchise for a while, and that this was much more Angie's idea than Alex's.

It sounded like Alex was getting ready to leave after nearly falling asleep when Angie's voice grew sharp. *"Bas, did you not see that?"*

"What?"

"The TV turned off."

Madelyn sat up straighter, covering her earbud with her hand as Alex claimed that it had been a mechanical fluke, while Angie insisted it was the ghost. Then—

"Do you hear that?"

"What?"

"Singing. The shower's on again too."

"I don't hear anything."

Madelyn didn't hear anything either. She paused the recording to retrieve her other earbud, and turned the volume all the way up. Rewinding a few seconds, she started the recording again, listening intently.

"Do you hear that?"

"What?"

"Singing."

She still didn't hear it. Pressing her hands over her ears, she closed her eyes and tried to narrow all her perception to the sides of her head.

"Just listen," came Angie's voice. A couple of seconds passed, and then Angie came through her earbuds again. Only this time, she was humming.

Madelyn's blood ran cold. She knew that tune. It was one of her go-to shower songs, from one of her favorite musicals. It was even nominated for a Tony Award for Best Musical.

In 2019.

Five years after Angie had recorded this.

Heart racing, Madelyn paused the recording and opened a new tab of her browser, typing in the name of the show and clicking on its Wikipedia link. Her eyes darted back and forth across the page, trying to make sense of what she'd heard.

Maybe it had premiered off-Broadway first. Or there had been a concept album, or a college production. Surely there was some way that this song would've been out in the world in 2014, where Angie could've heard it.

But according to Wikipedia, the show didn't premiere anywhere until 2016. Two years after this recording was made and Angie disappeared.

A laugh barked out of Madelyn without her realizing she was going to do it, and she slapped a hand over her mouth, shoulders still shaking at the ridiculous thought she'd just had. For a second, she'd almost wondered if maybe . . .

But no. That would be absurd.

Even if Angie did mention that it was a woman's voice.

Singing in the shower.

A coincidence, Madelyn was sure of it. There had to be some other explanation for Angie to have heard this song in 2014. Sung by a woman. In the shower.

Just like Madelyn had a couple of nights ago.

Scrubbing a hand down her face and probably making a mess of what was left of that morning's mascara, Madelyn looked down at Potato, still snoozing away on her pouf. "It's impossible," Madelyn whispered, and the little dog raised her head, tail wagging curiously. "Right, spud? There's got to be a reasonable explanation. It can't be . . ."

She shook her head, refusing to say it out loud. She was tired and weirded out from Alex's revelations over the past couple of days. And she had to admit that part of her really wanted to be the one to help him solve the mystery of what had happened to his friend. Not only for him and Angie, but for the connection that it would create between the two of them.

She scrubbed back a couple of minutes in the recording and listened again. And again. And again.

Every time, the melody was clear.

Her head began to pound, and she pulled out her earbuds, dropping them on the table and slumping back in her chair. It wasn't possible. It just wasn't.

But it was the only thing that made sense.

Angie had been hearing *her*.

Ten years before she ever moved in.

Somehow—and the thought resisted even taking form in her brain, but she forced the pieces into place, mental muscles straining against a conclusion that couldn't possibly be true, yet was the only one she had—

She was Angie's ghost.

CHAPTER TWENTY-FIVE

Celebrating pandemic-style (ie in sweatpants in my backyard, LOL) with @thekelsey_od because GUESS WHO JUST GOT HIRED AT @raymondrealtygrp??? Congrats, Kelsey!!! So pumped to be working with one of my besties!!!

—Instagram post from @piper.j.carden, June 2020

Madelyn called in sick the next morning.

The odds of a sub actually following her lesson plans for the day were about as good as the odds that the sub would actually *know* the Latin pronunciations she'd intended to teach her students—they weren't that hard if you knew the rules of Latin, which the average sub did not—but she diligently emailed them in anyway. Maybe she'd get lucky.

Which was more than she could say for these recordings.

She'd half listened to several of them the night before, but today she started over again from the beginning, notepad in hand. Today would be more efficient than last night. After rearranging the audio files in order by date, she downloaded an audio player that allowed her to see the waveform and control the speed of the playback, allowing her to easily skip over the long periods of silence and ambient noise. This time, she would listen to the story as it unfolded instead of jumping around in time. If there was another explanation for what she'd heard last night, this would be the way to find it.

Although . . . she was surprised to find that part of her didn't *want* there to be another explanation. As much as it freaked her out to consider that Angie could somehow hear her, ten years before she'd come to East Henderson, once the idea caught in her head, she couldn't get it out. All night, she'd tossed and turned until her blankets were a tangled mess. Eventually, Potato got fed up enough to jump to the floor to sleep in her crate, which Madelyn had finally fished out of the garage yesterday and placed beside her bed. But by the time her alarm went off in the morning, the theory had absorbed into her bloodstream, and she thought it might hurt if she had to give it up.

Still, there was a lot to go through, and after Madelyn got past the novelty of hearing Alex's younger voice on the recording, she quickly got bored.

She pulled out her Switch and started playing *Tetris*, giving her eyes and hands something to do while she listened to Angie and her dad, Angie and Alex, the TV, assorted music—Angie liked the angsty-girl rock that Madelyn had been into in high school; her dad favored music from the '70s and '80s—and occasionally Angie's dad muttering angrily to someone he called Chelsea, who never spoke back and Madelyn suspected wasn't there at all. She guessed Chelsea was Angie's mom, and from the sound of it, she'd really screwed her dad over when she left. Or at least he thought she had.

Most of it was mundane. Small talk between Angie and her dad, sarcastic teenage ribbing between Angie and Alex, the occasional argument. Exactly what you'd expect to hear in a normal household with a single father and a teenager.

But sometimes, Madelyn would pause her game, rewind the audio, and play it again slower. Gradually, as the hours slipped past, her notebook pages filled up. Snippets of song lyrics or bits of melodies, which Madelyn ran to her piano to notate even though she thought she recognized most of them. Times of day, places, stray comments that she thought could mean something.

The picture formed quickly, and as impossible as it seemed, it was too clear for her to pretend she didn't see it.

It really was her that Angie had heard all those years ago. She knew it in the songs Angie hummed, the places in the house where Angie heard them, the times of day, the strange phenomena that Angie reported outside of the singing.

The scratching in the hall: Potato digging at the wall.

The clanking of the pipes in the bathroom: Alex tinkering under the sink.

A strong smell of burned sugar in the kitchen: a catastrophic attempt at homemade Moon Pies that she'd intended as gifts for her fellow teachers at the start of school, but which all wound up in the garbage.

Still, even as the disturbing questions in her mind grew larger and louder, excitement buzzed in her stomach. As bizarre as this was, it was also incredible. She had no idea what it meant, or how it was happening, but somehow, she and Angie were linked in a way that defied time.

Why her? Why now? Was it something about her specifically, or was it more about the house itself? She kept hoping to find the answers in the recordings, but no matter how hard she listened, she couldn't find any.

With only two files left, Madelyn put down her Switch and allowed the white noise to play as she went to make herself a fresh pot of coffee, although she should probably switch to decaf this time. Her whole body felt like it was vibrating, but whether that was from the caffeine in the pot she'd already consumed or from her discoveries in the recordings, she couldn't be sure.

Male voices caught her attention as she drummed her nails on the countertop, waiting for the coffeepot to finish gurgling. Hurrying to her laptop, she stopped the playback and scrubbed back to the beginning of the sounds. Angie's father, Cameron, was clear, but the other voice was new, although not unfamiliar. Madelyn knew that voice.

Scribbling notes, Madelyn listened as the men discussed some sort of debt, with Cameron begging for more time and the other man holding fast. Although he claimed to be sorry about the circumstances of their arrangement, Madelyn didn't hear any remorse in his voice.

Her heart stuttered to a stop when Cameron finally said his name, confirming her suspicions.

Give me two weeks, Doug. Please, I'm begging you.

Doug Raymond. Of course. Who else would it be?

Their conversation ended with Angie's dad being given two weeks to come up with the money, or else. And that was it. Anxiously, Madelyn scrubbed forward in the audio, but there was nothing else in that file.

Only one more was left, and it was a fraction of the size of the others. When she loaded it into the player, it was only a few seconds long. That had to be a mistake, right? None of the others, except that very first sound test, was less than two hours, with most stretching on for much longer. She deleted and reloaded it, but it still came up as the same brief length. Sighing, worrying that her last possible clue in this mystery was corrupted, she pressed Play, expecting garbled audio or static, or maybe an error message.

Instead, after a pause and a shaky breath, she heard Angie's voice more clearly than she had in any of the previous hours of audio, like she was speaking directly into the recorder. Only sixteen words.

"This is Angie Stewart, September 24, 2014. If anything happens to me, it was Doug Raymond."

CHAPTER TWENTY-SIX

You may have heard some rumors regarding claims made by a disgruntled former employee about our company. While we wouldn't typically discuss former employees like this, in this instance and in the face of so much disinformation, we believe it is warranted. So to be clear: Piper Carden resigned for personal reasons at the beginning of March 2021. Kelsey O'Donnell was recently terminated for poor performance and untrustworthy behavior, neither of which had anything to do with Ms. Carden's departure, despite Ms. O'Donnell's claims to the contrary. Ms. O'Donnell's attempts to damage our company's reputation in the community are nothing more than petty vindictiveness brought on by her own misguided actions. We hope this clears up any confusion, and we apologize for any anxiety that Ms. O'Donnell's underhanded tactics may have caused. If you have further questions regarding this situation, feel free to take them to your leader, but please do not engage in spreading these rumors any further. There is no substance to them whatsoever. Hopefully if people stop paying attention to Ms. O'Donnell's slanderous claims, she will lose interest.

—Raymond Realty Group internal memo, May 2021

"Miss Zhao, wait!"

Madelyn cringed, scrunching her eyes shut for a second before smoothing her face and turning around. "Oh, hi!"

She'd been avoiding Alex all day, eating lunch in the cafeteria instead of in her classroom, taking her planning period in the library, and bringing her coffee in an insulated mug from home instead of getting it from the teachers' lounge. But she'd risked a dash to her car during seventh period for her anxiety meds, since her chest had felt like a clenched fist since she woke up that morning.

That had been her mistake.

It wasn't that she didn't want to see him. She craved him like a good book and a warm blanket. But she couldn't tell him about that recording. It would destroy him to know that Angie had asked for his help and he'd never answered. But she didn't know how she could *not* tell him either.

Her only option was to push him away.

Her smile felt glued on as she met his eyes, which only made her feel worse when she saw the genuine concern in them.

"Did you need something?" she asked, hating the coolness in her voice. Her stomach twisted as his face fell, hurt flickering through his eyes. She wanted to touch his cheek, tell him that none of this was his fault, that something was going on here that she didn't understand, that she was only trying to protect him.

Instead, she kept her face expressionless as she checked her watch.

"Sorry," he said, his tone indicating he wasn't exactly sure what he was apologizing for. "I just wondered if you wanted to get coffee after school today. The last couple days have been . . . a little unusual. I thought it might be nice to hit the reset button."

"I can't," she said curtly, not meeting his eyes. If she did, she might lose herself in their dark depths. "I have to go home."

"Oh," he said, his voice wavering slightly. "Okay. No problem. Some other time, then."

Madelyn nodded, lips pressed together. She couldn't think of anything else to say, so instead she spun away without a word, staring at the floor as she ducked into her classroom.

As the students packed up after eighth period, Madelyn checked her phone again. She'd been hoping to hear from Kelsey today—she'd left her three messages since listening to Angie's recording—but her phone had remained frustratingly silent all night and all day today.

Still no word. She sighed, putting her phone face down on her desk, then immediately picked it back up and checked again. She couldn't help it.

If anything happens to me, it was Doug Raymond.

The bell rang, marking the end of the day, and the students filed out of her classroom. Madelyn slumped back in her desk chair, checking her phone again. Where was Kelsey? Why wasn't she calling her back? Madelyn had said in her messages that this was important.

Her phone rang, and Madelyn sprang upright, certain that she was about to find some answers. "Hello?"

There was a pause, and then a mechanical voice said, *"Hello. If you would like information on consolidating your credit card debt—"*

Madelyn hung up, slamming the phone down on the desk a little too hard, as if it were the phone's fault that it wasn't Kelsey. "Screw you," Madelyn said out loud, flipping off her phone.

"Whoa, what did they ever do to you?"

Madelyn spun in her chair to see Alex standing at the door of her classroom, hands in his pockets. Today he was wearing a brown sweater vest over an orange collared shirt. A goddamn sweater vest. A person should not be allowed to be this adorable. Frankly, it was obscene.

Madelyn curled her hands into fists, nails digging into her palms. No more flirting with Alex. Not until she had some answers for him that wouldn't make things worse.

"Nothing," Madelyn said, forcing a smile. "Telemarketer."

"You know you can silence those calls," Alex said. "Especially if they're pissing you off that much."

Madelyn shrugged. "It's not so bad."

"Tell that to whoever was on the phone." Alex took a tentative step into the room. "So, I wanted to apologize," he said, his eyes not quite meeting hers.

"Apologize? For what?"

"I think I came on a little too strong. All the stuff with Angie, and your house and her bag . . . I realize we've only known each other a few weeks, and that was a lot. Probably too much. So I wanted to apologize for dumping all of that on you, and to let you know that I'm going to back off."

"Back off?"

"Yeah," Alex said, his cheeks reddening. "I'm going to give you your space. Which I realize I'm not doing right now. But starting whenever I leave this classroom, I will stop bothering you."

"Bothering me?" Madelyn's brain felt sluggish, able only to echo back to him what he'd said. She didn't want him to back off. She wanted him to back *on*, or whatever the opposite of *back off* was. She didn't want to hurt him, but that didn't mean she wanted to lose him entirely.

He gave her a sad smile. "I can tell when I'm making someone uncomfortable. And I'm sorry for doing that to you."

Madelyn's mouth gaped, but before she could find the right words, he'd turned and walked out of her classroom. For a moment, she sat glued to her chair. Had he broken up with her? After one date?

She picked up her phone and texted Syzygy. I think I just got dumped.

TIL you were dating someone?

Alex.

WTF.

He apologized for unloading too much of his baggage on me.

AND???

And . . . that's it. He said he'd leave me alone.

Three dots appeared, then disappeared. A second later, her phone rang. Syzygy.

"Hey," Madelyn said listlessly.

"Is he still there?"

Madelyn shrugged. "Probably headed to his car."

"You absolute imbecile."

"What?"

"How far is the parking lot?"

"I don't know, like a couple minutes?"

"And how long have you been talking to me?"

"Um—"

"Please tell me you're not still sitting in your classroom like a shrub."

"I can't just—"

"Move your ass."

Syzygy had always had an uncanny ability to get Madelyn moving when she would've otherwise stayed frozen in place. It was probably because of them that she'd ever managed to walk away from Ralph at all.

Now she found her feet moving almost of their own volition, taking her out of her classroom and down the hall, toward the exit to the teacher lot. She wasn't sure what she'd do when she got there, only that she didn't want Alex to leave thinking that he'd ruined something between them. She didn't want him to leave at all.

Pushing her way through the double doors to exit the school, she spotted him moving toward his car. She wasn't sure if he was moving twice as slowly as usual, or she was moving twice as fast. Either way, she caught up with him right as he was pulling his keys out of his bag.

"Alex!"

He turned toward her, and she realized too late that it was *definitely* her moving twice as fast, because she barreled into him with enough force to send them both slamming into the side of his car. Her elbow hit the window, sending a flash of cool pain followed by numbness down her arm.

"Sorry! Sorry," she said, rubbing her arm as she disentangled herself from him. His messenger bag had swung around his body, and now hung between them like a shield.

"Um, hi?" He smoothed his hands down his clothes, blinking at her with an expression caught between confusion and—she hoped—hope.

"You aren't bothering me," Madelyn blurted. She realized, now that they were face to face, that she hadn't actually planned out what to say to him. She just hadn't wanted him to leave thinking that she didn't like him.

"Oh," Alex said, blinking.

"And I don't need space."

"Clearly," Alex said, a bemused smile playing on his lips.

"But I . . . have some stuff right now, okay?"

"Stuff," Alex repeated, and she wondered if maybe she wasn't the only one cursed to awkwardly echo instead of contributing anything meaningful to the conversation.

"But I don't . . . it's not anything about you, all right? Not anything bad, I mean," she said. Oh God, was she even making sense? Was she making it worse?

But he smiled, and her heart turned from lead to feathers. "Are you sure?"

"I—"

Either fate had a wicked sense of humor or it hated her entirely, because as soon as she opened her mouth, she caught movement out of the corner of her eye. Someone was standing at the edge of the parking lot, waving at her from the open door of a blue Prius. A woman with dark, curly hair and an expression like she was delivering a war telegram.

Kelsey.

"Crap," Madelyn hissed under her breath. Once Kelsey had her attention, she gave her a small nod, then got back in her car.

"You okay?" Alex said, glancing over his shoulder to see what had grabbed her attention. Madelyn was glad that Kelsey was already out of sight. Her car remained where it was, waiting for Madelyn to join her.

"Actually, I need to go," Madelyn said reluctantly. Obviously, Kelsey wanted to talk, and for some reason, she'd driven all the way out to East Henderson instead of calling. She wouldn't have done that if it weren't important.

Something like disappointment flashed across Alex's face, but he was polite enough to tuck it away almost as soon as she caught it. "No problem. I'll see you tomorrow?" He took another step away from her.

She hated this. She didn't want to hurt him, but she also didn't want to be someone who wasn't honest about how they felt, or who played games with other people's emotions. She knew too well how it felt to be with someone like that, and how miserable it was. She couldn't do that to Alex, even if her motives were pure. So either she needed to end this for good, or she needed to let him know she was in. Even if "in" was way more complicated than she wanted it to be.

Screw it all. Maybe they were doomed to crash and burn, but at least it wouldn't be because she hadn't tried. Stepping forward, she hooked a hand around the back of Alex's neck and rose up on her toes, lifting her face to his. She could feel his surprise as their lips met, but it quickly turned to eagerness as his mouth opened to hers. He tasted of coffee and, underneath, spearmint gum, and his lips were even softer than she remembered. His hair was like silk between her fingers, and that stupid sweater vest was so soft she wanted to curl up in it and purr.

She allowed herself two blissful seconds before pulling away, gasping even though it had been only a moment. "I don't need space," she repeated breathlessly. "I'm sorry."

He blinked at her, lips still slightly parted. She could tell he wanted to talk, to discuss *them*, whatever that meant. But she didn't have any answers right now, other than that she desperately wanted *them* to be a thing.

Better to not talk at all. Better to let the moment be a moment, and hope more would come soon.

Before he could say anything, she turned and speed-walked back toward the school, hoping Kelsey understood that she wasn't ignoring her, but was just waiting for Alex to leave. She didn't want him to think she was ditching him for someone else, even though technically, that's exactly what she was doing.

As soon as she saw Alex's car pull out of the lot, Madelyn exited the building again, walking straight to Kelsey's car, which was still parked in the same spot. She knocked on the passenger window, and Kelsey unlocked the door.

"Well, this is a surprise," Madelyn said, dropping into the seat.

"Sorry about that," Kelsey said, swiveling her head to scan the parking lot. "This just felt safer than calling."

"What's going on?"

"You remember what I said about Raymond's playbook?"

"Yeah . . ."

"Well, I think we might be going another round." Kelsey slumped in her seat, shrinking into her oversize black sweatshirt. She looked like she was trying to disappear.

"What do you mean?"

Kelsey fiddled with her key chain, a beaded turquoise seahorse. "I got a letter from his lawyer. Again. Seems someone knows we talked."

Madelyn's stomach dropped. "Who?"

"I don't know. I told you, he's got flying monkeys everywhere. Who did you tell about our meeting?"

"No one," she said. She hadn't even told Alex about Kelsey. Syzygy knew, but they didn't count. Not only would they never say anything, but they didn't even know anyone in East Henderson.

"Well, someone figured it out. I've been reminded in no uncertain terms that I am legally bound not to discuss the case. And that if I willfully break the terms of our agreement again, they'll make me regret it. I'm paraphrasing, but that's the gist."

The blood drained from Madelyn's face. Everyone had warned her that Raymond was powerful and paranoid, but she hadn't dreamed that he might actually be spying on people. She was seized by an overwhelming urge to look behind her, as if there might be a man in a trench coat and sunglasses hiding in the back seat, but a quick glance confirmed she was being absurd. "Oh, Kelsey. I am so, so sorry. I swear, I didn't—"

"You may want to check your mail when you get home. If I got one of these, I wouldn't be surprised if you did too."

"I will. Listen, the reason I called—"

"I'm sorry, Madelyn, but I don't think I can talk to you anymore. It's not you. I just . . . I can't go through that again." Kelsey's eyes jumped briefly to the mirror. They hadn't stopped darting around since Madelyn got in the car. "But I didn't want to just . . . disappear. I wanted to tell you what was going on with me. I figured I owed you that."

Madelyn nodded, her throat tight. They both knew she was thinking about Piper. "Thank you, Kelsey. If there's anything I can do . . ." She trailed off, unable to come up with a promise that wouldn't be empty.

Kelsey gave her a tight smile, her eyes glassy. "Just don't give up on her, okay? Promise you'll keep digging, and don't let them shut you up."

"I promise." She wouldn't give up on Piper *or* Angie. Of that much, she was certain.

Kelsey leaned over the console between the seats to give Madelyn a tight hug. Her curls tickled the side of her face, and Madelyn heard her quietly sniff back tears. "Thank you for listening to me," Kelsey whispered. "It means so much."

"Of course," Madelyn said. "It's the least I could do."

Kelsey drew back, giving her a sardonic smile. "It's really not. Most people do a lot less."

She unlocked the doors, and Madelyn got out of the car, shivering slightly even though it wasn't that cool. She felt like she was living in a movie. The kind where not everyone had a happy ending. "Take care of yourself," she said. The words rang hollow in her ears.

"You too."

Madelyn closed the door as Kelsey turned on the car, but before she could walk away, Kelsey rolled down the window.

"And Madelyn?"

"Yeah?"

"Be careful. They're watching you."

Before Madelyn could think of a response, Kelsey pulled out of the space and was gone.

CHAPTER TWENTY-SEVEN

Don't have a ton of sympathy for her, TBH. She signed up to work there. Either she didn't do her research, or she was willing to look the other way in exchange for a paycheck. Sure, it sucks to be in her position, but she got there all on her own. Next time, maybe don't work for fascists.

—comment by deusexmacaroni replying to post FORMER EMPLOYEE SUED BY RAYMOND REALTY on r/RottenRaymond

---

Madelyn's mind reeled the whole way home. Who had talked to Raymond about her? Was it someone she knew? Someone she trusted? Or was it a complete stranger eavesdropping on her conversations without her even realizing it?

She thought of the places she'd talked about Doug Raymond. With Alex in the coffee shop, and again in the hardware store. With Nat at the coffee shop, and then in the library. The possibilities made her stomach twist.

She checked her mail when she got home, her heart in her throat. Nothing from Raymond Realty Group. But that didn't necessarily mean she was in the clear.

The afternoon passed in a haze. During Potato's walk, Madelyn found herself sizing up the people around her. Was that woman really taking a selfie, or was she filming Madelyn? Was that man looking at her too much? Was that guy *really* stopping to tie his shoe, or was he trying to eavesdrop?

Everyone looked like a spy. Everything felt like a threat.

She cut their trip to the park short, nearly dragging Potato back home in her haste to get inside, away from prying eyes. Away from the flying monkeys.

Back at her house, she walked from room to room, shaking out her hands to try to still the feeling of buzzing beneath her skin. Kelsey's voice kept playing over and over in her mind. *They're watching you.*

No matter what she did, she couldn't shake the sensation of eyes on her back, tracking her every move.

She hadn't even fully decided to call before she was reaching for her phone. She tapped the video icon by Syzygy's name, then chewed on her lip until their face appeared on the screen.

"Hey, what's up?" Their short hair, shaved on the sides and currently dyed a rainbow of pastels, was pulled up in a purple scrunchie on the very top of their head, making them resemble a brightly colored onion. They didn't wait for an answer before setting the phone on the counter, so Madelyn could see them moving around the kitchen they'd once shared making dinner.

"Kelsey came to see me after school."

"Really? All the way from Lancaster?"

"She said it felt safer than talking on the phone."

"That sounds a little extreme."

"It is. Someone knows we met. She has no idea who, but somehow, Raymond found out. She got a threatening letter, and now she says she can't talk to me anymore."

"Holy shit."

"I'm not going to lie, Syz, I'm kind of freaking out."

"Um, you and me both, babe. What are you going to do?"

"Keep checking my mail, I guess. See if I get a letter too."

"Even if you don't, Mad, I think you need to drop this. It doesn't feel safe. Three people are missing, and the one who's still around had to move to freaking Amish country to get away from them, and apparently that *still* wasn't far enough. I don't want you to have to change your name and go live in a bunker just to be able to sleep at night."

"I don't either, but he can't just get away with all of this."

"People do every day, Mad. It's how the world works. If you have enough money, you can get away with anything."

"Which means this whole thing is pointless," Madelyn said, her shoulders slumping. "Even if I *could* get to the bottom of what happened to Angie and Piper, there's nothing I can *do* about it. Not if Raymond is determined to cover it up." She sighed. "I was stupid to think I could change anything."

"Slow your roll, Little Miss Anxiety Spiral." Syzygy was moving again, running water and clanking dishes. When they returned to the screen, they were twirling a forkful of linguine in red sauce. "Also, did you take your meds today? You're a bit more nihilist than usual. That's supposed to be *my* thing."

Madelyn wrinkled her forehead. "I'm honestly not sure about the Effexor. I took my BuSpar a little while ago, though." She could mentally picture her pill organizer on the bathroom counter, but couldn't remember if she'd opened it that morning. She'd just been so distracted lately.

"Okay, well, maybe let's allow for the possibility that you're a bit unregulated right now, so things may feel a bit worse than they actually are. He may be powerful, but he's not invincible. So let's not rush to the worst possible conclusions."

Madelyn pursed her lips. After two years of living together, Syzygy could always tell when she was off-balance. Madelyn found their extremely specific talent both helpful and deeply annoying. "There's something else too," she admitted, then told Syzygy about Angie's recording. "So you can see why I'm feeling a bit pessimistic at the moment."

"Wow," Syzygy said, eyes wide. They'd pushed their plate aside to lean in as she talked, resting their chin on their hand, so their face took up most of the frame. "What does Alex think about all this? Does he have any theories?"

Madelyn made a show of studying her nail beds, chewing on the inside of her cheek.

"Mad. Please tell me you told him what you heard."

"I was going to. I wanted to wait until I was sure."

"Sure about *what*? It's literally a recording of her voice."

"Sure that I knew what happened. And that he wouldn't freak out."

Syzygy groaned, giving Madelyn a glimpse of a mouthful of half-chewed food. "You have got to be kidding me."

"It's been ten years, Syz," Madelyn argued. "There's probably nothing he can do about it now, and I didn't want him to feel worse about what happened."

"She was his best friend, Madelyn. He deserves to know. She *wanted* him to know."

"In 2014. Not *now.*"

"That is not your decision to make. If it were me, wouldn't *you* want to know?"

Madelyn pressed her lips together. Of course she'd want to know. Otherwise she'd wonder forever.

But this was different. Alex was fine now. He'd gotten over Angie and made a good new life. Why would she mess with that? All that would accomplish would be hurting him more, and probably cause him to hate her in the process.

"I'm sorry, but that is bullshit," Syzygy said when Madelyn tried to explain her reasoning. "Has he done anything to make you believe he'd be mad at *you* for trying to find out the truth about his friend?"

"Ralph would have said it was me inserting myself into other people's business."

"Ralph was so up in your business I'm surprised he wasn't wiping your ass for you, so I am uninterested in what he would have said about literally anything."

Madelyn laughed, but unexpected tears stung the backs of her eyes. Syzygy was right, and Madelyn hated knowing that she'd given such a big chunk of her life to someone who was so immensely not worth it. Maybe when she was forty, dating an indisputable asshole for six years wouldn't seem like such a big deal, but at twenty-three, it felt like forever.

"Hey, Mad, listen," Syzygy said, their voice suddenly taking on a serious tone. "That's not a reflection on *you*. You know that, right? Ralph picked you because you're a good person who sees the best in people. Those are *good* qualities. It's not your fault that he used them against you. That's entirely on him."

"I know." Madelyn sniffed. And she did, or at least a part of her knew. But the rest of her still felt a little broken. He was the one swinging the hammer, but she had shattered all the same. And she was mad that she hadn't been stronger. And mad that she was mad, since that meant he was still taking up space in her brain. Which was stupid, and made her feel stupid for being mad.

Sometimes she hated having a brain.

"You should tell him," Syzygy said.

"Ralph?"

"No, Alex, you ding-dong."

"I kissed him today."

"You *what*?"

Madelyn nodded, swallowing hard. "When you told me to go after him, I chased him into the parking lot and kissed him."

"Oh my God, Mad, why did you not *lead* with this? Tell me everything. What did he say?"

"Nothing."

"Nothing?"

"I kind of ran away."

"You . . ." Syzygy closed their eyes for a second. "Okay, let me get this straight. You gave him the impression you weren't interested, enough for him to gracefully bow out of the race. Then you chased him down and kissed him. Then you *fled the scene*?"

"Well, when you put it like *that*, it sounds weird."

"It *is* weird, you goober. Why the hell are you calling *me*? You should call him."

"But how will he react when he finds out about . . ." Madelyn flapped her hand around wildly. "All this?"

"I have no idea. But has he given you any reason to think he's a bad person? Has he sent up any red flags at all? Pinged your asshole radar?"

"No," Madelyn admitted. "And I've been looking."

"Then let's assume he will react like a good and reasonable person. And also, he likes you. And may I reiterate, she was his *best friend*. He deserves to know."

"You're right," Madelyn breathed out. If she was honest with herself, she'd known she needed to tell him ever since she listened to Angie's last recording. She just needed someone to push her over the edge, and she could always count on Syzygy to be that person.

Her phone buzzed with a text. Madelyn stared at it, holding her breath, then responded before she could change her mind.

"You need to get off the phone with me and call him right now," Syzygy continued to rant. "I cannot *believe* you have let literal hours pass with no communication. That poor boy is probably so turned around he's arranging his furniture on the ceiling."

"I can't call him."

"Madelyn, you are going to give me a stroke."

"I can't call him," Madelyn repeated, taking a deep breath, "because he just texted me inviting me to come over. And I said yes."

CHAPTER TWENTY-EIGHT

FROM: sebastianag@gmail.com
TO: angiemae@gmail.com
SUBJECT: HBD

Dear Angie,

It's your birthday today. If you're out there, you're officially an adult. What's it like? As you know, I've still got a couple months to go. Do you have all the answers to life's questions now? I hope so. I'm sick of having no idea what I'm doing.

I leave for school in a few weeks. It's weird to be starting college without you. I know it sounds stupid since you've been gone almost two years now, but I think I always figured you'd be back by now. It didn't feel right finishing high school by myself, and it doesn't feel right to be doing this alone either.

I know it's been a while since I've emailed. And I really don't know what to say now. It's pretty clear that you don't want to talk to me. I don't even know if you're getting these. FWIW, I'm sorry about our fight. It wasn't worth it. I wish I could take it all back.

Anyway, happy birthday. I miss you a lot. And maybe it's dumb, but when I blow out my candles in a couple months, I'm going to wish for you to come home.

Come home, Angie.

Love,
Bas

Madelyn jogged up the short walkway to Alex's front door and rang the bell, shaking the nerves out of her hands. The address he'd texted her was a modest duplex about fifteen minutes from her house, with faded beige siding and a maroon front door with a fleur-de-lis brass knocker. A small mound of yellow mums perched in a brown pot on the front step, and Madelyn wondered absently if Alex had bought them himself, or if his mother or grandmother had brought them over. She liked the idea of a man buying fresh flowers for his front porch, even if it wasn't really a porch.

She shifted nervously from foot to foot, trying to run through her breathing exercises, but barely had time to get through one cycle before Alex swung open the door, dressed in dark-green basketball shorts and a faded gray T-shirt with the sleeves cut off. "Madelyn!" he exclaimed, like he was surprised to see her even though this had been his idea. "Thanks for coming over."

He led her into a comfortable living room furnished with a cream-colored sofa and a gnarled coffee table that looked like it was made out of tendrils of smoke. Two tall black bookcases stood against one wall, filled with neatly arranged books and a few small potted plants. A tryptic of abstract paintings hung over the couch, brightening the room with swirls of green and blue and black.

"Your place is really nice," Madelyn said, surprised. She'd expected an apartment like her male friends from college: cheap fake-wood TV stand, beer stains on the couch, sports posters on the wall in snap-on frames, maybe a minifridge as an end table. Alex's place was small, but it felt like the home of a grown-up.

"Not really," Alex said, blushing slightly. He gestured to the coffee table. "My abuelo made that before he passed, out of a piece of driftwood he pulled out of the river. And my sister painted those." He pointed to the paintings. "She got obsessed with TikTok DIY art videos one year and gave us all paintings for Christmas."

"That's still really good," Madelyn said. She'd tried a couple of those art trends before. They'd all wound up in the garbage.

Alex seemed to check himself, then shook his head. "I'm sorry. I'm terrible at taking compliments. I mean, thank you."

"It's okay. I suck at it too. I blame oldest child syndrome."

"You too?"

Madelyn nodded, and Alex grinned. "How many siblings did *you* have to make feel better about themselves?"

"Just one, but she really wanted me to work for it."

Alex laughed. "I've got three. My sister is a junior at UPenn, and my brothers are actually at the high school this year. You missed having them in choir by the skin of your teeth."

"Do they sing?"

"One can but pretends he can't, and the other can't but thinks he can. It's a very convoluted family secret."

"I *really* want to meet your brothers now."

"That's definitely within the realm of possibility," Alex said, his smile widening.

Heat rushed to Madelyn's face. Had she casually asked to meet his family? She wasn't even sure that they were actually *dating*. One dinner and two kisses—one of which had been an ambush—were not a relationship. Hardly meet-the-parents worthy.

And then there was all this Angie stuff complicating things. And the Piper stuff, which he barely even knew about. Who knew how he'd react when she told him about all *that.*

She could feel her brain preparing to launch itself into a shame spiral, but Syzygy's voice popped into her head, blocking her path. *He sounded happy about it, right?*

Yes, her brain begrudgingly admitted.

So maybe don't go hurling yourself off Embarrassment Cliff yet. You like him. He likes you. He doesn't seem to be an axe murderer or a raging narcissist. Stop self-sabotaging.

Madelyn had told them once that she sometimes pictured them as her shoulder angel, and it helped keep her from spinning out. Syzygy's response had been to ask what they were wearing, and to sigh dramatically—*What's a person got to do to get a harp around here*—when Madelyn said their normal clothes. She'd promised to envision them carrying a rainbow ukulele from then on, which both pleased them and weirdly worked to calm her even more.

"Can I get you anything?" Alex asked, moving through the living room into the small galley-style kitchen and opening the fridge. "I have water and, um, water. Sorry, I didn't plan very well for this. It was kind of an impulsive text."

"I would love some water," Madelyn said, trying to take in everything about Alex's home without looking like she was snooping. It was a typical rental kitchen: black appliances, dark laminate counter speckled to look like granite, cheap tile on the floor. But it was clean, which was more than she could say for her kitchen at the moment, and the fridge was covered with photos of groups of dark-haired kids and adults she assumed must be Alex's family, and—to her delight—a few cards that were obviously from students, the outsides printed with generic THANKS, TEACHER! messages and the insides filled with loopy preteen handwriting.

She spotted a photo of Alex and Angie as teenagers close to the fridge handle, then cut her eyes away. Guilt churned in her stomach. "I have something to tell you," she blurted as Alex handed her a glass of water. She took a long sip.

"Oh. Okay," he said, sounding slightly surprised. His text had said he was hoping they could talk, but he probably wasn't expecting a confession.

"Um, can we sit down for a minute?" Madelyn gestured to the living room, and he followed her to the couch. He flopped comfortably into what she assumed was his typical seat, sinking into the cushion and angling his body to face her, one arm draped across the back.

Madelyn perched on the other end, back rigid, hands clasped in her lap. Her heart machine-gunned against the walls of her chest. She took a deep breath, trying to figure out the best place to start. "Angie's bag . . ." The words revealed themselves to her sluggishly, like they were being dragged through wet cement before forming in her brain. "There was something inside that I think she wanted you to have."

Slowly, awkwardly, she stumbled through the past couple of days. Finding the recorder, listening to the audio files, Angie's final message about Doug Raymond. About Piper, and Kelsey, and her visit earlier that afternoon. "I think you're right. They didn't run away because of bad credit. Something happened to them, and it has something to do with Doug Raymond."

Alex blew out a long breath, pressing his hands to the tops of his legs and straightening his arms, like he needed to stretch out the knots of Madelyn's story. "Wow. I'm . . . not really sure what to say."

Madelyn nodded, her stomach still turning. "It's a lot."

"Yeah."

It was truer than he realized. She hadn't even dropped her biggest bombshell yet. *Also, I think I'm her ghost.*

She knew he deserved to know, but there was no way to make those words sound sane, no matter how she tried to arrange them. It took no effort to imagine how he'd look at her—the furrowing of his brow, the curl of his lip, the distancing in his eyes as his interest cooled.

You're so weird, Ralph used to say. *Most guys want girls who are into normal stuff. It's a good thing you've got me to put up with all your crazy.*

And that's what she'd sound like, when she told Alex. Crazy.

"Hold on," Alex said, rising from the couch and exiting the room. He returned a minute later holding a laptop, which he opened as he sat back down beside her. This time, he sat closer, their hips nearly touching. "Okay, what did you say your cousin's name was?"

Madelyn blinked, off-balance. "Piper Carden."

"Pi . . . per . . . Carden," he said slowly, typing her name into his search bar.

"What's going on?" Madelyn had imagined more of a discussion as he processed what she'd told him. Maybe bewilderment at all the bizarre layers she had found, maybe anger that she hadn't told him right away. Hell, she'd *kissed* him and then run away like he was diseased. Shouldn't he want to talk about *that*?

Apparently not, because he was already skipping from one link to another like rocks off a pond, opening and closing tabs so fast she could barely read a few words on each page before he was on to the next. "There's nothing here," he muttered, frowning. "Nothing *useful*, anyway."

"No?" Madelyn felt almost dizzy at how rapidly he was scrolling through each page. She wasn't the world's fastest reader, but she wasn't slow either. "I can't even tell what we're looking at."

"Oh, sorry," he said, pausing his frantic browsing. "I taught myself to speed-read in college. I thought it would help studying go faster. Turns out, it absolutely does not, but it *can* be helpful in trying to find information on a specific topic. I'm not reading every word on the page, just scanning for keywords."

"Oh, thank God," Madelyn said. "I was beginning to think you were an android."

He laughed. "I wish. That would probably make my life a lot easier. Far fewer pesky feelings to get tangled up in."

Did he glance at her when he said that? She couldn't be sure.

He sighed, running a hand through his hair. "Okay, you googled, I googled, you went to the library . . . maybe we're going about this the wrong way."

He typed in a new URL, and she raised an eyebrow. "Really?"

"Hold on, let me see . . ." He typed Piper's name into his Facebook search bar.

Madelyn's eyes widened. "That's her!" She pointed at the top search result. Madelyn had never sent Piper a friend request, not wanting her parents to see it, but she'd definitely stalked her profile. Her profile link said that Piper and Alex had one mutual friend.

Alex laughed incredulously. "I can't believe that worked. I mean, I *can*—this isn't a tiny town, but it's not big either. And I've been here my whole life. So I'm probably within a couple degrees of like, eighty percent of East Henderson. But also . . . I can't believe that worked."

His hand shook slightly as he clicked on her profile to see who their mutual friend was.

"Wyatt Schaefer," Madelyn read out loud.

"We went to high school together," Alex said. "Honestly, I don't even know if he still lives here. I don't think I've talked to him since we graduated."

They both leaned in toward the screen as they scanned Wyatt's Facebook profile, which didn't tell them much, then jumped over to LinkedIn, which revealed that Wyatt had worked for Raymond Realty Group for two years as an accounts manager. "That must be how they knew each other," Madelyn said, nearly bouncing in place.

"Maybe. But that doesn't mean that he knows anything," Alex cautioned. He switched back over to Facebook and pulled up a private message window. He wiggled his fingers briefly over the keyboard before typing out a brief message, asking if Wyatt would be open for meeting up sometime soon to catch up.

"You think he'll go for that?" Madelyn asked dubiously. If someone from high school messaged her out of the blue, asking her to meet, she'd assume that they'd either been hacked or were trying to recruit her to an MLM.

"We were a pretty small high school class," Alex said. "Everyone kind of knew everyone. I think he'll—"

He was interrupted by a chime from his computer.

> Bas! Awesome to hear from you, dude. Would love to get a bite sometime. I'm done working by 4 most days. LMK when works for you.

Bas, Madelyn mouthed. He'd told her that he stopped using the nickname after Angie disappeared.

"Yeah," he said softly. "High school nicknames are kind of hard to shake. Whether or not you want to keep them around."

Madelyn hadn't realized she'd said anything out loud. "I'm sorry."

He shrugged stiffly. "It's fine."

It didn't seem fine. His whole body had tensed at the name. She wondered what he would do if he ever heard Angie's recordings. If he heard the two of them hanging out, poking fun at each other, watching movies together.

If he heard the last thing she'd said to him.

Alex was already typing again, setting up a place and time to meet with Wyatt. They went back and forth a few times, then Alex glanced up at Madelyn. "Next Thursday okay?"

Madelyn couldn't believe that he was all right waiting a whole week; she felt like she might spontaneously combust if she didn't get answers soon. "He can't meet up sooner?" She hoped she didn't sound too anxious.

"It's already been ten years," Alex said. "It's not like we're in a hurry."

But Madelyn was. Her mind drifted back to the thing he didn't know, the thing she couldn't bring herself to tell him quite yet.

I'm Angie's ghost.

"Actually," Alex said before she could figure out how to push back without being weird, "he did mention that he's free tomorrow. I just figured that was too soon. Would you rather do that?"

"Yes," Madelyn agreed, relieved. "Tomorrow is perfect."

The knot inside her loosened a little, only to promptly tangle itself right back up again.

One step closer to answers meant one step closer to telling Alex the truth. Her confession echoed through her mind like a drumbeat.

I'm Angie's ghost. I'm Angie's ghost. I'm Angie's ghost.

Either he'd think she was crazy, and he wouldn't want to be with her . . . or he'd realize she was the reason that he was fighting with his best friend the night she disappeared. And he wouldn't want to be with her. All roads led to the end of whatever this thing between them was.

She just wanted a little more time in the reality where it was still a possibility.

Still, sometime soon, she'd have to tell him that something bound her and Angie together. Something outside of time, something she didn't understand but couldn't deny.

And she couldn't shake the feeling that if she was somehow linked to Angie, if it was *her* voice Angie had heard in the past—her voice *Alex* had heard in the past—then they were supposed to help her. Angie.

And if Angie was still out there, then Alex was wrong. They *were* in a hurry. Because ten years had already gone by, and they couldn't afford to lose another second.

CHAPTER TWENTY-NINE

> Congratulations to this month's Raymond Realty Rockstar, PIPER CARDEN! Piper came to us fresh out of college a couple years ago, hit the ground running, and hasn't slowed down since. "We all love Piper," CFO Brendan Walker says. "She's always game to take on a new task, constantly thinking ten steps down the road, and has a smile that can light up a room. I don't know what we'd do without her." Thanks for helping the Raymond Realty engine run smoothly, Piper!
>
> —Raymond Realty Group internal newsletter, November 2020

It felt strange to walk into a bustling sports bar for a conversation about missing women, but Alex had let Wyatt pick the place, and as far as Wyatt knew, they were just old friends catching up. So Mayday Brewhouse it was, an oak-and-brass-style pub with flat-screen TVs in every corner that, on a Friday night, were all tuned to the Phillies game.

Madelyn clutched her purse in front of her as Alex escorted her through a churning sea of red jersey–clad baseball fans, to where Wyatt had claimed a table behind a thick pillar with only a partial view of the TVs. At first, she'd offered to drive herself, but now she was glad that Alex had insisted on picking her up, since she wasn't sure she could have located them if she'd come on her own.

Wyatt stood to shake hands with Alex, then Madelyn, offering an apologetic smile. "I forgot about baseball," he admitted, half yelling to be heard over the din. He was a slightly built man, with short strawberry-blond hair and a trim beard, and nervous bright-blue eyes. When Madelyn shook his hand, he gripped hers firmly, staring at her intently with a grin that felt a little too eager.

They settled into their chairs and studied the menus as a waitress brought over a bowl of fresh popcorn and glasses of water. For a few minutes, they made small talk as Alex and Wyatt caught up on the basics of their lives since high school, and Wyatt asked Madelyn polite, empty questions. He asked how she was liking East Henderson so far, and she gave innocuous answers about her job, her neighborhood, her adventures in home repair.

Her insides buzzed with anticipation. She didn't want to make generic small talk. She wanted answers.

The waitress arrived, a middle-aged woman with a smile like a sea turtle. "You guys ready?" She gave her tablet a few preparatory taps with a stylus, then turned expectantly to Madelyn, thin blonde hair swinging around her chin. "Ladies first."

After ordering a cup of soup—her stomach felt like it was trying to eat itself, so soup was about all she could manage—Madelyn leaned toward the waitress, lowering her voice as much as she dared. "Is there a quieter table we could move to?" She cut her eyes to the nearest cluster of Phillies fans, who were making up creative new insults for one of the players on-screen, although she honestly couldn't tell whether they considered their target friend or foe.

The waitress chuckled, shaking her head. "During playoffs? This *is* the quiet section."

"Really?" Madelyn looked around the crowded restaurant in dismay. There were so many people here. So many ears.

"Come back for an Eagles game; this'll seem like nothing."

Madelyn smiled tightly, breathing through her nerves as the waitress moved on. *No one is watching you,* she reminded herself. She scanned the people surrounding them. All eyes were glued to the TV. *It's safe to talk here. No one is listening.*

Of course, that's what she'd thought the first time she'd met with Kelsey too.

After the waitress had finished taking their orders and departed back to the kitchen, Wyatt turned to Madelyn. "So how long have you two been together?"

"Oh, um . . ." Madelyn faltered, not sure how to answer that question. *Were* they together? She honestly had no idea. And tonight definitely wasn't a date, although it was clear that Wyatt assumed otherwise. "Actually . . ."

"We met a few weeks ago," Alex interjected smoothly, which was both an answer and not an answer at all. He glanced at Madelyn, then leaned forward, his hands folded on the table. "Listen, there was actually something specific we both wanted to talk to you about tonight, Wyatt," he started.

Wyatt's forehead wrinkled slightly, his eyes curious. "Oh yeah?"

"I know this may seem like a really strange thing to ask, but I saw that you used to work for Raymond Realty," Alex said. "Madelyn is renting from them now, and we had some questions about the company."

Wyatt gave Madelyn a small smile. "I mean, I wasn't super high up and it's been a while, but sure, I'll answer what I can. What did you want to know?"

Alex took a deep breath, catching Madelyn's eye. *Here goes nothing,* his face seemed to say. "Did you know a woman there named Piper Carden?"

Wyatt blinked, leaning back in his chair and tilting his head. "Yeah, a bit. We weren't close, but we worked together occasionally. Why?"

His smile hadn't faded, but Madelyn thought she detected a slight shift in his tone. Was it cooler? More guarded? Then again, she'd met this guy only a few minutes ago. Maybe she was being paranoid.

"We were wondering if you had any idea where she is now," Alex said. "We'd love to talk to her." They'd decided ahead of time to tread lightly around the shady conspiracy theories. It wasn't just that they didn't want to scare Wyatt off. If Doug Raymond really *was* behind all these disappearances, he could do the same thing to them. They needed to be careful.

Wyatt shrugged, spreading his hands. "I wish I knew, but I really don't. After she quit, we didn't stay in touch."

"So she *told* you she quit?" Madelyn asked.

Wyatt shook his head. "Not personally, no. I believe my manager told me."

"Did it seem weird that she didn't tell you herself? Or give any notice?"

"Not really. As I said, we weren't close, and lots of people left without notice. And she hadn't been happy, so I wasn't shocked that she'd quit."

Lots of people left without notice? Madelyn made a mental note to circle back to that, but right now, she was more interested in the last thing he'd said. "Why wasn't she happy?"

Wyatt's brow creased, his expression growing uneasy. He shifted in his chair, leaning forward. "I'm sorry, I really don't understand what's going on here." He looked from her to Alex. "I thought you just wanted to get together and catch up."

"I did," Alex said, his answer coming a little too fast. "It's just that . . ." He looked at Madelyn, clearly at a loss.

"It's my fault," Madelyn jumped in, coming up with an explanation on the fly. "I got a little freaked out when I heard about Piper and the lawsuit. And I think Alex, um . . ."

"I thought it might be reassuring for her to know a little more about what happened," Alex finished. "And since I saw you worked there, I thought you might know something that could help shed some light on the whole thing."

"Ah. Sure," Wyatt said, although his expression was still skeptical. "I mean, I really don't know much. We all knew about the lawsuit, of course, but we weren't supposed to talk about it, so it's not like I had any details."

"What do you mean, you weren't supposed to talk about it?" Madelyn asked.

"It was just policy," Wyatt said. "Whenever the company got some bad press, management advised us to ignore it until it went away. No fanning the flames, you know."

Their food arrived then, and they all leaned back to allow their waitress room to set it out. Madelyn's soup was accompanied by a large slice of buttery garlic bread. She ripped off a small corner and chewed it, mulling over what Wyatt had said. How much bad press did a company need to get to warrant making an entire policy about it? And even if it *was* a reasonable policy not to engage with bad press publicly, restricting employees' private conversations felt extreme.

"So you couldn't even talk to each *other* about the lawsuit?" she blurted once the waitress left.

Wyatt raised an eyebrow, his burger halfway to his mouth. "I don't know that I'd say *couldn't*. It was just discouraged."

"Discouraged by who?"

"Leadership," he said again.

"Doug Raymond?"

"It is his company." Wyatt took a huge bite of his burger, shoving so much food in his mouth that he seemed to have trouble chewing it.

Madelyn wondered if he'd done it so that she'd stop asking him questions. If so, he'd need to try harder. "And that didn't seem strange to you?" she pushed.

Alex shot her a warning look, but she pretended she didn't see. She could tell Wyatt was getting irritated, which meant he probably wouldn't agree to meet with her again, making this her only chance to get answers. If she couldn't find out anything new from him, then she was out of ideas. And they'd never find Angie.

Wyatt frowned, dropping his half-eaten burger on his plate. "Look, was it the best place to work? No, but what place is? I may not agree with everything they did, but they paid on time and I liked most of the people I worked with, which is more than I can say for some other places I've been. I didn't talk about the lawsuit because it had nothing to do with me. And frankly, I kind of feel like this dinner doesn't either."

"Wyatt, it's not like that—" Alex started to say.

"No, it is," Wyatt cut him off, standing abruptly and tossing his napkin onto the table. His face was quickly turning a deep shade of red. "I was really excited when I got your message, you know? I don't keep in touch with a lot of people from high school. I've been looking forward to this all day." He shook his head, his lip twitching. "What a waste, huh?"

"Wyatt, I'm sorry," Madelyn said, half rising from her seat as well. "I got carried away. Please, sit back down and—"

"I don't think so," Wyatt said, narrowing his eyes at her. "I don't know what your deal is, but you're going to have to find someone else to interrogate. I'm done." He turned to Alex, who was sitting frozen at the table, his food untouched. "Have a nice life," he mumbled, his eyes dropping to the floor. He pulled his wallet out of his back pocket and pulled out a couple twenties, dropping them onto the table, then shuffled quickly toward the door without making eye contact.

Madelyn looked at Alex, stunned. "Should we go after him?"

He shook his head, slumping in his seat as the Phillies fans erupted around them, pumping their fists and smacking each other on the backs in response to whatever had happened in the game. It felt like Madelyn and Alex were in a totally different world than everyone around them. "No," Alex said, "he's right. We *were* using him for information. Which he doesn't even have. He has every right to be pissed." He let out a humorless chuckle. "Everyone made fun of him in high school. He didn't have many friends. Angie thought he was gross." He shook his head in disgust. "Turns out, *I'm* the one who's gross."

"No you're not," Madelyn insisted. She didn't think Alex could be gross if he tried.

"I used to think I was being such a good person by being nice to him when everyone else avoided him. Like I was performing community service or something."

"That's just high school," Madelyn said softly. It didn't make it okay, but she also didn't want him thinking he was worse than anyone else when it was the same stupid game that everyone played at that age.

"Yeah, but I'm still doing it." He looked at her with a grim smile. "Not really an excuse for that, is there?"

"You're trying to help Angie," she said, determined to keep him focused on their goal. "And her dad. And Piper. We both are. And we're close, I can feel it. At least three people are missing, and Doug Raymond is at the center of it, somehow. Maybe Wyatt didn't have the answers, but I'm sure if we keep looking—"

"I'm not going to keep looking," Alex said. His face seemed sunken, his eyes hollow. Like he'd aged decades since they'd first entered the restaurant. He met her eyes, his expression weary. "I think I'm done, Madelyn." There was no bitterness in his voice. Only sadness.

"No," Madelyn said again, keenly aware that she'd been repeating that word a lot tonight. "You can't be done. Angie left us that message because—"

"She left *me* that message," Alex interrupted. "Ten years ago. And I missed it. But there's nothing I can do for her now."

"But the ghost," Madelyn argued. "You *heard* it. It told you to help her."

I *told you to help her,* she added silently, but she couldn't tell him *now* that she thought she was Angie's ghost. He was already upset. Knowing that Madelyn was part of the reason for all this—or deciding she was crazy—would only make him feel worse. She'd tell him later, when it wouldn't feel like kicking him while he was down.

"Maybe it did," Alex said sadly. "But I didn't do anything about it. And now it's too late. I'm just going to have to live with that."

He pushed his untouched burger away from him, then nodded at Madelyn's half-eaten soup. "I think I need to go get some air, but you take your time. Text me when you're ready to go, okay?"

"I'm done," Madelyn said, wadding up her napkin and tossing it on the table as the baseball watchers roared their frustration at the game. She pulled out her wallet, but Alex waved her away.

"My treat."

"You didn't even eat anything."

He shrugged. "It's the least I can do for all your help."

"I *didn't* help," Madelyn said, more to herself than to him. She felt empty, like a drain had opened inside her. Was this really how it ended? No answers, no justice. Not even a decent theory about what had happened to Angie, or to Piper. All that time and effort invested, and now it was just . . . over.

After paying the bill, they drifted out of the restaurant side by side, not speaking. Madelyn felt dazed during the ride back to her house, like she wasn't fully in her body, like part of her was still sitting at that table searching for answers to questions she didn't even fully understand.

If this was it, what was the point of Angie hearing her voice all those years ago? Why were they linked? Did any of it mean anything?

And if she really was Angie's ghost, then why had she asked Alex to help her all those years ago, knowing he was doomed to fail?

CHAPTER THIRTY

Kelsey O'Donnell 9:03 AM: Hey, you there?

Kelsey O'Donnell 9:07 AM: Piper?

Kelsey O'Donnell 9:48 AM: Sorry, got pulled into a meeting. Brendan tells me you're out sick. Do you need anything? Meds, OJ, soup?

Kelsey O'Donnell 9:57 AM: You're making me nervous. I've texted you like ten times this morning.

Kelsey O'Donnell 10:34 AM: Okay if I still haven't heard from you by lunchtime, I'm coming over to your house. Please let me know you're okay.

Kelsey O'Donnell 11:22 AM: I'm leaving for lunch in about ten minutes, and I'm driving straight to your house. You'd better answer your door.

Kelsey O'Donnell 12:06 PM: WHERE ARE YOU??? You didn't answer your door. There's no way you could have slept through how loud I was knocking. It's been hours. PLEASE RESPOND.

Kelsey O'Donnell 2:25 PM: Now Susan is telling me you actually QUIT? WTF????

Kelsey O'Donnell 2:26 PM: Well if you quit (seems sus but) I guess it's pointless to keep slacking you. But if you can see this, PICK UP YOUR DAMN PHONE.

—Slack exchange between Kelsey O'Donnell and Piper Carden, March 2021

"Oh no. Oh *no.*"

Madelyn stood in her front entryway, aghast. While they'd been at dinner with Wyatt, Potato had been busy. In a way, Madelyn envied the singular focus of dogs, who once locked in on a task, would stop at nothing until it was complete.

But mostly, she wanted to launch Potato into orbit. Indefinitely.

"Bad dog. *Bad* dog," Madelyn said as she waded through a sea of drywall crumbs to where Potato had burrowed a sizable hole into the wall outside the bathroom. In her nervousness over meeting Wyatt, Madelyn must have forgotten to crate her, and judging by the size of the hole, Potato had been working studiously since the moment she left.

Rather than cease her efforts, Potato doubled down, shoving her face into the fist-size hole she had created, little paws a blur of motion. The dog-deterrent spray that Madelyn had been using had clearly not had any effect. Potato's stubby brown tail pinwheeled in excitement as she strained to tunnel her fluffy body fully into the wall.

Madelyn snatched her up before she could wedge herself all the way in, holding her out in front of her with both hands like a diseased football. *"No,"* she said again, even though it was clear Potato either didn't know or didn't care what the word meant.

Taking care not to actually throw her, despite her annoyance, Madelyn deposited Potato in her crate, then returned to survey the damage. It was far from a neat hole; Potato had used every digging tool at her disposal, and the edges of the drywall were equal parts ripped and chewed. Somehow she'd also managed to spread bits of drywall all over the hall and into the living room. A few more minutes and she may have actually managed to get inside the wall, which would have been a disaster. Madelyn couldn't even begin to think of how she would've coaxed her back out.

"Wow. It's like the end of *The Shawshank Redemption* in here," Alex said from the front door.

Madelyn looked at him, both surprised and relieved that he was still here. After their disastrous dinner, he'd driven her home, but she'd honestly forgotten that he'd walked her to the door. Potato's antics had shoved every other thought from her head.

"Help," Madelyn said, gesturing at the hole in the wall. She wasn't supposed to use so much as a picture nail. Or have a dog at all. Doug Raymond would flip his shit if he saw that her dog had tried to Jules Verne her way through his house.

Alex picked his way through Potato's drywall shrapnel to join her by the hole. "It's not that bad," he said after a few seconds of examining the damage.

Madelyn puffed out an incredulous breath. "You can practically see the high school from here."

"It's an easy fix. We just need to cut a patch of the drywall so we can match the paint. Unless you have some here . . . ?"

Madelyn rolled her eyes. Doug Raymond would sooner leave her a map to Atlantis than touch-up paint. He was hardly a DIY guy.

"Okay, so tomorrow morning, I can come by and we'll grab a square of drywall—"

Madelyn made a keening noise akin to a kitten caught in a bear trap.

"We will fix it," Alex said. He looked like he was fighting a laugh, and Madelyn tried not to resent him for his amusement at her

suffering. He registered the look on her face and added, "It really isn't that complicated. And cutting the patch won't make it any harder to fix, I swear."

Madelyn didn't really buy it, but considering her only other options were to either vanish in the middle of the night like Angie or fess up to Doug Raymond, she decided to put her faith in Alex's home-repair skills. "All right," she agreed, feeling deflated. Literally nothing about this day was going according to plan. Not the meeting with Wyatt, not her house, not her whatever-it-was with Alex.

At least they worked together. Which meant he probably wouldn't ghost her when he inevitably decided that she was more trouble than she was worth.

Which would hopefully be after this weekend, since she didn't have the faintest clue how to patch drywall. She supposed she could watch a YouTube tutorial, but that hadn't helped her much last time.

"Hey," she said, as Alex turned to the door. Eager, she was sure, to get as far away from her and her stupid baggage as possible. "I'm sorry about Wyatt."

He shrugged, giving her a small smile. "Truth?"

How was she supposed to respond to that? Did people ever actually opt *out* of the truth? "Sure."

"I appreciated that you pushed so hard. I wouldn't have."

"Because you're capable of reading social cues."

"No, because I would've chickened out." He sighed, crossing his arms as he leaned against the doorframe. Madelyn found herself staring at the vein tracing its way up his biceps, vanishing under his sleeve, and had to tear her eyes away.

It would make this all a lot easier if he weren't so damn *pretty*.

"I didn't have a lot of friends in high school," Alex said.

"Really?" The question came out like an accusation, but Madelyn was genuinely stunned. He was smart, kind, and *deeply* hot. Also bilingual. How was he not swarmed by admirers as a teenager?

If he noticed her incredulity, he was polite enough to ignore it. "After Angie disappeared, I didn't have any energy for . . . well, anything, honestly."

"I'm sure people understood."

"*No one* understood," Alex said with a dry laugh. "I mean, you've met teenagers, right? There's no grace period. I pulled away, and no one chased after me."

Nitwits, Madelyn thought.

"So when Wyatt agreed to meet tonight . . . I don't know. I guess I felt kind of . . . validated?"

Madelyn would happily validate him all night long and straight on through the next day, but she wisely refrained from telling him that. Instead, she said, "That makes sense."

"Anyway, I don't think I would've pushed for answers the way you did. And I appreciate that." His dark eyes bored into hers, and she had to fight to catch her breath. But she couldn't forget that the night had been a dead end.

"I just wish we'd actually gotten some answers," Madelyn said forlornly. "But it's dead ends all around. An oubliette of questions."

Alex laughed. "I love the way you phrase things."

Madelyn gave him a tight-lipped smile. "I'm a regular hoot."

"You remind me of Angie," he said, almost absently. Then the weight of what he'd said settled around them, dropping a wet blanket over the crackling static in the air.

"Well," Madelyn said after a long pause, "I'm sorry I'm not her."

It was the wrong thing to say. She knew it the second the words left her lips. But once it was out there, she couldn't take it back, so it hung there between them like a poisoned cloud.

She was not expecting Alex to step toward her. So close she could count the individual hairs attempting to push through the smooth skin on his chin, freshly shaved earlier today but flirting with shadows tonight. So close she could smell the few sips of beer on his breath, note the shades of pink in his tongue when he licked his lips.

Oh God. Had she not screwed things up between them? Was this thing still . . . a *thing*? She desperately hoped it was.

"I'm glad you're you," he said. His voice was heavy, his eyes bottomless pools of smoky brown quartz. His eyes locked on hers, stealing the breath from her lungs.

Her heart was so loud it could be heard from space.

"Me too," she said faintly, and she didn't even have time to think about what a silly response that was before his lips were on hers, his hand cupping the back of her neck, then sliding up to bury his fingers in her hair.

Her body was electric, every inch of her skin charged with pulsing heat. Her hands came up to grip his arms—*God*, those were good arms, firm and lean with the perfect smattering of soft dark hair—then slide around his back, pulling him close. She opened her mouth to his, and his hands traveled down her back, leaving burning trails of fire along her skin. She pressed into him, seized with the desire to be closer, closer, *closer*. Every atom of space between them was a chasm, too far to bear, and she did her best to eliminate every one.

They moved across the living room, collapsing onto the couch, a cheap hand-me-down that Syzygy had bought for a hundred bucks off Facebook Marketplace and that Madelyn had taken with her when she moved out, because even a good teacher's salary wasn't enough to buy new furniture. The understuffed cushions immediately surrendered and stiff springs dug into her back, but Madelyn did not care because all her senses were attuned to Alex, who was lying on top of her, kissing her like she was the last breath of air in an infinite sea.

"Okay?" he breathed against her lips as his hand slid up her leg, fingers toying with the hem of her dress. With the warm weather lately, she'd been favoring stretchy jersey dresses and lightweight jackets, since that was easy to throw on in the mornings and looked professional while still feeling comfortable. A wardrobe choice she was extremely grateful for now.

"Mm-hmm," she managed to vocalize, then gasped as his hand traveled higher, his touch against her bare skin igniting a flame that started low in her belly and then radiated out, sending shivers down her legs, into her toes.

His shirt was loose at his waist; she slipped her hands underneath, running her fingers along the firm muscles of his stomach, relishing his soft gasp against her mouth.

Everything about him felt amazing, from the warmth of his skin to the slow questing of his lips to the gentle way his hands explored her body. It had never been like this with Ralph. With him, everything was a performance, like she was constantly auditioning for his approval, waiting with bated breath to see if she'd passed whatever test he'd set for her. Not like this, where she could abandon thought, chasing sensations wherever they led.

At some point, his shirt fell to the floor, and the lights were turned off, although she couldn't recall which one of them had done what. The hem of her dress had worked its way up to her waist, and she hooked one leg around his, wishing she could hold him there, fitting against her, forever.

Against her back, something buzzed. And then buzzed again. And again.

"Sorry," she said, digging her phone out from between the couch cushions.

Alex laughed, his breath a warm puff on her neck. "All good," he said, pressing a kiss into her collarbone.

She blinked at the screen, willing it into focus. It was her dad, FaceTiming. No thanks.

She tapped to decline the call as Alex gently tugged the strap of her dress off her shoulder, continuing to work his way down her body.

A shiver went through her.

"Hello?" Her dad's voice. "Madelyn? Are you there? Why is it so dark?"

Shit.

CHAPTER THIRTY-ONE

FROM: sebastianag@gmail.com
TO: angiemae@gmail.com
SUBJECT: Big day

Dear Angie,

Hey. It's been a while. But of course you know that.

I graduated from college today, and you weren't there. I knew you wouldn't be, but I still found myself looking for you. Will I ever stop doing that? It's been nearly six years, and I'm still scanning crowds for your face. Do you do that too? Or have you moved on?

That's a dumb question. You've had plenty of time to come back if you wanted to. And you're an adult now. You're free to make your own decisions. Obviously you don't want to come back here.

I should stop looking. That would be the healthy thing to do. It's probably what you'd tell me to do.

But I can't help it. I still miss you. Every day. And I'll keep looking, even though I know you're gone.

Love,
Bas

"I'm going to go," Alex whispered from across the now well-lit room, pulling his shirt and shoes back on as Madelyn tried to talk her dad through navigating his password manager. Fortunately, she'd accidentally answered the phone with the camera facing the ceiling, so he hadn't seen anything that would require Madelyn to fake her own death.

Turned out her dad needed help getting back into his Netflix account on his TV after accidentally logging out. "Hi, honey! I'm here too!" her mom chirped, appearing behind her dad's shoulder. "You look a little flushed. Are you feeling okay?"

"I'm fine, Mom," Madelyn said, hoping her mom didn't follow up with a question about why her hair was so disheveled. It was bad enough that they'd been interrupted by her parents; the last thing she needed was her mom interrogating her about it within earshot of Alex. She walked into the kitchen, careful to keep the camera facing away from him.

She tried not to let her disappointment show on her face. A few minutes ago, she'd been wrapped around Alex like a burrito. Now she was hunched over her phone trying to figure out why her dad had twelve different passwords saved for Netflix.

See you tomorrow, Alex mouthed as he reached the door.

She cast him a regretful look, wishing she could apologize for messing up their night, but he smiled and shook his head. He didn't say anything, but she understood: *We're good.* As he quietly slipped outside, pulling the door shut behind him, he blew her a tiny kiss, sending all the blood in her body straight to her face.

"That one didn't work either, Peanut," her dad's voice announced, his face filling the entire screen.

"Okay, try the next one," she said absently, watching Alex's headlights sweep across the front of her house as he pulled out of her driveway.

"I can't remember which one I was on," her dad admitted.

Her mom popped back up behind him. "Your face is still so red! How much water have you had today?"

After she got off the phone—she had to unearth her digital thermometer to prove she wasn't feverish before her mom would hang up—and let Potato out of her crate, Madelyn felt restless. She wasn't sure what to do with herself. Well, she knew what she *wanted* to do, but Alex was long gone, and no matter how much she wished she were the type of girl who had enough confidence to ask him to come back, she wasn't.

Instead, she poured herself a glass of wine and played her Switch for a while, passively killing monsters and completing side quests, but gave up after an hour, when she realized she wasn't any calmer than she had been when she started.

Frustrated, she refilled her glass and opened her laptop. If she wasn't going to have sex tonight, she might as well get a head start on work for next week.

She opened her email before she logged into her school portal, mostly out of habit. It was all junk—marketing newsletters that she should really just unsubscribe from. She went down the list, checking them all to mass delete.

Her mouse hovered over the last one. The genetic testing company where she'd found Piper was running a half-off sale.

She didn't care about the sale, but found herself clicking through to the site, logging in to see her messages. She scrolled through her correspondence with Piper, sadness swelling in her chest. She wished they'd had more time. That they'd met earlier. Or at all. They'd never even seen each other in person. Only as pictures on a screen.

She paused at one of Piper's last messages. She'd forgotten about this one.

It was just a photo. A selfie of Piper flashing a peace sign in front of a chain-link fence. The subject read simply Work. She remembered it seeming a little odd at the time. Piper never sent photos without a message.

But now she saw that underneath the photo were numbers. She'd ignored them before, assuming they were just some strange artifact that the email server had tagged onto the photo.

40.15029183486955, -75.67273623931226

Coordinates? she now wondered. She typed them into her search engine. Sure enough, it was a spot on the northeast edge of East Henderson, up toward Pottstown.

Why had Piper sent this to her? What would she find there?

She had no idea. But she knew she had to check it out.

She texted Alex. I may have found something. Piper sent me a location. No idea what's there.

His response came almost immediately. When do you want to go?

Tomorrow? After drywall?

I'm in.

The next morning came too early and too bright. She wasn't hungover, exactly, but her body was keenly aware of exactly how much wine she'd consumed before face-planting into bed the night before. Alex wasn't due to come pick her up until ten—he wanted to swing by the hardware store on their way to check out the mysterious coordinates—so she took her time getting ready, chugging two full glasses of water before making her coffee, then optimistically changing the sheets on her bed.

You jinxed it, Syzygy texted as Madelyn rummaged through the half-unpacked boxes still jammed into various corners of her house, looking for her candles. She could've sworn she still had some that smelled like jasmine and vanilla, which Ralph hated and therefore made them her favorites. All this prep means you are definitely not getting within ten feet of that bed.

Whatever happened to being sure he was into me???

He IS into you. I'm just saying, the universe is not fond of careful planning. It's going to mess with you, whether or not either of you wants it to. Those are the rules.

Your patients are going to love you.

Damn right they are.

I was kidding, you jerk.

I wasn't, you horny strumpet. Godspeed.

She found the candles in a box in her office labeled Misc. Crap, which made her want to punch her past self in the face. Would it have killed her to actually organize and label her stuff *before* she moved?

She grabbed a Sharpie as a favor to her future self, and was halfway through listing the contents of a box labeled simply Stuff, when a noise caught her attention. It sounded like it was coming from the closet, a faint rustling sound.

Oh God. Did she have *mice*? That was the last thing she needed right now.

Grabbing a pair of scissors out of her desk drawer—unlikely to be much use against a mouse, but she felt like she needed something in her hand—she edged toward the closet, scanning the floor for any hint of movement. Nothing caught her eye, but shuffling noises continued to come from the closet. She had nearly reached the door when something heavy clattered to the floor, with a sound like an explosion. A surprised screech ripped from her lips, and she jumped back, horrified at what she might find inside.

"Madelyn?"

The voice was muffled, and it took her a second to realize it was coming from outside. Gradually, her pounding heartbeat softened enough for her to become aware of the sound of someone knocking on the front door. How long had *that* been going on?

"Madelyn, are you okay?"

She looked at her phone and saw she'd missed half a dozen texts from Alex. Somehow she'd gone from having plenty of time to losing track of time entirely. "Coming!" she called, hurrying out of her office and through the living room. "Can you please come look in my office closet?" she asked the second she opened the door.

Alex blinked at her, his hand still raised to knock. "Um, okay?"

"There's a mouse or something in there. I think it knocked down my shelves."

"A *mouse* knocked down your shelves?"

"Or a possum. Or a freaking capybara or something. I don't know. It sounds huge, whatever it is." In the back of her head, Madelyn was aware that she'd intended to act cool when he showed up, but that was off the table now. All that mattered was that he rapidly exit whatever beast had invaded her closet.

"Capybaras are native to South America," Alex said conversationally as he moved past her into the house.

Madelyn stared at him like he'd sprouted a third eye. "Well, this one is native to my closet."

"I just meant that it's probably not a capybara."

Was he being cute? She couldn't tell. She'd lost her entire capacity for flirting. "Please, can you go check?" was all she could think to say. Her voice came out like she was five years old. Later, she knew, she'd be mortified that she'd shriveled like a raisin in the face of a rodent in her closet, but right now she didn't care.

She realized she was still clutching the scissors, and tried to hand them to him, but he waved them away, opting for an empty box and a broom instead. "It's probably more afraid of us than we are of it," he said as he squared off against the closet door.

"Oh good, so it's a *traumatized* possum."

He glanced back at her, one eyebrow raised. "There really is no defusing this, huh?"

She nodded at the box in his hand. "Let's get rid of the intruder and then I'll let you know if I'm defused."

Planting his feet, Alex wiggled his fingers like he was getting ready to play flag football with Madelyn's uninvited guest rather than trap it in a box. Then he lunged for the door and yanked it open, squaring his shoulders dramatically with the doorway and bellowing, "SHOW YOURSELF, VARMINT!"

Madelyn couldn't help herself. As freaked out as she was, she burst out laughing. *Varmint?* She wasn't sure she'd ever heard anyone utter that word outside of *Looney Tunes*.

Shoulders shaking as she covered her mouth with her hands, she peered around his body, both dreading and anxious to see the damage to the closet and the culprit apprehended.

Her laughter faded as soon as she got a clear view.

It looked . . . fine.

Everything was neat and put away, exactly as she'd left it. No sign of her craft supplies crashing to the floor, despite the calamitous banging she'd heard. No indication that anything had disturbed the contents at all. And definitely no possum, capybara, or anything else.

Alex turned to her, his expression bemused. "Maybe it got out?"

"No, this can't be right," Madelyn said, pushing past him to examine the shelves for herself. All her stuff was fine: her sewing machine, her baskets of ribbon and washi tape, her stacks of paper, her plastic bins of thread and fabric. Nothing had so much as budged from when she'd first organized it after moving in. "But I *heard* it," she muttered, more to herself than to Alex.

"Déjà vu," he said softly. Madelyn looked at him, and found him studying her with a strained expression. "You sounded like Angie. This was her room, you know."

Angie. That must be it. She hadn't heard something in her closet right now. She'd heard Angie rummaging through *her* closet, ten years ago.

"Maybe it's the ghost," Alex said with a tight smile. He had no idea how close he was to the truth.

Madelyn forced a laugh. "Yeah, maybe." She still didn't know how to tell him. It seemed more impossible with every passing day. Especially after last night, when they'd almost . . .

What would he do when he finally learned the truth? Would he be angry? Hurt? Betrayed?

Even if he didn't think she was crazy, she'd lose him. She knew it in her gut. He'd hate her for keeping it from him, and he'd have every right.

Still, she had to tell him. The secret was eating away at her. She couldn't hold it in any longer. She just needed to find the right time. It wasn't now; not when they had an actual clue to follow, and he wanted answers just as much as she did. She didn't want to make it awkward for him or, worse, make him want to give up entirely.

Later, once they'd found some answers—or hit another dead end—she would tell him. No matter how much she dreaded his response.

"It was probably something outside and I thought it was in here," Madelyn said, waving a hand toward the window. "Sorry about that."

"No problem," Alex said, although his shoulders still seemed tense. Madelyn kicked herself for being such a wimp and not just dealing with it herself before he got here. Now he was stuck reliving painful memories, and it was her fault.

"Are you ready to go?" she asked brightly, stretching a smile across her face. She wanted to get back to where they were before she'd reminded him of how much their whole relationship was tied up in his missing best friend. Even though their plans for today centered around another missing woman who may have been targeted by the same man, it still felt a little more comfortable than trying to investigate Angie directly.

"Yeah," Alex said, replacing the scissors on her desk and dropping the box on the floor. "Yeah, let's get out of here."

After cutting the square of drywall for the paint match, Madelyn followed Alex to his car, pretending she didn't notice how eager he was to leave.

CHAPTER THIRTY-TWO

FROM: dougraymond@raymondrealty.com
TO: vpcontact@lmp.org
SUBJECT: Re: Issue

The thorn in our paw has been removed. I'll tell my people she quit. Shouldn't be a problem. Sorry for the inconvenience.

Regards,
Doug Raymond
CEO Raymond Realty Group

After stopping by the hardware store for paint and drywall supplies, they followed directions on Alex's phone to the location from Piper's email. The map took them down winding back roads to the north side of East Henderson, past the pristine new Darley Estates development with its giant blue Raymond Realty signs, until they eventually turned down a gravel road leading to a sprawling commercial construction site, surrounded by an industrial chain-link fence.

They drove a slow lap around the property, searching for an entrance, but all the gates were closed, and no one appeared to be on the site. After circling the entire thing once, Alex parked the car near what seemed to be the main gate, and they both got out to peer through the fence.

A large sign on the fence announced the North Ridge Business Park, "coming soon" from Raymond Realty Group. It was weathered and faded, forgotten and discarded by time.

"This is so weird," Alex said, pacing back and forth in front of the fence and rising up on his toes to see into the site. "Some of the work in here looks recent. Like that foundation over there looks like it was just poured." He pointed across the lot. "But at the same time, this site looks abandoned." He walked over to the sign and peered at the papers posted in clear plastic sleeves. "These permits are current, but this place looks like a ghost town."

He shook his head, looking perplexed, then pulled out his phone. "Hold on a sec, I think I might . . ." He trailed off, frowning as he poked at his phone for a few seconds. "Never mind. No signal."

Without the ability to get through the gate, there wasn't much to do. After a few minutes of peering through the fence, they climbed back in the car. They tossed theories about the stalled construction back and forth throughout the drive back to Madelyn's. Maybe it was a historic site. Maybe Raymond Realty had hit some sort of environmental restriction. Maybe the zoning had changed.

Nothing felt right, though. And none of them explained why Piper would have sent that location to Madelyn. Or what might have happened to Piper afterward.

When Alex pulled to a stop in front of Madelyn's house, he held out an arm before she could get out of the car. "Hold on. Let me check something . . ." He fiddled with his phone, then smiled triumphantly. "Awesome, he *is* still running that company."

"What company?"

"The one who pulled the permits. It's Angie's dad's old company."

"You mean *Raymond's* company," Madelyn corrected. She remembered the article she'd read in the library that mentioned Raymond Realty acquiring Cameron Stewart's company.

"It was, but not anymore. Raymond Realty only ran their own crews for a couple years, then sold them all off. Cheaper for them to pay contractors rather than employees. The guy who bought this company was one of Angie's dad's workers. He stayed on through the acquisition, and then took over after Raymond off-loaded it. I worked for him for a while in college. I've still got his number."

He tapped the contact, then put his phone on speaker, balancing it on the dashboard between them.

Madelyn hovered close to him to hear. He shifted his weight so that his arm brushed hers, sending a shiver through her skin. She wondered if he felt it too, this hyperawareness of where her body was in relation to his, like they each were pulled by the other's gravity.

"This is Laird," a gruff voice said over the speaker.

"Laird, hi, this is Alex García."

"Alex! Good to hear from you, dude." Laird's voice instantly shifted from businesslike to casual, although the roughness remained. "How've you been?"

"Good, thanks. Hey listen, I had a question I hoped you might be able to help me with."

"Shoot."

"I was up north of town and passed some signs for a project of yours, but it looks like—"

"The Raymond property?"

"That's the one."

Laird's sigh was clear through the phone. "That project was a real kick in the balls."

"'Was'? So you're not still working on it?"

"Yes and no. Ground to a halt during the pandemic. Which wasn't unusual; plenty of jobs went tits up in 2020. Lots of companies couldn't make their projections and went under. We only barely made it out."

"So they ran out of money?"

Laird laughed, but it didn't sound like he was amused. More annoyed. "If they ever had any to begin with. Getting paid on that job was like trying to redeem a coupon at a meth lab. Even with work drying up left and right, I was relieved when they pulled the plug on that one."

"Wow," Alex said, exchanging a look with Madelyn. "I always thought Raymond Realty was rolling in money."

"They sure want folks to think that, don't they?" He paused, and Madelyn could practically hear him shrug. "I dunno, man. It isn't like their checks bounce or anything. Just always have to chase them around the playground a few times before they'll hand them over. They probably pay their assistants more to give us the runaround than they pay us."

"Why?" Madelyn said.

"Who's that?" The gruffness was suddenly back.

"Sorry, Laird, that's my friend Madelyn. She's here with me. We're trying to figure out what's going on with that property."

"Why do you care?" Laird's tone had shifted from friendly to suspicious.

"He's my landlord," Madelyn said. She glanced at Alex, not sure where to go from there, then decided to go for broke. "And I don't like him and want to know what he's doing with my money."

Laird barked out a laugh. "She's not from around here, I take it?"

"Moved here last month," Madelyn said.

"Yeah, Alex will tell you, folks from East Henderson don't offer up those sorts of opinions about Doug Raymond. At least not without using a lot more words to beat around the bush."

Madelyn looked at Alex, who nodded. "As I said, small town," he said quietly. "Word has a way of getting back to people."

"And some people have their ways of getting back at the ones sayin' the words, if you know what I mean," Laird added.

"I'm not going to say anything," Madelyn promised. With everything she was learning about Doug Raymond, she would prefer to never interact with him again.

"I can vouch for her," Alex added.

"As long as you're sure," Laird said. "I've got a business to run here, you know."

"I know." Alex's shoulders relaxed, and he cast Madelyn a pleading look, as if to ask her not to throw any more wrenches into the call. "So getting back to Madelyn's question—"

"Why be such a turd about paying? Alex, my man, I know you're an innocent kid, but even you've gotta know that some people shit just because they like the smell."

"I . . . am gonna need a little more than that, Laird."

"He got off on it. He messed with us 'cause he could. He knew we'd put up with his bullshit because we needed the money, and he liked seeing us have to chase after it like donkeys with a carrot."

"So you don't think he was covering something up?" Madelyn asked. Alex looked at her, and she wondered if he could hear the disappointment in her voice. Even though she knew it would almost certainly not be that easy, a part of her had hoped that Laird held the key to a vast conspiracy, one that went back at least ten years and tied directly to Angie.

Instead, she'd found a mean little boy with a magnifying glass, burning ants because they couldn't fight back.

"Covering something up?" Laird repeated, sounding surprised. "No, nothing like that. Like I said, the checks always cleared. And you hardly cover something up by pointing at it. Best way to keep people in the dark is by never giving them a reason to open their eyes." He chuckled. "I mean, the guy's a shitheel, don't get me wrong. But he's not Walter White. The only master plan he's got ends in *-bate*."

Madelyn felt herself deflate, even as Alex snorted beside her. So that was it, then. Another dead end.

"Well, thanks, Laird," Alex said when Madelyn didn't respond. "Sorry to have bothered you."

"Nah, it's okay. Always good to hear from you. Let's grab a bite soon, so long as you promise not to get more mud on my table. Talk to you la—"

"Wait a second," Alex interrupted, straightening his shoulders. "I want to make sure I'm clear on this. So you stopped working on this project in 2020?"

"2020 isn't really a year one forgets, Alex."

"All work? You didn't keep any part of the contract open? Or start a new one?"

"We closed out the tab."

"So you *didn't* renew the permit on this job two years ago?" Alex asked, his voice raising in pitch. "Because the permit posted up there has your name on it."

"Oh, that," Laird said, sounding unconcerned. "That's nothing."

"Nothing?"

"Yeah, Raymond called me up a little while after we closed out the project and asked if I could renew the permit. Said it was for tax reasons. Told me he'd pay me a couple hundred bucks to say it was still going. I said I wasn't going to say it was going if it wasn't. We went back and forth a bit, and settled on I'd get the permit if he'd commit to a full day of work on the property once every three months." He laughed. "Must've been some tax break. But hey, it gave my guys one more paid day off once a quarter."

"So the job *has* been going on?"

"Oh, no. One day a quarter, my crew gets the day off, and I head up there to catch up on paperwork. He hired my company to work on his property. So I work. For my company. On his property."

Madelyn grinned. That was the first glimmer of justice they'd heard in this whole story.

"Then who just poured a foundation out there?"

"Poured it when? This year?"

"This *week*, probably."

"Wasn't us," Laird said firmly. "I'm never lifting so much as a splinter out of my little finger for that man again. He must have found some fresh meat."

"Is there a way we could figure out who it is?"

"You could call over to accounting at Raymond, see who's getting the checks. If it's someone I know, I may get in touch with them. See if there's a gentle way to tell them they've got a 'kick me' sign on their back."

"Will do."

"I wish I could give you a good contact over there, but the guy I deal with now is dull as cow's teeth. They used to have a great girl handling the account, real funny, sharp as a knife in cheese. I think she moved on, which is a shame. Mostly for me. Can't recall her name now . . ."

"Piper?" Madelyn guessed, her throat thick.

"Yes!" Laird sounded delighted. "That's it. Piper. Did you know her too?"

"I did," Madelyn said. Her brain buzzed like it was filled with bees. This had to be it. Piper's last project. This strange, stagnant business park that had been shut down since 2020, yet was still inexplicably on the books.

What were they doing in there? What had Piper found that they needed to cover up?

"Thanks, Laird," Alex said with a concerned glance at Madelyn. "You've really helped us out."

"Any time, Alex. You take care now."

After ending the call, he turned to her. "Well? What do you think?"

Madelyn didn't know what to think. This felt like a major piece of the puzzle, but she still had no idea where to place it. Why would Raymond have poured so much money into a dead site? What was he hiding? What had Piper found? And what did Angie and her father have to do with any of it?

Madelyn recalled something Kelsey had said, about unfamiliar people coming into the office for top-level meetings. At the time, she'd chalked it up to the generally frigid atmosphere toward her: just one more thing no one bothered to tell her about. But what if it was something more than that? What if those meetings were about covering something up? Something that had to do with this site, which Piper knew about and Raymond needed to keep quiet?

But what could it have been? Madelyn racked her brain, but couldn't come up with any decent theories.

"I think . . . ," she said slowly, then sighed. "Honestly, I have no idea. But whatever happened, it all keeps coming back to Doug freaking Raymond."

CHAPTER THIRTY-THREE

FROM: vpcontact@lmp.org
TO: dougraymond@raymondrealty.org
SUBJECT: Re: re: Issue

Keep your people in line, Doug. We can't keep cleaning up your messes.

"It's *got* to be connected," Madelyn said as she unlocked her front door. She was talking in circles, she knew, but she reasoned best out loud. Not that it was helping her make sense of any of the pieces they'd found.

First Angie and her father disappearing ten years ago, owing money to Doug Raymond.

Angie leaving her bag with Alex before she vanished, with a message that Doug Raymond was behind it.

Piper disappearing seven years later, while working on a project for Doug Raymond.

The abandoned North Ridge construction site, kept active by Doug Raymond.

Kelsey being silenced. By Doug Raymond.

The only thing they all had in common was Doug Raymond. But what did that mean? What reason could he possibly have had to go after a teenage girl and her father? They couldn't have been the only ones who owed him money. There had to be more to it. Something was still missing.

"I keep coming back to the recording," Alex said. Far from being irritated at Madelyn's need to keep walking back and forth over the same well-trodden path, he had fallen into step right beside her. "She said, 'If anything happens to *me*.' Not her dad. Not *us*. Her. If it really was about money, wouldn't her dad have been the target?"

"That's a good point."

Alex followed her inside, the plastic bag of supplies from the hardware store dangling from one hand and his toolbox in the other. Madelyn had her own basic tool set, but didn't have anything specifically for drywall. He set it all on the kitchen table as Madelyn rescued Potato from her crate and attached her leash.

"Plus," Alex said, trailing after Madelyn as she carried Potato back outside, "she *knew* she was in trouble. That's why she left that recording for me."

"Maybe Raymond threatened her?"

Potato finished doing her business and circled around to sniff her creation, which was Madelyn's cue to scoop her up and bring her back inside. She placed her on the floor, then walked into the kitchen, opening the fridge. "Water? Soda?" Her eyes fell on the half-full box of Cabernet on the counter, left over from her poor choices earlier in the week. "Wine?"

Alex sank onto the couch and checked his watch. "What time is it, noon?"

"It's Saturday. Land of eternal five p.m. Also we're hard-boiled detectives now, so we probably should've been sipping from flasks this whole time."

"You've convinced me. Wine it is."

Madelyn poured what she deemed an appropriate afternoon-size portion of Cabernet into two stemless wineglasses and brought them over to the couch, where Potato had made herself comfortable on a pillow beside Alex and was now industriously licking his arm.

"You've made a friend," Madelyn observed as she sat beside him. Potato glanced briefly at her, then resumed her licking.

"I'm probably salty. I was not expecting it to be this hot." He pulled at the front of his T-shirt, wafting air-conditioning onto his chest.

Madelyn got hit with a wave of his scent, spicy pine mixed with salt and sweat. She felt suddenly intoxicated in a way that had nothing to do with the midday wine. A little burst of heat rippled through her, raising gooseflesh on her arms.

She cleared her throat, willing her body to calm down, and took a long sip of her wine. "Climate change is mad at us."

"Can you blame it?"

"Nope."

Alex shifted, picking up Potato and moving her onto the floor. "Okay, little one, that's enough for now, I think." Potato yipped in halfhearted protest, then wandered over to her toy box and selected a stuffed squeaky toy that looked like a radish. She shook it violently, its floppy green leaves slapping the sides of her head, then lay down to gnaw on her plush kill.

He picked up his wine and settled back into the couch, except now their arms were touching when they definitely weren't before. He'd somehow managed to move closer to her without making it look like that's what he was doing. Sneaky.

Madelyn's heart fluttered. They hadn't yet talked about what had happened between them last night, but it hadn't left her thoughts. Every time she looked at him, her brain immediately zapped back to this couch, his weight on top of her, his taste in her mouth.

Was his mind still there too? What did he think about it? Did he want to pick up where they left off, or pretend it never happened?

His knee brushed hers. She was wearing another sundress—no cardigan this time, since the temperature was on track to top eighty degrees today—and she had to swallow her shiver at the feel of his skin against her bare leg.

"Madelyn." His voice was low, and when she looked at him, he was turning his wineglass in his hands, staring at it like he hoped it might tell him his future. "I want you to know that I really appreciate your help. I've never really been able to talk with anyone about . . . about what happened. I don't know that I can ever express to you how much it means to me."

Oh no. Oh *no*. This was the type of statement that always ended in a *but. I appreciate your help, but I think I need to take some time for myself. I like talking to you, but I think we're better as friends.*

She braced herself for the crushing disappointment. "It's fine," she said, her voice coming out a little brighter than she'd prefer. "I mean, it's really not a big deal. I was already invested because of Piper. And you've helped *me* so much, showing me around school, fixing my sink. So it's kind of quid pro quo, honestly." She was speaking rapidly, trying too hard to sound okay in a way that only made it more obvious that she wasn't.

She also wasn't looking at him, staring instead at Potato as she determinedly squeaked her radish. So she wasn't prepared when he reached out and took her hand. Her breath caught in her throat.

"Wait, hold on," he said, chuckling under his breath. "Will you please let me finish?" His thumb rubbed slowly back and forth across her knuckles, leaving trails of fire in its wake. "What I was *trying* to say was that I appreciate your help with all this . . . but I hope you know that's not the only reason I like you."

"You . . . what? You like me?"

"Come on," he muttered, a blush rising to his cheeks. "You couldn't figure that out after last night?"

Madelyn shrugged, starting to feel silly. "I don't know, it was impulsive, you could've been being polite—"

"Polite?" Alex set his wineglass on the coffee table, then turned to face her, keeping his other hand tight on hers. "Madelyn, polite is shaking hands, or telling an old lady you like her hat. It is *not* getting half-naked in your living room and sticking my tongue down your throat."

Heat flooded Madelyn's face. Good God, the way her temperature shot up twenty degrees in an instant. Even though she had the memory of Alex actually *doing* those things, it was another experience entirely to listen to him describe it. She shifted on the couch, antsy, like her skin was sending off sparks. "Oh," was all she managed to say, her voice sounding a little hoarse.

He slid closer, heat radiating off him. Or maybe that was her; she couldn't tell anymore. She breathed him in, drunk on his scent, his skin, his closeness.

"I wasn't just being polite," he said softly, his free hand coming up to brush her hair off her neck, then to stroke the skin it bared. "Actually, if you'll recall, I was kind of rude." His breath was downy feathers against her skin.

"I do not recall."

His fingers lightly traced the line of her jaw. Her eyelids fluttered, threatening to close.

"I didn't ask if I could kiss you," he said. "I'm sorry. I should have."

"I didn't ask you either. In the parking lot. So I think we're even." She felt floaty, like gravity was swirling all around the room. It was almost a tipsy feeling, but her wineglass was still mostly full. Could you get drunk on a person?

Alex's other hand was now drifting slowly up her arm. "Even so, I still should have asked," he said. "Next time, I will."

She paused her blissful floating, holding his gaze. "*Next* time," she said, trying to be clear so he'd get her meaning, "the answer will be yes."

He grinned, his dark eyes falling to her lips. "Madelyn, may I ask you a question?"

"Yes."

She couldn't wait any longer. This time, she was the one to close the last of the distance between them, to pull his mouth onto hers, to slide her fingers into his hair.

He responded hungrily, pressing her back onto the couch as he kissed her. With one hand, he explored the length of her body, pausing occasionally for a soft "okay?" Always followed by her own murmured consent before he'd taken his next breath.

Madelyn felt like she was spinning, and not just from the way Alex felt on top of her, although that definitely was a factor. Ralph had never asked her if *anything* was okay. He just always assumed it was. Whether that meant plucking a book from her hands when she was reading or pushing her back on the couch when she was watching TV, it had never occurred to him that she might rather continue her own activity than engage in his.

She wasn't used to being with someone who cared what she wanted. Much less someone who made it a point to ask her.

Placing her palms on his chest, Madelyn pushed him into a sitting position, rotating her own body in tandem so that she straddled his lap. His hands slid up her arms, and he hooked his thumbs under the thin straps of her dress. "Okay?"

She nodded, and let her head fall back as he pulled the straps off her shoulders and kissed down her neck. He was working his way down her sternum when she opened her eyes—

And jumped off Alex's lap.

"Crap," Madelyn shrieked, falling onto the floor and tugging her dress straps back into place. She had totally forgotten that there was a double window above the couch, and while last night the lights had been off and it was dark outside, *now* it was the middle of a sunny Saturday afternoon. And her blinds were open.

Outside in the cul-de-sac, several of her neighbors were supervising kids, taking walks, chatting in driveways. And she was about to get naked in front of all of them.

"Are you okay?" Alex said, alarmed, before following her gaze and balking at the window. "Oh shit."

"Yeah."

"Do you think they saw anything?"

"Dear God, I hope not. I really do not want to lose my job."

He laughed. "You're not going to lose your job for making out with someone on your own couch."

"You don't know. People are weird about this stuff. *You're* fine. You're the hot Spanish teacher who has lived here forever. I'm just the new trollop."

"Hey," he said, reaching down a hand to help her up. When they were eye to eye—or eye to nose, since he was half a head taller than her—he tipped her chin up and kissed her lightly on the lips. "You are in no way a . . . did you really say *trollop*?"

"Um, I plead the fifth."

"That's not a word you hear every day."

"I had a British roommate for the past two years."

"Oh, well, that explains it."

"I'm serious, though," she said, taking a step away from him, her eyes darting to the window. "I can't do this here."

"Could you do this . . . somewhere else?" Alex said, raising an eyebrow. He took her hand, stepping back toward the hall. "Remember I've been in this house before. A bunch of times. And I'm pretty sure it has other rooms."

"Other rooms, huh?" she said, following his lead.

They rounded the corner into the hall, and he pulled her closer, his hand drifting from her hand to her waist. "I don't want to be presumptuous," he said softly, his breath tickling the side of her neck, "but they may even have furniture that's more comfortable than a couch."

"You know, I think you're right," she said, her fingers teasing their way under the hem of his shirt as they stepped into her bedroom.

He sucked in a breath through his teeth as her nails grazed lightly up his ribs. He backed her toward the bed, trailing soft kisses along her jaw.

Something small and fluffy caught her ankle, and she tumbled backward, bringing Alex down with her. They landed in a heap on the mattress as Potato bounced excitedly by the bed, eager to play the wrestling game too.

"Nope," Madelyn said, disentangling herself from Alex to scoop Potato up and deposit her in the hall. "Not puppy time," she said firmly, closing the door and exiling Potato to the other side.

She turned back to the bed, running a hand nervously through her hair and ignoring Potato's plaintive whines from the other side of the door. "Sorry about that."

Alex grinned. "I'm not. It's pretty comfy over here." He'd shifted so he was reclining against her headboard, his long legs stretched out in front of him.

"Oh yeah?"

"Yeah. You should come check it out."

She was already back by his side. She smiled as he pulled her to him. "Okay."

CHAPTER THIRTY-FOUR

I love to shoot. Love to carry. Unless I'm in my pajamas, I'm probably carrying, and even then, it's not a guarantee I'm not. But safety is incredibly important to me. Incredibly important. If you can't be responsible with a gun, you shouldn't have one, period. That's just common sense.

—Doug Raymond in *Pennsylvanian Handgunner* magazine, October 2018

The barking outside her door was what finally pulled Madelyn out of bed.

"Shut *uuuup*," she groaned, reluctantly sliding out from under Alex's arm and fumbling through the rumpled blankets in search of her dress. She found it jammed down into the crease between her mattress and footboard and tugged it on over her head.

"I didn't say anything," Alex said, giving her a playful smile. He lay stretched out on her bed, the sheets tangled across his waist, one hand behind his head on her pillow. His tousled hair now stuck up in every possible direction, making him somehow even more beautiful.

Of course she'd enjoyed the sight of him since the first time she'd spotted him in the school library, but looking at him like this, the lean muscles of his stomach and chest, the veins running down his bronze arms, took her breath away. Every inch of him was perfection. Even the parts of him that weren't perfect . . . were perfect. The twisted scar along his shin, the tan lines that sliced across his biceps, the pronounced knobbiness of his knees. She wanted to bask in him—as she had done for the better part of the past hour.

But now her dog was being a right little stinker, and had to be dealt with.

"I wasn't talking to *you*," Madelyn said, swatting Alex's foot as she slid off the bed and walked to the door.

"Bring the little Tater Tot in here," he said. "We can snuggle."

"You and Potato?"

"I'd kind of hoped you might fit in there somewhere too. Unless you're dying to go patch drywall."

"I mean," Madelyn said, opening the door to the hall, "I *was* really looking forward to—oh my *God*."

All the playfulness evaporated from her tone, replaced by horror. "Alex!" she screeched, unable to put into words the sight that had greeted her in the hall.

He was already moving toward her, scrambling off the bed and pulling on his boxer shorts in one swift motion. He came up behind her and stopped short. "Holy shit," he breathed.

He knelt down, extending a shaking hand toward Potato. "Here, girl. Can you bring that to me?"

The little dog wagged her tail, tongue lolling out of her mouth, but stayed where she was. Obviously, she didn't want to hand over her discovery. And who could blame her? She'd never get a treat like this again.

"C'mon, spud," Madelyn said, her voice trembling. She crouched beside Alex, trying to smooth her face. "Give it to me."

She deeply, *deeply* did not want to play tug with it.

Alex took a tentative step toward her, but Potato wasn't having it. She picked up her toy and scampered into the living room, settling on her pouf.

Madelyn covered her face with her hands, her breath coming in quick, short gasps. "Oh my God, she's going to drag that thing all over my house and I'm going to have to burn all my furniture."

"Just the carpet," Alex said, moving toward the kitchen with slow, deliberate steps. "What's her favorite food?"

"Um, anything I'm eating. Cheese is a safe bet. Or bacon."

"Do you have any bacon?"

"I don't know. Probably not. Bacon is expensive." She couldn't think straight, or tear her eyes from her dog. Where the *hell* had that thing come from?

"Gotcha." Alex opened the fridge and peered inside, then emerged with a stick of string cheese. He removed the wrapper and waved the cheese at Potato like a wand. "Here, sweet girl. Want a treat?"

"Don't give her the whole thing. It'll give her gas," Madelyn said automatically. As if *that* were a thing to be worrying about right now.

Alex furrowed his forehead at her, but obediently broke a smaller piece off the stick, placing the rest on the counter. "Come on, Potato. Don't you want cheese?"

Potato had been watching him carefully the whole time, and had surged to her feet when he'd opened the string cheese. Her tail wagged hopefully, her doggy mouth hanging open in an expectant grin. She took a couple of tentative steps toward Alex, but then looked at Madelyn and immediately hopped back, protecting her prize. She repeated this dance a couple more times before deciding to pick it up and carry it to Alex, although once she reached him, she was faced with a dilemma: how to get cheese without dropping her toy.

They both continued their gentle coaxing as the tiny gears in Potato's head whirred. They watched her puzzle through her situation, before she finally let her new toy fall to the floor and lunged for the cheese.

Immediately, Madelyn scooped Potato up in her arms, holding her tight as she chomped happily on her cheese, and as Alex knelt down to examine what she'd left on the floor. He didn't touch it, but instead peered at it, tilting his head from one angle to another. "I need my phone," he mumbled, then retrieved it from the coffee table and walked back toward the bedroom.

Madelyn clutched Potato to her chest, feeling frozen in place. "Where did you *get* that, sweetie?" she asked, surprised to find she was on the verge of tears.

"Madelyn, I think you need to come see this." Alex's voice sounded strained, like his windpipe had constricted to half its size.

Still carrying Potato, Madelyn rounded the corner to where Alex was shining his phone light into the hole in the drywall they'd cut out that morning, which Madelyn now saw had been widened by aggressive chewing. She crouched down and peered in, then gasped, breathing in a throat full of dust. She fell back hard on her butt, coughing violently.

She dropped Potato, but Alex grabbed her before she could scamper back into the living room to retrieve her discovery: a skeletal human hand, with two fingers still attached.

Taken, they both now realized, from the extremely dead person encased in Madelyn's wall.

PART FIVE

And if it was, I didn't mean it

CHAPTER THIRTY-FIVE

Last week, I was served with a lawsuit by my former employer, accusing me of stealing and disseminating company secrets. To say I was shocked is an understatement. To be clear, the only company secret I have discussed since I was unjustly terminated was why Raymond Realty Group is covering up the disappearance of my friend, Piper Carden. She's been missing for over two months now, not that they want you to know that. Piper, if you're out there, I'm not giving up. And to my former coworkers turned spies: I hope you take a good look. I have nothing to hide. But I think RR does.

—since-deleted Facebook post from Kelsey O'Donnell, June 2021

Alex held it together long enough to pick up the bones on the living room floor using an inside-out gallon-size ziplock bag, which he then sealed and set on the counter next to the rest of the string cheese, far out of Potato's reach.

Then he ran to the bathroom and threw up.

Madelyn sat in the hallway, stunned, her back pressed against the wall opposite the hole. No wonder Potato had been obsessed with this strip of wall since she'd moved in. She must have smelled . . .

Madelyn pulled in deep breaths through her mouth, fighting the bile rising in her stomach. More sounds of retching drifted out of the bathroom. "You okay?" she called, her voice hoarse from coughing.

She heard him spit into the toilet. "Nope. You?"

"Nope."

Potato trotted over to Madelyn inquisitively, obviously at a loss for why the humans weren't thrilled about the buried treasure she'd found. Madelyn looked around, searching for something big enough to block the opening in the wall without Potato being able to move it. She settled on a wicker basket full of throw blankets, which she dragged in front of the hole. Later, she'd have to donate the basket and all its contents to a thrift shop, because there was no way she could ever cozy up again in a quilt that had shared space with a dead body.

By the time she finished blocking the hole, Alex emerged from the bathroom, skin still tinged slightly green. "It's her," he said, sounding miserable. "Angie." His face crumpled on her name, and he took a long, shaky breath as he slumped against the wall. He looked like he might collapse.

"We don't know that," Madelyn said. She felt like her bones were made of overcooked spaghetti, but at least she didn't suspect that the bones in the wall belonged to anyone she knew. Of the two of them, Alex had the better excuse to fall apart right now. Which meant she had to hold it together.

"I should've looked for her," Alex said, eyes fixed on the basket of blankets blocking the hole. "She *trusted* me. She left me that message. And I let her down."

"It might not be her," Madelyn said firmly, taking him by the arms and positioning her face right in his line of vision, so he had to look at her. "It could be anyone."

Piper, her brain screamed, but she shoved the thought away. She could not process the possibility that the cousin she'd come to East Henderson to find had been in her wall the whole time.

"No matter who it is," Alex said, shaking his head, "Doug Raymond killed them. Which proves he's capable of murder. Angie could be in a different wall."

Please God no, Madelyn thought. One corpse in her house was plenty. If there were more, she'd have to burn the place to the ground and start over.

But her freakout could wait until later. Right now, she had a dead body to deal with and a panic attack to defuse. "Plus if it's Angie, then where is her dad?" she pointed out. "There's only one body in there." That sounded callous, but she was already running at a mental deficit. She couldn't brain enough to be gentle.

He nodded slowly, but she couldn't tell whether she was getting through to him. He stared right through her, eyes fixed on the wall. "I need to look back in there," he said finally.

"Are you sure?" She knew it was absurd, but she felt like the basket was all that was keeping something terrible from escaping into her house. She couldn't shake the mental image of a handless skeleton crawling out of the wall like a monster from a horror movie. Plus, Alex had hurled up the entire contents of his stomach the last time he'd looked in there.

"I'll be okay this time," he said, jaw set. "I need a closer look. If it's her, I think I'll know."

Madelyn wasn't so sure. The body was wrapped in a blue plastic tarp, which Potato must have upset in her eagerness to get to the bones within. The right arm and shoulder were visible—no hand, since Potato had claimed it—along with most of the head. But there was no hair, no skin, no clothing that Madelyn could see. Whoever had dumped the body there had probably removed anything identifying first.

But since she couldn't think of an even remotely sensitive way to say that to Alex, she moved aside.

He knelt by the wall and moved the basket, holding his breath. There wasn't much of a smell beyond a general mustiness, but he must not have wanted to breathe the dead-body air. Madelyn didn't blame him.

"Find anything?" she asked as he moved his phone light back and forth. It struck her that he was still in his underwear, and hers was still somewhere on her bedroom floor. How long ago had they been twisted around each other in her bed? Thirty minutes? An hour? It felt like a lifetime had passed since then.

He shook his head, then moved the basket back. Only once he was standing again did he finally take a breath. "I can't even tell if it's a man or a woman," he said, his chest heaving as his lungs caught up on oxygenating his body. "Maybe if I could see under the tarp, but I don't want to touch anything."

"Me neither," Madelyn agreed. She'd seen enough crime dramas to know you're never supposed to disturb the scene. Barring, of course, canine interference. "We should call the police."

"No!" Alex practically shouted.

Madelyn jumped, her eyes widening. She'd never heard him so much as raise his voice before.

"Sorry," he said quickly. "But even if this isn't . . . her . . ." He swallowed, Adam's apple bobbing for a second, before he could continue. "Odds are that Doug Raymond did this. This is his house."

"Isn't this the smoking gun, though?" Madelyn was confused. "As you said, this is his house. Won't he be the obvious suspect?" If the police investigated Raymond for murder, maybe they'd finally learn what happened to Piper. Maybe it would even lead them to the truth about Angie.

But Alex frowned, shaking his head. "If the system was fair, sure, but it's not. Raymond has spent a ton of money getting law enforcement on his side. I'm telling you, if we call the police now, it's more likely that *we* go to jail than him."

"Well, then, what do we do?" Madelyn was feeling frantic. She could *not* live here with a dead person in her wall. Plus wasn't it illegal to not report human remains? By not calling the police, were they committing a crime?

"I don't know, just . . . just give me a minute, okay?"

"We can't just *leave* it there."

"I know."

"And we can't move it ourselves. That's a felony."

"I *know*."

"So what—"

They were both cut off by the sound of bells chiming through the house. Someone was at the front door.

CHAPTER THIRTY-SIX

PROS: Worked with some great people. Food in the cafe was pretty decent. CONS: CEO is a petulant tyrant who demands cult-like loyalty. Needs to chill out.

—Glassdoor review from former employee of Raymond Realty Group

---

Potato made a beeline for the couch, jumping up onto the back to bark out the window as Madelyn and Alex exchanged panicked looks. For a second, they stood there, paralyzed by the knowledge that they were three feet away from a dead body, there was a human hand in a baggie on the kitchen counter, and they both looked and probably smelled like they'd just had sex.

That last part really wasn't a big deal in light of the rest, but still felt like a thing Madelyn should panic about.

The doorbell rang again, followed by a knock. "Madelyn Zhao?" an unfamiliar male voice called.

Madelyn unfroze first, darting into the kitchen to grab the hand off the counter. She threw it into the cabinet under the sink, where she kept her cleaning supplies. Whoever was at the door was unlikely to look in there. "Sorry," she whispered, hoping that the owner of the hand would understand why she was treating their detached appendage with such irreverence.

She turned to find Alex still staring at the wall, wide-eyed. "Put on your pants!" she hissed at him, grabbing a hooded sweatshirt off the back of a chair and zipping it up over her dress to hide the fact that she wasn't wearing a bra. She wasn't wearing underwear either, but she didn't plan on giving the stranger on her doorstep the opportunity to notice that.

She peeked through the peephole on the front door. She didn't recognize her visitor, who seemed to be wearing a uniform of some sort. She couldn't make out the words on his blue windbreaker, but no one wore that style of jacket without being forced.

Maybe he was a delivery guy. Maybe if she didn't answer, he'd drop whatever he had on the step and leave.

He knocked again. "Ms. Zhao, I know you're home."

Her stomach churned. He didn't *act* like a delivery guy. She felt like she was in a mobster movie, being hunted by goons.

At least the hole in the wall wasn't visible from the door. One small thing to be grateful for.

She glanced over her shoulder to be sure that Alex had moved into the bedroom to find his clothes, then opened the door.

"Madelyn Zhao?" the man asked. He was probably in his midthirties, about her height and slightly stocky, with thinning blond hair that was receding sharply at the temples. He didn't *look* like a hit man. Not that she had much of a frame of reference.

Still, she had to fight the urge to block the doorway with her body. But that would make her look suspicious, when currently, this man probably couldn't care less about her. She could now read the embroidery on his jacket: KEYSTONE COURIERS. He was just there to drop something off, that was all.

"Can I help you?" She kept her voice calm, even though her body felt electrically charged. Her heart hammered against her ribs so hard she wondered whether he could hear it.

He was sent by Raymond Realty. He had to be. Kelsey had said she might get a letter. Now here it was.

She couldn't shake the feeling that it was somehow related to the body in her wall. Even though no one could possibly know what they'd found, there was no telling her anxiety that.

"Confirming that you are Madelyn Zhao?"

"That's right." Should she have admitted that? Maybe she should've refused to answer.

He's just a courier, she reminded herself. Just because she knew there was a dead body in the house didn't mean anyone else did.

Except the person who had put it there.

"This is for you," he said, holding out an envelope with her name typed on the front. Once she'd accepted it, he pulled out a digital pad for her to sign, then gave her a perfunctory smile. "Have a nice day."

"You too," she said automatically as he turned and walked back to his car, which he'd parked on the street. She looked down at the envelope in her hand. Her name was the only thing on it.

Alex emerged from the hallway, now fully clothed, and he'd made at least a cursory attempt at smoothing his hair. "Are they gone already?"

She nodded and held up the envelope. "It was a courier."

"What's that?"

"I'm guessing it's phase one of the playbook."

She dead-bolted the door and slid her finger under the envelope flap. Inside was a single typed sheet, printed on Raymond Realty letterhead. The text was brief.

> Dear Ms. Zhao,
>
> It has come to our attention that you have been making material changes to the property you have rented, located at 906 Gazelle Ln. We remind you that your lease prohibits you from making any such alterations to the property, including but not limited to cosmetic

changes such as paint, fixtures, and flooring, as well as amending the existing structure in any way.

Additionally, we have learned that you have been making public inquiries about Raymond Realty Group which are defamatory to our company. Raymond Realty Group has long been a trusted and valued member of the East Henderson community, and we take any attempt to damage our reputation seriously.

Please cease and desist from any and all slanderous and disparaging activity regarding Raymond Realty Group immediately. Failure to comply with the terms outlined in this letter will be considered a violation of your agreement with Raymond Realty Group, resulting in its prompt termination. We also reserve the right to pursue any and all legal remedies available to us should your actions result in material damages for Raymond Realty Group.

This letter shall serve as your final notice on these matters.

Regards,
Joshua Torres
General Counsel
Raymond Realty Group

She read it through three times before looking up to find Alex looking at her. "Well?" he asked.

Madelyn shook her head, disgusted, and handed him the letter. "Just like Kelsey said. Total bullshit."

Alex scanned the page, his face darkening. "That asshole." She assumed he was talking about Doug Raymond, but then he added,

"No wonder no one wanted to keep in touch with him after high school."

"Wyatt?" she guessed.

"Has to be. You heard him last night. He really didn't think the company did anything wrong."

"You really think he would have reported that conversation to a company he doesn't even work for anymore?"

Alex shrugged. "I don't know, but that's the only way they could've found out, right?"

Madelyn ran her hands through her hair, trying to recall their conversation at the restaurant. Had they even mentioned the work they needed to do on the house in front of Wyatt? She wished she could remember. Kelsey had gotten her cease and desist letter before they'd even met with Wyatt, so maybe Madelyn's had already been in the works before their dinner. But if that was the case, why wait until today to deliver it?

This whole thing made her feel like she was losing her mind.

She took the letter back from Alex and sank onto the couch, reading it over again. The language sounded so harsh. *Defame. Slander. Disparage. Terminate.*

This was how it had started for Kelsey. She'd asked questions. And they'd taken everything.

Her hands started to shake. Alex sat beside her, taking her hands in both of his. "It'll be okay."

"I can't afford a lawsuit," she said, her voice trembling. Raymond Realty had hundreds of millions of dollars. She got excited when she could afford name-brand canned soup.

"They're not going to sue you," he said. "They only want to scare you so you'll stop looking." He nodded over at the hall, and the secret they now both knew lay hidden within the wall. "Probably so you won't find *that*."

"Except we already have." Her insides were thrumming like a freight engine. Everything felt too tight, too hot. She remembered the sweatshirt and unzipped it, peeling it off and throwing it aside as she struggled to breathe.

"I can't stay here," she said, gasping for air. It felt like the walls were closing in. Walls lined with dead bodies. "Oh God, what am I going to *do*?"

"You can stay with me," Alex said. The suggestion came so fast, he must have already been thinking about it. "I've got a pullout couch I can sleep on. You can have my room."

She looked at him, slightly bemused in the midst of her panic attack. "You . . . do remember what we were doing an hour ago, right?"

He smiled sheepishly. "I don't want you to feel pressured. Like I expect anything. This isn't moving in together. This is just giving you a place to crash because your house is . . ."

"Haunted?" Madelyn suggested when he trailed off.

Alex's eyes lit up. "Oh shit, do you think *that's* the ghost? Maybe it was here when they moved in. Maybe the body isn't related to Doug Raymond at all."

Now wasn't the time to tell him that she thought *she* was the ghost. She gave him a tight smile. "Maybe."

"Anyway," Alex continued, "you don't have to. I just wanted to offer, since I know you don't know a lot of people here yet, and—"

"I'd love to," Madelyn said hurriedly. Truthfully, she didn't want Alex to leave her sight. Not just because they'd slept together, although she'd be lying if she didn't admit the thought of staying at his house immediately sent her thoughts galloping back down that path. But she felt safer with him around. Stronger. Less alone.

Plus she couldn't afford a hotel, especially one that would allow her to keep Potato with her, and she couldn't even begin to think of how she'd explain to someone else the reason she needed a place to crash. Not that she knew anyone else in this town well enough to ask. Her only other sort-of friend was Nat, and this was a much bigger favor than borrowing a shirt.

"Are you sure?" Alex asked. "I can go pick up some food and we can talk about—"

"I'm sure," Madelyn said firmly. She didn't want to stay in her death house for a second longer than was necessary. She couldn't even imagine *eating* in here. "Let me throw some stuff in a bag, and let's get the hell out of Dodge."

CHAPTER THIRTY-SEVEN

I won't lie; it's disappointing. I thought the people of Pennsylvania were smarter than this. I thought they valued freedom more than this. Very disappointing day, to be sure.

—Doug Raymond on the results of the 2022 Pennsylvania gubernatorial election

---

"I think it used to be a closet," Alex said suddenly, breaking the comfortable silence they'd been sitting in since they'd finished making up the sofa bed and following Potato around while she explored the new space.

It had taken Madelyn only a few minutes to pack. She felt like monsters were nipping at her heels, and didn't want to stay in her house a second longer than was necessary. They'd left in such a hurry, she'd even forgotten her keys, but that wasn't such a big deal. Her parents had mailed her a hide-a-key rock the week after she'd moved in, which she'd placed in the front flower bed. At the time, she didn't think she'd ever need it. One of the many things she'd been wrong about.

Alex had talked her into stopping by Wawa for hoagies on the way over, but hers was still wrapped up in the fridge. Her appetite was nonexistent. Every time she considered eating something, all she could think of was that hand dangling from Potato's mouth.

Once they were convinced Potato wasn't going to attempt to destroy Alex's house, Madelyn had dropped onto the edge of the sofa bed, utterly exhausted. Somehow this had evolved into her napping with her head on Alex's pillow while he sat beside her, feet stretched out in front of him, one hand idly running through her hair while he scrolled his phone with the other.

Now she opened her eyes, angling her neck to look up at him. He wasn't looking at his phone anymore, and was instead squinting slightly, focusing on something only he could see.

"What?" Madelyn asked groggily. She felt like she'd been hit by a truck.

"In the hall. I think there was a linen closet there. He must have taken out the shelves and then drywalled over the whole thing."

Blearily, Madelyn pushed herself upright. She tried to figure out the relevance of what he'd said, but her brain felt like pudding. "Okay . . ."

He turned to look at her, and there was fire in his eyes. "When Angie lived there, it was a closet. Which means that whoever that body is, it was put there *after* she disappeared."

Madelyn's eyes widened. "Oh."

"Yeah," Alex said. His jaw was tense, like he was gritting his teeth. "So, not her ghost then. But maybe *her*."

"Maybe not," Madelyn reminded him. "It could be—" *Piper,* her mind whispered. How long did a body take to decompose? Was three years enough time to turn someone from a person into a skeleton? "Anyone," she finished, stuttering slightly. "Just because we only know about a couple missing people doesn't mean there aren't more."

"True," Alex said, sounding unconvinced. He draped an arm across the back of the couch, and that was all the invitation she needed to snuggle into his chest, her eyelids still drooping. Why on earth was she so sleepy? After the day they'd had, she'd been prepared to never sleep again, but it was like each of her eyelashes weighed a thousand pounds. Holding them up was a herculean effort

She stifled a yawn. "What should we do?" It was almost rhetorical. They'd done everything they could think of to find answers, and had run out of breadcrumbs to follow.

She was sure Kelsey had told her everything she knew. Even if Wyatt wasn't the one who sold her out to Raymond, he couldn't be trusted. She doubted Laird had much else to offer. Nat had no love for Raymond, but didn't seem to know more than anyone else with an internet connection.

Yet they had to do *something*. She couldn't live in a house with a literal skeleton in the closet. Nor could she stay at Alex's forever, as tempting as that option seemed right now.

"We could talk to Raymond," Alex said quietly.

Madelyn chuckled sleepily. "Sure, then we'll go hang out with Putin."

"I'm being serious."

She frowned, lifting her head to look him in the eye. "Why?" Her tone indicated that there was not a good answer to this question.

"He's the only one who knows what happened."

"Assuming it was him."

"Angie said—"

"Angie recorded that before she disappeared. Before Piper disappeared. Plus she was *sixteen*. Everyone is overdramatic and stupid at sixteen."

"Angie wasn't stupid."

"That's not what I—"

"Wait, are you telling me you *don't* think Raymond did this?" His arm wasn't around her anymore. He had shifted his position, sitting cross-legged on the flimsy mattress with his shoulders squared toward her.

She mirrored his position, now fully awake. "No, I'm saying we don't *know*. We've been assuming it's him because he seems the most likely, but we also haven't considered anyone else. What we *do* know is that Raymond is super rich, petty as shit, and immune to consequences. He threatened to evict and sue me. And he brags about carrying his stupid gun every time he opens his mouth. So what I'm *saying* is, why on earth would you want to piss someone like that off? And once you did, what makes you think he'd tell you the truth?"

"I can get him to talk," he said, his face determined.

She laughed incredulously. "He's a multimillionaire megalomaniac with no conscience. You're a seventh-grade Spanish teacher. Unless you are secretly the Punisher, I don't see that happening."

"Well, what do *you* suggest?" This was a tone she'd never heard from him before. He was irritated. With her.

She threw up her hands. "I don't know! I don't know, okay? I've lived in this town for less than two months and just found out there's been a corpse outside my bedroom the entire time; I stupidly decided it was a good idea to rent from the fucking Godfather, who is now threatening to ruin my life; my dog tried to eat a literal human hand in my presence; and now I'm fighting with the only person I even *know* in this freaking place, because he wants to go get himself shot in the face by store-brand Donald Trump." To her dismay, hot tears brimmed in her eyes. "All of our choices suck," she said, her voice breaking as the tears spilled over. Great. Now she was crying *and* ranting. Nothing like torpedoing your brand-new relationship two hours after consummating it.

"Hey," Alex said, his face softening, "I'm sorry. You're right. There are no good options here."

"Why do you make it sound so much more eloquent than me?"

"Well, I am a professional speaker and language expert, you know."

"Wow, you really finessed that job title into dust there, didn't you?"

He laughed, and Madelyn found herself smiling through her tears. She marveled that they could laugh in the middle of this horribleness. Ralph used to get mad if she showed even the barest *hint* of a smile when they fought. He assumed she was gloating, or making fun of him, or not taking the situation seriously enough. She wasn't used to feeling . . . comfortable.

"We don't have to figure it out right now," Alex said, settling into the couch and guiding her back under his arm. "Today was a lot."

"You can say that again."

"Today was a lot."

She groaned. "You are twenty-six. Why are you talking like you're the opposite of that?"

"What's the opposite of twenty-six? Thirteen? Negative twenty-six?"

"Sixty-two."

He paused for a second. "How?"

"You reverse the numbers."

"Oh. And I was supposed to track with that?"

"It made sense in my brain." Her words were getting fuzzier. With the adrenaline draining out of her, she was drifting off again.

She thought longingly of the wine she'd abandoned on her coffee table. She'd taken only a couple of sips before setting it down to move on to other activities. At the time, she'd assumed she'd come back to it later, a lazy postcoital drink. Why couldn't *that* have been the way this day had gone?

"Today wasn't *all* bad," she said, letting her hand trail down Alex's chest.

She felt his sharp intake of breath when her fingertips found the front of his waistband, but instead of following her lead, he grabbed her hand, lifting it to his lips. "You're right," he whispered, kissing her fingers. "Part of today was *amazing*."

And yet he did not seem to be receiving the signals she was very obviously sending.

She sat up straighter and leaned in to kiss him, but he pulled away, sliding off the couch, leaving her alone on the paper-thin mattress.

"I think I'm going to take Potato for a walk," he said, already moving toward the kitchen table, where she'd dropped the leash. "Give you some peace and quiet."

"But—"

"You were napping before. I shouldn't have woken you up."

But she was awake *now*, dammit. And if she had to choose between sleep and Alex, she'd never close her eyes again.

"Alex, wait." She slid off the mattress as he scooped up Potato and clipped on her leash. "I'm not tired."

"I'm feeling antsy anyway. I need to get some energy out, I think. Work up a bit of a sweat."

Was he even hearing himself? "I think there might be another way to accomplish those goals."

But it was like her words didn't even register. He opened the front door, then kissed her on the forehead like she was five. "Rest up. I'll be back later."

Before she could even wrap her brain around what had happened, he was gone.

CHAPTER THIRTY-EIGHT

These people ask me, "Doug, you came from nothing. You know what it's like to live paycheck to paycheck. Wouldn't it have been better if you'd been paid more?" And you know what I tell them? Hell no. *Hell* no. I built my business from the ground up. I learned the value of hard work. I'm very successful now, very rich. You think that would be the case if I'd been given handouts? If I had it easy? These young people today, they're getting soft. They want to get something for nothing. So no, I don't think the minimum wage is too low. If anything, it's probably too high.

—Doug Raymond on the *Big Questions* podcast, April 2017

—

Despite her annoyance that Alex had missed signals so strong they could've been detected by the International Space Station, Madelyn *was* tired. Spite kept her awake for fifteen minutes after he left, before exhaustion drove her back to bed. When she woke up, the air was filled with a scent that was both spicy and a little bit sweet, causing her mouth to water. She followed it into the kitchen, where Alex stood at the counter, mashing up avocados in a metal bowl. Potato sat at his feet, tail wagging hopefully. On the stove, steam spilled from the edges of a covered pot, carrying the delicious smell.

"What are you making?" Madelyn said, resisting the urge to lift the lid and shove her nose inside.

"Guacamole," he said. "For the tamales." He nodded toward the stove.

"You made tamales?" Madelyn couldn't even have asked Ralph to boil a pot of water without him acting like he was dying. And even though she *knew* by now that Ralph wasn't normal, that he was manipulative and controlling and that everything he said was self-serving in some way, she was still surprised sometimes when other people weren't like him.

"I'm warming up tamales," Alex corrected. "My siblings and I help my mom make a giant batch of them every couple months and she always sends me home with a bunch for my freezer. Tonight felt like a no-cooking night."

"So you *did* make them, just not today."

"I assisted. Mostly, I was on rolling duty."

"Dude, let me be impressed." She plucked a tortilla chip out of the open bag on the counter and dipped it in the guacamole.

"Wait, I haven't added the—"

"Too late," she said, popping it in her mouth. It was delicious, creamy and fresh with just the right bite of lime. "Um, this is amazing, don't add anything," she said with her mouth full. At her feet, Potato shifted her attention to Madelyn with pleading eyes. Madelyn broke off a corner of the chip and dropped it onto the floor, where Potato eagerly hoovered it up.

"I'm glad you like it, but you are incorrect," Alex said, dumping in a pile of chopped onions and tomatoes from a nearby cutting board.

After he gave it all a stir, she sampled again and had to admit that he was right. The veggies *did* make it better. "This is so much better than the stuff from the store," she said, scooping up another heap of guacamole.

He froze halfway to the sink, holding the dirty knife and cutting board. "Please tell me you don't buy that prepackaged green goop from the supermarket."

"Not often, considering we get paid like characters in a Dickens novel."

Alex groaned. "That stuff is mostly sour cream and preservatives. It's barely even got avocado in it. Calling it guacamole is a crime against my ancestors."

She raised an eyebrow. "I did not take you for a food snob."

"If anything, I'm a word snob. I don't like when people use the wrong words for things."

"I'm understanding more and more why you became a Spanish teacher."

He grinned. "Guilty as charged."

The tamales were finished steaming, and they both loaded their plates and carried them to the small table, dropping a couple more chip fragments on the floor for Potato. In addition to the guacamole and tamales, Alex also had a bowl of homemade salsa—"all I did was throw a bunch of ingredients in a food processor," he insisted—and had heated up a bowl of refried beans, which he said also came from his family's big cooking days. He could never eat all the food his mom sent home with him but had learned he could freeze the beans in ice cube trays, then store them in gallon-size freezer bags to reheat as needed.

"How much of your freezer is food from your family's cooking days?"

"Most of it," he admitted.

Even though Alex kept stressing how much work he didn't do, Madelyn couldn't help but marvel at the differences in how they lived. Most of her dinners consisted of rolling up tortillas and peanut butter, microwaving ramen noodles, or dumping jarred sauce over pasta. Neither of her parents had been much of a cook, and she'd never bothered to take it upon herself to learn. She envied Alex's casual comfort in the kitchen, and how his version of a thrown-together easy meal was her idea of fine dining. She envied his family cooking days, which she envisioned as sepia toned and in slow motion.

She tried her tamales, then closed her eyes in bliss. "This is divine."

"Thanks, I put a lot of blood and sweat into reheating them."

She laughed, loving how easy it was to talk to him, to *be* with him. Ralph was never easy. Everything felt like a contest with him, or like there was something to prove. Sometimes, when he started getting amorous, she would give in so she wouldn't have to talk to him for a while. She'd check out, let him use up his energy—he never paid much consideration to hers—and then enjoy the silence once he was done.

How had she spent such a long time with someone like that, when people like Alex existed? Even though she kept searching for an opportunity to revisit their earlier activities in her bed, she also enjoyed all the other parts of being around him. Talking, laughing, eating. The type of stuff she'd do with Syzygy. She'd always assumed that all the effort she had to put into her relationship with Ralph was normal, that romantic relationships were different from friendships, that she wasn't *supposed* to want more.

No wonder Syzygy had always hated Ralph. He'd made her world so much smaller than it should've been.

"So how have you enjoyed your first few weeks as a teacher?" Alex asked around mouthfuls of food. "Minus, you know . . . all the other stuff."

Madelyn laughed. "Is that what we're calling it now?"

"Honestly, I don't know *what* to call it. Can we just pretend it doesn't exist for a few minutes?"

That sounded good to her. She would like to pretend it didn't exist for a lot longer than that. Forever, preferably.

She thought about his question for a minute. "I like it a lot," she said slowly.

"But?"

"But these kids *really* want there to be a pecking order. I was not prepared for how much everyone needs to be the main character of choir. It's like a blood sport."

"Yeah, middle school is ruthless," Alex agreed. "I think I would sooner chew off my own finger than go back to that time of life."

"That bad?"

He shrugged. "It could've been worse. At least I had Angie. We had each other's backs." He cast his eyes down, poking at the remainders of his food with his fork, and Madelyn knew his thoughts were drifting back to the body in her wall. If they'd ever actually left.

"It might not be her," she said softly.

"Yeah. I know." But he sounded defeated, like he didn't really believe what he was saying.

Madelyn's chest was tight. She had to tell him. She'd already kept this secret for too long. It may not be a good time for it, but she was beginning to think there might never be one. "Alex?"

"Yeah?"

"About Angie's ghost . . . I think I know who it is."

His eyes widened, and he leaned forward in his chair. "What? How?"

"I've actually known for a while. But I didn't want to say anything because . . . well, I wasn't sure you'd believe me."

"Are you kidding? Why wouldn't I believe you?"

"I mean, it's kind of . . . out there."

"We're talking about a ghost. I think 'out there' is assumed."

"And I didn't want it to make things weird between us."

He took her hand across the table, gently rubbing his thumb over her fingers. "I wouldn't worry about that. In case you haven't noticed, I'm kind of into you."

We'll see about that, Madelyn thought, taking a deep breath. "The thing is, I think Angie's ghost . . . I think it's . . . me."

Alex didn't drop her hand, but his fingers grew stiff and still on hers. "What?"

She tried to explain how she'd figured it out through listening to Angie's recordings, realizing that the songs Angie's ghost was singing were songs she sang, some of which hadn't even been composed yet. How other things then began to fall into place, sounds and smells that Angie observed that Madelyn could trace to things she'd done since moving in.

How she thought that maybe some of the strange things she'd been experiencing lately might actually be Angie, also unwittingly making ripples through time.

"I can't explain it," she said after she'd run out of secrets. "I don't know how or why it's happening. But she and I are linked somehow. Which means *I'm* the voice you heard telling you to help her. My voice, now, ten years later. And I wouldn't have asked you to do that if she was dead."

Alex had gradually retracted as she spoke, pulling his hands back into his lap, and then crossing his arms, studying her with an impenetrable expression. He hadn't spoken, but listened silently, his face stony.

Now he opened his mouth, then hesitated, like he wanted to speak but couldn't find the words. Finally, he said, "Why didn't you warn her?" His words were sharp.

Madelyn blinked, taken aback. She had been prepared for a lot of reactions, even anger, but she wasn't prepared for an accusation. "I'm not doing *any* of it on purpose. It just happened. I would've warned her if I could, but I don't have any control over what she hears and what she doesn't."

"But you think you're the one who spoke to me. You said you wouldn't have told me to help her if she was dead. Which means you think you did *that* on purpose."

"I don't know how any of this works," she said. "And I can't prove anything. Maybe I will find a way to communicate intentionally, but I haven't yet."

"So let's say you do. Why communicate with me? Why not tell her to answer the phone when I call, or leave me a message, or, I don't know, buy a Taser or some pepper spray or something she could use to defend herself. Why not *help* her?"

"I don't know!" Madelyn's eyes were starting to water—stupid crying reflex when she got upset—but she didn't care. "I'm not going to defend myself against something I haven't even *done* yet. I've done everything I can to figure out what happened to her. You think I wouldn't warn her if I could?"

Alex scrubbed his hands over his face, sighing deeply. "You're right," he said, the fire leaving his voice. "I'm sorry. I just—why you? If it's not a ghost, if it's possible to talk to someone across time, why you? Why not me? You never even met her." He didn't sound accusatory anymore. Just sad.

"I don't know," Madelyn said, her heart sinking. She knew that this would be hard for him to hear, but she hadn't anticipated that he'd wish *he* were the ghost. "Maybe there's a reason it's me."

"Or maybe that house is just two tin cans on some sort of temporal string, passing fuzzy messages back and forth for no reason other than simple physics."

"I don't think there's anything simple here," Madelyn said.

"Maybe not that we understand. But that doesn't mean it's not happening."

"Yeah, I guess."

He tilted his head, as if a thought were just occurring to him. "In which case, you weren't *telling* me anything at all. You could've been talking to your TV, or on the phone, or to your dog. You could've already said the words I heard and not even have realized it." He said it matter-of-factly, like he was giving an update on the weather. Even though if what he was saying were true, it meant that all possibilities were back on the table. Including that it was Angie's body they'd found earlier that day.

"Alex, I—"

"It's fine," he said. "It's not your fault. It is what it is." He gave her a tight smile, then glanced down at her mostly empty plate. "Are you done? I think I'm just going to clean up and go to bed. The day is catching up with me."

She nodded wordlessly, and Alex whisked away her plate, carrying the dirty dishes over to the sink. She followed him, intending to help, but he shooed her away, telling her that she was his guest and his mother would never let him hear the end of it if he let a pretty girl clean up after him. He said it playfully, but Madelyn got the sense that he also wanted an excuse to stop talking for a while, so she left him alone.

She thought about waiting for him on the sofa bed, but worried that felt like she was expecting something, and there wasn't anywhere else to sit except at the table. She returned to the bedroom, Potato trailing behind her. She texted him, I know you're tired, but can you come let me know when you're done? I'll be up for a while.

She wished she'd brought her Switch, but video games had not exactly been at the top of her mind when she'd been fleeing the dead body in her house. She examined Alex's bookshelves, figuring she'd pass the time reading until he was ready to talk.

And they *needed* to talk. They still hadn't decided what they were going to do about the body at her house, or the cease and desist letter she'd received, or Doug Raymond in general. Nor had they discussed the fact that they'd had sex, which Madelyn was coming to believe was going to be only a onetime thing, based on everything that had happened since then.

She selected a red-covered science fiction novel she'd heard was funny—she couldn't handle anything heavy right now—and settled onto the bed, lifting Potato up to snuggle beside her.

The writing was sharp and intriguing and hilarious, and by the time she checked the time again, she was several chapters in and an hour had gone by. Her text message was marked as read, but Alex hadn't responded.

Marking her page with the dust jacket, Madelyn slipped off the bed and walked to the open doorway to peer out.

Nearly all the lights were out, although the vanity light in the bathroom was on, the door cracked, presumably acting as a night-light. It wasn't that late; had he really ignored her text and gone to bed?

Sure enough, when she walked into the living room, she found him stretched out on the sofa bed, fast asleep.

CHAPTER THIRTY-NINE

I hired a Raymond Realty Group realtor to help me buy a house based on the high reviews, but that was a mistake. Only showed me homes WAY out of my price range and were far too hung up on their "Platinum guarantee," which they could never adequately define. Felt like a scam.

—one-star Yelp review of Raymond Realty Group

—

In the morning, there was a note on the table.

Didn't want to wake you. Gone to run some errands, then to my family's house for lunch. I'll try not to be there too long. Help yourself to anything. I'll be back this afternoon. - A

P.S. You talk in your sleep. It's adorable.

Madelyn felt her face warm, wondering what she'd said, hoping desperately that it hadn't been part of the dream she'd had about him.

She texted him to say she was up and had gotten his note, then looked around the empty house. What was she going to do for half the day until he came back? She'd barely brought anything from her house, just a handful of clothes, basic toiletries, and dog food for Potato. She didn't even have her laptop here.

After taking Potato outside and feeding her breakfast, Madelyn showered and got dressed, selecting wrinkled yoga pants and a tank top from the backpack she'd hastily stuffed with whatever her hands touched first from her dresser. Alex had transformed his bed back into a sofa before he'd left, and she settled onto it, tucking her feet underneath her and pulling out her phone. She'd been thinking all morning about what to do next, even if Alex wasn't around to help.

She scanned through her messages, then fired off a text to Nat. Hey, do you know if there's a way for me to look up when my house was remodeled? Do they have records of that at the library?

The response came a few minutes later. What kind of remodel?

A small one. I think there used to be another closet.

Why would someone cover up a closet?

Madelyn almost laughed, wondering how Nat would react if she texted her the real answer—to hide a body. Instead, she sent a shrug emoji.

That may be hard to track down, Nat wrote. They probably didn't even pull a permit for it. I'll see what I can find out, but don't hold your breath.

Thanks. Madelyn thought for a minute, then added, You don't happen to know any extremely cheap yet still good lawyers do you?

What the hell did you do???

Nothing. But my landlord is threatening to sue me.

WHAT

Yeah. He sent a courier to my house yesterday with a letter accusing me of all sorts of stuff I didn't do. But he also has a bajillion dollars and I have like, two.

What an asshole. What did you do to piss him off?

I asked unflattering questions about him.

That'll do it.

Yup. Hence my need for a bargain basement lawyer.

I don't think I've got anyone, but I'll keep thinking on it.

Thank you.

Are you home now? I would be freaked out to be alone at home after my landlord threatened me.

No, I'm at a friend's house.

Cute coworker friend????

Madelyn smiled. Maybe.

Oooh. The plot thickens. Sorry you're dealing with this though.

Thanks. Me too. Madelyn shook her head. Nat didn't know the half of it.

Without anything else to do, Madelyn texted with Syzygy for a little bit, then retrieved her book from the bedroom and read for a while. Around one, her stomach growled, and she walked into the kitchen to retrieve yesterday's hoagie from the fridge.

Carrying the sandwich to the table, she checked her phone. Still nothing from Alex. *No rush, but any idea when you'll be home?* she texted.

Three dots appeared, indicating he was typing a response, but then went away. She waited, but they didn't reappear. He must not be in a place where he could text. Probably at lunch with his family.

After finishing her hoagie—still delicious, even though the bread had gotten a little soggy overnight from the oil and vinegar—and throwing away her trash, she returned to her book, losing herself in the story. Every so often, she'd check her phone, but it remained silent. No texts from Alex, no updates from Nat. Not even any spam email.

The book wasn't long, and the pages went by fast. Before she knew it, she'd reached the end, and Alex still hadn't called or texted. She checked the clock. Five p.m. He'd said he would come home after lunch. Either lunch had gone absurdly long or something had happened.

She texted him again. Then called. No response.

Now she was getting worried. She didn't have her laptop, but Alex's was charging on a shelf in the bedroom. She opened it, hoping fervently that it was unlocked, but no such luck. The cursor on the log-in screen blinked at her, asking for a password.

She closed her eyes, trying to think through her options. She didn't have her car here, so she couldn't go far. She didn't have Alex's parents' phone number, so she couldn't talk to him that way. She supposed she could get a rideshare, but she didn't have an address either. Unless . . .

Syzygy wrinkled their nose when they answered her FaceTime. "Aren't you shacking up with your new boy toy? Is Bang Town really so boring that you have to call me twice in one day?"

"He's not here," Madelyn said hurriedly. "I think something is wrong. I need you to do me a favor."

Syzygy's face morphed instantly into business mode. "Of course, love. What is it?"

"I don't have my computer here and Alex's is locked. Can you log in to my school account and look up a student file for me?"

"Isn't that . . . kind of illegal?"

"Only if you tell someone."

Syzygy shrugged. "Hell yeah. Damn the man. Just a sec." They stuck their phone in a stand and disappeared for a minute while they went to get their laptop. While they were gone, Madelyn texted them the school district website, along with her faculty log-in.

"All right," Syzygy said when they returned, eyes focused off-screen as they typed. "I am . . . in. Yes. Welcome, Madelyn Zhao. What am I doing as you?"

"Go to Student Records and look up, um, hold on." She couldn't remember the twins' names. She pulled up Alex's Instagram and scrolled through his photos until she found one of him with his siblings. He'd tagged them in the caption. She clicked through to the first profile. "Carlos García. I need the address and phone number on his file." Alex didn't live with his parents, but his brothers did.

Syzygy rattled off the information, then turned to look intently into the screen. "Madelyn, are you okay? You sound . . . not good."

"There's a lot going on right now, Syz," Madelyn said. She'd told them about Alex and the cease and desist letter that morning, but not about the body in her wall. The fewer people who knew about that, the better. "I have a bad feeling about it. Like something awful is going to happen."

"Listen," Syzygy said, their voice somber. "You know I'm here for you. Always. Just a couple hours away. No questions asked."

"I know," Madelyn said, grateful tears pricking her eyes. "I appreciate it."

"I'm serious, love. Don't be a martyr. If you need me, you know how to find me."

"I do."

"Let me know when you get in touch with Alex." No jokes now. Madelyn must look more stricken than she thought.

"I will. Thank you."

"Of course. Anytime."

After ending the call, she dialed Alex's mom's number, which was listed as the primary contact on his brother's school file. She answered on the first ring. "Hello?"

"Hello, Mrs. García? This is Madelyn Zhao. I'm friends with your son Alex."

"Sebastián? You know him? Do you know where he is? Is he all right?" His mother's voice was breathless, frantic.

Madelyn's stomach dropped to her knees, her throat going instantly dry. "I'm sorry. Are you saying that Alex didn't go to your house for lunch today?"

"No!" Mrs. García sounded on the verge of hysterics. "No, he was supposed to be here, but he never arrived. I've tried calling him, texting him. Nothing. I called the hospital, they don't have him. I called the police, but they say they cannot do anything until he is missing twenty-four hours. They say he is an adult, probably not missing at all. Probably just doesn't want to come over. But I know my son. He is not like this. He would not do this." Her accent became more pronounced the more upset she became. By the end, she was practically wailing.

"No, he wouldn't," Madelyn agreed quietly. Her hands were numb. All her blood felt like it had left her body. All day long, she'd been sitting on the couch, reading a book, biding her time, and all that time, Alex had been missing.

Her mind flooded with images of the body in the wall. Of Alex in the wall.

Suddenly, she felt like she might be sick.

"I'm so sorry, Mrs. García," Madelyn rasped, her throat growing thick. "I will let you know if I hear from him." She hung up, then sank to the floor, clutching her phone to her chest, her breath coming in short, strained gasps.

Alex was missing.

There was a body in her house.

And if she didn't find Alex soon, she had a horrible feeling that he'd be next.

CHAPTER FORTY

You're driving with race cars here. The slow lane here is the fast lane anywhere else.

—Raymond Realty Group internal newsletter, August 2020

Madelyn paced back and forth across Alex's living room, Potato trailing eagerly behind her, convinced they were playing some sort of game. She tried to recall if he'd agreed that he wouldn't go confront Doug Raymond, or if he'd just agreed to stop *talking* about confronting Doug Raymond, and found it infuriating that she couldn't remember.

Where else might he have gone without telling anyone? Madelyn could come up with only one place, as much as she hated the idea of going back there.

She pulled out her phone and texted Nat. I'm so sorry to keep bothering you, but are you busy right now?

No, what's up?

I need a ride, and it's not the sort of thing I want to call a Lyft for.

Color me intrigued. Where are you, and where are you going?

Madelyn texted the addresses, and Nat replied a minute later with a thumbs-up. **Totally doable. Be there in 15.**

Half an hour later, Nat rolled to a stop in front of Madelyn's house, peering curiously over the steering wheel as Madelyn tried to wrestle her panic attack into submission. Her yellow Fit sat alone in the driveway. There was no sign that Alex was here, but that didn't mean he hadn't stopped by. There was still a chance she might find a clue inside.

"Looks like someone's home," Nat observed.

"Actually, this is my house," Madelyn admitted. "That's my car."

Nat looked at her with raised eyebrows. "Did I just give you a ride of shame?"

"I wish," Madelyn said wryly. "Little more complicated than that, unfortunately." She took a deep breath, steeling her nerves, and opened the door. "Thanks for the ride."

"You sure you don't need anything else? I can wait."

"No, I'm fine," Madelyn lied. "Really." If she needed to go anywhere else to look for Alex, she had her car now. Not that she had any idea where to go.

Her hand shook as she fumbled through the front flower bed, searching for the fake rock. She sighed as the key fell into her hand, relief and disappointment swirling inside her chest in equal measure. Alex must not have come here after all.

Or he left. Or he put it back before going inside.

Or something awful happened to him. And someone *else* put it back.

Horrible visions of what she might find when she opened the door flashed through her head. She imagined her cream couch stained red with blood, Alex's lifeless body sprawled across the carpet.

She pulled in deep breaths, working up her courage, then turned her key in the lock.

A mixture of relief and disappointment flooded her when she stepped inside. Everything looked precisely as they'd left it. She crept into the hall to peek at the hole. The basket was still in front of it, drywall dust still on the floor. She checked the bedroom, the office, the bathroom. All undisturbed and empty.

"Alex!" she called desperately. "Where are you?"

Nothing.

She wandered through the small house, double- and triple-checking under her bed, in the closets, behind the curtains. Every space she thought could possibly hold a person. Except one.

Grimacing, she slid the basket of blankets away from the hole in the wall and turned on the flashlight on her phone. Crouching down, she shined the light inside the cramped space.

The body was as they'd left it, tarp pulled partially down, handless arm jutting out to one side. No Alex, thank God.

That reminded her, the hand was still under the sink. Unless someone had moved it. She hurried to the kitchen and yanked open the cabinet door, praying it was still there.

It was gone. Either Alex came back and got it, or someone else had been here.

Neither option was good.

Did you come get the thing from under the sink? Madelyn texted Alex, knowing he wouldn't respond. She stared at her phone, willing him to answer. But it remained stubbornly silent.

Madelyn slumped onto the floor, leaning back against the cabinets. "Angie," she said quietly, feeling a little ridiculous, but not knowing what else to do. "I don't know if you can hear me, but my name is Madelyn. I think I'm your ghost. Except I'm not a ghost. I'm a real person, and I live in your house. I know your friend Bas. We work together. He teaches Spanish now. I call him Alex." She took a deep breath, heart pounding. "We've been looking for you. And I think he might be in trouble, and I don't know what to do. So if you're still out there somewhere, Angie, now would be a great time for you to come back. Because I really need your help." She shook her head, feeling ridiculous. "If you can even hear me."

It was absurd. Even if Angie *could* hear her in the past, Madelyn didn't know how she could help. She didn't even know if she was still alive. For all she knew, Angie was sitting three feet away from her, buried in an old linen closet.

Still, it made her feel a tiny bit better to talk to someone else who cared about Alex as much as she did. Even if she wasn't there.

Her phone buzzed in her pocket, causing her to jump in surprise. *Angie?* she wondered wildly.

No. That would be ridiculous. Chiding herself for getting so excited, she pulled out her phone, only to have her heart rate immediately surge again when she saw Alex's name on the screen.

Hey.

HEY???! WHERE THE HELL HAVE YOU BEEN???

Long story. Can you come meet me? I'm at the North Ridge site.

What are you doing at North Ridge?

I'll explain when you get here.

You should call your parents. They're really worried about you.

Ok.

Is everything okay??? You sound weird.

I'm fine. Are you coming?

She growled in frustration. Would it kill him to give her even a tiny bit more information? He knew how freaked out she was. He could've at *least* answered her question about the hand. Why was he being so taciturn?

But if the only way she was going to get answers from him was to drive out to the stupid construction site, then she'd drive out to the stupid construction site. Okay. I'll be there soon.

She waited for a response, or even an emoji react, but he didn't send anything.

Taking one last look around her house, she locked up and went to her car, dialing Syzygy as she drove. "Anything?" they asked the second their face appeared on the screen. They were in the car too, probably on their way to the bar for a shift.

"Turns out his parents haven't seen him at all today," Madelyn said, speaking quickly. "So I went to my house and I think he stopped by earlier, but he's not there now. But then he texted me and said he's at that sketchy construction site we went to yesterday."

"The hell?"

"Yeah, it's all super weird."

"So where are you going now?"

"I'm going to meet him."

"At the creepy-ass abandoned construction site?"

"Yeah."

"Madelyn, I know you like this guy, but this pings *all* my true crime red flags."

"Alex wouldn't hurt me."

"Why, because he's charming and good looking? So was Ted Bundy."

"Syz, I know you're looking out for me, but I swear Alex is not that guy. He's not Ralph."

"Good, because Ralph would *totally* murder you and bury you at a creepy-ass abandoned construction site."

"He would not."

"You're right, he's probably too lazy to bury you himself. He'd get his current girlfriend to do it instead."

"Syzygy."

"Sorry. Focusing. Where is this place?"

"It's kind of in the middle of nowhere?"

"This plan keeps getting better."

"Shut up. It's not like it's a hole in the woods. It's just kind of out away from the rest of the town."

"Okay. But so you know, if you get murdered, I'm going to come out there and kill you."

"Fair."

"Let me know when you get there?"

"I will."

After getting off the phone, Madelyn spent the rest of the drive turning what she knew over and over in her head. Angie and her dad disappeared. Doug Raymond owned their house. There was a body in the closet. The closet was covered up after they lived there. Piper Carden worked on the accounts for North Ridge. North Ridge was being kept open, even though no work was being done there. Piper Carden disappeared. Kelsey O'Donnell tried to find her. Kelsey was threatened and silenced. Madelyn was now being threatened and silenced. And now Alex was at North Ridge.

How was it all connected? She couldn't find the common thread, and felt like she was losing her mind.

When she was a few minutes away, she checked her phone at a stoplight. A new text from Alex had come in while she was driving. Park where we did yesterday. Gate is open now. Go in and turn left at the dumpster. I'll find you.

Again, what was with the robotic texting? And how did he suddenly have enough signal to text from North Ridge in the first place, when it was a dead zone yesterday? It all felt wrong. She opened the glove compartment and pulled out her emergency anxiety meds, popping a couple in her mouth and swallowing them dry. She normally got this prescription refilled only a couple of times a year, but at the rate she'd been going lately, she'd be out within a few more days.

The sun was almost finished setting when she parked beside Alex's car, her mind overflowing with questions. How had he gotten the gate open? How had he gotten here in the first place? And what was up with this freaking construction site?

Remembering that she'd promised to text Syzygy when she arrived, she pulled out her phone, only to remember again that there was no signal out there. Great.

Keeping one eye on her phone bars, she walked through the gate, following Alex's directions. North Ridge was enormous, the size of a small subdivision. What could possibly have justified Raymond holding on to it all these years? It had to be costing him a fortune.

"Alex?" she called.

A second later, his voice sounded up ahead. "Madelyn?" He sounded almost surprised, which was weird considering he'd just texted her directions.

"Where are you?" she called, beginning to jog toward where she thought she'd heard him. He didn't answer, but he hadn't sounded like he was too far away. She peered inside partially framed buildings as she passed by them, before coming into an open space that had been leveled and framed for foundations, but didn't have anything built yet.

A single floodlight illuminated the area, propped up on a tall metal stand.

She froze, all the blood draining from her face.

She'd finally found Alex.

"It's about time," Doug Raymond said, calmly pointing a gun at her. "We were beginning to think you'd never get here."

CHAPTER FORTY-ONE

> You'd better believe I'm carrying. It's my God-given right under our mighty Constitution, and quite frankly, I have a hard time trusting anyone who has a problem with that.
>
> —Doug Raymond on *Up Close and Cynical with Joe Dabny*, April 2022

"Be a doll and go join your boyfriend," Raymond said, gesturing with the gun.

Alex was down on one knee, legs awkwardly woven through a grid of rebar that had been laid in preparation for a new foundation. His hands were zip-tied in front of him, binding him to the grid. One eye was blackened and swollen shut, and he had a fresh piece of duct tape over his mouth, which Raymond must have put in place right after Alex called out to her. His good eye went wide when he saw her, and he pulled hard against his restraints, so they cut into his skin, turning his hands white.

Madelyn couldn't breathe. She glanced down at her phone, but there was still no signal. Raymond chuckled. "Sorry, not a lot of signal out in these parts, sweetheart. A few patches here and there, if you know where to look, but they're few and far between. We were gonna run the whatchamacallit, the fiber thing, but then everyone lost their freaking minds over the flu and the government shut everything down, and well . . ." He shrugged. "Never got around to it."

"What's going on?" Madelyn asked, her heart in her throat. What was Alex doing here? What had he done that day?

"Well, it's a funny story." Raymond chuckled. "I was coming out of church with my family, looking forward to a nice lunch, when he comes charging up to me, demanding to speak with me. Never mind that he's scaring my grandkids, my wife. No, Romeo here doesn't care about any of that. He just wants his way. So, to avoid causing a stir, I stepped away. And you know what this nutjob showed me?" He shook his head, an incredulous smile on his face. "A human hand. Actual bona fide human remains, sealed up tight in a plastic baggie like a ham and cheese sandwich. Well, obviously I couldn't let him keep waving *that* around. He was upsetting people enough as it was. But of course, I couldn't just let him leave with it either. When a man keeps a bag of body parts in his car, all bets are off as to what he might do. I knew I needed somewhere private, somewhere we could have an honest chat. So, long story short, here we are."

Madelyn looked at Alex in disbelief, her heart sinking. After their whole conversation last night, he'd done it anyway? "You went back to my house without telling me?" she said, as if that mattered anymore. She knew it was silly to feel betrayed now, when much bigger things were at stake. But she'd trusted Alex, and he'd lied to her.

"I think you mean *my* house," Raymond said slowly, his eyes narrowing. "Which you have not taken very good care of, I might add. I thought I told you not to go messing with my walls. And I'm *sure* I told you no pets allowed."

"I didn't do anything wrong," Madelyn said, knowing as she said it that he wouldn't care. He'd probably made up his mind about how tonight was going to go long before she got there.

"Funny," Raymond said, without a hint of humor in his voice. "That's what he said too. Now, hurry along." He gestured with the gun.

Not seeing any other options, Madelyn took a slow step toward Alex.

"Wait," Raymond interrupted. "You can leave your phone there." He winked at her. "Just in case."

Madelyn abandoned her phone and picked her way around the rebar grid, toward Alex, who was shaking his head wildly, urging her away. As she got closer, she could see the angry red marks on his wrists where he'd strained against the ties, and the crusted blood on the side of his face, blending into his dark hair. How long had he been here? Raymond said he'd been waiting for him outside church that morning. That was hours ago. What had Raymond been doing to him all this time?

More zip ties were scattered around him in the dirt. "Go ahead and grab a couple of those and tie yourself up next to him. And don't try anything cute. I'm already cranky that I'm missing pot roast night with my grandkids for this."

With trembling hands, Madelyn reached for the ties. As she bent down, she paused to tug at the tape at the corner of Alex's mouth, picking at it with a fingernail until she got a good grip.

"What did I say about—"

Madelyn ripped off the tape before Raymond could finish telling her to stop, then hurriedly scooped up a handful of ties, holding them up to show Raymond. "I'm doing it! I'm doing it!" she said, pressing her right wrist to the cold metal and looping a tie around it.

"Don't do it," Alex hissed. "You can still get away. Please, *go*."

"Knock it off," Raymond called, sounding almost bored, the gun still pointed at them.

Then, without warning, he squeezed the trigger.

A crack like thunder split the night.

Alex screamed, collapsing onto his side, writhing in pain. Dark blood pumped from the wound in his leg, in which Madelyn thought she glimpsed white splinters of bone.

"Alex!" Madelyn yelled, dropping the zip ties and pressing her hands to the wound. She cast around for something she could use to stanch the bleeding, but there was nothing.

"Leave him," Raymond barked.

"You want to shoot me, fucking shoot me," Madelyn snapped, pulling off her tank top and tying it around his leg. Alex groaned and cried out, gritting his teeth against the pain. Blood seeped instantly through the fabric, soaking her hands. She remembered hearing that a tourniquet was a last-ditch solution, and should be used only when there were no other options. That using one often meant sacrificing the limb.

She hoped Alex would forgive her.

"I'm sorry, I'm sorry," Madelyn repeated as she grabbed two zip ties off the ground. With blood-slicked hands, she strung them together, then looped them around his leg, over the tank top, pulling them as tight as she could.

Alex let out an awful wail that grated against the inside of her head, then trailed off into gasping, shuddering breaths.

"I'm warning you," Raymond called.

"O-*kay*," Madelyn snarled, grabbing a zip tie and securing one wrist to the grid. She tried not to pull it so tight that it cut into her skin, but didn't dare make it so loose that she could slip out. Part of her knew that Raymond had no intention of letting either of them survive the evening, but she couldn't bear the possibility that he might hurt Alex more because of something she did.

She fumbled with the other tie, but this one was harder, since she had to use her already bound hand to do it. One end kept snapping out of her grip before she could insert it into the other. She almost had it when—

"Wait."

It wasn't Raymond this time, but a female voice. And a familiar one.

Madelyn looked up in shock, her jaw dropping. Nat stood beside Raymond, arm outstretched, holding a gun to his head.

"Drop it, dickweed."

What the hell was she doing there? How had she even known where to find them? Madelyn blinked at her in uncomprehending relief, half expecting her to vanish like a mirage at any second.

Raymond let his gun fall to the ground, where it landed in the dirt with a muffled thump. His eyes glistened with rage.

Nat kicked the gun away, then tossed Madelyn a pocketknife, which bounced off the metal and landed in the dirt a couple of feet away. "Go ahead and get yourselves out of here," she said, her voice low, not taking her eyes off Raymond.

Madelyn didn't need to be told twice. Snatching up the knife, she pushed the blade open with her thumb and cut through her ties, then Alex's. His were harder to wedge the knife in, and he winced when she pulled the knife through the plastic. Blood seeped from shallow abrasions where the ties had cut into his skin.

"Come on," Madelyn said, looping his arm around her shoulders and struggling to get him upright. "We've got to get out of here."

"What?" Alex groaned, his face pale. His head lolled on his shoulders. "What's happening?"

"You're going to be okay," Madelyn said, "but you have to stand up. I know it hurts, but I can't lift you on my own."

Obediently, Alex tried to get his good leg under him, but it buckled, and he pitched forward, crying out in pain.

"Bas!" Nat cried out, alarmed.

Madelyn looked up sharply. *Bas?*

Alex blinked, squinting against the darkness, his whole body going tight with shock as he noticed Nat for the first time. *"Angie?"*

PART SIX

And if I did, you deserved it

Ten Years Ago

Angie lurched forward, nearly smacking her forehead on the steering wheel as her car jerked to a stop in the driveway. She didn't remember the drive home, and hadn't even realized she had arrived until she was rocketing into her driveway. Her heart felt like galloping horses in her chest.

A murder. She had witnessed an actual *murder*.

And the man who committed it owned their house.

She crashed through the front door, feeling like a tornado was tearing through her brain. "Dad! Dad, where are you?"

She heard the bedroom door slam. The yelling started before he reached the living room. "What on earth were you *thinking*, young lady, taking the car by yourself? You don't even have a *license*! What would have happened if—"

He froze when he saw her. Angie didn't know how she looked, but it must have been bad, because his face shifted from furious to concerned in the blink of an eye. "Honey, what's wrong? What happened?" He rushed to her, grabbing her by the arms and leaning in to examine her face.

"I'm sorry, Dad. I shouldn't have taken the car. I shouldn't have—I'm so, so sorry."

"Did you get in an accident? Are you okay?" He glanced over her shoulder, toward the window facing the street, as if he expected to see the car shattered into pieces and scattered across their lawn.

She shook her head. "No, it's not the car." She squeezed her eyes shut and pressed her shaking hands over them, trying to block out the horrible images that kept playing over and over in her brain. When she took her hands away, they were damp. She had no idea when she'd started crying.

"Honey, you're scaring me. What's going on?"

After a few shuddering breaths, she managed to tell him what had happened when she arrived at Raymond Realty. The story came out in halting, fragmented pieces. As she spoke, her father's face grew paler and paler, until it was practically gray.

"We have to call the police," Angie said, remembering that she hadn't been able to complete her 911 call. "My phone—"

"Do you have any evidence?" her father interrupted sharply. "Photos or videos?"

She shook her head. "It all happened so fast—"

"That's fine, honey, that's fine," her father said absently, although he seemed anything but fine. He looked haunted, like the subtle valleys of his face had deepened into chasms all at once. "We can't go to the police," he said quietly, almost to himself.

"What?" Angie blinked at him, confused. "But Dad, he *killed*—"

"I believe you, sweetie, I promise," her dad said, "but getting the police to believe us is another story. Doug Raymond is a very rich man, and he has a lot of powerful friends."

"But . . . I saw him do it. I'm a witness." He'd killed that woman right in front of her. Her blood had been on his face. It was probably still on the carpet of his office. Surely that would be enough for the police?

But her dad was shaking his head. "I wish that meant more, honey. But without proof, and with his connections, I don't think it's going to be enough. Especially considering how much money I owe him."

"What does money have to do with it?" Falling behind on rent was hardly in the same category as *murder*.

"More than it should," her father said, frowning. "I told you that I'd been doing some work for him, to try to pay back what I owe. I've seen how he works. You have to trust me when I tell you, Doug Raymond operates by a completely different set of rules than we do. The police are a dead end." He met her eyes, his expression intense. "Are you *sure* he saw you?"

"Positive." She swallowed, remembering the look on his face when their eyes met. Pure feral rage.

"Okay," her dad said, bobbing his head in a steady nod. "Okay."

Without another word, he disappeared into his room, leaving Angie standing bewildered in the living room. Did he just . . . go to bed? Had she broken her dad?

But then he emerged a few seconds later, clutching a crumpled green duffel bag with faded brown straps. He tossed it toward her, and it landed at her feet. "Pack what you can. We leave in ten minutes."

"What? Leave? Why? Where are we going?"

"We can't stay here. He knows who you are. He knows where you live. You just saw him kill someone. You're not safe here. We have to go."

"Go where? For how long?" This was all happening too fast. She couldn't make sense of it.

"I don't know," her dad said, already heading back to his room, presumably to pack his own suitcase. "I'll figure it out."

"Dad," she called after him, her thoughts a jumble. "How are we supposed to—"

"I'll figure it out," her dad repeated from his bedroom, his tone firm. "Nine minutes."

There wasn't time to think. There wasn't time to do anything. With shaking hands, Angie picked up the duffel bag, and ran to her room to pack.

CHAPTER FORTY-TWO

"It's not rocket science, but it ain't easy": Raymond Realty CEO Doug Raymond on his company's meteoric rise, the thrill of making his first million, and being the architect of his own success.

—*East Henderson Herald* profile, December 2016

—

"Angie?" Madelyn repeated, looking incredulously from Alex to the woman she'd known as Nat. All this time wondering whether Angie was alive, and it turned out she'd been texting with her the entire time. In her head, she ran back over every encounter with "Nat" since they'd met, struggling to make sense of their relationship. Why had she lied?

"I thought you worked at the library," Madelyn said, unable to keep the hurt out of her voice. Was there no one in this town she could trust?

A look like remorse flickered across Nat's—*Angie's*—face, but Madelyn didn't know how to take that. As it turned out, she didn't know this woman at all.

"I never said I worked there," Angie said quietly. "You assumed. I just didn't correct you."

A fire lit inside Madelyn. She knew she should feel happy that Angie was alive, and relieved that she'd come to their rescue. But she wasn't about to take the blame for being manipulated. Not again. "You told me your name was Nat," she said. "You pretended you didn't know Alex. You *wanted* me to believe you were someone else. Why?"

"Because I didn't know if I could trust you yet," Angie said, her eyes darting to Alex.

"You . . . you know each other?" Alex seemed like he was barely hanging on to consciousness by a thread, his words coming out like they were dipped in wax. Still, he was fighting his way forward, toward Angie, despite Madelyn's attempts to steer him in the opposite direction.

Angie's eyes softened as she looked at him and nodded. "I'm sorry I couldn't tell you," she said, her eyes growing glassy. "I wanted to."

"I didn't get your recording," he admitted, his voice growing thick. "If I'd found it earlier, maybe—"

"It's okay," Angie said. "I was just a stupid kid trying stupid things. But there's nothing you could have done."

"I'm sorry about our fight," Alex said, his words slurring slightly. "You were right. I was an asshole. I should've helped you."

"That was ten years ago, Bas," Angie said. A smile tugged at her lips.

"I know. But I'm still sorry."

"This is all very heartwarming, but can we please get on with it?" Raymond said, rolling his eyes. His hands were still up, but in a half-hearted way, like he was only playing at being held at gunpoint.

Angie turned her eyes back to him, her gaze hardening. "Sure thing, asswipe. Let's get on with it. What's with the zip ties? What were you going to do to my friends?"

Friends. Was that what they were? Madelyn felt like she couldn't be sure about anything anymore.

Raymond shrugged, pressing his lips together in an innocent frown. "I wasn't going to do anything to them."

"Could've fooled me," Alex mumbled, sagging against Madelyn.

Anger flashed across Angie's face. Moving lightning fast, she smacked the butt of the gun against the side of Raymond's head, sending him staggering as she steadied the barrel back on him. His hand went up, clasping his cheek. "You *bitch*," he seethed.

"One more time, turd weasel," Angie said, unfazed. "What was the plan after they tied themselves to that grid?"

"The new foundation," Alex said, his voice so quiet only Madelyn could hear it, as she struggled to maneuver him to safety.

Madelyn's eyes widened. "He was going to bury us in concrete," she realized, chest clenching as she imagined the horror of that experience. "He's done it before. That's why he keeps the permits for this place current. So he has a convenient place to hide the evidence."

"That's preposterous," Raymond sniffed.

"Is it?" Madelyn challenged. "What happened to Piper Carden? Is she out here somewhere? Let me guess: she figured out you were using this place for something other than a tax write-off, so you killed her?"

"It's weapons, isn't it?" Angie said. "Not just body disposal. That's just a fun perk. But a big site like this, away from prying eyes, where large vehicles can go in and out without anyone batting an eye . . . pretty good space for gunrunning, right?"

"You kids watch too much TV," Raymond scoffed. "Accusing me of all this nonsense. I only needed you two to sit still long enough to see reason. That's all."

"Reason?" Angie repeated, her voice raising in pitch. "Is that what I saw you do to that woman in your office ten years ago? Show her reason?"

Something clicked behind Raymond's eyes. "Angelina Stewart," he said slowly, his lips curling into a slow grin. "Almost didn't recognize you. Did you change your hair?"

"I grew up," Angie said through gritted teeth. "No thanks to you."

"You're slippery, I'll give you that," Raymond said. "Always wondered where you slithered off to."

"Maybe your goons are just really bad at hide-and-seek," Angie said.

Morbidly, that reminded Madelyn of the corpse in her wall. "Who is in the wall of my house?" she asked abruptly. "Whose body did you hide there?"

Angie's eyes whipped to her. "Excuse me, there is a *what* in the wall of your house?"

"It can't be Piper," Madelyn said, narrowing her eyes at Raymond. "You already had this place when she disappeared. You would have disposed of her here. Not in the wall of your rental property."

"It's her, isn't it?" Angie said, staring daggers into the side of his head. "The woman from that night. She was your first, wasn't she? You didn't plan it. It just happened. And I saw you. And then you had to hide her *and* deal with me."

She laughed, rolling her eyes. "We really did you a favor, didn't we, clearing out that night? You probably arrived right after we left, huh? Because you needed to get rid of me. And probably get rid of my dad too, just in case. But we weren't there. And we'd left our phones, which you knew meant we didn't want to be followed, and weren't coming back. Which suddenly provided you with a perfect body-hiding space."

"I don't know what you're talking about," Raymond grumbled, but he was starting to seem flustered, red creeping up the sides of his neck.

"Who was she?" Angie asked, digging the muzzle of the gun into his split cheek, causing him to wince. "I looked for years and could never figure it out. No missing people from East Henderson that day. No one went missing from your company, or your family, or your social media. I looked through all the missing persons records I could get my hands on and didn't find her. It's like she was a ghost." Angie gave a disgusted chuckle. "Except ghosts don't bleed like that, do they, Doug?"

Raymond groaned. "Blah blah, either shit or get off the pot, but either way *shut up*."

"Who was she?" Angie shouted, leaning in to belt into his ear, spraying drops of spittle on his face. "You unbelievable mother*fucker*, can't you answer a single goddamn question?"

"Maybe if you'd say anything that wasn't utter crap," he scoffed. "Now, kids, I'm going to cut to the chase. You don't want to shoot me. I'm a very powerful man. If anything happens to me, there will be consequences. Major consequences. And you don't want that. But I don't exactly want you spreading your ridiculous conspiracy theories about me either. So because I'm also a reasonable man, I'll make you a deal. I'll hand you each ten thousand dollars, cash, if you'll just sign a statement agreeing not to bring this up with folks. My lawyer can draw it up right quick, very standard, nothing fancy. We can be done with all this foolishness tonight."

Alex gave a weak laugh, stumbling a little against Madelyn. "Yeah, no worries, man. It's forgotten," he said, sarcasm dripping from his voice. "Where do I sign?"

Madelyn glanced down at his leg. She wondered how long it had been since she put the tourniquet on. She wondered if she'd gotten it tight enough. She wondered how much blood was too much.

"You have got to be kidding me," Angie snarled, shoving him again with the gun. "Ten *years* I've been running from you, and you offer me ten thousand fucking dollars? At the very least give me some goddamn answers if you're going to try to buy my silence like it's a goddamn Goodwill couch."

"I never told you to run. And I certainly didn't ask you to come back," Raymond said, shrugging again in that infuriating buffoonish way.

"Why *are* you back?" Alex suddenly asked, lifting his head from where it had been hanging listlessly a second before. "It's been ten years. Why now, Angie?"

To Madelyn's surprise, Angie looked directly at her. "Because she asked me to."

Ten Years Ago

Everything felt important. Angie turned in a circle in her room, taking in her shelves of books and figurines and mementos, the sketches and posters taped to her wall and pinned to her bulletin board, her framed photos and stuffed animals and boxes of jewelry and accessories.

Her dad said they had to go, but not when they were coming back. How long would they be gone? Where were they going? What would she need?

She looked at the empty duffel bag on her bed. It seemed so small.

"I guess socks and underwear are a good idea," she muttered to no one in particular, pulling open her top dresser drawer and dumping the entire contents into the bag. But now it was nearly half-full, and she hadn't even packed any clothes yet. She scooped out the mismatched socks and ratty training bras and threadbare underwear that had gotten shoved to the back of the drawer, leaving only what she still actually wore. "That's better."

Her brain felt like it was on fire, and her skin crawled with fear and a horrible eagerness. She didn't want to go; she didn't want any of this to be happening. But she also felt energized, electric. She needed to run, or scream, or smash something. She needed to move, and she couldn't move until this bag was packed.

"Need to be smart," she reminded herself. Into the bag went T-shirts, jeans, sweatshirts, sneakers. In went a small makeup kit, toothbrush, deodorant, hairbrush, fingernail clippers. Lip balm. Tampons. Body lotion.

She left her fun jackets, her bulky sweaters, her heavy combat boots and chunky earrings. She left her posters and candles and yearbooks. She left her journals and sketchbooks, her DSLR camera, her novels and comics and manga.

Everything that made her *her*. She would leave it all behind. There just wasn't room to bring it with her.

Bas. She hadn't told Bas. He needed to know. It didn't matter that they'd fought. He would worry when she didn't show up at school. She picked up her phone and dialed his number.

Her dad appeared in her doorway with three minutes to go, pulling a giant rolling suitcase behind him. His eyes went wide when he saw the phone by her ear. "Whoa whoa whoa, what are you doing? Put that down," he said, making a frantic *put it down* motion with his free hand.

"I'm calling Bas," she said as it rang.

"Hang up *now*," he said, and started to move toward her as if he were going to do it himself.

"Okay, fine, I'm hanging up, jeez," she said, ending the call midring.

Her father breathed out a sigh, some of the tension leaving his shoulders. "We have to leave our phones. And our tablets. We can't risk them being used to track us."

"What? Why? Can't we put them in airplane mode or something?" Angie felt like she'd been doused under ice water. Her phone had all her pictures, all her videos. It had her log-ins for all her social media, all her contact information. She couldn't just *leave* all that.

But her dad wasn't budging. "I think there are still ways to track a phone in airplane mode."

"Dad, he's a *Realtor*; he's not Batman."

"Angie, I do not have time to argue with you about this," he said sternly. "The phone stays, and that's final."

"Can I at least *text* Bas and—"

"No. No more communication whatsoever." His eyes narrowed. "Actually, go ahead and give me the phone now." He held out a hand expectantly, clearly not trusting her to follow his orders once he left the room.

She groaned in frustration, but powered the phone off and handed it over. *I'll get a new one,* she tried to tell herself. *All that stuff is in the cloud. It's not gone forever. Just for now.*

Still, she couldn't bring herself to leave with nothing to remind her of the people she was leaving behind. She didn't have many physical photos; printing and framing photos was never much of a priority for her since she could access it all digitally. There was a framed family photo of the three of them before her mom left by the side of the bed. Angie's hair was in pigtails; she was probably about ten. And a five-by-seven amusement park print of her and Bas grinning on either side of a person dressed as a chocolate bar, taken on a class trip to Hershey Park last year.

She pulled the Hershey Park photo out of its flimsy cardboard frame, which had been gathering dust on her dresser for months, and scanned her bookshelf for something that she wouldn't get sick of, since it could be her only entertainment for . . .

She didn't want to think about how long it might be.

We'll come back, she assured herself again. *This is only temporary.*

Forcing herself to make a decision, she grabbed tattered paperbacks of *The Princess Bride* and *Jurassic Park*, along with a worn copy of *The Authoritative Calvin and Hobbes* whose cover was no longer attached to its pages. Both photos went inside *Calvin and Hobbes*, the wood frame of the family picture dropped unceremoniously on the floor.

"Angie!" her dad called from the living room. "Come on!"

She glanced at her watch. Time was up. "Coming!" She dropped the books in the duffel bag and zipped it shut, then looked around her room one last time. Tears warmed her eyes, but she sniffed them back. She couldn't afford to cry now. That could come later.

Angie.

"I said I'm coming!" she called, before she realized that wasn't her dad's voice.

My name is Madelyn. I . . . your ghost.

The words were fading in and out, like they were being swept toward her on an invisible tide. She had to strain to hear, and still suspected she was missing some pieces. Goose bumps rippled over her body, along with an unexpected flush of annoyance. After everything, *now* her ghost decided to introduce herself?

"Sorry, Madelyn, now is not a great time," she muttered, heaving the duffel bag off her bed. It was a good thing it had wheels. It weighed a thousand pounds.

. . . live . . . house. I know . . . Bas. We work . . . teaches Spanish.

"What the hell?" Angie said out loud. These were very non-ghostly things for her ghost to be saying. And what on earth did she mean, that she knew Bas? If she knew Bas, why couldn't he hear her? And what was the thing about teaching Spanish? What did that have to do with anything?

He . . . in trouble.

"Bas is in trouble?" Angie repeated, alarmed. Why would Bas be in trouble? He didn't know anything about what she had seen tonight, or even about all the money they owed to Doug Raymond. "Why is he in trouble?"

Help . . . me.

"Help you do what? I need more information. *Please*," Angie begged. She waited, straining her ears, but the ghost had gone silent. Angie picked up a stuffed dragon and hurled it at the wall, imagining it smacking her ghost in the face. "I don't know what to *do* with any of that, you cryptic bitch," she yelled.

"Angie!" her dad barked again. "What the hell is taking so long?"

"One second!"

Okay, okay, she had to think. Bas was in trouble. Why would he be in trouble?

She couldn't think of anything other than that Doug Raymond would decide to go after Bas in order to get to her. It still felt far-fetched, but she couldn't come up with any other theories, at least not with the few seconds she had left.

But her dad had taken her phone. What else could she—

The recorder. She climbed up on her bed, grabbed the voice recorder from its most recent hiding place behind her curtain rod.

"Angie!"

She had only seconds before her dad dragged her out. What could she say?

She held the recorder up to her lips and pressed Record. "If anything happens to me, it was Doug Raymond."

She would've said more—told him to be careful, to watch his back, maybe figure out some way to contact each other—but her father appeared in her doorway, his face red. Quickly, she hid the recorder behind her back.

"Young lady, get in the car *right now*."

She nodded mutely as he grabbed the handle of her duffel bag and dragged it out behind him. She needed to get this recording to Bas. She needed him to find it. How?

Her eyes landed on her canvas bag of ghost-hunting supplies jammed in the top of her closet. The strap dangled down, partially wedged between stacks of shoeboxes filled with old postcards, art projects, birthday party favors. All the random stuff from her childhood that she'd saved, only to abandon now.

She yanked at the strap, and the bag came loose, along with most of the boxes. They tumbled to the ground with a crash, spilling pieces of her past like trash across the floor.

And that's what they were now, she supposed. Just trash.

She shoved the recorder inside one of the bag's many pockets. Maybe when Bas noticed she was missing, he'd come to her house looking for clues. He knew what this bag looked like. She picked up a

Sharpie and wrote *BAS* on the bag in big block letters, just to be safe. He'd find it, and he'd find the recording, and he'd be safe.

She was debating where to leave the bag to be sure he'd find it, without drawing attention from anyone else who may show up at the house, when she had an even better idea. She ran outside, where her dad was heaving her duffel bag into the trunk. His was already in there, along with a toolbox, their winter coats and snow boots, and a shovel. A gold necklace that she recognized from her mom's jewelry box winked at her from a plastic grocery store bag. She peeked inside and saw more jewelry, a watch, and some of her dad's collectible comics that she'd never been allowed to read, still in their plastic sleeves.

Holy crap. Did he think they'd be gone for *months*? He'd packed the car like they were going to be living out of it. But . . . they were coming back, right? When it was safe?

Her dad was holding the door open for her. She clutched the bag to her chest, feeling the world closing in around her. "I need to make a quick stop," she said.

Her dad shook his head. "I packed a cooler of stuff from the kitchen. It's in the back seat."

She glanced in the back of the car and spotted the cooler peeking out from under a pile of blankets and pillows. "No, not for food. I just need to see Bas real quick." If he was home, she could tell him what the ghost had said. If not, the bag would have to do. But at least this way, she'd be sure he'd get it.

"Angelina, I told you, we don't have—"

"Two minutes, I swear. And his house is on the way to the highway anyway. We literally have to drive right by it." Her eyes filled with tears as she realized the truth of what she was about to say. "He's my best friend. And I don't know when I'll see him again. Please, Dad."

He sighed, his expression softening. "Fine. Two minutes. Then back in the car."

"I promise," Angie said, buckling her seatbelt. "I'll be so fast, they'll barely remember I was there."

CHAPTER FORTY-THREE

FROM: angiemae@gmail.com
TO:
SUBJECT:

Bas,

Here I am, writing another email I will never send. My drafts folder is giving my spam a run for its money. My dad doesn't know I still access this account sometimes. He'd probably flip out if he did. But I'm careful. Even if they got in here, what can they learn? Ooooh, I have access to the internet. Big deal.

But just in case, I can't tell you where we are, or what we're doing, or what our plan is. I'm not sure we even have one. We're surviving, I guess. If you can call this survival. I used to think East Henderson sucked, but it's nothing compared to this non-existence I'm living now.

I miss you. I miss our movie nights and the way your pants were never long enough and your big dumb smile. I miss your mom's cooking and your dad's laugh and the way your abuela would always pinch my cheeks, even though I hated that. I miss the scratch of your sister's pencils in her sketchbook, and Carlos's bad singing, and Miguel's even worse jokes. I even miss the way the cafeteria always smelled a little sour, and the bus was always a little stuffy, and the pool at the Y always felt a little too thick in the summer, like too many kids had peed in it. I miss my home. And I miss you, because you were the one who made it feel like home.

Throwing this one onto the pile. Maybe someday I'll be able to send it. But by then, you probably won't even remember me anymore.

Love,
Angie

"You heard me?" Madelyn said. She couldn't believe that had actually worked.

"Yeah, and you really could've given me a little more to go on, you jerk," Angie said. "Couldn't have dropped like, the date into that message? Maybe a last name?"

"I'm so sorry," Madelyn said. "I didn't think—"

"Relax, I'm just messing with you," Angie said with a wink. "Took me forever to put it all together, but I got there eventually. And once I figured out who you were, it was easy enough to keep an eye on you." She frowned at Raymond. "Good thing, since I see this shitstain hasn't changed at all."

"I keep trying to tell you people, I'm just a businessman," Raymond grumbled.

"So was Al Capone," Angie said dryly.

"Look, what do you want? Is it more money?" Raymond asked. "Fine, I'll go up to twenty thousand. Twenty thousand apiece to sign your names and walk away. I think that's a pretty sweet deal."

"No one cares what you think, you sniveling puddle of vomit," Angie said. "I want answers. Who was the woman I saw you kill ten years ago?"

"And what happened to Piper Carden?" Madelyn asked.

"And how many . . ." Alex started to say, but then he trailed off, his body going limp as he finally lost consciousness.

"Alex!"

"Bas!"

Everything happened at once.

Madelyn tried to hold him up, but her angle was wrong and he was too heavy. Her legs buckled as he tipped toward her, deadweight in her arms.

Angie lunged forward, instinctively reaching toward him.

And Doug Raymond, taking advantage of her momentary distraction, wrenched the gun out of Angie's hand, pointed it at her head, and pulled the trigger.

Three Months Ago

"Twelve-ounce Cubano, two shots of espresso?"

Angie startled slightly, but gave the friendly barista a tight smile. "Yup, that's me." She'd been coming into this coffee shop a couple of times a week for the past few months. They had good coffee and reasonable Wi-Fi, and it was easy to get in a few hours of work tucked into one of the cushy armchairs in the back of the seating area.

But he knew her order now. She'd become a regular.

Clearly, it was time to move on.

Every location got a new hair color, a new name, new accessories, new makeup. At first, she'd tried to become invisible by being as plain as possible. She stopped wearing makeup, dressed in muted colors, wore her hair loose and lank. But gradually, it became evident that if nothing else about her was memorable, people actually paid *more* attention to the parts of her she couldn't change: her face, her shape, her height.

Now, she had fun going the other direction. She was the woman with the bright hair, the bold makeup, the eclectic wardrobe. All things she could change. As soon as she swapped out one of them, *poof.* She was someone else.

But she'd just recolored her hair bright red, after a two-week experiment with mossy green, swapped out her makeup from glittery pastels to warm earth tones, and dipped into her extensive collection of fashion glasses. And yet, under all that, he recognized her.

Too bad. She really liked this place.

She took her order number on its wire stand to an empty table and opened her laptop, determined to savor her last visit before beginning the search for a new place. After spinning up her VPN—today, she'd be in the Czech Republic, she decided—and opening an incognito window, she began running down her regular list of searches.

- Doug Raymond
- Raymond Realty
- Doug Raymond crime
- Raymond Realty crime
- Doug Raymond charged
- Raymond Realty charged
- East Henderson Pennsylvania
- East Henderson murder
- East Henderson missing person
- East Henderson body found
- East Henderson human remains
- Sebastián García
- Alexander García
- Madeline East Henderson Pennsylvania

Her fingers froze, hovering over the keyboard. Until now, a quick glance at the search results had told her nothing had changed since the last time she'd looked, but this one was different. She clicked on the link, which took her to a Facebook post from the official East Henderson Middle School account.

> So excited to welcome Madelyn Zhao into the East Henderson family as our new choir director for the 2024–2025 school year! So happy to have you as an East Henderson Tiger, Ms. Zhao!

The post included a photo of Madelyn Zhao, a grinning Asian woman with stick-straight dark hair and wide brown eyes, holding up a sign on which she'd written PROUD TO BE A TIGER! in orange marker. She looked close to Angie's age, maybe a little younger, and wore a flowery wrap dress with flutter sleeves that would've looked ridiculous on Angie but that Madelyn somehow managed to make look chic.

Angie barely looked up when the barista dropped off her coffee, too lost in her own thoughts. This could be her. After all these years of questioning, she might finally have an answer.

She closed her eyes, trying to think of what else the ghost had said, or if she'd given any indication of what Angie should do next. She'd said something about work right around when she'd said the thing about Spanish. That would fit with Madelyn Zhao, since Bas taught at the middle school. But she didn't recall the ghost giving her any other instructions beyond *help me*, which was so ambiguous it made her want to tear out her hair.

But that was okay. She'd been waiting for years for a sign that it was time to go back. This was probably as good as she was going to get.

"Okay, okay, okay," Angie chanted to herself, wiggling her fingers over her keyboard before opening her email. She fired off a quick message to her boss, saying she was sick and taking the day off. She'd taught herself to code years ago, which had been easy enough to spin into remote work once she'd figured out how to fudge all the tax information for her paperwork—currently she was Sydney Brewer, borrowing the identity of an infant who had passed away in 1984. Every couple of years, she'd invent a new résumé and jump to a different company, always into a faceless developer role where she could keep her head down and blend into the digital scenery.

It wasn't the life she'd imagined for herself as a kid, but it was better than she'd feared back when she and her dad had been sleeping in their car on the side of the road, rationing out graham crackers and constantly looking over their shoulders.

Had it really been ten years? Ten years of running, hiding, waiting?

Shoving her laptop back in her bag, she stood and walked briskly toward the exit, waving a distracted goodbye to the barista as she pushed open the door with her hip. "See you next time!" he called after her.

"No you won't," she muttered, walking through the door for the last time.

After ten years, she was finally going home.

CHAPTER FORTY-FOUR

Race cars don't quit. They make pit stops.

—Raymond Realty Group internal newsletter, February 2016

Madelyn screamed, hands flying to her face, her eyes squeezed shut as she waited for the earsplitting bang of the gunshot.

It didn't come.

She scrambled out from under Alex's limp body, craning her neck to get a clear look at what was happening. When they'd fallen, they'd landed in a heap behind a stack of mortar bags, blocking her view. Hurriedly, she scooted on her hands and knees around the bags, not wanting to waste time standing up. Did Raymond have second thoughts about shooting Angie? Had she gotten the gun away from him at the last second?

They were still standing where they'd been when she'd fallen, face to face in the middle of the dirt road. But now Raymond was examining the gun, looking disgusted. "You stupid bitch. You didn't even remember to load your own gun?"

"Oh, I remembered," Angie said. "Just decided not to."

"That's the dumbest shit I've ever heard."

She shrugged one shoulder. "Never really liked the things."

The gun on the ground, Madelyn wanted to yell, but didn't dare. *Angie, get the gun on the ground!*

As if he'd read her mind, Raymond's head swiveled, his gaze locking on his gun, lying several yards away.

"Angie, the gun!" Madelyn screamed.

Angie's head spun toward her. By then, Raymond was already in motion.

Angie threw herself at Raymond, already halfway to his weapon. She was faster, but at twice her size, Raymond wasn't going down easily. He stumbled away from the gun, Angie hanging on to his back like a feral cat. She hooked an arm across his throat, locking her hand into her opposite elbow.

He wrenched at her arms as his face reddened, unable to break her hold. They crashed into the floodlight, sending it toppling. A beam of light cut sharply across the sky before splashing over the ground.

Raymond wove in and out of the light, eyes bulging. Angie dangled behind him like a cape. "Go to sleep, you greasy freaking yak," she gasped, straining to keep her grip. He punched and clawed at her legs, clamped around his broad middle.

Then, abruptly, he stopped trying to throw her off. His expression changed from desperate to smug.

Madelyn's heart stopped. What was he—

Without warning, he threw his body backward.

"Wait!" Madelyn cried. But it was too late.

He tipped over like a felled tree, smashing on top of Angie. Her body slammed into the ground with a dull thwack.

Madelyn hurried toward them on all fours, staying out of the light. For a second, she feared Angie may be dead or unconscious, but then she saw Angie's arms moving, fumbling to get him off her.

He rolled off, moving stiffly. Angie had taken the brunt of the impact, but he was clearly in pain.

Still, he was better off than she was; she rolled to her stomach, struggling to get her arms under her. She gasped, her face red, fighting for air in awful, grating gulps. The fall must have knocked the wind out of her.

Raymond stood, blocking Madelyn's path to Angie, scanning for the gun. Madelyn searched the ground around her. Was it nearby? Could she get to it first?

She couldn't find it. It was lost to the darkness.

Raymond changed tactics. He kicked Angie's shoulder, knocking her back onto her side. She winced as she hit the ground, letting out a weak cry.

He stepped over her weakly flailing body, one foot on either side of her waist. "Should've stayed gone, bitch," he rasped. She must have done a number on his throat.

"Are . . . you going . . . to kill me?" Angie wheezed, still unable to take a full breath. "Like . . . you killed . . . her?"

He laughed, an icy sound that made Madelyn's blood run cold. "By the time I'm done with you, you'll wish you got off that easy." He grabbed a fistful of her shirt, lifting her shoulders off the ground. She latched on to his arm, legs kicking as he hauled her up. He paused, slowly curling his fingers into a fist, making sure she saw, before he swung down.

Angie lifted a hand in a weak block, turning her head. His fist crashed into her face, splitting her cheek. All at once, her body went limp, as though her strings had been cut. Blood welled from the cut on her face, dripping down her jaw.

"Stop!" Madelyn finally reached them. She grabbed Raymond's arm before he could punch again, hugging it to her chest like wrestling a snake. His elbow dug painfully into her sternum. "Leave her alone!"

He snarled, dropping Angie and pivoting to smack Madelyn, open-palmed, across the face. Tears blurred her vision. Heat blossomed across her cheek. But she held tight. If he got the gun, that was it. He'd kill them all. The only way to get out of this alive was to stop him now.

He struck her again, and again. Tears streamed down Madelyn's face. She tasted metal. Her skin was on fire. A high-pitched tone swelled in her ears. She couldn't see anything.

A meaty hand tugged at her arms. She refused to let go; he wrapped his fingers around the index and middle fingers of her right hand and twisted, hard.

Madelyn screamed, dropping his arm as pain stabbed through her. Her fingers jutted out at a wholly unnatural angle from her hand, already starting to swell. She hugged her throbbing hand to her chest as she stumbled away from him, blinking rapidly to clear the tears.

Angie was sitting up now, scooting away from Raymond crab-style across the dirt. "How many people have you killed?" she spat as he closed in on her. Her voice sounded like it was coated in sand. "How many are buried here?"

"Three more after tonight," Raymond snarled, grabbing her ankle and yanking. She kicked at him, but her elbows buckled and she crashed to her back. He flung her leg across her body. She clutched at the dirt reflexively as he stomped on her wrist.

Madelyn heard a sickening snap.

Angie's scream pierced the night, and she crumpled in pain. Raymond leveraged himself on top of her, fitting his hands around her neck. "I've had enough of you," he said, pressing his full weight onto her throat.

Madelyn's hand burned. Her fingers were broken, possibly in several places. Even moving her arm hurt. "Stop!" she yelled through her tears, but he had no reason to listen.

She stumbled toward him, kicking anywhere she could as Angie turned purple underneath him. Her blows just glanced off him. "You stupid women," he said through clenched teeth. "Can't ever just do as you're told."

Madelyn rammed her knees into his side, trying to push him off Angie, but it was no use. Her leverage was terrible, and she was dizzy with pain. Her body started to shake. Her legs felt heavy, like moving through molasses. He may as well have been a boulder.

Veins burst under Angie's skin. Her eyes bulged. She didn't have much longer.

I'm sorry, Madelyn thought tearfully, looking from Angie to Alex. He hadn't moved from where he'd fallen. Maybe he was already dead.

Raymond glanced at her over his shoulder, his eyes gleeful. To her horror, he winked. "You're next, sugar." Angie's legs kicked feebly.

Revulsion rippled through Madelyn. He couldn't just *do* this. He couldn't just kill people and get away with it.

Except he could. He always had. Maybe he always would.

She looked around for something, anything she could use as a weapon. Maybe she could still find the gun—

The sound of a siren sliced through the night. Madelyn's head whipped around. Headlights bobbed toward them from the entrance to the site. A blue light flashed in the windshield as the siren grew louder.

Raymond released Angie, raising his hands above his head as he rose up off her. He didn't look scared, though, just annoyed. Madelyn remembered what Alex had said about the police in this town. That most of them were in Raymond's pocket.

Were they being saved? Or had Raymond just gained an accomplice?

She raised her own hands too, hoping desperately for the former, as the car rolled to a stop and a voice yelled, "Freeze, police!"

CHAPTER FORTY-FIVE

I didn't get where I am by playing it safe. I got here by playing it smart.

—Doug Raymond, *Fox & Friends* interview, June 2020

—

Hope flooded through Madelyn. She knew that voice.

It can't be . . .

A shadowy figure emerged from the car, backlit by its headlights. Their arms were outstretched, holding a gun. "Hands where I can see them!" the officer yelled. Their voice was low and marginally feminine, with a touch of a British accent. "Especially you, Bad Santa."

Now Madelyn *knew* she knew who it was.

"Don't you know who I am?" Raymond barked, practically foaming at the mouth. "You cannot speak to me like this. I was assaulted by these savages, who then attempted to extort me. I demand that you arrest them at once."

"Assault and extortion, eh? By these little women? Louisa May Alcott would never." They were working their way toward Raymond and Angie in a roundabout way, keeping out of the pool of light cast by the flood.

Raymond shielded his eyes against the harsh light. "Who are you? What's your badge number? I'm going to have a word with your supervisor."

"I think not." The "officer" finally stepped into the light, taking three quick strides until they were right in front of Raymond. "And yes, I know exactly who you are, you misogynist piece of shit," Syzygy said as they pressed their gun—which Madelyn could now see was not a gun at all, but Syzygy's trusty Taser, Jubilee—to his neck.

Raymond shuddered as the current zapped through him, then collapsed into an undignified heap on the ground. Madelyn stared at him, waiting for him to leap back up like a monster in a movie, but he lay still and silent. Finally.

Madelyn stared at Syzygy in disbelief. "What are you *doing* here?"

"Saving your ass, apparently," Syzygy said, taking in Angie retching on the ground, Alex's bloody leg, Madelyn's twisted hand. "What the hell happened?"

After Syzygy checked on Alex and Angie to make sure they were both still alive—pulses were strong, they reported, although they'd both seen better days—Madelyn did her best to fill them in. As she spoke, she retrieved a few of Raymond's beloved zip ties to bind his hands and feet before he woke up, although Syzygy had to help her secure them in place, since Madelyn could use only one of her hands. Syzygy listened in horrified fascination, interrupting every now and then to utter a string of oaths comparing Raymond to everything from a moldy slice of damp white bread to a desiccated turnip.

"Your turn," Madelyn said when she was done. "How are you here right now?"

"You really thought you were going to announce you were going on a solo quest to rescue your boyfriend from a supervillain at an abandoned construction site and I was *not* going to make a cameo appearance?"

"Can you please speak in plain sentences? I am in *so* much pain."

"All right, well, basically, I started driving right after you had me break into your school account because you sounded terrified and did *not* instill any confidence that you were making good choices, downloaded a police siren and lights app from the car, and cranked my speakers up as loud as they would go. Also I held my iPad against my windshield like *this*." They shoved a hand straight out in front of them, palm out, their other hand by their chest, miming driving. "Good thing you couldn't see inside the car or I'd have looked deeply stupid."

"Am I still sharing my location with you?" She'd been meaning to turn that off.

"Bloody right you are, and judging by the sight of you lot when I tracked you down, it's a damn good thing I didn't hit much traffic. Wound up losing your signal about half a mile down the road, but fortunately there's sod-all else out here, and your car pretty much glows in the dark." They nodded at Madelyn's mangled hand. "Might want to get that looked at, love."

"Angie and Alex need a doctor too," Madelyn said. "But we don't get any reception out here."

"I can take you all to the hospital," Syzygy said. "It'll be faster than getting an ambulance out here. But we may want to figure out what we're doing about him first," she said, nodding at Raymond. "He's going to be right cranky when he wakes up."

"And it's our word against his," Madelyn said, her stomach sinking. He'd tried to tell Syzygy that they had assaulted him and tried to extort him, when he'd thought they were a police officer. What was to stop him from telling the real police the same thing? Sure, they all were a lot more injured than he was, but he could claim self-defense. Or just claim wealth, and let the police make up their own excuses.

"Actually," Angie rasped from the ground, sounding like she had gargled shards of glass. "It's not."

"Oh shit, love, I thought you were out cold. My bad," Syzygy said, kneeling beside her and gently helping her into a sitting position.

"Just wishing I was," Angie croaked. Bruises were already beginning to darken around her neck, her cheek was smeared with blood, and her wrist lay limply in her lap, red and swollen.

Madelyn suspected Angie would look even worse in the morning. So would she, most likely. Her face was already beginning to feel puffy from where Raymond had hit her. She wouldn't be surprised if she woke up tomorrow with two black eyes.

Angie took a few careful breaths, wincing as she did. Madelyn wondered how many broken ribs she had. "I took some precautions this time," Angie said. She let out a tiny laugh, then groaned. "Fool me once," she whispered.

Madelyn wasn't sure what she meant, but she could ask more questions later. For now, they were all in dire need of medical attention.

It took some doing to get Alex into the back seat of Syzygy's Honda Civic, with Syzygy doing most of the lifting and Madelyn and Angie trying their best to assist with only one working arm each. But eventually, they managed to get him in and buckled, and only a little worse for wear, his injured leg elevated as best they could across the seat.

Madelyn collapsed into the front passenger seat, then remembered Angie had to fit too and pressed herself as far as she could toward the center console. It would be a tight squeeze, but they'd manage. She peered at her through the open door. Angie was leaning against the side of the car, looking like she might topple over any second. "Come on, get in," Madelyn said as Syzygy settled into the driver's seat.

To her surprise, Angie shook her head. "You go on," she said, closing the door. She gave Madelyn a weary smile through the open window. "I'm good."

"Good? Are you insane?" Angie looked like death warmed over, and was probably minutes away from passing out. She was the opposite of good.

"I swear I'm okay," Angie said, obviously suppressing a groan. She nodded at Raymond's prone form. "Just need to get this sorted."

Madelyn remembered Raymond's gun, lost somewhere in the darkness, and narrowed her eyes. "You had better not be about to do something stupid."

"I'm *not*," Angie insisted, glancing past her to Syzygy. "Is she always like this?"

"Worse," Syzygy said merrily.

"No wonder Bas likes you," Angie said, glancing fondly in the back seat. "You're the opposite of me." She looked back to Madelyn. "Thanks for looking out for him."

"Thanks for coming back," Madelyn said.

Angie grinned, her teeth rimmed pink with blood. "My pleasure." She stepped back from the car, holding her broken wrist gingerly with her other hand.

Madelyn wanted to argue with her more, *force* her to come to the hospital with them, but Syzygy shook their head. "She can take care of herself," they said softly.

So Madelyn just turned around to watch Angie, looking small and alone in the darkness, as Syzygy steered the car out of the site. Too soon, she was gone, disappearing into the night once more.

Ten Years Ago

"Cameron?" Doug pounded on the front door—*his* front door—but there was no answer. No sounds came from inside the house. The driveway was empty, save for his BMW, with its sole, silent passenger.

"I'm going to come in if you don't open up!" Doug warned, his hand already in his pocket, closing around his keys.

No answer.

"Fine," Doug grumbled, fumbling with the keys in the dull light of the streetlamp. There were so many keys, so many houses. It was *exhausting*.

At least once the paperwork was signed—thank God *that* had gotten wrapped up before Abigail had started acting like such a bitch—he'd have more exciting responsibilities, and could off-load these pocket-change clients with their pathetic shoestring budgets onto someone else.

He was sick of pretending he cared about the little guy. It was about time he got to play with the big boys.

He found the right key and fitted it to the lock. The door swung open. Doug waited, but was greeted by only silence.

He stepped inside, smacking the wall until he found the light switch. He grimaced when he saw the state of the house. Filthy. Disgusting.

It hadn't been like this earlier today. It *wouldn't* be like this anymore.

"Cameron!" Doug barked, his voice swallowed up by the dull walls, the shabby carpet.

He waited, but there was no one there. Cameron and his daughter, the insufferable brat, were gone.

He moved farther into the house, looking around, nudging the detritus on the ground with the toe of his shoe. After all, this was his property. His investment. He had every right to be here, and if Cameron didn't like it, well, then he should have paid his rent on time, shouldn't he?

Doug Raymond couldn't be blamed for the irresponsibility of others. It wasn't *his* problem people were so goddamned irresponsible that he had to step in and take over, was it? No, he was doing them a favor. Without him, where would they be?

Nowhere.

In the kitchen, he paused. Two phones, side by side on the counter, along with an iPad. He picked one up. It had been powered down. Odd.

He turned it on. It greeted him with a setup screen, asking him to pick a language.

So, they'd wiped their phones and left them behind. Interesting.

He checked the bedrooms, holding his breath. The girl's room was a wreck, rubbish coating the floor. Cameron's room was only marginally better. Doug grimaced at the rumpled bed, the clothing strewn across the floor.

He wasn't an idiot. It was clear that Cameron and his daughter had fled, taking their meager possessions with them.

Good. Cameron knew what Doug was capable of. If he'd decided to run, that meant he was scared. He wouldn't let his daughter say anything. At least not for now.

If they became a problem later, Doug would deal with it. He had the resources now to do that.

In the meantime, this was his house. And if they were gone, he would use it as he saw fit.

Sweat ran down his brow as he hoisted Abigail out of the trunk of his car and dragged her inside. She was heavier than she looked. Must have indulged in more Entenmann's than she'd let on.

Once he was in the living room, he let her fall to the floor, wiping his brow with his sleeve. He locked the front door. What he did in his house was his own business, no one else's.

He looked around, searching for a place to put her. Obviously he couldn't keep her at the office. As it was, he would need to call in a cleaning crew first thing to deal with the mess. And of course, he'd have to pay them double to keep their mouths shut. Maybe triple.

No matter. He could afford it now.

Abigail had been a liability. He saw that now. He appreciated her connections, and he had enjoyed the look of her for a while, but it was stupid to have a woman like that in control of such a delicate part of an operation. When he was in charge, he'd do things differently. Until then, he'd just tell them that Abigail . . . had a change of heart. Went to go discover herself, or some other such nonsense.

But he, Doug Raymond, was ready to step into her place. She'd been the wrong choice from the start. Anyone could see that. He'd do it better.

He walked through the house—holy heavens, it was small—and settled on the linen closet across from the bathroom. He dumped the sheets and blankets out on the floor. Cameron wouldn't be needing them anymore.

The shelves were a little trickier, but he was eventually able to wriggle the bottom one loose, and he didn't think he needed to remove the others. Abigail wasn't very large.

Her body was beginning to stiffen, but he managed to get her inside with a few swift kicks.

He wiped a hand across his brow. Fucking women.

He closed the door, then slumped against it, his breathing heavy.

It was Abigail's fault, of course. She'd come in with her tight skirts and low-cut tops, her intentions on display for the world to see. But then when he'd taken the obvious next step, waiting until they were alone in order to remain discreet, she'd had the audacity to act *offended*? As if *he* were the one in the wrong?

She'd left him no choice, really.

Eventually, there would be an investigation into Cameron's disappearance. Nothing he couldn't handle, though. Police salaries were thin. He could afford to make this go away without even breaking a sweat.

In the meantime, though, he was fine. No one knew about Abigail. No one knew about the Stewarts.

He was still Doug Raymond. And in this town, he was a fucking god.

CHAPTER FORTY-SIX

FROM: angiemae@gmail.com
TO:
SUBJECT:

Bas,

I realized something while I was reading your last email. You have a whole life I wasn't there for. You've had friends, roommates, girlfriends (yes, I've seen your Instagram. Friendly word of advice: the mustache is doing you no favors). You went to college, had jobs, got your own place.

I don't know you anymore. You've grown up, and I missed it.

But I haven't. I've been in this weird limbo all this time. I've tried to have a life, but it's hard when I can't tell anyone the truth about who I am. I feel stuck. Like I stopped being me the night I left. So even though I don't know you anymore, I think you might still be the only person out there who really knows me.

Isn't that strange?

Anyway, I miss you too. So, so much.

Love,
Angie

Over Syzygy's protests, Madelyn convinced them to drive to a Philadelphia hospital forty minutes away instead of the county hospital ten minutes away. "You put his leg in a *tourniquet*, Mad, every minute counts," Syzygy argued.

But Madelyn was adamant. "Philadelphia." She already knew Doug Raymond owned the police and judges of East Henderson. She wasn't going to risk that he owned the doctors too.

Even by emergency room standards, Madelyn and Alex were an alarming sight. Syzygy sprang out of their seat and ran inside the second they parked the car, returning with a gurney and two orderlies in gray scrubs before Madelyn could even finish extracting herself from her seatbelt.

"What did you *say* to get them out here so fast?" Madelyn whispered as the orderlies carefully lifted Alex onto the gurney. He was semiconscious now, moaning loudly whenever someone touched him.

"I said my friend was outside trying to cut off a guy's leg," Syzygy said with a shrug. They noticed Madelyn's horrified expression and winked. "Kidding."

"*Are* you?"

"Probably."

Once inside, Alex got whisked immediately through a set of double doors that proclaimed in large letters AUTHORIZED PERSONNEL ONLY, while Madelyn sat in the waiting room with Syzygy, waiting for her name to be called. A receptionist brought over a set of clean scrubs for her to change into, since Madelyn was still in her filthy sports bra and yoga pants. No wonder she kept getting odd looks.

When she came out of the bathroom, she was presented with paperwork for Alex, which Madelyn realized she couldn't fill out beyond his name. She'd left her phone at North Ridge.

"I'm sorry," Madelyn said, handing the clipboard back to the receptionist. "I don't know any of this."

The police arrived soon after. Apparently when two people arrived in the emergency room looking like they had barely survived a Michael Bay movie, standard operating procedure was to call the cops.

It took Madelyn a few minutes to realize from their questions that they thought she and Alex had hurt each *other*. Then another few to convince them that they hadn't. Eventually, they realized that whatever had happened that night was far more complex than would fit on their notepads. They promised to come back later to take her full statement, and had her repeat her phone number three times, even though she kept telling them she didn't have her phone.

"Please, can you give me any information on my friend?" she kept asking every medical professional who passed while she waited.

But no one knew anything.

The police moved on to Syzygy next, hoping that maybe their lack of injuries indicated a simpler story. Unfortunately for them, they didn't know that Syzygy was allergic to simple. "My version of events?" they mused. "Well, to be honest, I think it all started back when Madelyn introduced me to her boyfriend Ralph—"

"Ralph?" One of the cops checked his notes. "Is Ms. Zhao"—he pronounced it *za-how*—"currently dating this 'Ralph' in addition to Mr. García?"

"Oh, dear God no," Syzygy said, blowing a light raspberry. "This was, what, 2020? But of course they'd been together since high school, which meant that his talons were in her *deep* by the time I entered the picture."

Madelyn was finally taken to an exam room then, and was almost sad to miss Syzygy's explanation of how every detail of the past four years of her life was necessary context for the events of the past few hours.

An exam, an X-ray, and a series of shots that felt like being stung by wasps later, Madelyn had her fingers set by an orthopedist, then wrapped in what seemed like enough gauze to circumnavigate the earth. "Do you think you could get me an update on the man who came in with me?" Madelyn asked the nurse when she came in with her discharge paperwork, same as she'd asked every other person she'd seen.

"What's his name?"

"Sebastián Alejandro García. He goes by Alex. He was shot in the leg and—"

"Actually, yes, I *have* seen him," the nurse said, recognition lighting up her eyes. "What's your relation?"

"He's my . . . friend. And we work together," Madelyn said. It seemed silly after what they'd been through that weekend that she still didn't know what she and Alex were to each other. She'd literally given him the shirt off her back to save his life. And yet somehow the word *dating* seemed too presumptuous.

The nurse pursed her lips. "I'm sorry, dear. But we can only give out that information to family."

"Oh. Okay." Madelyn's eyes watered, but she tried to hold it in. Worry buzzed in her stomach like bees. "Can I see him?"

The nurse shook her head reluctantly. "Also just family."

Madelyn nodded stiffly, forcing a tight smile. "Oh. Okay. That's fine. I just wanted to check." She was blinking as fast as she could, but couldn't seem to push the tears back into her eyes.

The nurse gave her a sympathetic look, then leaned closer as if sharing a secret. "But if you happened to swing by the recovery wing in a day or two . . . you may be glad you did."

"So he's going to be okay?" Madelyn asked eagerly. She felt a thousand pounds lighter. "He didn't lose too much blood?"

"I don't recall saying any of that," the nurse said with a shrug. "Just that you may enjoy a trip to recovery."

With Alex in the hospital and a dead body still in her house, Madelyn and Syzygy decided to split a hotel room that night rather than drive the three hours back to Syzygy's apartment. Madelyn considered showering, but was so exhausted that instead, she passed out fully clothed face down on the bed.

In the morning, after first stopping at Alex's house to check on Potato, Syzygy drove Madelyn back out to North Ridge to pick up her car. She dreaded what she might find. Would the police be waiting to arrest her? Would Raymond be waiting to kill her? By the time they parked beside her car, still where she'd left it, her hospital scrubs were soaked through with sweat.

But everything looked exactly as it had the night before, except now the gate was closed. And when Madelyn opened the door of her car, her phone sat on her front seat, along with Alex's.

A folded note was tucked underneath, written on one of the fast food napkins Madelyn kept in her glove compartment.

Found these. Thought you'd want them. -Nat (fashion police)

Madelyn sighed in relief. So Angie was okay. She couldn't wait to tell Alex.

She followed Syzygy back to the hospital, where they headed straight to the recovery wing. She gave her name to the receptionist, and this time, she was greeted with a smile. "You're on his list," the receptionist said, handing her a visitor sticker.

She heard Alex before she saw him, and followed the trail of rapid Spanish to his room. As she suspected, both of his parents were there, along with his grandmother and all three of his siblings. They filled the small room, but as soon as his mother spotted Madelyn in the doorway, she waved her in, ushering her over to Alex's bedside.

"Are you Madelyn?" she asked hopefully. When Madelyn nodded, she took Madelyn's good hand in both of hers and gave it a tight squeeze. "I am so happy to finally meet you, mija. Thank you for finding him. Thank you for taking care of him. Gracias de todo corazón."

"I didn't do much," Madelyn said, her face growing warm.

"Don't listen to her, she's concussed," Alex said, smiling laboriously at her from his bed. Both wrists were bandaged from where the zip ties had cut into his skin, and his leg was suspended in front of him in a heavy cast. Dozens of metal pins stuck out of it at every angle, making Madelyn wonder how much of his leg was left in there. But even with the cast, he looked so much better than the last time she'd seen him. One eye was black, and he had gauze covering the cuts on his face, but gone were the grayish undertone to his skin, the listless droop of his head. If he wasn't tethered to the bed, he looked like he may try to leap out of it to give her a hug.

"What happened to you?" Alex said, his eyes widening as he took in the bruises covering Madelyn's face. "You get in a fight or something?" He scrunched his eyes in what Madelyn thought was a drugged attempt at a wink.

"You should see the other guy," Madelyn said, smiling so wide her cheeks hurt. She'd been so worried that she'd been too late, that he'd lost too much blood, that she'd come back to find him in a coma or missing a limb. "You look like you're feeling better."

"Oh, I am *extremely* high," Alex said cheerfully. "I can't feel anything right now. They tell me I should be grateful for that."

"They're probably right," Madelyn said with a glance at his leg.

"Did you see that I'm a human pincushion now?"

"I noticed, yes."

"So it turns out you suck at tying tourniquets. But that's okay, because now I get to keep both my feet." He stared intently at his leg for a second, then shrugged, turning back to her. "I was going to wiggle my toes for you, but I can't feel them. I swear I could, though."

"I believe you." Madelyn felt like she might collapse with relief. She wanted to crawl in bed next to him and wrap her arms around him, resting her head on his chest to revel in the music of his heartbeat.

Alex introduced her to everyone in the room—she recognized them all from pictures, but this was their first time seeing her—and caught her up on his prognosis, with a few corrections from his family whenever he went off on a drug-induced tangent. It turned out that while the bullet had shattered his tibia, it had managed to miss the major arteries. Still, fishing out the bone fragments and resetting the leg had required a fairly extensive surgery, and he'd likely need physical therapy to get him walking again.

"Your shirt didn't pull through, though," he added, giving her a somber nod. "I appreciate its sacrifice."

Madelyn laughed, resting her good hand lightly on the edge of the bed. He glanced down, then edged his fingers forward to rest on top of hers. "Hey," he said softly, pitching his voice for only her to hear. "I'm sorry for how I acted with you at my house."

"It's okay," she said quickly. It felt silly to bring that up after what they'd been through last night. And if anyone was in the wrong, it was her. She shouldn't have kept throwing herself at him when he clearly didn't want to. That was gross, and she should have backed off after the first time.

"No, I want to explain," he said. "I shouldn't have lied to you."

"Lied?" She tilted her head, trying to recall what he was talking about. "About what?"

"About not going to confront Doug Raymond. I knew I was going to do it anyway, even though you told me it was a stupid idea." He grimaced down at his leg. "Obviously."

She shook her head. "It wasn't stupid. I was just scared. And I really should apologize to you. I shouldn't have kept trying to . . . you know." She glanced around at his family filling the room. She hoped the bruises covered the blush rising to her cheeks. "I could tell you didn't want to. I'm sorry I didn't take the hint."

"Oh, I wanted to," Alex said, running his thumb gently over the back of her hand. "I just didn't feel right being with you, knowing I wasn't being honest."

She smiled, carefully threading her fingers through his. "You want to be with me?"

He squeezed her hand. "I really, really do."

Madelyn's heart felt like it might burst with joy. If the room wasn't full of people, she would have leaned over and kissed him.

His sister's phone rang, which reminded Madelyn of his phone in her pocket. She pulled it out to return to him and, as she did, noticed a text had come in from *Maybe: Angie.*

Hey Bas, it's me. Angie. Text me when you get this, okay?

Hurriedly, Madelyn pulled out her own phone to see if she had gotten a text too. She had. Several, actually. The first one had come in last night, from the contact she still had saved as *Nat—fashion police.*

I'm okay. Took care of everything. You'll see tomorrow.

Then another one, a few minutes later. Found your phone. Left it in your car. Bas's too. Figured you could get it to him.

The last one was from this morning. Not sure if you got your phone yet, but whenever you get this, can you let me know if Bas is okay?

Madelyn handed Alex his phone, then texted back. He's okay. I'm with him now. Broken leg, but he's going to be fine. Thank you for finding my phone. Are YOU okay?

The response came almost immediately. Turn on your TV. Channel 4.

Madelyn frowned at the text, wondering if Angie would always be so cryptic. "Hey, Alex, do you mind if I turn on the TV?"

He handed her the remote, and the TV mounted near the ceiling came to life midway through a breaking news story.

"—video uploaded late last night that has since gone viral, with over half a million views at the time of this report, depicting multimillion-dollar East Henderson business owner Doug Raymond threatening and assaulting a group of three unidentified young people. In the video, Raymond appears to confess to a series of crimes, including what sounds like murder, although the veracity of the footage is still under investigation. Shortly after the video was released online, Raymond was discovered by authorities outside a northern Philadelphia police station. He has since been taken into custody, and is being treated for minor injuries. More on this developing story throughout the day."

OMG, Madelyn texted Angie, her jaw hanging open. What is even happening right now?

Three dots appeared, then went away, then returned before the response came through.

Hopefully? Justice.

EPILOGUE

Three Months Later

"Don't worry, I'm on it." Angie set her bowl of popcorn on the coffee table and unfolded herself from the couch, padding into the kitchen in her bare feet to retrieve the open bottle of wine from the counter. She started to return to the living room, then grabbed a second, unopened bottle for good measure.

"I still can't believe you haven't seen this," she said as she topped off all their glasses, then settled back into her seat.

"I can't believe you're still into horror movies," Bas—she was trying hard to remember that he went by Alex now, but her mind still defaulted back to Bas—said around a handful of popcorn. Now that Angie and Madelyn were living together, he was constantly at their apartment.

At first, Angie hadn't been sure she wanted to stay in East Henderson after everything that had happened. But even though she'd been so anxious to get away as a kid, she now found herself yearning to make up for the time she'd lost. Maybe she would never get to graduate from high school with Bas, or dress up for prom, or paint her face and stumble around like a zombie in the high school's haunted-house fundraiser at Halloween. But that didn't mean there was nothing left for her here.

Meanwhile, Madelyn hadn't wanted to go back to her house after the body was removed. The FBI eventually identified the remains as a woman named Abigail Norris-Graham, who had ties to several major arms traffickers operating throughout the United States.

The coroner's report indicated that the cause of death was blunt trauma to the head. Raymond refused to say anything about the circumstances that led to her death, stubbornly claiming that he didn't know anything, even after the forensic report identified some of his skin cells under her fingernails.

But Angie had watched it happen. She didn't know why he'd killed her. But she knew how, and she was more than happy to describe what she'd seen to the FBI.

It was Madelyn's idea for her and Angie to move in together. She didn't want to rush things with Alex, but wasn't ready to go back to living alone. Besides, Madelyn had joked, in a way, they'd already been living together for ten years.

Angie shrugged. "I find horror movies soothing."

Alex rolled his eyes, shaking his head.

"Actually, I can see that," Madelyn piped up. She was snuggled into Alex's side, his arm curled around her. His leg, now in a regular cast following the removal of his fixator earlier in the week, was stretched out on a kitchen chair in front of him. "It's a good distraction from all the real-life stuff."

"So's a comedy," Alex said, but Madelyn shook her head.

"Not in the same way. Comedies are happy, but they don't give my anxiety anywhere to go. Horror lets me channel it somewhere else for a while."

"See, I knew I liked her," Angie joked, smiling at Bas. "She gets it."

"That's actually a thing, you know," Syzygy piped up from their spot on the floor by Angie's legs. "There have been studies. Horror movies activate the parasympathetic nervous system, which can be really helpful for chronically anxious people like our girl here." They grabbed a piece of popcorn from the bowl they were sharing with Angie and tossed it at Madelyn, who stuck out her tongue at them. The popcorn bounced off Madelyn's knee and landed on the floor, where it was immediately gobbled up by an enthusiastic Potato.

"Not you too," Alex said, frowning at Syzygy in mock betrayal.

"Who, me?" Syzygy said, then shook their head, sending their thick crown of hair swishing. Today, it was various shades of blue and green, which Syzygy called their "mermaid hair." "No, I'm just here for the company. These movies scare the knickers off me. If you lot let me pick, we'd be rom-comming it up right now."

"Gross," Angie said, wrinkling her nose.

Syzygy leaned their shoulder against her leg. "You're calling *me* gross? You're the one who picked the movie with the dead ghost children."

"At least the dead ghost children don't make me watch them tongue kiss anyone."

"I should hope not; they are *children*."

"You know what I mean."

"What's your problem with kissing? I would've thought you rather liked kissing," Syzygy said with a knowing smirk.

Angie felt herself blush. "I don't like *watching* it."

"Okay, but what if—"

More popcorn flew across the couch, spraying them both. "Will you two stop flirting so we can unpause the movie?" Madelyn said as Alex laughed.

She was one to talk. Madelyn and Alex had been inseparable since he got out of the hospital. He'd dragged Angie with him—or more accurately, convinced her to pilot his wheelchair—to sit in the front row for Madelyn's winter concert a few weeks ago. When it was over, he'd presented Madelyn with a dozen red roses and pronounced the concert "spectacular," which meant he really *must* be in love, since to Angie, it just sounded like a bunch of twelve-year-olds with cracking voices singing "Sleigh Ride."

It was a little weird for her at first, seeing him so wrapped up in someone else, but she was getting used to it. She liked seeing him happy.

She liked seeing him at all. She hadn't realized quite how much she'd missed him until he was back in her life.

Potato bounded over, sniffing wildly around Syzygy on the floor, searching for every last kernel as they started up the movie again. They had the subtitles on, since no one except Alex spoke Spanish, but that didn't stop Angie from stealing peeks at Syzygy whenever she could. She coiled a lock of their hair around her finger, and Syzygy readjusted their position to give her a better angle, draping an arm across Angie's lap and resting their head on top.

Warmth spread through Angie as she ran her fingers through their hair. This thing between them was still new, having started not long after she and Madelyn moved in together, but it already felt more comfortable than any of her past relationships. Maybe because this time, she didn't have to lie about her name, who she was, why her life looked the way it did. This time, she could just be Angie.

She still had a hard time believing that her years of running were finally over. But not even Raymond's massive pile of money was enough to save him once the FBI got involved.

It turned out that the FBI had been keeping an eye on Raymond for years, and were more than happy to step in once the stream of evidence started flowing. Identifying Abigail was only the beginning. Madelyn turned over her messages from Piper, and the FBI quickly determined the image in the message with the coordinates of North Ridge also contained encrypted financial documents. It turned out that Piper had become suspicious of the way the North Ridge books were being managed, and had started quietly documenting what she saw as a pattern of fraudulent accounting practices. She was concerned that Raymond Realty Group was using its development projects as a front to cover up criminal activity, and meticulously logged every discrepancy she could find.

Madelyn said she had no idea what Piper intended to do with her findings, or why she'd decided to send them to her. Maybe she just wanted to have access to them in case she got fired. Maybe she planned to take it all to the police. Maybe she was planning to post it online. They'd never know.

Piper Carden's remains were found embedded in one of the abandoned foundations at North Ridge. After Madelyn and Alex gave their statements detailing what Raymond had done to them, the FBI scanned the area with ground-penetrating radar. Piper's cause of death was ruled to be a gunshot wound to the head, although she also had been shot in the back. The bullet was matched to a gun registered to Doug Raymond.

Piper wasn't the only body they found at North Ridge. There were five in all. Two were Raymond Realty employees who had gone missing in a similar manner to Piper, while their former coworkers were told that they quit. They just didn't have a friend like Kelsey to look for them.

The FBI never released the identities of the other two.

Once the truth of Doug Raymond's criminal actions started to emerge, there was no stopping it. Dozens of former employees came forward alleging harassment and intimidation tactics, verbal abuse, and discrimination in the workplace. They hadn't been permitted to talk about any of it after leaving the company, since most were pressured to sign nondisclosure agreements similar to the one Raymond had forced Kelsey to sign, but the investigation into Raymond empowered them to speak up anyway.

Of that number, a smaller percentage had information about other, even more sinister activities. As of Angie's last count, Raymond was facing more than forty separate criminal charges, ranging from money laundering to gunrunning. She didn't know how many of them would stick—as much as she wanted the justice system to be fair, she knew there were still infinite loopholes available for those who could afford it—but the sheer number encouraged her.

But probably the icing on the cake was the discovery that Raymond actually didn't own Raymond Realty at all anymore. He'd signed over his company in late 2014 to LMP Inc., a national property management corporation with suspected ties to organized crime. The *Philadelphia*

Inquirer was the first to break that story to the public, and after that, as other news organizations picked up the scent, the rest of the pieces fell quickly into place.

In addition to being a high-ranking manager within LMP, Abigail Norris-Graham had also been the chief liaison between the corporation and their numerous illicit contacts. Murdering her had put Raymond in a very precarious position, and journalists theorized that LMP had used it as leverage to wrest control of his company away from him in exchange for covering up what he'd done. He'd been permitted to remain on as CEO and still collected a generous salary, but had no claim anymore to the company's substantial assets.

Angie had always wondered what he was overcompensating for with all the flashy cars and military-grade guns. Now she knew.

At first, Angie was frustrated when she realized she'd never know why Raymond had killed Abigail that night. But eventually, she realized that it didn't matter. Abigail could have smiled wrong, or laughed wrong, or made the wrong joke, or worn the wrong shoes. Or she could have done nothing wrong at all. There was no such thing as behaving well enough to placate men like Raymond. They would always find an excuse.

It had taken weeks to convince her dad that Raymond was no longer a threat to them. He was certain that he would somehow buy his way out of consequences as he always had, and that Angie should go back into hiding before he could come after her. It didn't help that he thought her plan to catch Raymond was asinine.

"You planted cameras to film yourself being *assaulted*?" he'd shouted, so loud she had to pull the phone away from her face. "What were you *thinking*?"

"I had it under control," she said. "I needed him to think he was winning so that he'd confess."

"He *was* winning! I watched the video. He could have killed you."

"He didn't, though! I was fine."

"Young lady, my definition of *fine* does not include multiple broken bones and two missing teeth."

It was true; she'd gone to a walk-in clinic for X-rays, and wound up in a wrist brace for a month. "It looked worse than it was."

"Just *promise* me you will never do anything like that again," he'd pleaded. "My blood pressure can't take it."

"Your blood pressure is fine," Angie said, rolling her eyes. "But I don't think I'll have to. I think it's finally over."

Her dad wasn't so sure, but as the days turned into weeks, then the weeks into months, he gradually conceded that maybe this time was different. Maybe Raymond had walked far enough into the deep end that he'd finally sunk. Her dad still hadn't worked up the courage to return to East Henderson, but Angie was sure he'd get there eventually.

It was okay, though. He was living in Oklahoma now with a woman named Jackie he'd met at the garden center a few years before. She had two grown kids of her own, and no desire to get married again, which suited her dad just fine. When the news broke about Doug Raymond's arrest, Angie's dad finally told Jackie the truth about his past, and Angie had met her for the first time over Zoom just a few weeks ago.

The movie ended, and Angie looked eagerly around the living room. "Well?" She'd probably seen this movie a dozen times, but was always curious to hear others' reactions.

"Not bad," Alex said, sounding surprised. "I actually liked that one."

"Quite depressing, though, wasn't it?" Syzygy said. "You'd never get that ending in a rom-com."

"I don't know," Madelyn said, her voice distant. "I feel like there's room for romance in a ghost story." She looked up at Alex and smiled, then at Syzygy and winked.

"Ours wasn't really a ghost story, though, was it?" Angie asked.

"Also, point of order, that was *not* what I said and you both know it," Syzygy said, sounding miffed.

"Wasn't it, though?" Madelyn asked, ignoring Syzygy. "I mean, sure, neither of us is dead—"

"I should bloody well hope not," Syzygy said, giving Angie an exaggeratedly suspicious once-over.

"Oh my *god*, Syz, can you shut up for like two seconds so I can be profound?"

"Oh, sorry, were you being profound? Must've missed it. Apologies, please start over and I promise to be appropriately reverent."

Angie enjoyed watching the two of them together. There was a hominess to their relationship, an utter lack of pretense. They never tried to impress one another or earn the other's affection. They simply loved each other for who they were.

It reminded her of her and Bas, the way they used to be. The way she hoped they might someday be again.

"Anyway, I just meant that even though we weren't ghosts in the *traditional* sense, we still haunted each other," Madelyn said. "We both had unfinished business that needed to be resolved before we could move on. Isn't that a ghost story?"

Alex kissed her fondly on the top of the head. "I think you're *really* reaching," he said, smiling down at her. "But I appreciate the effort."

Angie narrowed her eyes. "After all this time, you're *still* pissing all over other people's ghost stories?"

He shrugged. "I just feel like you might be using the term a little too loosely."

Her popcorn bowl was empty, so she threw a couch cushion at him instead.

"Ow!" he yelped, swatting it away from his face.

"Oh hush, you big baby. It didn't even hit you."

"It's the *principle* of the thing."

Angie made a dramatic show of flipping him off, and Alex rolled his eyes. "Well, *you* haven't changed a bit."

For some reason, that made her deliriously happy.

"Don't mind him," she told Madelyn. "He's always been a skeptic."

"Here's what I wonder," Syzygy said, leaning forward to brace their elbows on their knees. "From a purely scientific perspective—"

Madelyn and Angie groaned in unison.

"No, shut up, hear me out," Syzygy said. "What *was* happening in that house? I mean, you obviously did actually hear each other. That's not a psychological phenomenon; it's absolute fact. Angie, you heard Mad's atrocious shower singing—"

"Hey!" Madelyn interjected, at the same time as Alex said, "Well, *I* like it."

"And Mad, you heard evidence of Angie's abject clumsiness."

Now it would've been Angie's turn to be offended, except that Syzygy was right.

"So what I'm wondering is . . . why? And how? Is this a measurable phenomenon? Is it quantifiable? Can it be repeated? I have so many questions." Syzygy was speaking fast, their eyes alight with curiosity.

"I have a theory," Angie said. She'd been chewing on an idea ever since she'd learned the identity of the woman she'd seen Raymond murder. "I think it was Abigail."

Madelyn recognized the name first. "Abigail, like body-in-my-wall Abigail?" She tilted her head, nose crinkling slightly.

"That's the one," Angie said. "I realized something about her full name. Abigail Norris-Graham. Her initials are ANG."

"Oh my God," Alex said, his eyes going wide. "That time with the Ouija board. When we thought it was spelling your name."

Angie nodded. "Maybe she *was* trying to answer my questions. Maybe it really wasn't either of us."

"Well, it wasn't *me*," Alex insisted, still a little defensive, even after ten years.

"But Abigail—sorry if this sounds a bit crass—but she wasn't in the wall yet," Syzygy said. "I mean it's a fascinating theory, that maybe you two were communicating over some sort of spirit-realm telephone held together by a pissed-off ghost. But wouldn't she have had to be, well, a ghost already?"

"Some would argue that time is just a construct," Madelyn said. "Maybe ghosts aren't bound as tightly to it as humans."

Angie exchanged an amused look with Alex over her head. As much as horror was Angie's thing, science fiction was Madelyn's. Of course she'd be the one to introduce "time as a construct" into the conversation.

"Maybe," Madelyn continued, "it's something like the Block Universe theory, which posits that what we perceive as linear time is actually all happening at once, and once we're no longer bound by a physical body—"

"Okay, Stephen Hawking, can we put a pin in the quantum theorizing?" Angie said, shaking her head. "Some of us did not finish high school."

"It is an interesting hypothesis," Syzygy mused.

Angie shoved their shoulder. "*Excuse* me, I believe you're supposed to be on my side now."

Syzygy held up their hands in surrender. "Right, my bad. Hush, you!" they barked at Madelyn in mock sternness.

Angie caught the look they exchanged with Madelyn, though, and knew the two of them would be circling back to this topic later. Not that she minded, as long as she didn't have to listen to it. She'd spent ten years dissecting everything that had happened leading up to the night she left. She was happy to be done with it now.

"Well, regardless of why it happened," Alex said, raising his wineglass, "I'm glad to be here with you all now."

"Hear, hear," Syzygy said, lifting their glass as well.

Madelyn and Angie joined the toast, exchanging a smile that was just for the two of them.

Ghost to ghost.

ACKNOWLEDGMENTS

Much like Madelyn in *You Shouldn't Be Here*, I know what it's like to doubt myself. To second-guess every little choice and action, wondering if maybe *this* is the thing that screws everything up for good. And I experienced a *lot* of doubt when writing this book. It can be easy as an author to lose perspective on your own work, especially when you don't have the luxury of time to step away from it. Thankfully, I also know what it's like to have my own Syzygy and Alex: the team that helps get you through it when you're not sure you can do it on your own. And my team is truly the best. This book would not exist without them.

Thank you to my agent, Holly Root, my stalwart champion for so many years, and always the sharpest tack in the room. Thank you for always having my back, my front, and my middle.

Thank you to Alyssa Moore and the team at Root Literary for being such consummate pros, always. I'm so proud to be part of your team.

Thank you to my editor, Megha Parekh, for being such a joy to work with, and for getting excited about this story back when it was just a weird nugget of an idea. Thank you to Wes Miller for your enthusiasm, your brilliant editorial mind and thoughtful suggestions, and for validating the eastern Pennsylvania vibes that I tried so hard to capture. (Sorry not sorry for making you hungry.) And thank you to Kellie Osborne, Sarah Engel, and Ashley Little for your keen eyes, meticulous attention to detail, and impeccable research skills. You're the reason I won't be waking up at 4:00 a.m. panicking about continuity errors.

Thank you to Nicole Burns-Ascue, Miranda Gardner, and the entire production team at Thomas & Mercer for shepherding this book through the production process, and delivering such a beautiful final product at the finish line.

Thank you to Caroline Teagle-Johnson for the absolutely stunning cover for *You Shouldn't Be Here*, which made me gasp in delight the first time I saw it. And thank you to Jarrod Taylor and the T & M design team for coming up with the many clever visual details that really helped bring this story to life.

Thank you to Stef Sloma, Andrew George, and the rest of the Thomas & Mercer marketing team for your tireless work in helping this book find its readers.

Thank you to Heather Baror-Shapiro for traversing the globe in search of new opportunities for my stories, and thank you to Jasmine Lake and Mirabel Michaelson for seeing their potential in other media.

Thank you to Megan Beatie, Allyson Cullinan, and the publicity team at Thomas & Mercer for being such fantastic cheerleaders and wingpeople, seeking out amazing opportunities, and always helping me put my best foot forward (rather than tripping over it).

Thank you to Sarah Brown for helping me plot out this entire book on your couch, for always having a pep talk ready to go whenever I was in the throes of self-doubt, for driving me to events and workshops and retreats all over the place and hanging out with me so I wouldn't have to be by myself, and for all the other million other ways you have always supported me throughout my entire writing journey. I can wholeheartedly say that I would not be where I am without you.

Thank you to Amy and Nathan Fritz, Melissa Hogan, Jon and Heather Fulk, Dan and Summer Watt, and Danny and Lydia Craig for your integrity and commitment to the truth when it would've been so much easier to turn away. Without you, the idea for this book never would have been born.

Thank you to Myra Simmons, Erica Rodgers, Kristin Tubb, Alisha Klapheke, Mandy Buehrlen, and Meredith Lyons for being the best sounding boards, writing buddies, shieldmaidens, sages, cheerleaders, and friends I could ask for. Being a village is not always easy or rewarding, and I hope you each know how much I value that you choose to be part of mine.

Thank you to all of the family and friends who have encouraged and inspired me and supported my work. I am blown away by your support, and so tremendously grateful.

Thank you to Fezzik and Astrid for being such dutiful fluffy assistants. I could have written this book without you sharing my desk chair and sitting on my laptop, but it wouldn't have been nearly so cuddly. Special thanks to Fezzik for inspiring Potato, the best character I've ever written.

Thank you to my brilliant, talented children for sharing your passions and interests with me, for asking questions that make me think, and for caring so much about the world around you. Thank you for making dinners, for watching puppies, for talking to me about your stories and being excited when I talk about mine. You make me proud every day. I love you, and I love being your mom.

Thank you to Greg for being a true partner, for sharing your time and talents and knowledge with me, for splitting the mental load, for walking alongside me every step of every day. Thank you for loving me, for growing and learning and questioning with me, for challenging and uplifting me, for supporting me in a million different ways, for making me laugh, and for never running out of things to talk about. I love you, and I love our life together.

And thank you to you, reader, for lending me your time, your heart, and your imagination. There are so many amazing books out there that you could have picked up, and I am honored that you chose mine.

ABOUT THE AUTHOR

Photo © 2022 Amanda McNeal

Lauren Thoman is the author of the Mindy's Book Studio selection *I'll Stop the World*. She lives outside Nashville, Tennessee, with her husband, two children, a fluctuating number of rescue and foster dogs, and a somewhat alarming quantity of fish. Her pop culture writing has appeared in numerous online outlets including *Parade* and *Vulture*. When she's not writing, she's probably on the hunt for tacos or coffee, poking around her flower beds, or buried underneath a pile of dogs. For more information, visit laurenthomanwrites.com.